HATCH

ALSO BY KENNETH OPPEL

Bloom

Inkling

Every Hidden Thing

The Nest

This Dark Endeavor

Such Wicked Intent

Half Brother

The Boundless

Airborn

Skybreaker

Starclimber

Silverwing

Sunwing

Firewing

Darkwing

Dead Water Zone

The Live-Forever Machine

THE OVERTHROW   BOOK 2

HATCH

KENNETH OPPEL

ALFRED A. KNOPF
NEW YORK

THIS IS A BORZOI BOOK PUBLISHED BY ALFRED A. KNOPF

All rights reserved. Published in the United States by Alfred A. Knopf, an imprint of Random House Children's Books, a division of Penguin Random House LLC, New York.

Knopf, Borzoi Books, and the colophon are registered trademarks of Penguin Random House LLC.

Visit us on the Web! rhcbooks.com

Educators and librarians, for a variety of teaching tools, visit us at RHTeachersLibrarians.com

Library of Congress Cataloging-in-Publication Data is available upon request.
ISBN 978-1-9848-9476-2 (trade) — ISBN 978-1-9848-9477-9 (lib. bdg.) —
ISBN 978-1-9848-9478-6 (ebook)

The text of this book is set in 12-point Adobe Garamond Pro.

Printed in the United States of America
September 2020
10 9 8 7 6 5 4 3 2 1

First Edition

For Nathaniel

It's going to be okay.

They were rising. They were getting out. Beyond the metal walls of the elevator, Petra heard the rattle and clack of cables, pulling them higher.

Up, up, up, she chanted inside her head.

Her heart beat against the cage of her ribs. She stared at the control panel, wishing they could go faster. Sweat prickled her back. The elevator was packed with anxious teenagers, jostling against each other in their color-coded jumpsuits. She did another quick head count: they were all here, no one left behind. Not even Seth. She found him in the crowd, still in his hospital gown. They'd rescued him just in time.

Up, up, up.

Soon the elevator would jolt to a stop.

Soon the doors would open.

Soon they'd be free.

Beside her, Anaya squeezed her hand. Petra squeezed back. She was so grateful to have her oldest friend in the world with her. It didn't matter that Anaya looked different now; it was still Anaya. And she, Petra, was still the same, despite everything.

I am still me. The thought was like a rope she clung to. Like the elevator cable lifting them out of here. If it frayed and snapped, all was lost.

It's going to be okay.

From deep below came a rusty squeal. The elevator wobbled, and Petra touched her hand against the wall. Like she was comforting it. Giving it a little bit of encouragement: *You can do it, elevator.*

"Are we too heavy?" she whispered to Anaya.

She didn't know why she was whispering.

"It's a freight elevator," her friend said. "We should be fine."

Nothing they could do about it now anyway. They were still rising, and that was all that mattered.

Up, up, up.

On the control panel there were only two buttons. The top one was lit: a pale flickering light beckoning them to the outside.

The elevator shuddered and stopped.

She turned hopefully to Anaya. "We there?"

With a frown, her friend shook her head. "Too soon."

Too soon? Petra felt like they'd been in here forever. She stared at the doors, willing them to snap open. They didn't.

"Something's wrong," Anaya said.

"We stuck or something?"

Frantically, Petra stabbed at the top button, then gasped as the elevator dropped a little. From below came the anguished sounds of metal twisting. It sounded like it was being *chewed*. She didn't want to think about the kind of teeth that could eat metal. She didn't want to think about what would happen if those teeth chewed right through the elevator cable.

Another downward tug. The elevator suddenly seemed a lot smaller, the air thinner. She gulped back the panic blooming through her body.

"We've got to get out of here," she said, looking at the ceiling.

The elevator shuddered violently, and the light blinked out.

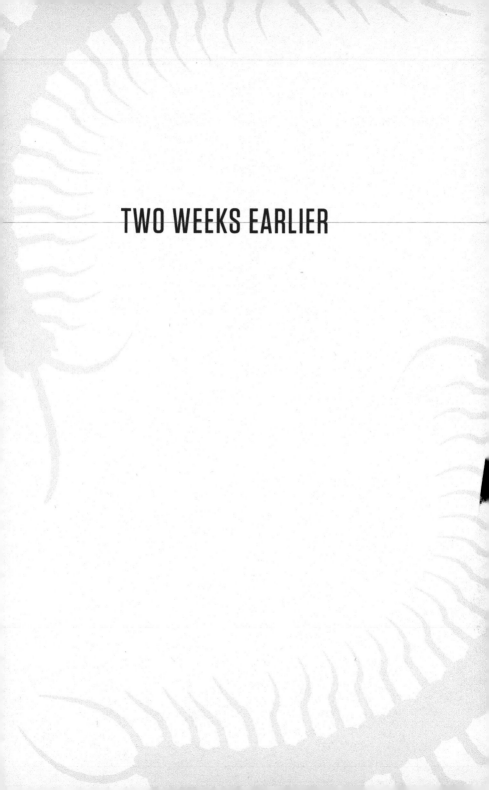

TWO WEEKS EARLIER

CHAPTER ONE

ANAYA

THIS WASN'T NORMAL RAIN.

It came as a sudden deluge, pockmarking the water and misting Anaya's view of the battered city across the harbor. It lashed down on the field of Deadman's Island, where she stood with Mom and Dad, Petra and her parents, Seth, and Dr. Stephanie Weber. And it wasn't *right*.

Just minutes ago, all her attention had been focused on Stanley Park, where the cryptogenic grass and vines were dying. Yesterday they'd been sprayed with an experimental herbicide, and now they were wilting and cracking. Up till now, nothing had been able to kill these plants. They'd spread worldwide, crowding out crops, sending strangling vines into houses, waiting underground to trap and eat animals and people in their acid-filled sacs. But the herbicide that Dad and Dr. Weber had created—it *worked*. And seconds ago, Anaya had been cheering along with everyone else on the army base who'd rushed out to witness this huge triumph.

But now came the rain. Mostly it was real rain. She could feel it, wet against her face. But among the raindrops were ones that were too big to be normal. They didn't soak into the earth but bounced and settled on the grass like gleaming translucent beads.

"Hail," Mom said.

Her mother was a pilot, and Anaya knew she'd seen all kinds of severe weather. Hail in May was weird but not impossible. And Anaya *wanted* it to be hail. But near her feet, one of the gleaming beads quivered, swelled, then—

Burst.

She stepped back with a gasp as something swift and wet uncoiled from inside. It happened so quickly that she couldn't tell the thing's size or shape—except that it seemed too big to come from such a tiny space. In a second, it had burrowed into the earth and disappeared.

"Did you see that?" she cried.

"Eggs," Dad said, kneeling down as more of them hatched. Their squirming cargo slithered into the grass. He lunged and caught something in his cupped hands, but it squirted between his fingers and was gone.

"Holy crap," said Seth. "What are they?"

"There's hundreds of them!" Petra gasped, stamping with her foot.

Anaya's shoulders jerked at the sound of a gunshot. Across the field, a soldier fired a pistol uselessly at the ground until someone yelled at him to stop.

"They're everywhere!" she heard another soldier shout.

"We need specimens," Dr. Weber was saying with remarkable calm.

Anaya spotted several more trembling eggs nestled among the blades of grass. She snatched the coffee cup from Petra's father and splashed out the contents. Dropping to her knees, she scooped up the eggs and snapped the plastic lid back on.

"Good thinking," said Dad.

"Let's get that to the lab," Dr. Weber said. "Fast."

As quickly as it had come, the rain subsided. Anaya rushed toward the main building. She felt like she was clutching a grenade. Against the waxed paper was a sudden churning.

"I think they're hatching!"

She sped up, bolting through the doors, down the corridor, and into Dr. Weber's laboratory.

"In here," Dr. Weber told her, opening a large glass terrarium that contained some samples of black grass.

Anaya lowered the coffee cup inside. Very quickly she snapped off the lid. Several tiny translucent creatures spilled out. Dr. Weber sealed the terrarium. Wriggling at the bottom, the things looked like they were trying to burrow through the glass.

"They all want to get underground," Seth said.

"They're larvae," Dad remarked, leaning closer. "Trying to find somewhere safe to grow. And they're not all the same." He turned to Dr. Weber. "Stephanie, can you get that magnifying camera working?"

With a joystick, Dr. Weber angled the small camera mounted above the terrarium. She flipped a switch, and on the monitor loomed some kind of blunt-faced worm.

"Looks kind of like a borer worm," Anaya said.

Growing up with a botanist dad, she'd been shown all sorts of things—not simply weird plants but the freaky creatures that ate them. She knew it pleased Dad that she'd never been one of those kids who squealed at the sight of bugs. He'd taught her to look longer and closer.

"Yeah," Dad agreed. "A flat-headed borer larva."

"So these things are from Earth?" Seth asked hopefully.

"They just fell from the freaking sky in raindrops!" Petra told him.

"I just want to know for sure!" Seth retorted.

"These definitely aren't from Earth," Dad said. "Borer larvae aren't segmented like this, and they don't have lateral fins." He pointed at the long ridges that ran the length of the thing's body.

"They might be for digging," Dr. Weber remarked.

When the worm opened its wide mouth, Anaya took a sharp breath.

"Oh my God," said Petra.

Inside were spiraling blades that looked like the turbine of a drilling machine.

On the monitor another creature now plunged into view. This one had an oversized head, which was mostly taken up with a pair of black-dot eyes. Its narrow body was like a chain of armored blocks, each sprouting spiky hairs. Below its head was a big hump, and through the translucent flesh, Anaya made out something dark and bundled.

"What's that?" she asked, pointing.

"I think those might be the beginnings of wings," Dad remarked. "This one might be a flyer. What else have we got in there?"

Dr. Weber panned the camera across the terrarium. There were a couple more of the bulgy-headed creatures, a few more worms, and then a grub-like thing so blobby Anaya couldn't tell which end was which.

"This little dude's a puzzle," Dad remarked as the camera zoomed in. Dad had always had a habit of calling his specimens endearing names. *Rascal. Scoundrel. Smart aleck.* "He's still completely undifferentiated."

"Meaning?" asked Sergeant Diane Sumner. Petra's mother worked for the Royal Canadian Mounted Police and liked to understand things as quickly as possible.

"Meaning it's hard to tell what the heck it is," replied her husband, Cal Sumner, who was a nurse practitioner at the Salt Spring hospital.

As Anaya watched, the grub thing flopped over to a worm that was busily bashing its head against the floor. She still couldn't tell which end was which until the grub thing unhinged its jaws and inhaled the worm whole.

"That just really happened," Petra said, sounding horrified.

Bloated, the grub was motionless for a few seconds, maybe stunned it had eaten something as big as itself. Its body twitched. Then it flumped over to one of the black-eyed bugs and ate that, too. It finished off all the other larvae in the terrarium. Its swollen body bulged as if its prey were still alive and thrashing around inside. Then it became very still.

"Did it die?" Anaya heard Mom ask.

"What's all that goo?" Seth said.

A pale fluid oozed from the thing's flesh, and at first Anaya thought it must be injured, but the fluid quickly hardened into an opaque gray coating.

"A cocoon?" she asked, squinting.

"It's entered the pupal stage," Dad said.

"Looks more like a shell," Dr. Weber commented. "Hard."

"How could it turn itself into an egg?" Petra asked. "It just hatched!"

"Whatever it is," Dad said, "this troublemaker's definitely a work in progress."

"I don't want to see him when he's finished," said Petra.

"Dr. Weber?"

Anaya turned to a lab technician at a nearby workstation pointing at her monitor. On it was a weather broadcast showing a huge white swirl over the Pacific Ocean. Its eastern edge covered the west coast of North America, including Vancouver.

"That's one heck of a system," said Mom.

"It's like that big rain a couple of weeks ago," Seth said.

In a time-lapse visual, the enormous swirl of cloud expanded, swelling across North America, billowing toward Asia, bellying down to swallow up South America.

"Except this time the rain is eggs," said Anaya. "Not seeds."

"Is this it?" asked Petra. "Are they invading?"

They.

Anaya stared at the creatures behind the glass. "These aren't them, are they? The cryptogens?"

That was the name they'd given them. It meant "species of unknown origin." Maybe it was more scientific than the word *aliens,* but it was no less scary.

"Not a chance," said Dr. Weber, nodding at the terrarium. "These things aren't higher-order life-forms. They're oviparous. Egg layers. Insects, by the looks of it. It's definitely a new invasion, but not the big one."

"Just another bit of an alien ecosystem," Dad said. "First they sent down the flora; now we're getting some fauna."

"Step away from your workstations!"

Anaya jolted at the booming voice and spun around.

Colonel Pearson strode into the laboratory, soldiers fanning out behind him.

"What's going on?" Dr. Weber demanded.

He knows, Anaya thought with a clenched heart. *Pearson knows what we are.*

"I want all your records, your hard drives, all external storage units," Pearson told the lab staff.

Anaya saw them glancing nervously at Dr. Weber as they pushed back their chairs and stood. Soldiers immediately took over the computers, tapping keys, unplugging devices.

"Colonel Pearson," Dr. Weber said, "this is completely unacceptable!"

Her voice was filled with indignation, but Anaya had the feeling she would not come out the winner in this battle.

"This lab," she told the colonel, "is under the authority of the Canadian Security Intelligence Service."

"Not anymore," Pearson said. "I want a full briefing on your findings. And I mean *all* your findings, Doctor. The parents will be detained in their apartment for the time being." He nodded to the soldiers nearest him. "Take the children downstairs to the holding cells."

"What's all this about?" Sergeant Sumner said in her steeliest RCMP voice.

"Come with me," a soldier said to Anaya.

Instinctively, she stepped toward her father, but the soldier tugged her smartly away and unclasped handcuffs from his belt.

"You're not serious!" Dad exclaimed. "Handcuffs?"

"Arms behind your back," the soldier snapped at her.

She'd been brought up to be respectful and obedient, but right now she was overwhelmed by confusion—and anger.

"This is crazy! We helped figure out how to kill the plants! And you're arresting us?"

"You've got no cause for this!" Dr. Weber said.

"I have ample cause, as you know," said Colonel Pearson.

Because we're only half human, Anaya thought.

Sergeant Sumner took out her phone and began dialing. "I'm calling my superintendent."

Pearson himself snatched the phone from her hand. Sharply to his soldiers he said, "Cuff them all. Now!"

Anaya felt the loops of steel close coldly around her wrists.

"Ow!" Petra cried out as a soldier snapped her arms behind her back.

"There's no need for this!" Mr. Sumner objected.

"Don't touch them!" Anaya heard Seth shout. And then someone cried out in pain.

When she turned, she saw that Seth had ripped off the bandages on his right arm, revealing his feathers. Their tips bristled, razor-sharp. They were longer than the last time she'd seen them on Cordova Island. Their colors were even more vibrant now, exploding along his arm in a dazzling pattern.

On the floor, a bright line of blood led to the soldier who'd tried to manacle Seth.

"You cut me!" the soldier snarled, cradling his wounded hand.

Immediately, three other soldiers had pistols out, aimed at Seth.

Everyone knows now, Anaya thought numbly. This past week, they'd tried so hard to keep their changing bodies secret: Seth's feathered arms, Petra's growing tail, her own clawed feet.

Seth pulled back his bristling arm, ready to lash out again.

"Seth!" Dr. Weber yelled. "Don't!"

"You crypto freak!" the injured solider spat at Seth, and Anaya saw the hatred in his face—and the fear.

"Lower your arm, boy!" Pearson barked at Seth.

"Don't shoot him!" Petra wailed.

"Seth," croaked Anaya, hardly able to breathe. "Stop!"

Slowly Seth dropped his arm to his side. At once, two soldiers smashed him against the wall and manacled him.

Anaya was given a hard shove toward the exit.

"Hey!" she protested.

"Stop this!" Dad shouted, and grabbed the soldier, but immediately two others pulled him away, twisting his arm behind his back so he winced in pain.

"You can't do this!" Mom shouted at Pearson. "You can't separate us from our kids!"

A scuffle broke out between Petra's parents and the soldier escorting Petra from the lab. Anaya gasped as Sergeant Sumner actually punched a soldier in the face—and was instantly wrenched away and handcuffed, along with Mr. Sumner.

Anaya was pushed through the doorway into the corridor. With a last backward glance she saw Mom's beautiful face compressed in anguish, and Dad looking more furious than she'd ever seen. Then she lost sight of them. She felt like a long, invisible tether had snapped, ripping a hole in her belly.

Beside her, Petra called out, "Mom?"

And this was what started Anaya crying. Because her friend's voice was filled with the childish hope that her mother, even now, could somehow protect her. Anaya knew that Petra had never gotten along with her mom, and yet she was still the person Petra wanted most right now.

"Don't worry!" Anaya heard Sergeant Sumner call out from the lab. "We'll sort this out! The RCMP knows where I am."

"This is a big mistake," Seth shouted as he, too, was marched into the corridor.

The soldiers escorted them through a fire door and down several flights of stairs.

"I'm a freaking hero, okay!" Petra yelled, her voice echoing off the concrete walls. "I got the dirt that's killing the plants. What'd you guys do? Huh? You can't treat us like this!"

Then her voice broke and she was crying again and saying she wanted to go home, couldn't they just let her go home?

Anaya took a breath, tried to stop herself from shaking.

Downstairs now: a dim concrete corridor with windowless doors.

The guard unlocked one of these doors and shoved her inside, alone.

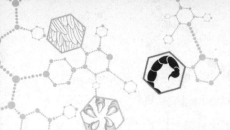

CHAPTER TWO

PETRA

THERE WAS NO WINDOW, no clock, and Petra had lost track of how long she'd been inside. Her eyes felt rusty from crying. Itchy, too, because she was allergic to her own tears, thanks to her stupid water allergy. Her face was probably a mess.

She'd cried herself out, but panic still paced around inside her, like a hungry animal looking for a chance.

She tried to keep her breathing slow and steady, but it was nearly impossible. She was in a cell, a *jail* cell. A metal bed with a thin mattress. A seatless toilet. A fluorescent bar in the ceiling. And outside, the earth was crawling with those squirmy things. They must be everywhere by now! What were they going to *turn into*? Her eyes kept darting to the corners of the ceiling and floor, afraid she'd see them scuttle inside her cell.

Where were her parents? For the first little while, she'd expected the door to fly open and her mom to breeze in and say everything had been sorted out. Mom could be a royal pain when she dug her heels in; she'd have made some calls and busted some heads and everything would be all right. Or Dr. Weber would've pulled strings. After all, she worked for CSIS, and that was even more important than the RCMP. But as time dribbled on, Petra's hopes withered.

She wished Anaya and Seth were in here with her. Seth especially. She felt calmer when he was around. Safer, too. He'd tried to protect her and Anaya when they were getting handcuffed. If the three of them were together, they could talk at least. It would stop her freaking out inside her own head.

How had Colonel Pearson even found out about them?

They'd tried so hard to keep everything secret. It had to be their social worker, that sneak Carlene. She'd been in the room when Dr. Weber had first told them about their cryptogenic DNA. Carlene had tried to hide it, but she'd looked horrified. It *was* horrifying. *You try having alien DNA inside you, Carlene.*

Petra could feel her tail squashed in her leggings. It was long enough now that she had to kind of shove it down a pant leg. It made a bulge. Sometimes it even twitched on its own. Which was why she'd started wearing a skirt, to make sure it stayed hidden.

And her legs. Her skin had gotten all scaly and then sloughed off, leaving baby-smooth skin underneath. She didn't mind the smooth skin, even though it was definitely weird. It was like having dolphin skin. And it wasn't only her legs anymore.

She lifted her top a little bit and saw how her stomach was getting rough. Her fingers crept around to her lower back: same.

It was upsetting to touch. It was like being some weird kind of reptile.

Would all of her skin slough off? Even on her face?

I will not think about this now.

And her tail, how long would that thing get?

Stop it.

If only Dr. Weber had chopped it off when she'd asked.

When the cell door swung wide, her heart gave a hopeful jump, but it was only a female guard with a tray of food.

"What time is it?" Petra asked.

No reply.

"Where's my mom and dad?"

Nothing.

"Those things that came down in the rain, are they all over the place? What's going on out there?"

Silence.

"Why won't you answer me?" Petra demanded.

The guard had obviously been told not to engage. Her eyes wouldn't even meet Petra's. By now, everyone on the military base must know she and Seth and Anaya were cryptogen hybrids.

"This is probably against the law," Petra said. "Just so you know."

The guard locked the door behind her. After eating, Petra felt swamped by exhaustion. On the hard bed she actually fell asleep. When she woke, there was another tray of food waiting for her by the door. Lunch or dinner? How long were they going to keep her locked up? She paced. She used the toilet. She picked at the scaly skin on her stomach and touched the new, smooth skin underneath. She wished she could change her clothes. Another meal came. She worried some more, slept some more.

The only way she had any sense of time was by keeping track of food trays. Five. She figured she'd been in here almost two days.

The next time the door opened, a pair of guards entered. This was new.

"Turn around so I can handcuff you."

"Why?" she demanded.

No reply.

"Where are we going?"

No answer.

"You guys suck," Petra said.

But she felt almost elated to be marched down the corridor. At least she was out. At least she was going somewhere. She looked at the windowless doors and wondered if Seth and Anaya were behind any of them. No point asking. She was escorted into a big, white, windowless room.

In one corner, a man adjusted a video camera on its tripod. Two soldiers flanked the inside of the doorway. In the middle of the room, behind a table, sat Colonel Pearson. Next to him was Dr. Weber.

At the sight of her, Petra broke into a hopeful smile. Dr. Weber wasn't wearing handcuffs. Which was a good sign. After all, she was CSIS. She'd stick up for her, and Seth and Anaya. Maybe she'd already convinced Pearson that they were perfectly innocent.

On the other side of Dr. Weber sat a man she'd never seen before. His military uniform was not festooned with colored bars like Pearson's. He had a big, jowly head with pouchy eyes that held zero warmth. He looked like a corrupt Roman emperor. Or at least the actor who'd played one on that TV series her family liked. His name tag said RITTER.

Petra looked back at Dr. Weber and asked, "Where's my mom and dad?"

It was Pearson who replied. "We're questioning them separately."

"What about Seth and Anaya?" she asked.

"They're detained as well."

"You can't just lock people up."

She tried to decipher the colonel's silent gaze, but in the end her eyes slunk away to Dr. Weber, who offered her an apologetic, tight-lipped smile.

"Sit down," Pearson told her, nodding at the chair.

She glanced back at the soldiers by the door—armed, like she was dangerous!—and then at the guy behind the camera. The red recording light blinked on.

She sat. This was an interrogation. Her mouth was suddenly bone dry. She had to be as calm and likeable as possible. She was good at acting. She got main parts at school. She'd convince them she was helpful and friendly. A *friendly* alien. *Half* alien. She'd tell them everything they wanted to know. She tried to make her eyes look as large and innocent as possible.

Colonel Pearson said, "I've now been fully briefed by Dr. Weber and consulted with Dr. Ritter, who is heading up a special task force south of the border."

That meant the US. Petra wanted to ask what kind of task force, and what sort of doctor Dr. Ritter was, but she thought it was best to keep her mouth shut for now.

Dr. Ritter's large, fleshy hands patted a beige file folder in front of him.

"We have some new test results to share with you," he said. It sounded like he was chewing something, but she realized it was just his words. Maybe he'd been particularly hard-hit by black grass allergies and was super congested. Or maybe this was the way he always talked.

From the folder he took a big glossy photograph and slid it across to her.

Even before she saw it properly, Petra broke out in gooseflesh. It was obviously a picture of a skull. Inside were the bright silver folds of a brain, like a giant, gleaming walnut.

"This is me?" she asked, her words clicking in her dry mouth.

Dr. Weber nodded. "It's from the MRI scans we did last week. Before we went to the eco-reserve."

Petra felt a panicked tightening in her chest. You didn't get shown a picture of your brain unless there was something wrong with it. She couldn't handle some new freakish thing about her body. She tried to imagine this was a picture from a textbook. Didn't work.

"The area of interest is here," Dr. Ritter said, pointing. "The occipital lobe. That's the part that governs vision and perception."

"Why's it blurry?" Petra asked, looking automatically to Dr. Weber.

"Sometimes you get small glitches," she replied. "Or that's what I initially thought. But when I looked at Seth's and Anaya's scans, I realized theirs had exactly the same blurred area."

Petra swallowed. "Why?"

"Whatever's there was interfering with the MRI's radio waves," Dr. Ritter told her in his chewy voice. "Luckily the good doctor here also did some functional scans using a different frequency. Those came out very clearly indeed."

From his folder Ritter took another picture and laid it on top of the first. This one was a grid of four close-ups, all from slightly different angles.

"Here," said Ritter, pointing to a silver shape.

Petra bent closer, an oily fear spreading through her stomach. Nestled in the wrinkles of her brain was an object that reminded her of a sea polyp with wavy little arms.

She didn't know anything about the brain, but her gut told her this thing did not belong. Her mind was desperately trying to telescope her away from her body. Somewhere outside this room, a hundred kilometers away, would be good.

"Is it a tumor?" she heard herself ask hopefully.

She'd never thought a brain tumor would be best-case scenario.

"No," said Dr. Weber gently.

She wanted her parents. She didn't want to see any more. There was alien DNA in each and every one of her cells, she was growing a tail, her skin was peeling off—but *this* thing, it was like a little animal living *inside* her.

"I'm gonna be sick," she mumbled.

Dr. Weber began to stand, but Colonel Pearson said no and nodded at one of the soldiers. Quickly the soldier moved a small garbage can beside Petra. She turned and retched. Nothing came up but strings of liquid. She spat. Her eyes watered and her nose ran. The last time she'd thrown up, her mother had held her hair out of the way. She'd rubbed her back and said kind things.

If she'd expected Colonel Pearson's expression to soften, she was mistaken. Dr. Ritter made a phlegmy sound in his throat and folded his fleshy hands.

"You okay, Petra?" Dr. Weber said kindly.

"What is it?" she asked. "That thing in my head."

Dr. Weber turned to the colonel. "It's obvious that these children are completely innocent and don't pose any kind of threat to—"

"That's not obvious to me at all," Dr. Ritter said. He stabbed his thick finger at the photos of her brain. "*That* is a transmitter."

Startled, Petra looked at Dr. Weber, who nodded reluctantly.

"It produces radio pulses. That's why our MRI images were scrambled."

"And Seth and Anaya have one, too?"

"Correct," Ritter said. He sat back in his chair, studying her. His gaze was so intense, it was like he was trying to bore his way inside her skull.

"Hang on," she said. "You don't think I'm actually sending *messages* to them!"

"We know you are," Pearson replied tersely.

"When?"

"The morning the black grass started dying, the same morning the second rain fell. Around five a.m., my comms team picked up a powerful radio pulse coming from inside the base. It lasted just under two minutes. We tracked the signal to its source: the apartment where you were all sleeping."

CHAPTER THREE

SETH

"HOW COULD I BE sending a signal if I was asleep?" Seth asked, bewildered.

From behind the table in the white interrogation room, Colonel Pearson watched him silently, waiting. So did Dr. Ritter, his eyes cold and intent in his saggy face.

Did they actually expect him to answer his own question? Since he'd been shown those pictures—that thing inside his brain—Seth's thoughts had scattered like puzzle pieces. He was still scrambling to fit them together.

A transmitter in his brain.

A radio signal sent from his head at five in the morning.

While he was asleep—

And dreaming.

He'd definitely been dreaming. He remembered the dream vividly. Over the years he'd had so many like it, but this one had been unique. He'd been flying and had seen his own feathered arms. Below him, Anaya leapt across a field; in a lake, Petra surged through the water. He'd been overwhelmed by an incredible sense of speed and purpose, and right before the dream ended, he'd felt the familiar ache building in his head—and then a sudden release, all the pain torrenting out of him into the sky.

Had *that* been a transmission? The one Pearson said they'd picked up?

"As I've been saying," Dr. Weber told the two men, "none of the kids are even aware of transmitting."

Seth was so glad she was here. When he'd first come into the room and seen her, he'd felt a surge of relief. She was here to fight for him, to make sure these military guys didn't think he was some kind of dangerous mutant.

"Are you communicating with them, Seth?" Dr. Ritter asked in his chewy voice.

"No!"

Dr. Weber said, "My theory is that Seth and the others, since birth, have been transmitting biological data to the cryptogens so they could determine if the kids were thriving in Earth's environment."

"Which could only mean their endgame is colonization," said Colonel Pearson. "And that means an invasion."

"But only when the conditions are right," said Dr. Weber. "The children didn't thrive. At puberty, two of them developed acute allergies. Seth, his entire infancy, suffered from fragile bones and had frequent fractures. It wasn't until the first big rain that the environment became more favorable for the children."

"And the cryptogens," said Ritter. "They're essentially terra-forming our planet, reshaping it for themselves. If they've been collecting biological data from these hybrids, as you suggest, they might easily be collecting other important data from them. With their cooperation."

"I'm not telling them anything!" Seth insisted.

"It also seems clear," Dr. Ritter went on, "that the structure in their brains isn't simply a transmitter. It's also a receiver." His lightless eyes settled on Seth. "Dr. Weber has told us you have some very interesting dreams."

Seth looked over at her, feeling a stab of betrayal. Why had she gone and told them about his dreams? The most personal things that belonged to him. And not a lot belonged to him. He didn't want to share them, and certainly not with Ritter.

Bluntly, Colonel Pearson asked, "Did you dream the morning the second rain fell?"

"It's all right, Seth," Dr. Weber said to him. "There's nothing you need to hide."

Before today, *everything* was about keeping secrets. Hiding his feathers. Cutting Anaya's claws. Concealing Petra's tail. Telling no one. Just a few nights ago, Dr. Weber had talked about moving them off the base for their own safety, so the army wouldn't discover their secret.

And now she was urging him to tell the truth. Or was she actually inviting him to play innocent and give Ritter and Pearson as little as possible? He felt terribly confused.

Testily, Ritter turned to Dr. Weber. "You said you could make him cooperate."

Seth frowned. Had they made some kind of deal? A horrible doubt wormed through him. Had he totally misunderstood things? He'd assumed she was on his side. But then why wasn't she banging on the table and demanding they let him go, or at least take off his handcuffs? And why wasn't *she* wearing handcuffs? Who was she actually working for?

"What's going on?" he asked.

His voice came out broken. That morning on the field—was it even forty-eight hours ago?—she'd asked him if she could be his foster mother, and he'd said yes. He desperately wanted her to be that person again, the one willing to give him a home, the one he could trust.

"Seth," she said calmly, "we've got new life-forms literally raining down on the planet. The colonel and Dr. Ritter want to know as much as possible about what we're facing. I agreed to help them with these interviews so I could be present, and be your advocate. They've promised me that the three of you will be safe."

Ritter cleared his throat. "*If* they cooperate with us. And if you can't assist us, Dr. Weber, you'll be removed from the room."

Fear forked through Seth. He didn't want Dr. Weber removed. Even if he wasn't sure whose side she was on.

"Yes," he blurted. "I dreamed that morning. Right before I woke up."

"Describe it."

He told them about the feathers on his arms. How he'd soared through the air. He told them he'd seen Petra swimming and Anaya bounding.

"I think we need to keep in mind that these are *dreams*," Dr. Weber said. "We have no idea of their importance, if any."

Ritter ignored her. "In these dreams are you aware of communicating with the cryptogens?"

"No."

"But you are aware of their presence?"

"Sometimes, yes. It's like someone's watching."

"You're flying in your dreams. Where are you going?"

"Toward them, I guess."

"Why would you want to do that?"

He hesitated. "Because it feels like I'm going somewhere good."

That was probably a mistake. He wished he could take that back.

"In your dreams do you speak at all? Are there words?"

"No."

Ritter leaned closer across the table. Seth could hear his nostrils make a little whistling noise.

"What do you say to them?"

"I told you, nothing!"

Over his lifetime, Seth had spent a lot of time like this. Sitting in a chair, in a crappy room, answering questions and talking to people who sometimes took notes. He would have to tell them personal stuff about how he felt, and what he'd been doing. He was always trying to convince them of things. That he was well behaved. That he was a good guy. A good bet. That he wasn't dangerous. That he deserved to have someone care for him.

His eyes strayed to Dr. Weber—did *she* still care about him?

Ritter leaned back and looked up at the ceiling. "Doesn't it seem convenient," he said, chewing on his words like he was enjoying some tasty food, "that the *moment* we discover how to kill the plants, a new wave of cryptogenic life pelts down?" His gaze dropped back on Seth. "Maybe they're watching. Or someone's *telling* them."

"Not me," Seth said, hating Ritter. "Anyway, you guys picked up our signals, right? Shouldn't you *know* what I said?"

"The transmission was coded," Ritter replied.

"Wow," Seth said. "With all your modern technology and everything."

"Seth," Dr. Weber warned, "I don't think being sarcastic is useful here."

"Aren't you supposed to be on my side?" Seth said, surprised by the anger in his voice. Then he jerked up straighter as Ritter slammed his fleshy palm against the table.

"What—do—you—tell—them?"

"Nothing!"

"What do they look like?"

"I've never seen them!"

Ritter reached inside an attaché case on the floor and pulled out Seth's sketchbook. The only grown-up Seth had shown that book to was Dr. Weber. Because he trusted her. Ritter slapped it on the table.

"That's private," Seth said, half rising from his chair.

"Sit down, Seth," said Pearson.

The soldiers at the door took a few steps closer, hands on their firearms.

Seth sat. The soldiers retreated.

"You don't seem to understand your situation," Colonel Pearson told him. "You're being detained as a threat to national security under the War Measures Act."

"I haven't done anything! Except help rescue people—and collect the soil that's killing the plants!"

"You're transmitting information to a hostile force."

"You just said you don't even know what I'm transmitting!"

Seth winced as Ritter opened his sketchbook and started paging through it. That dead gaze of his passed over his pictures like greasy fingers.

"It seems you have very detailed knowledge of what the cryptogens look like. And don't tell me these are all made up."

"Some of them are," he insisted. "I've been drawing that stuff since I was a kid. But some of it is stuff I saw in my dreams."

"A flying creature, an aquatic one, and a land-based one,"

Ritter remarked. "One with feathers, one with a tail, one with claws and fur."

"We can't know this is what the cryptogens actually look like," Dr. Weber said.

Ritter said, "On the contrary, I think Seth knows a great deal about them."

"I don't," Seth insisted.

"I'm told your feathers are very impressive. Do you think they'll form wings?"

"I don't know," Seth said.

"Do you hope they might?"

All his instincts told him to say nothing, just shrug. He looked at Dr. Weber. She'd told him to tell the truth. Maybe she didn't care what happened to him after all. So why not? If she wanted him to tell the truth, he'd tell the truth.

He said, "Yes."

"Did you know that second rain was coming?"

"No."

"Do you know what else is coming?"

"Of course not—"

"Are the aliens already here on Earth?"

It was such a startling thought that Seth faltered. "No, I don't . . . I don't know!"

Ritter turned to the colonel. "We have no idea what kind of information is flowing between them, or what kind of threat they pose. They need to be transferred immediately to a secure location."

Seth's eyes flew to Dr. Weber, who looked as shocked as he felt.

"Colonel," she said, "you told me—"

"I told you they'd be kept *safe*. I didn't say *where*. Dr. Ritter will be taking custody of them now."

"Where?" Dr. Weber demanded.

"That does not concern you," said Ritter.

"It does concern me. You can't just disappear these kids!"

"Kids." Ritter smiled. "Are they?"

In shock, Seth stared at his unreadable face.

Dr. Weber said, "Of course they're kids. And they're completely innocent. You can't trample on their human rights."

Ritter looked at his hands like he might be contemplating trimming his fingernails.

"These hybrids have less human DNA than a banana. If a banana isn't human, neither are these kids. And if they're not human, how can they have human rights?"

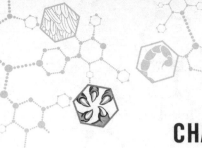

CHAPTER FOUR

BEHIND HER, ANAYA HEARD the soft boom of a heavy door closing. Without warning, her blindfold was tugged off. After so many hours of darkness, even the dim light of the corrugated metal tunnel made her squint. Seth and Petra stood blinking beside her.

It was such a relief to *see* them again. Automatically, she stepped toward Petra to hug her. A guard yanked her back by her handcuffed wrists.

"Hey!" she said, glaring at the five guards who encircled them.

She'd had enough of being prodded and *handled*. Blindfolded the whole time, she'd been shoved onto a helicopter, then an airplane, then another helicopter. Never had she had any idea where they were going. No one told them anything, not even what time—or day—it was.

"You two okay?" Seth asked her and Petra.

She nodded, and Petra muttered, "Yeah," even though she still looked a bit green from that last helicopter ride.

Anaya hoped they weren't going to be separated again. Back

on Deadman's Island, after her interrogation, she'd been locked in her solitary cell for at least another twenty-four hours. She'd gone over everything that had been said in that white, windowless room. The thing in her brain. Dr. Ritter's chilling words: *The fact is, we don't know what you are.* She'd felt like he'd just torn away her humanity.

"This way," the guard said now, giving Anaya a shove.

As if there were any other way to go. The corrugated tunnel dead-ended at a thick metal door that looked like the entrance to a bank vault. One of the guards pressed a buzzer, and after a moment, there was a loud clacking sound. It took two guards to haul the door open.

A wave of musty air crested over Anaya, and she was prodded inside a small vestibule. Behind a window of reinforced glass, a female guard regarded them before buzzing them inside.

Was this some kind of army base? She didn't see any sign, although the wall behind the reception desk did look like it had been hastily painted over. No Canadian flag, no American flag.

"Where are we?" she asked.

Without replying, the guards pushed them along a hallway. With a start, Anaya saw black grass growing out of a planter, then realized it was some kind of ancient plastic bamboo, mildewed with age.

They were brought to a set of elevator doors stenciled with the number 400. When they got on, Anaya checked out the old-fashioned control panel. There were four buttons, numbered 400 to 100. The guard inserted a key and pressed button 200, and with a jolt they started to descend.

So 400 was the highest level, and 100 the deepest. She didn't know if the elevator was just really slow or if they were going impossibly deep underground. Her ears popped.

When the doors rattled open, she felt like she'd entered a dingy hospital. Linoleum floors, pukey pastel colors on the walls, fluorescent lights set into stained ceiling tiles, and the sickly-sweet odor of mildew. She sneezed.

It had been a long time since she'd had an allergic reaction to anything. With the arrival of the alien plants, all her seasonal allergies had pretty much disappeared. But down here there must be mold or something. She sneezed again and wished she had a tissue—which would have been useless anyway since her hands were cuffed behind her back.

Lots of uniformed personnel moved around busily, some with clipboards, others dragging dollies stacked with boxes. It looked like they were still moving in. Everyone cut glances at her as she was marched past. The guards, she noticed, wore holsters, but the weapons looked stubbier than pistols, and she wondered if they were Tasers.

For the first time she realized no one had name tags or insignias on their clothing.

"Stop here," a guard told her in front of an open door.

When she saw Seth and Petra being taken farther down the corridor, she panicked. "Where are they going?"

Seth and Petra were all she had now. All during the long blindfolded journey, at least she'd *felt* their nearness as they'd jostled against one another. Whenever they'd tried to talk, they were promptly shouted at to stop.

She was prodded inside the room. There was an examination table, counters, a sink. It looked like a doctor's office, except it also had a shower stall. A wiry woman entered through a second door. A nurse? A doctor? She didn't introduce herself, only said, "Here," and handed Anaya two paper cups, one filled with water, the other containing a small pill.

"What's this?"

"Allergy meds. The air's filtered down here, but you're allergic to the mold spores."

She was surprised they knew this about her. Maybe they already had a huge file on her. Anaya swallowed the pill.

"Up on the table," the woman said, and drew a privacy curtain around it.

"I want to call my parents," Anaya said calmly.

Maybe this woman was a mother herself. Anyway, weren't prisoners entitled to a phone call? Wasn't that the law?

"Clothes off," she said. "Keep your underwear on."

Anaya took a breath. "I want to know where I am and why I'm here."

No reply. Anaya slumped. What had she expected? Milk and cookies and a phone? She knew she wasn't a simple prisoner. What was the phrase that creepy Dr. Ritter had used? *A grave threat to national security.* At least she wouldn't have to see him anymore.

"Clothes off," the woman repeated.

She kicked off her shoes. Her claws had already ripped through her socks. She was surprised by how quickly they'd grown. At the army base she'd been filing them down. At first, it was only the nail of each big toe that had tapered into a long claw. But now all her other toenails had darkened and sharpened, too.

She'd never forget her absolute horror the first time she'd seen those claws. What she felt now was nowhere near acceptance. More like resignation, and a tiny glimmer of wonder, too.

Next she peeled off her jeans. It was only a few days since she'd last shaved, but her calves had a thick covering of hair. Even her thighs were pretty much covered. They were also muscular in a way they'd never been before. Her legs had always been slightly too heavy for her liking, but now she felt an impatient strength in them. She'd been sitting for hours—days, really—and she wanted to move. She wanted to run and jump.

She glimpsed herself in a stained, wall-mounted mirror. Gone were the pimples and rashes that had once plagued her face. Gone were the puffy eyes, and the sneezing and wheezing. She hadn't used her inhaler in weeks. She looked so *healthy.* With her hair fanned untidily around her face, she was almost leonine.

Defiantly, she turned to meet the gaze of the woman—the

medic, or doctor, or whatever she was. She'd spent so much of her life wishing she could hide herself away, and she was done with that. She wasn't going to be ashamed of how she looked anymore.

"You going to file down my claws?" she asked.

She wasn't. But she did measure them, then checked Anaya's fingernails—which were starting to thicken and look bruised underneath the nails. She was going to have clawed hands, too. The woman plucked out a few strands of her leg hair and put them in a test tube. She opened a drawer under the examination table and passed Anaya a towel and a stack of fresh clothing.

"Shower and get dressed."

"I don't even get a wax?" Anaya asked, nodding at her legs. It made her feel better to crack a joke, like she had a bit of control. This got not even a grunt from the woman.

Anaya glanced at the clothing: a brown jumpsuit with short sleeves. On the breast was stenciled L9.

This did not seem like a good sign. If you gave someone a number, it was because you were taking away their name. And once you took away someone's name, it was a lot easier to take away whatever you wanted.

PETRA TURNED HER FACE into the shower, luxuriating in the hot water beating against her skin. She never, ever wanted to get out.

When the woman had told her to take a shower, Petra had sighed and said, "I'd love to, but I'm allergic to water."

"This water's safe for you," she'd been told curtly.

So she'd stepped warily into the shower stall, where a big plastic tank was mounted high up. The water inside had a suspicious yellow tinge. Petra had turned on the faucet and tested the drips with her finger, then her whole hand. She counted down the seconds. No reaction at all. Ecstatic, she'd stepped right under and taken her first proper shower since her allergy had started years ago.

She guessed this special water was like the stuff from the Cordova eco-reserve. When they'd rescued Anaya's father, Mr. Riggs, they'd had to cross a lake filled with acid-spitting water lilies. Somehow those lilies had changed the chemistry of the water, and Petra, to her amazement and delight, had been able to swim in it without getting seared like regular people.

Dr. Weber had said that, once she got the formula, she might be able to synthesize that water, but obviously these guys had beaten her to it. If she could shower every day, maybe things wouldn't be so bad down here.

She checked her amazingly smooth legs, then the rough patches spreading up her torso. She craned her neck to catch a glimpse of her tail, and shuddered as it twitched energetically in the water. *Oh, it's so hard being a teenage girl,* people were always saying. They had no freaking idea.

"Out," the woman in the white coat said.

Petra stayed in until she got barked at again and then reluctantly emerged in her towel. She saw the clothes waiting for her and sighed. The jumpsuit was a deeply hideous minty green. She'd look like a corpse in this. As she put it on, she noticed she'd been labeled W10, and that there was a Velcro flap in the seat.

"For your tail," said the woman. "When it gets longer."

"*How* long?" Petra asked in alarm.

"Remains to be seen."

No way was she going to let it stick out for everyone to gawk at. She guided it down her right pant leg, then pulled on the ugly black slippers they'd provided.

"Follow me."

The guard who'd stood watch outside now led her down a series of corridors. This place was a maze.

"Where's Seth and Anaya?" She wanted her friends back. Or were they planning on chucking her in a cell all by herself? "Would it kill you to answer me?"

Then she reminded herself, again, that she was going to be on her best behavior. Being snarky wasn't going to help her. She had to be cooperative. She had to show she wasn't a threat of any kind.

She passed doors stenciled with things like RESTRICTED AREA: PHONE AND WAIT and SENIOR OFFICERS ONLY. Through one window she glimpsed a huge faded wall map and antique computers.

In another room people were setting up more modern equipment. Everyone was hurrying, and she got the sense they were still getting this place ready. Was it all just for the three of them?

Twice her guards stopped to unlock doors barring the corridor. It was all done with keys, she noticed. No high-tech touch pads or retinal scanners. This place was definitely old—it sure smelled old—and she didn't think it was built to be a prison. In the corners of hallways were sad, discolored plastic plants.

As she was led toward a set of double doors, she frowned. From beyond those doors came echoing shouts and the unmistakable squeaky footfalls of a school gymnasium. One of the guards pushed the doors wide, and the sounds burst over her— along with the familiar smell of rubber and varnished wood. Colored lines were painted on the floor, basketball nets raised at either end.

And everywhere: kids.

Stunned, she walked inside. All the kids looked around the same age as her, and all wore jumpsuits that were blue or brown or the same vile green as hers. Various stations had been set up around the gym where kids were doing drills. She saw a boy with hairy arms doing a standing high jump onto a stack of truck tires. A girl with feathered arms slashed at a punching bag. Petra's eyes locked onto the swinging tail of a boy doing laps.

Back on Deadman's Island, Dr. Weber had said there were others like them. But Petra had no idea there'd be so *many*. The same terrible thing must have happened to all their mothers. And now the kids had been collected and brought here, like some crazy alternative school. The kids in blue were labeled with an A, the kids in brown an L.

She searched for Seth. For a lot of the blindfolded journey here, she'd been smooshed up beside him and been surprised how reassuring she'd found his warmth, and even his slightly musty smell. In the helicopter she'd felt so cold, like her whole body was coated in frost, and only Seth holding her hand had stopped her shivering.

A man in sweats with a clipboard was walking toward her. He was extraordinarily thick and muscular. With his square jaw, overly blow-dried hair, and neutral expression, he looked very much like an action figure. Or someone who should be hanging around with Barbie.

What she wanted to say was, *Let me guess, your name's Ken and you're a social worker who's super concerned about our safety.*

What she said instead was nothing. Because she was going to be cooperative and helpful.

"I'm Paul Samson," the man said. "I work for military intelligence."

"Oh," she said, taken aback that he'd actually told her his name and what he did. That was a first here. "I came with two friends. Are they here?"

He glanced at his clipboard. "Still in intake. They'll be along."

Petra looked around the gym. "How many of us are there?"

"Currently twenty-three at this facility."

At *this* facility? "How many facilities are there?"

This was met with silence.

"Okay, so *where* are we?" she asked instead.

"You're in an underground bunker that blocks all radio communication."

"Right. Because you're worried we're communicating with the cryptogens."

"Correct. You're being detained as threats to national and international security."

Petra had to bite back her smile, the idea was so insane. Paul's face showed no sign of amusement. He was blunt, but she was grateful he was actually talking to her and answering some of her questions.

"We're at war," he went on. "Our enemy has more advanced technology, and they're intent on our annihilation. We suspect you share many traits with the enemy—"

"Sure, but—"

"We don't yet know what you're capable of. We don't know what your intentions are."

"Oh, come on!" Petra said, then checked herself. She needed to control her temper.

"We don't enjoy detaining kids and separating them from their families," Paul said. "All of you are here for the greater good. I think you can understand that, Petra."

Her first name. Like some textbook maneuver to win her trust. She figured every kid had probably gotten this same speech.

"Yes," she said, trying to sound contrite. "I understand. You need to know as much as possible about our enemy. So we can beat them."

He regarded her carefully. "Exactly. You will be fed, and you will be safe, and you will be *here* until such time as we see fit."

Petra wanted to hate him, but she couldn't quite. He sort of reminded her of her mom. Very matter-of-fact. Following orders for the good of humanity.

"Are you in charge?" she asked.

"We're under the command of Dr. Ritter."

Her spirits plummeted. That guy with the freaky voice. Her eyes whipped around the room but didn't find him. Why was a doctor in charge, anyway? Wasn't it weird there wasn't a major or colonel or somebody running this place?

"We have some tests for you now," Paul said, and walked off. Her guard gripped her arm and steered her across the gym.

There were way more guards than kids here. All of them had Tasers holstered in their belts. She was led toward a corner of the gym with tables of equipment and a couple of white-coated lab techs.

"Sit down," one of the White Coats said, nodding to the empty chair beside a boy swigging from a water bottle. His face was flushed, like he'd just finished laps. His green jumpsuit said W2.

"Hey, W10," he said with a grin. And then in a fake whisper added, "I'm Darren."

Her eyes went straight to his arms. They were pleasingly

muscular, but what riveted her gaze were the gold-and-black tattoos that stretched from his fingertips to his upper arms, where they disappeared into his short sleeves. She squinted and looked closer. Were they tattoos?

"You don't have any patterning yet, huh?" he asked her.

"Patterning?"

"Your skin's shedding, though, right?"

"Mostly my legs so far."

"That's how it started with me, too. Then chest and back, and then arms. And after that, the patterns started coming in. Just kind of rising up through my skin." He stretched his arm invitingly toward her. "Want to touch it?"

The weird thing was, she did. There was something hypnotic about the pattern, the spiraling black bands with gold triangles in between. It almost looked like medieval armor, but so amazingly smooth.

"You'll be getting yours soon," Darren said, like he was trying to reassure her.

"Oh boy. Something to look forward to."

Darren had shaggy sandy hair and was handsome, in an obvious kind of way. It was weird meeting someone in a prison jumpsuit and not their usual clothes. She got a lot of clues about someone's personality from clothes. But Darren seemed pretty easy to read. He had one of those good heads where everything was the right shape and in the right place. When he smiled, his cheeks dimpled and his eyes lit up with bad-boy mischief. He was good-looking and knew it, and was undoubtedly popular, maybe even an alpha. Ruefully, she realized he was the kind of guy she usually went for. But right now she didn't even feel a flicker of interest. She wondered where Seth was.

The two White Coats were busy assembling small bottles and clinking glass things on a tray.

Darren looked at her. "You're still hiding yours, huh?"

It took her a second to realize he was talking about her tail. Automatically she checked for his. Obligingly he angled his chair.

It jutted from his Velcro flap. It was much longer than hers, muscular and knuckled, and flattened toward the end. It had the same markings as his arms.

"Whoa! How'd you keep it hidden before you got here?"

"Very baggy jeans."

She was catching a glimpse of what was coming her way, and she didn't feel ready. She looked back at his patterned arms. That she could handle. And hadn't she always wanted a tattoo? Once she and Rachel had snuck off to get one, but the parlor wanted a note from her mother—as if that would ever happen. The thought of Mom came with a stab of sadness, and she slowly pulled in a breath.

"I've gotta say, the flap's way more comfortable," Darren said.

His tail gave a swish and Petra gasped. "You can make it move?"

"Yep. Moves on its own, too. When I showered this morning, it nearly threw me off balance."

She nodded. "When I swam, mine was twitching like crazy."

"You *swam*? Where?"

When she told him about the lake on the eco-reserve, he looked at her with pure envy.

"Man, I'd love to go swimming. I guess we could now, if the water's changed. All us W's."

"W for Water," she said, and felt stupid that she hadn't figured it out earlier.

She looked out across the gym. She spotted some L kids in brown jumpsuits doing laps, running way faster than anyone else, and she thought of Anaya with her super-strong legs, how she could jump. L for Land.

Her gaze roved on, and her heart gave a happy squeeze when she spotted Seth in a blue jumpsuit. He had his arms stretched out, and a White Coat was measuring his feathers. A for Air. Beside Seth was a girl who looked familiar, though Petra couldn't figure out why. She had feathers, too. They weren't as long as Seth's, but their colors were even more vivid: purples and golds and greens and reds.

"The flyers," Darren said beside her, following her gaze.

"That's what you call them?"

He shrugged. "Seems pretty obvious. Runners, swimmers, flyers. I've even heard the guards saying it. Anyway, they're kind of weird, the flyers."

"What do you mean?" she asked, feeling indignant on Seth's behalf.

"They only hang out with each other."

She couldn't help smiling. Even in prison bunkers, there were cliques.

"Put this on."

A White Coat was holding out a plastic mask designed to cover mouth and nose. "What's this for?" Petra asked.

"It's a stamina test. Hold your breath as long as you can. We'll know if you inhale."

"Okay." Obediently she began pulling the mask over her face. "Is this to see how long I can stay underwater?"

"Yep," said Darren, putting on his own mask.

"You've done this before?"

He nodded. "I hold the high score."

The White Coat said, "Take one last big breath. And go."

As she held her breath, Petra tried to find Anaya. The gym was a bit like some bizarre science fair—with them as the exhibits. Grown-ups in white coats inspecting everything. Guards with Tasers in case anyone needed an educational jolt of high voltage.

She lost track of time. Above the door was a caged clock, but its second hand wasn't moving. When she glanced at Darren, he winked at her. So conceited.

She closed her eyes and pretended she was underwater. Often her thoughts flowed back to that swim in the lake, how she'd seen so clearly and swum so well, and how *good* it felt to be in water, period. She still didn't feel any need to take a breath.

When she opened her eyes, Darren's forehead was creased. His eyes flicked to her, and she could tell he was hoping she'd bail first. That wasn't going to happen. She winked at him. With a gasp, Darren sucked in a big lungful. His mask beeped. The technician made a note on her pad, then turned her attention to Petra, who counted out another fifteen seconds before sipping a dainty breath.

"We have a new high score," said the White Coat as Petra peeled off her mask.

"Good going," Darren said to Petra, but she could tell he didn't mean it.

She knew it was silly, but she felt ridiculously pleased with herself.

A different White Coat rolled a skinny table in front of them. "Arms up here. I'm going to put a drop of fluid on your skin. Tell me if there's itchiness or pain."

"What is it?" Petra asked suspiciously.

"We're doing a range of aqueous solutions."

Aqueous meant water, which meant major allergic reaction.

"No way, I'm—"

"It's okay," Darren told her. "I've done this one, too. You'll be fine."

"How long have you been here?" she asked him.

"Four days. I was one of the first. They were still putting in light bulbs."

With a glass pipette, the tech dropped a bead of cloudy liquid onto her outstretched forearm and then Darren's.

"Any itching?" the White Coat asked.

She waited apprehensively, then said, "I'm good."

"Me too," said Darren.

A second fluid was dripped onto her arm, then a third and fourth. To her surprise she didn't feel any discomfort with any of them. What was this stuff, and why wasn't it triggering her allergy? She glanced at Darren's tattooed skin. It really was strangely beautiful.

"Last one," said the tech. She dropped a dot of yellowish liquid onto both their wrists.

Almost right away Petra felt a sharp point of heat, steadily spreading.

"That one hurts!"

The lab technician promptly drizzled another solution on her arm. The pain stopped instantly, leaving only a red dot on her skin.

"I'm good," Darren said.

"Seriously?" Petra asked, looking over. The bead of liquid jiggled harmlessly on his unblemished skin.

"When your new skin comes in," Darren said, "this stuff won't hurt you either."

He tilted his arm and the drop slid like oil off Teflon and landed on the table. There was a hiss as it burned a small crater in the laminated surface.

Petra looked at the White Coat in shock, then anger.

"You *put* that on us?" Petra said, her voice rising.

The White Coat glanced over her shoulder to make sure a guard was nearby, and Petra checked her temper.

"The experiment was controlled. You're completely unharmed."
Petra looked at her forearm. The red dot was already fading.
Still . . .

"You are both very acid-tolerant," the White Coat said, like
this made everything okay. Like it was something that might help
them get a job later. The lab tech moved away and started typing
on a laptop.

"Pretty wicked, huh?" Darren said. "We're practically inde-
structible!"

He seemed awfully cheerful about being a freak in a bunker.
She wondered how much he'd been told about what was happening. About what exactly he *was*.

"How much do you know?" she asked carefully. "Like,
about—"

"That Paul guy briefed me when I got here. We're half alien.
Half *cryptogen*. Mom was abducted. My father's not my real
father—no big loss there. We're not allergic to the plant stuff.
Oh yeah, and we have transmitter things in our brains. Which
is why they buried us down here. I think that's about it. Am I
missing anything?"

"Bugs," she said.

"What?"

She told him about the second big rain, and the things she'd
seen hatch in Dr. Weber's lab.

"Holy crap," he said. "What'll they grow into?"

"Don't know," she said, then looked at his tattoos and his tail. "And we don't really know what we'll grow into either."

SETH RECOGNIZED THE GIRL right away.

Back on Deadman's Island, before they'd been discovered, Dr. Weber had shown them a video of a girl with feathered arms. She'd been in a hospital, crying.

She wasn't crying now. Her feathers were a blaze of color as she slashed at a narrow length of lumber resting between two sawhorses. In a few quick blows, she cut through it, and the jagged halves clattered to the floor.

He remembered how, on Cordova Island, he'd been able to slash down the black grass. His arms were like scythes. He'd never guessed there were others like him.

The girl stepped back, frowning. Her thick angled eyebrows and dark eyes gave her a slightly ferocious look. She was tall, with a strong jaw and wavy hair cut in a bob that seemed old-fashioned, like a silent movie star's. Seth tried not to stare. Her blue jumpsuit said A3. A thicker piece of lumber was set up for her.

"Her feathers are the sharpest," said the tall, regal-looking boy beside Seth. His name was Vincent and he'd introduced himself when Seth was first brought over. His feathers were all different shades of purple. Nearby was a girl called Siena, with red hair and a long, pale face, lightly freckled. She looked kind of like a vampire. Her feathers had just started to come in and were vibrant shades of blue, the same color as her eyes.

"Who is she?" Seth asked quietly, nodding at A3.

"Esta," Siena said. "She doesn't talk much."

"She seems really angry," Vincent said.

She probably had plenty to be angry about, Seth thought. Didn't they all?

There were lots of guards around them, way more than anywhere else in the gym. Paul, that hunk of vertical protein, stood watching with the White Coats as Esta demolished the next piece of lumber. When she was done, she went and stood off by herself. He wanted to talk to her, but he'd never been good at introducing himself.

"A4!" one of the White Coats said, and Seth had to check his own jumpsuit to realize that was him.

They'd stretched chicken wire across the sawhorses. Wood was one thing, but wire worried him. He didn't want to tear his feathers.

"Go ahead," he was prompted.

He took a careful swipe. Sparks danced off the tips of his feathers, and he looked around in alarm.

"Don't worry, it's just the metal alloy in your feathers," Paul told him. They seemed to know more about his feathers than he did. "Keep going."

Seth checked his feathers to make sure they weren't damaged. Metal alloy? His next swipe was harder. Sparks flew as he cut gashes in the wire. It felt good to swing his arms and feel their power. One more slash and he cut through the entire sheet of chicken wire. He looked over at Esta to see if she'd noticed. Briefly, her intent eyes met his.

"All A's, over here," one of the White Coats said.

When Seth saw the two punching bags hanging from the ceiling, his heart sank. Each had been dressed up in a soldier's battle armor with a happy face painted at the top. Someone's idea of a joke.

He and Esta were lined up in front of the two bags.

"A3 and A4, strike," one of the White Coats told them.

"I don't want to." He didn't want to attack something dressed up like a human. It would make him look like the enemy.

"It's only an exercise," said the White Coat, hardly looking up from his pad.

Without hesitation, Esta struck her punching bag. Her feathers cut through the fabric of the flak jacket and left a long gray gash in the armor beneath.

"Hold off." Two White Coats came closer to examine the damage.

"Went right through the ballistic nylon," said one.

"Couple of millimeters into the manganese steel plate as well."

They moved to one side and looked at Seth.

"A4, you're up."

"No," said Seth.

One of the guards stepped toward him, a Taser in his hand. Seth knew about those things. They shot out a wire and jolted you with high voltage.

"I urge you to comply," said a meaty voice behind him.

Seth felt a chill as he turned and saw Dr. Ritter. He'd never wanted to lay eyes on him again. *If they're not human, how can they have human rights?* Seeing him made Seth think of Dr. Weber, and how she hadn't been able to help him—or hadn't *wanted* to. He still wasn't sure which. After his interrogation, he'd never heard from her again. He'd been thrown back in a cell, then blindfolded and taken to this place. He'd actually hoped he might see her here, but no. She'd abandoned him.

"Sure," he said angrily. "I'll comply."

He flared his feathers to their full length and moved in on the punching bag. He slashed the flak jacket to ribbons. He was aware of the White Coats telling him to stop so they could study the damage, but Seth didn't feel like stopping. With another blow he cut a gash across the happy face, sending foam flying. A final chop of his left arm severed the rope holding the punching bag, and it thumped on the floor.

"How's that?" he demanded, turning to face Ritter. His pulse was loud in his ears. He felt a bit sick. He'd liked doing that, and it scared him.

He noticed that several guards had their hands resting on

their Tasers and were standing very alert. Even Vincent and Siena looked alarmed. But Esta gave a small nod, like she understood what he was feeling.

"Very impressive," said Ritter. "You four have given us a lot of data."

He came over and handed each of them a towel and a bottle of water, like a coach pleased with the performance of his star athletes.

"Have you ever flown?" Ritter asked them.

Seth shook his head, startled, but also intrigued. How many times had he dreamed of such a thing?

"Go ahead. Try. All of you."

Excitement pulsed through him. Did Ritter know something? Did he actually think it was possible? Seth flapped his arms, but when he heard snickering, he wondered if this was just a humiliation. He kept going anyway. He jumped and thrashed his arms harder, but down he came every time. Esta fared no better, and neither did Vincent and Siena.

". . . no way it's aerodynamically possible," one of the White Coats muttered.

". . . don't have the musculature . . ."

When he turned to glare at them, the muttering stopped.

"We'd like you to try gliding," Ritter said.

When Seth was on the eco-reserve, he'd fallen into the lake from way up high. He'd spread his wings instinctively and felt sure he was gliding for a second. Back on Deadman's Island, it hadn't been possible to try again, not when they needed to keep everything secret.

At the very end of the gymnasium was a blue high-jump mat.

"Take a run," Ritter said, "and when you reach the marker, open your arms and jump headfirst for the mat."

The first run was easy. The marker was placed within a meter of the mat and anyone could have jumped and belly flopped onto it. The White Coats moved the marker back a quarter of a meter and made them do it again. Each time, they increased the gap a bit more.

"Fast as you can!" Ritter shouted as Seth sprinted.

At the two-meter marker, he felt lift for the first time. When he opened his wings and pitched himself forward, he sensed the air bundling beneath his feathers, holding him, just for a second, before he skimmed down on the mat.

"I felt it!" he shouted to the spotter, unable to hide his excitement.

He rolled off the mat and watched as Esta launched, sucking in his breath in wonder. He could see her feathers bow as they took her weight. Her body was stretched straight, legs bending back like she'd dived from a great height, and she soared a few centimeters above the mat before touching down.

"It's amazing!" she said, turning her flushed face to him, laughing with delight. She was so beautiful suddenly that he couldn't speak.

"Let's do it again," she said.

If he could glide, maybe actual flight would come. That made sense, didn't it? If his feathers kept growing, he'd have more lift.

"That's it for the day!" someone called out.

Seth felt a pang of disappointment. He could've kept going much longer. But he glowed with the certainty that his wings had held him aloft.

THE TREADMILL SPED UP again, and Anaya kept pace.

Running had always been her most hated gym activity. At school she usually sat out because of her asthma. But in the past few weeks—once her allergies had virtually disappeared—her strength and stamina had improved massively. Even though she hadn't had a proper sleep in the past few days, she felt strong. She was so grateful to move. She actually felt *good*.

"They built a ton of these places during the Cold War," the boy on the machine next to hers said. "In case there was nuclear Armageddon."

His name was Charles and he wore a brown jumpsuit like hers. His label said L2, and according to him, he was one of the very first kids they brought here, nearly a week ago.

"They could just go underground and run the country from down here, until all the radiation cleared up. I did a school project on it."

Anaya figured Charles had probably done school projects on a lot of things, and gotten A's on all of them.

"This place is like a time capsule," he said. "I mean, wait till you see the cafeteria. There are *National Geographic*s from 1964. And the board games! There's Monopoly and The Game of Life, but the boxes have all these cartoony people in cardigans and bow ties, smoking pipes and smiling like lunatics. Also, they have LPs here. Like, *vinyl*."

He talked fast, even while running. He had a mop of black hair, very curly and faintly greasy. Glasses framed blue eyes that were never still for more than a split second. His fingernails were thick and black. He also had more arm hair than she'd seen on any teenage boy. And his thin face had serious stubble on it. He gave the impression of a very smart and very nervous meerkat.

She was still getting used to the fact that there were so many others like her. Nine in total, all in brown jumpsuits, each with the letter L stenciled on it. Within seconds of meeting Charles, he'd told her all about his allergies: pollens, foods, pretty much everything under the sun except the alien plants.

"Do you have any idea where we are?" she asked, surprised she could talk without losing her breath.

"They flew me out of Halifax, but I was asleep for a lot of it, so I don't even know how long I was traveling."

It was hard to imagine him ever sleeping. He seemed like he had coffee instead of blood.

"I don't think we're in Canada," she said. "All the signs I've seen here, they're only in English. They'd be in French, too, if this were a Canadian base."

"A very well-observed point," said Charles, and Anaya decided that he'd probably been on the school debating team. And thinking of school made her think of Salt Spring Island, and Mom and Dad, and *home*. She had no idea how far away, or even what direction, it was.

"We could be anywhere in the world," she said sadly.

"Nah. Jen, she's L3 over there? Doing the tire jumps? She's from Chicago, and she swears she wasn't traveling more than three hours. So we must be somewhere in North America."

The treadmill sped up again, and so did Anaya. Her legs felt like they had their own engine. She breathed smoothly and deeply.

"So what's going on topside?" Charles asked her. "They don't tell us anything."

She told him about the herbicide and the rainfall of crypto-genic eggs.

"Geez" was all he said. He was starting to sound a little out of breath now.

The machine beeped and sped up once more. Charles tried to keep pace, then slapped the red button. To Anaya's surprise, she was still okay. She looked straight ahead, concentrating, but was aware that a couple of White Coats had come over to watch.

The pitch of the machine was a high whine now. She thought she heard someone say *thirty-two* in hushed tones. Right now she really wanted to keep running, like she did in those euphoric dreams: racing and leaping, never wanting to stop.

"Man, you've got stamina," Charles said when she finally came off. "Did you run marathons or something?"

"Ha!" she said. "I wish."

But she was pleased by his compliment. *I like myself better like this.* The moment she had the thought, she realized how crazy it sounded. But it was true. She liked this new healthier, stronger version of herself.

She glanced down at the sneakers they'd given her to wear. The toes of both were ripped apart by her claws. When she looked up, Charles was watching her. He wasn't looking at her claws; he was looking at *her*. On the treadmill, she'd assumed he was just talkative and friendly. But this look was different. Quickly his eyes flicked away. Heat bloomed in her cheeks.

A White Coat came up and dropped new pairs of sneakers in front of them.

"L2 and L9. Your turn for tire jumps."

She was told to stand in front of two stacked tires and jump straight up onto them. The first time was easy. Each time she succeeded, they added another tire.

"You're good at this," Charles said as they both stood atop their tire piles. He brushed away his damp hair.

"You too."

From up high she could see the entire windowless gym. With

huge relief she spotted Petra and Seth. It was amazing how vulnerable she'd felt, being separated from them.

Charles topped out at four foot nine. Anaya kept going. Paul and Ritter had come over to watch.

"Go, L9!" Charles shouted out, and was told to be quiet by a guard.

She couldn't make the last tire, even after three tries. The White Coats took notes, their faces neutral. She was given a towel and a bottle of water.

"You did five four!" Charles told her. "You know what the world record is?"

"No."

"Five four. You just set it."

She grinned. "How do you even know that?"

"I spend way too much time reading *Guinness World Records*. Seriously, the old one was five three. You beat it!"

Dr. Ritter came up, his dead eyes regarding her. In his unnerving, chewy voice he said, "You're going to be extremely useful to us."

CHAPTER FIVE

"THEY'RE TRAINING US TO be soldiers," Darren said.

Petra frowned at him across the cafeteria table. "Did someone tell you that?"

"No, but isn't it obvious?"

He lifted his hands and raised his eyebrows, like only a moron could disagree. Petra wished he'd go away. He was nice to look at, but he was also a little annoying—mostly because she wanted to be alone with Anaya and Seth. Right now, she wanted it to be just the three of them.

But Darren had made that impossible. He'd glommed onto her as they'd been escorted from the gym to the cafeteria. Seth had already been sitting at an out-of-the-way table and had not looked thrilled to see Darren. And moments later, Anaya had headed over with a scruffy kid called Charles, a runner. He looked a bit like the main kid in that series about lunatic gamers who never shaved or slept and only drank energy drinks.

So much for just the three of them.

The cafeteria smelled of old socks and greasy, long-ago meals.

It made Petra feel both disgusted and hungry. The floor was alternating white and blue linoleum tiles. There were chrome-sided tables and lime-green chairs. The pink walls had faded posters of forests and mountains—maybe to make people forget there were no windows or fresh air.

At one end of the cafeteria was a little recreation area with shelves of books and board games, and some exercise machines. A few kids were playing foosball. Someone else was pedaling a stationary bike. No TV, no computers. No Wi-Fi. Obviously.

"I'm telling you," Darren was saying, "they've been drilling us here since day one. Laps. Tests. That's training."

"They're just studying us," Petra said. "They want to know what we're capable of."

"Think they can hear us with those?" Seth asked quietly, nodding at one of the security cameras mounted near the ceiling.

"Doubt it," Charles said. "This place was never meant to be a prison. And from what I've seen, it's very low-tech."

"Petra's right," Seth said. "They want to know what they'll have to fight one day. They're scared of us."

To make his point, he lifted his arms, which were now in casts. Petra had watched them doing it in the gym before they left. The White Coats had sleeved and plastered all the flyers' arms, wrist to shoulder, with a bendable joint at the elbow.

"They're being cautious," Darren said, nodding at Seth's casts. "Those feathers are super sharp. But Dr. Ritter knows we're not the enemy."

Petra saw Seth's eyes stray across the room and followed his gaze to a flyer sitting by herself. Petra recognized her now: she was the hybrid in the video Dr. Weber had shown them.

"Also, they *need* us, right?" Darren said. "Look what we can do." To Anaya and Charles he said, "You guys run and jump like freaking kangaroos. And you," he said to Seth, "your wings. Man! Those feathers can cut through anything." He turned back to her. "And you and me. We can swim in that acid water you're talking about. We're like underwater ninjas. They totally need us. We're *elite* forces!"

For emphasis, Darren leaned forward so his biceps hardened. Petra noticed that he seemed to pick a lot of positions where his muscles flexed. She hated that she always looked.

"Darren, they think we're *spies,*" Anaya said. "They're not going to give us *weapons.* They'd never trust us."

"But maybe we can make them," Petra said. "Trust us, I mean."

Anaya looked at her in astonishment. "You want to be a soldier?"

"Of course not! And you don't have to bite my head off. All I'm saying is, maybe if we just . . . *cooperate,* and do what they tell us, and answer all their questions and whatever, they won't think we're the *enemy.*"

"They don't even think we're *human,*" Seth reminded her. "Ritter said that to me!"

"Never said that to me." Darren smirked.

"They've been pretty good to us so far," Charles said. "Feeding us, keeping us safe."

"Good point," said Petra.

She'd been watching Charles. At first she'd thought he was a weird loner who latched onto new kids, but then she realized he was an admirer—of Anaya. His eyes were fixed on her. This was a first.

Grudgingly, she had to admit that Anaya was looking very pretty lately. Being a cryptogen hybrid agreed with her. Her skin was luminous, dark eyes bright, hair lustrous. She looked sleek and strong. Petra doubted Charles would be as keen if her face got all hairy. Still, she supposed Charles would get even hairier, so maybe they were made for each other. They could have super-hairy babies.

To make herself feel better, Petra did her pouty mouth, but Charles didn't even glance her way. For that matter, neither did Seth, whose eyes kept straying across the cafeteria to Esta. At least Darren noticed her pouty mouth.

"All I know," Darren was saying, "is that Ritter saved my life."

"What?" Petra said in surprise.

"Back in Austin, I fell into a pit plant," Darren said. "And I couldn't get out. It was super deep, and I was inside for, like, almost a whole day. Clothes and shoes all burned away."

Petra winced, not even wanting to imagine it.

"I thought I was going to die in there, but then I hear some voices, and I shout, and these two huge guys manage to cut the thing open. They drag me out, and I'm all naked and covered in acid, but absolutely fine. Then they see my tail and freak out big-time. They lock me in their trunk!"

"They locked you in their *trunk*?" she said.

"They thought I was an alien! Anyway, I can hear them talking about *getting rid of me*. And then we drive for a long time, and I'm thinking, *Great, I was going to die in a pit plant and now I'm going to die in a trunk.* But after a while we stop, and it's quiet. Finally the trunk opens, and Dr. Ritter's standing there with some soldiers. That's how I ended up down here."

Everyone was quiet for a moment, then Seth said, "Well, that's a beautiful story, Darren." His sarcasm was obvious. "Doesn't make him a good guy, though."

"And what makes him a bad guy?"

"We are in numbered *jumpsuits*, Darren," Anaya said. "They're calling us enemies of the state!"

"If I were running the military," Charles said, like he was giving a class presentation, "if I were running things—just hear me out on this, okay?—I'd probably do exactly what Ritter's doing. The cryptogens are obviously planning an invasion of Earth, sending down deadly plants, and now all these new bugs. And then there's us, these weird-looking hybrids with brain transmitters. For all we know, we might seriously be helping the cryptogens, giving them data without even knowing it. Whatever we're sending them, I don't think it's cookie recipes. If I were Ritter, I'd put us underground and study us, too. Absolutely."

Petra had to hand it to Charles. He was pretty persuasive.

"They dragged us away from our parents and locked us in a bunker!" Anaya said.

"Yeah, because they're trying to protect the entire planet!" Petra reminded her.

"I don't get you," her friend said, looking bewildered. "So you're okay with what they're doing to us now? Back on Deadman's Island you were—"

"I know," Petra cut her off. She didn't need Anaya telling everyone how she'd yelled and cried for her mother as they dragged her away. She took a breath. "I'm just trying to see it their way, from their point of view. I mean, Dr. Weber was studying us, right? Blood tests, MRIs. How's this so different?"

"She *cared* about us," Anaya retorted.

"Maybe," Seth said grimly, "she was *helping* Pearson and Ritter."

"No, she wasn't," Anaya protested. "She was only *cooperating* with them because she had to. She didn't want this for us!"

"They're *never* letting us out of here," Seth said.

"Do you have any evidence to support that?" Charles inquired.

Petra rolled her eyes. Charles was getting a little tedious now. He'd probably been *captain* of his debating team.

"Best-case scenario," Seth said, "the army beats back all the plants and everything else. Maybe we even help fight the cryptogens ourselves, just like Darren says. Brave child soldiers. Yay! We won. You think people are going to accept us afterward? You think they're going to thank us for our service and put us in Coca-Cola commercials? They will *never* accept us. They will *never* trust us. We spend the rest of our lives down here. And that's the *best*-case scenario."

"You have a very negative worldview," Charles said to Seth.

Seth shrugged. "Hasn't disappointed me so far."

To Petra he seemed to be retreating behind his eyes. It scared her. She wanted to say something to change his mind and bring him back to them. To her.

Across the room someone shouted, "Dinner!" At the far end of the cafeteria was a long metal tray slide, but the serving area had been walled over, except for a small hatch, which was now open. Someone on the other side pushed trays out along the slide.

"L's first!" the invisible server bellowed.

"That's us," Charles said to Anaya.

"Is it really gross?" Petra asked.

"Actually, it's pretty good," Charles said, and to Anaya added, "They know all about our allergies. We can eat everything."

The two of them went off together to get their meals. Petra looked at Seth. His gaze had strayed back across the room. To Esta.

WHEN IT WAS SETH'S turn to go get his meal, he made sure he arrived at the counter just after Esta.

The whole time he'd been watching her, she'd been drawing. She must've found pen and paper somewhere. It made him miss his sketchbook, left behind on Deadman's Island. Or maybe locked away here, where Dr. Ritter could page through it with his meaty fingers.

Standing behind Esta in line, watching her fold the sheets of paper into her pocket, he caught a sketch of wings and felt a sudden, strong pulse of kinship.

"I draw them, too," he told her.

She looked around at him, eyebrows raised quizzically. "Really?"

He nodded. "I've filled tons of sketchbooks."

Her guarded expression melted away. "Me too."

"We're sitting over there," he said. "If you want to join us."

She assessed their table. "The new girls."

"Anaya and Petra. We're from Salt Spring Island. We've been through a lot together."

"Who's the dude with the muscles?"

Seth was surprised she didn't already know. She'd been here longer than him. She really must keep to herself.

"Darren."

On first sight, Seth hadn't liked him. It was irritating, the way he carried himself, like his muscles were so big he couldn't possibly walk properly. He was an easy talker, which always made Seth suspicious. Years ago, in a foster home, Seth had known one of these confident, charming guys, but there was something in his eyes and grin just waiting to get angry so the bully in him could explode out. Darren had those same eyes, that same smile. Maybe Seth wasn't being fair. Maybe he didn't like him because he was handsome, the kind of guy girls like Petra always went for.

"Seems friendly enough," he added half-heartedly. "He thinks we're being trained as soldiers."

Esta sniffed.

"That's what I thought. Charles I just met, too. Seems pretty smart."

Reluctantly, Esta said, "Okay."

They got their meals and carried their trays over to the table.

When they arrived, Darren was saying, "But seriously, don't you guys want to *fight* these things? Better than waiting it out down here."

"This is Esta," Seth said as the two of them sat down at the end of the table, across from each other.

Everyone said hi except Petra, who gave a quick, closed-lip smile. Seth had no idea why she was being unfriendly. She turned her back on Esta and resumed her conversation with Charles and Anaya and Darren. That suited Seth. He wanted Esta to himself.

He took a bite of his lasagna, then another. It was surprisingly good, and he realized how hungry he was.

"Did your parents ever see your drawings?" Esta asked him.

"Foster parents."

"Did you know your real mom at all?"

"A bit." Every time Seth thought of her, he felt the same clench in his chest, like a muscle that would never get tired. "She gave me up pretty early. After that it was a foster home. Foster *homes*." He took another bite of lasagna. "How about you?"

"My mom was only eighteen when she had me. When I was six months old, she dropped me off at my aunt's and that was it. She never came back."

"So your aunt brought you up?"

"Yeah, but she didn't want to. She hated my mom. My aunt was always telling me how wild and selfish she was. My aunt already had two kids of her own. And they all thought I was a freak."

"Because of your feathers?"

"Yeah. Were you born with them, too?"

"They cut mine off."

Esta nodded and took a bite of buttery garlic bread. "Same here. My aunt still thought I was weird, though."

"Did you get a lot of broken bones?"

"When I was little, yeah, I felt like I was always in a cast. Leg. Wrists. Arms. The hospital called Children's Aid the first couple of times. Until they realized my bones were just frail."

He remembered the exasperation of his various foster parents whenever he was in a cast. A broken arm or leg meant he wasn't much help around the house. The opposite. He'd liked how much extra time it gave him to draw, though.

"Did you dream a lot?" he asked her. "About flying?"

She nodded, her eyes widening as she chewed.

She didn't need to say anything more. He could tell how much she loved those dreams. From the moment he'd seen her, he'd felt connected. At first, it was the sheer thrill of meeting someone else who had feathers. But now he realized how much the two of them shared.

"When I was little," she said, "I told my aunt about the dreams, because of the headaches at the end, but I could tell it bugged her, so I stopped. But then she started finding my drawings. She told me they were wicked. I think she thought they were devils or something."

"My foster parents got freaked out, too."

Esta grinned. "I got better at hiding them. But after the big rain, my aunt and uncle noticed I wasn't allergic to the pollen. They all were. They caught me eating the berries on the vines."

"I did that, too! They tasted so good."

"So good! Then the feathers started growing back."

"Were you excited?"

"Yeah, but it was scary, too."

He noticed they'd both stopped eating, they were talking so fast. He hadn't looked at anything but her face for a long time.

"Mine came in all at once," he told her.

"Seriously? Mine weren't that fast. A couple poked out each day, but it was super painful. My aunt and uncle were freaking out. They thought I was some kind of monster. Or devil, I guess."

"What'd they do?"

"They didn't want to take me to the hospital. They were too ashamed. Worried what people would say. They just kept bandaging my arms. But one day a neighbor noticed the blood leaking through my sleeves and took me to the ER herself."

He almost told her he'd seen her there in the hospital, on the video Dr. Weber had shown them. But it seemed like an invasion of her privacy. She'd been so upset and scared.

"After that," Esta said, "it was all doctors trying to figure it out, and then my aunt and uncle disappeared and no one could reach them. Then these guys in uniform showed up at the hospital, and I ended up on a helicopter here."

"It sounds terrible."

"At least I know what I am now. And why."

There was an excited tingling at the base of his skull. He felt so close to her, it was like they hardly needed to speak.

"What's the thing you hope for most?" he asked.

He must've been whispering. He could barely hear himself.

"The thing that kept me going?" she whispered back.

He nodded, knowing exactly what she was going to say next.

"That one day I might fly for real."

ANAYA TURNED WHEN THE cafeteria doors opened and eight guards came inside.

"Dormitories!" one of them called out.

"Bedtime," Darren said.

"Trays on the racks," the guard shouted. "Form two lines. Boys on the right, girls on the left."

"How retro," Anaya said, glancing over at Seth and Esta. The two of them had been talking nonstop. Their meals weren't even finished. They were speaking so quietly that Anaya wondered if they were even speaking at all. For a second, they gazed at each other like they were in a trance, and then suddenly they noticed that people were getting up. Both of them blushed.

Anaya felt her own cheeks heat, like she'd barged in on something private. Petra was watching them, too, with an expression that Anaya had never seen on her face before.

Jealousy. It took her totally by surprise. All through the meal, she'd noticed Petra doing her pouty lips thing and had assumed it was for Darren. It never took Petra long to have an admirer. And Darren was exactly the kind of guy Petra liked. And maybe the big lips were also for Charles, just to get his attention and prove that she was still the prettiest, even if she did have a tail. But all along, the pouty lips had been for Seth.

For Anaya, Seth was like the best big brother you could have, and she'd assumed Petra felt the same. She couldn't quite believe her friend had a crush on him. She usually went for the handsome, confident dudes. The Darren models.

Esta stood abruptly and went to return her tray.

"Guess we get to see the dorms now," Seth said, watching her go.

He obviously hadn't caught the jealous look on Petra's face. He was completely clueless—just like Anaya had been until a few seconds ago.

She almost felt sorry for Petra. Her friend was so used to getting what she wanted. But right now, all Seth wanted to look at was Esta. Which made sense. She had feathers, like him, and they clearly had a lot to talk about. And Esta really was very pretty. No wonder Seth was mesmerized.

She glanced at Charles, a bit sad she didn't feel the same fascination with him. It was very nice having an admirer—if she could even call him that. But she wasn't getting much of a sparkly feeling. Maybe it would come later.

As she headed over to the cafeteria doors, she hoped the dorms weren't gross. She suddenly realized how much she wanted to lie down on something soft and sleep. After everyone had lined up, Dr. Ritter entered the cafeteria, and the room somehow seemed a little dimmer. He looked directly at her.

"L9. You'll be coming with me."

"What for?"

Ritter didn't answer. A guard with buggy eyes pulled her hands behind her back, cuffed her, and marched her through the doors.

"What've I done?" she asked, to no reply.

"Tell us where she's going!" Seth demanded behind her.

Being separated suddenly from her friends was like being dragged away from her parents all over again. And now it was nighttime, which made things even worse. The corridor was almost deserted. Wasn't it too late for an interview or a medical examination? And why the handcuffs?

She tried to breathe, tried to pay attention and make a map in her head. She passed a red door that said FIRE EQUIPMENT, a row of dented gray lockers, a room labeled TOOL CRIB.

A set of double doors marked A-200 led to a landing with stairs going up and down. The way down was labeled with a sign:

LEVEL 100

VAULT / MACHINE ROOM / MORGUE

Morgue? A terrible musty smell welled up from below. Despite the allergy meds, she sneezed.

"Up," said Ritter, to her relief.

The sign pointing up read:

LEVEL 300

SITUATION ROOMS

What exactly was a situation room? Brown linoleum treads on the steps, just like at school. Half landing. Sharp turn. Up again.

She was marched past the double doors to Level 300 and kept going. She read the sign leading up:

LEVEL 400
COMMUNICATIONS / MEDICAL

Medical. Her stomach gave a twist.

At the very top of the stairs, the guards pushed through a final set of double doors. A sentry was stationed behind his desk.

This place was like a maze, corridors branching in all directions. She passed doors stenciled with big red letters: OPEN WITH EXTREME CAUTION and TELECOMMUNICATIONS ROOM. Through a wire-reinforced window she caught an eerie glimpse of a dentist chair surrounded by flex lamps and mildewed trays. Right next to it was a door that said SURGICAL SUITE.

Another turn, another corridor. At the open doorway of a small, bare room, Anaya paused. A woman in a hazmat suit stood beside a square hatch. At her feet was a bunch of gear, including pruning shears and a chain saw.

"Make sure you get it all!" the woman yelled into the hatch.

From inside came an echoey reply: ". . . wouldn't have thought they'd grow down so deep."

"Yeah, they're fast!" the woman said, reaching inside and scooping up a tangle of pruned black vines. Some of them were still twisting.

Dr. Ritter pulled Anaya past the open door, his face tight with displeasure.

"Doors stay closed at all times," he told the guards.

"Yes, sir," they replied promptly.

Anaya couldn't believe that the cryptogenic vines were getting inside, this far underground. They must've been coming in through an air shaft. Anaya took a mental snapshot of the hallway. A shaft meant a possible way out.

The corridor dead-ended with an elevator—definitely not the one she'd arrived in. A sign on the doors said ANTENNA FARM ACCESS.

What was an antenna farm? The guard with buggy eyes turned a key in the lock, and the doors opened immediately. The control panel had only two buttons: 400 and G. Anaya's heart stuttered. G for Ground.

"Yes, we're going to the surface," Ritter told her, pulling out a pollen mask and fixing it over his mouth and nose. The guards did the same.

"Why?"

Were they letting her go? The thought careened around her head like a bird trapped in a room. Ritter watched her impassively, as if she were behind glass in a museum. The two guards avoided eye contact with her. She was getting used to being treated like a criminal. The elevator rattled as it slowly rose.

When the doors jerked apart, she was ushered into a small room with a concrete ramp leading to a set of heavy doors. The guards opened them, and cool, invigorating night air bounded toward her, tangy with pine needles.

Any hope of being released was quickly doused when she saw the large fenced enclosure. In the stark wash of electric lights, antennae and satellite dishes jutted into the air. Half a dozen White Coats turned to look at her with a touch of annoyance, like she was a late party guest.

"Let's get on with this," one of them said, sneezing behind his mask.

Everyone was wearing pollen masks, but there was still lots of sniffling and coughing.

"Bring her over," said a White Coat next to a dentist chair. It was bolted to the concrete deck. Lots of little trays around it.

"Why am I out here?" Anaya asked.

It was hard to imagine anything good happening in a dentist chair. Her handcuffs were removed, and she was forcefully seated. Her arms were yanked around back of the chair and refastened at the wrists. No matter how tightly she held herself, she couldn't stop trembling.

"I thought you were worried we'd transmit to the cryptogens if we were outside!"

Ritter nodded. "Tonight that's exactly what we want you to do."

She looked at him, bewildered.

"You're helping us with a very simple tracking exercise."

"How?"

Ritter chewed through his words with particular relish. "The organ in your brain transmits to the cryptogens, and if they transmit *back* to you—as we believe they do—we might be able to find the source of their signal. We'll be using two other antenna farms to triangulate the incoming signal. And then we have their location."

That sounded reasonable enough, and Anaya's body relaxed the tiniest bit.

"Why me?"

"According to the MRI scans, your brain has the biggest transmitting structure. Your signal might be the strongest."

"It only happens when I'm asleep, though," she said.

"Yes, we're aware of that."

She felt a prick in her right arm and turned to see a medic holding a syringe.

"Just something to sedate you."

"I don't want to be sedated! I didn't give permission!"

"Relax," Ritter told her.

Anaya's eyes darted all around. People were staring at monitors and equipment, murmuring to each other. Within a few seconds, she felt weirdly calm, more observant. She heard, quite close, a train's whistle. It was comforting to think of a train moving through the night. The fact that it was still running seemed like a good sign. The world hadn't totally fallen apart.

Beyond the fence, darkness weighed heavily. Anaya sensed forest all around. She smelled it—along with the faintest whiff of the sickly perfume from cryptogenic vines. She imagined them curled through tall pines.

Drowsier now, she tilted her head back and saw stars. The lights of a plane drifted downward across the sky, and she heard the deepening drone of its engines. Coming in for landing. So there was an airport not too far away, and a city.

Remember this, she told herself. Her eyelids drooped. She didn't think she was fully asleep, though. She still smelled pine needles, felt the cool air on her face—

And she was moving through the forest, running. It was so good to be free from the chair, her hands unmanacled. In the back of her head, she felt the familiar pressure, just shy of pain, that always came when she had the dreams.

She heard faraway human voices:

"Okay, she's transmitting."

"Signal's strong."

Running and bounding through the forest, Anaya saw her furred arms, her clawed hands. Past the trees, someone was waiting expectantly for her.

More distant voices:

"We've got an incoming signal!"

"Make sure all directional antennae are synced."

"Power boost on three, please."

"Triangulating now."

The voices suddenly evaporated.

Deep inside Anaya's head, someone else was talking. It wasn't so much a voice as a presence. It had the smell of soil after a big rain. And with the smell came a color, a flicker of amber light. The sounds in her head were like a language she had never heard. Somehow she caught their *feeling*. There was curiosity and concern. Most of all there was urgency. The sounds reshaped themselves. In the darkness of her head, she could almost *see* it happening. A single word:

—*Help*.

And then human voices intruded again.

"We've got a fix!"

"You sure?"

"Nailed it!"

Suddenly Anaya's head was empty, as if a small, shy animal had just bolted from its warren. She felt a pang of loss.

"Let's get her inside fast," she heard Ritter say. "I don't want her transmitting anything else."

She was aware of being hoisted out of the dentist chair. Half walking, she opened her eyes. She was already inside the elevator, a guard supporting her on each side. Ritter watched her closely.

"What did you experience?" he asked.

She was still dopey, but a small, steady part of her mind cautioned her.

"I was sort of half awake the whole time. I dreamed I was running in a forest." They already knew this stuff anyway, so she figured that was safe.

"Did you see anything else?"

"Claws on my fingers. Fur on my arms." Again, old news.

"Did you hear anything?"

One word. *Help.*

Was someone offering help or asking for it? She had no idea. What she felt most strongly was the feeling emanating from that one word, like an amber glow.

It felt like kindness.

"No," she lied. "I didn't hear a thing."

CHAPTER SIX

THE GUARDS HAD LONG ago turned off the dorm lights, but Petra was still wide-awake. She'd been assigned a top bunk and they were triple-deckers, so she was practically squished against the ceiling. It was too warm, and she was in a room full of strangers, and the nauseating smell of lemon disinfectant wafted out from the bathroom. They'd been given basic toiletries, and a change of underwear to sleep in. It was like some terrible summer camp, except that she had no personal possessions, was deep underground, and could never leave. And her best friend wasn't even here.

Petra's worries bounded like wild animals unleashed into the night. Where had they taken Anaya, and why wasn't she back yet? What were they doing with her? *To* her?

She felt intensely alone and homesick. She missed her own bed and pillow. It seemed frivolous, with the world being invaded and all, but she did. This mattress was super thin, and the pillow was too fat and hard, and she was sorry if she was whining like

Goldilocks, but she missed her duvet, too. She'd chosen it four years ago when she'd thought lilac was a good idea, and now wished she'd chosen white, but she would've given a lot to have it against her now.

Earlier she'd heard a girl crying herself to sleep, and that had almost started Petra going. She wondered if Mom and Dad were still on Deadman's Island, under arrest. Part of her hoped they were. Probably they were safer on a military base than anywhere else. Not that anywhere was safe anymore, with the plants, and now those freaky bugs hatching all over the world.

She turned onto her side and clamped her eyes shut, but she started seeing the patterns on Darren's arms, writhing hypnotically. She thought of Darren's tail. What had happened to him was going to happen to her. Her own body would change, and there was no way of stopping it, nothing she could do.

She opened her eyes. Better this way. Harder to go down a black hole of panic. She stared at the rows of triple bunks, the humps of sleeping girls. She saw the empty bottom bunk that was Anaya's and wanted her friend back *now*.

And that made her think of her other friend, Seth, which made her angry, but this was better than being crushed by panic. At dinner he'd ignored everyone but Esta. By the end, the two of them weren't even talking, just gazing at each other like actors who hadn't heard the director yell, "Cut!"

Seth used to look at *her*—or at least sneak little glances when he thought she wouldn't notice. But not the way he'd looked at Esta, like they were having some kind of silent conversation. As corny as that sounded.

He'd just *met* Esta. She, Petra, had known him a lot longer. He'd *held her hand* in the helicopter. Sure, it was only holding hands, and maybe it was silly, but it had *meant* something to her. And she was sorry if she didn't have *feathers* like Esta, but honestly. It was ridiculous. What kind of guy was he, if he could lose interest so quickly?

Light cut across the dorm as the door opened, and Anaya walked in a little unsteadily. The door closed and locked behind her, and Petra climbed out of bed and rushed over to her friend.

"You okay?"

"A bit dizzy."

Petra helped her to the empty bunk and squished in beside her. In the dim glow of the night-light, she studied her friend's face.

"What happened?" she asked, then listened as Anaya told her about the antenna farm, the dentist chair, the drugs, and the signal-tracking experiment.

"I think one of them talked to me," Anaya said.

Petra felt an electric tingle. She knew the answer but still asked: "One of *who*?"

"One of *them*," Anaya said. "A cryptogen."

"You're sure it wasn't a dream?"

Anaya shook her head. "This was totally different. This time someone was actually there. At first I couldn't understand the sounds. It was like they were looking around my brain, trying to figure out *how* to talk to me."

"Like translating?"

"Yeah. I think it was hard for them. Maybe that's why I only got one word."

Petra swallowed. "What word?"

"Help."

She was so confused, it took a few moments to gather her thoughts. "It makes no sense, Anaya. They're invading us! Why would they help us, or need our help?"

"It felt like both. Offering and asking. The way she said it."

"Whoa, hang on," said Petra. *"She?"*

Anaya looked surprised, too. "It felt, well, motherly."

In the dim light, her friend's eyes looked wet. Petra squeezed her shoulder. "Maybe you just miss your mom."

"Maybe, but . . . no, I definitely got the sense she was *like* me." She frowned. "I think she wanted my help."

Petra let out her breath. "These things are trying to wipe us out!"

"I know, it's crazy, but I trusted her."

Petra almost clamped her hand over Anaya's mouth. "Don't say things like that! You didn't tell Ritter this, did you?"

"No. I lied to him."

Petra's shoulders dropped in relief. "Good."

"I thought you were all for cooperating with Ritter."

"Yeah, I am, but if they even *think* we're friendly with the cryptogens, or *helping* them, we'll never get out of here."

She knew she was contradicting herself but was also convinced that their only hope was making Ritter believe they were loyal *humans,* that they wanted to *destroy* the cryptogens. If Anaya started blabbing about how they might actually be *nice* aliens and want to help, they were sunk.

"During the test," Anaya said, "I heard one of the army guys say they got a fix. They found the source of the cryptogens' signal!"

"Are you serious? So where is it?"

Petra had always imagined the cryptogens in a spaceship somewhere, darkly orbiting the planet. But with a chill she wondered if maybe they were closer than she thought. Could they already be here, hidden on Earth?

"They didn't say."

"But wherever they are, this is good news, right? If we know where they are, we can attack them—maybe even do a surprise attack! We can fire missiles into outer space, can't we?"

"I'm not sure," Anaya answered wearily, and Petra couldn't believe her friend wasn't more excited.

"This is *good* news," she said, jostling Anaya. "This means we have a chance. Maybe we can actually beat them!"

"THIS IS INCREDIBLE," SETH said, keeping his voice low. He leaned closer across the cafeteria table, his half-eaten breakfast forgotten. "You actually *talked* with one of them!"

"Well, she talked to me," Anaya said. "It was so quick."

He noticed she referred to the cryptogen as a she. "And she was friendly?"

Anaya looked uncomfortable. "It was just a feeling I got."

"Yeah," said Petra. "I'm sure all they want is to come down and help us build more Walmarts."

"Look," Anaya replied, "maybe you're right—maybe they want to confuse us."

Seth tried to imagine what it would be like to have their words, their language, inside his head. Gooseflesh prickled his neck. He realized he felt envious.

"We're not telling anyone else about this, okay?" said Petra.

"These things in our brain must be pretty powerful," he said, "if we've been transmitting to them, wherever they are. And if they can *talk* to us . . ."

His thoughts strayed, and he took a sip of his water, his mouth suddenly dry. He found Esta across the cafeteria. He'd been thinking constantly about their conversation yesterday, especially the strange thing that had happened at the very end.

"If the cryptogens can communicate using these things in our brain," he said, pulling his attention back to Anaya and Petra, "why can't we?"

He watched their faces carefully. Petra was already shaking her head.

"No," she said, looking frightened. "You're talking about—"

"Listen," he said, "yesterday with Esta, there was this moment I wasn't sure we were actually *talking* anymore. It was only for a few seconds. I mean, I *heard* her. But I'm not sure her mouth was moving."

"Okay, I get it," Petra said, and she seemed almost angry now. "So why don't we test this little theory. Anaya, whisper something to Seth, but don't tell me what it is. And, Seth, you tell it to me"—she rolled her eyes—"*telepathically.*"

Seth leaned in as Anaya cupped her hands and spoke softly into his ear.

"Did you hear that?" he asked Petra.

"Nope. I'm good to go. Zap away."

He wished her eyes weren't so skeptical—it was distracting. Her pouty mouth was distracting, too. For a second he felt at a loss. With Esta it had just happened without him realizing—if it had happened at all. Maybe he *had* imagined it.

"You finished?" Petra said. "'Cause I'm getting nothing."

"I haven't even started!"

He took a deep breath and tried to turn down the volume in the cafeteria. He focused on Petra's left eye—he'd been looking at Esta's eyes when it happened. The darkness of Petra's pupil helped him concentrate, and he was suddenly aware of a shimmer at the very bottom of his vision. It reminded him of the light coming from underneath a closed door at night. He was aware of a pungent, salty scent. It seemed to belong to the light, beckoning him. Silently he spoke the words Anaya had told him.

He blinked and saw Petra inhale sharply. Her cheeks flushed a deep red.

"I heard you," she murmured.

He was aware of his heart beating hard. "What did I say?"

"*These gluten-free pancakes are gross. Is that right?*"

Seth's giddy pulse tripped over itself, then recovered. He nodded.

"Oh my God," said Petra, holding her hands to her cheeks. "We're telepathic now?"

"Why're you blushing?" Anaya asked her.

"It was just . . . so personal. Like having someone whisper right into your ear. No." She shook her head. "More like having a person show up inside your head. And there was a kind of flicker of light that came with the words." She frowned. "And a smell."

"What was it?" he asked.

"Like woodsmoke."

He nodded. "You smelled like a beach at low tide."

She wrinkled her nose. "That doesn't sound too nice."

"No, it was unforgettable. And totally personal, like it could only have been you."

"Last night," Anaya was saying excitedly, as if she'd just

unlocked a memory, "when I heard the cryptogen in my head, I saw a pulse of amber light and smelled wet soil."

"Maybe it's some kind of sensory fingerprint," Petra said.

"And the light's a kind of beacon," he added. "But the other person has to want to talk. You can't just barge in and read people's thoughts. It's like a phone call, not mind reading. You have to want to talk."

"I want to try now," Anaya said excitedly.

Seth faced her and waited. At the periphery of his vision came a quick glimmer of light. A smell filled his head, so appropriate and, somehow, familiar that he smiled. And with the scent came silent words, blossoming in his head. But their edges were unclear. He squinted, trying to bring them into focus.

"Think I got it. You said—"

"What did I smell like?" Anaya wanted to know first.

"Your light was green, and you smelled like a lawn that had just been mowed. Your words were kind of hazy, though. But you said, *Do we tell anyone?*"

There was a moment of silence as they all regarded each other.

"We should tell Ritter," Petra said.

He looked at her, startled. "Are you crazy?"

Her face clouded with annoyance. "No, I am not crazy, Seth. This is important information. The cryptogens are telepathic. That's something you'd want to know about your enemy, right?" She shot a look at Anaya. "And I don't want to hear about how some of them might be nice and friendly."

"Ritter'll want to do tests on us," he said.

"They're *already* doing tests on us," Petra retorted. "That's all anyone does with us, including Dr. Weber. It's not like Ritter's going to drill into our brains or anything!"

"No?"

He couldn't believe how naive Petra was. Maybe having an RCMP officer for a mother made her trust people in uniforms.

"You think Ritter actually cares what happens to us?" he asked her.

"Look," Petra said, "we are at war, and we're all on the same side, right? We're all on the *human* side? So we should be doing everything we can to help! And that means not keeping secrets that might help us fight these things."

"First thing he'll do is split us up," he said. He was absolutely sure of this. "He won't want us talking behind their backs. He'll worry we're plotting in secret." He lowered his voice even more. "And if we want to get out of here, that's exactly what we should be doing. Making a plan. The telepathy gives us an advantage, and I'm not giving it away."

He looked over at Anaya, who hadn't said anything in a while.

"You agree with me, right? You didn't tell Ritter about talking to the cryptogen. So why would you tell him about our telepathy?"

"If it were Dr. Weber," Anaya replied, "I'd tell her everything in a heartbeat. But not Ritter. Shouldn't we tell the other kids, though? They have a right to know."

He shook his head. "The more kids we tell, the more likely someone tells Ritter. I can see Darren doing it. He's already acting like he's in the army. I heard him say 'Yes, sir' to Ritter in the gym. He practically saluted."

"What a numbskull," Petra said.

"So we keep it just the three of us," said Anaya, "for now."

"I think this is a mistake," said Petra stubbornly, "but if we keep it secret, that means no telling Esta either."

"She might've figured it out already," he said, remembering how she'd blushed before leaving the table.

"Well, if she hasn't, don't tell her," Petra said pointedly.

Seth felt himself revolt. "We can trust her."

"No exceptions, Seth. Back me up on this, Anaya."

"She's right," Anaya said.

Seth shrugged. "Fine. Just the three of us."

From the corner of his eye he saw Darren strutting toward them, his sleeves rolled back to show off his muscled arms. Seth ate another forkful of his omelet. It was filled with cheese and mushrooms and green peppers and was really very good.

"So, what's new?" Darren asked, dropping down beside Petra.

Seth caught her eye for a split second.

"Nothing," Petra said.

CHAPTER SEVEN

—*IT'S YOUR BIRTHDAY IN* two days, Anaya said to Petra as they did laps. She was keeping to a slower pace so they could run side by side.

—*Which means it's yours in eight,* Petra replied.

Their silent talking had become a habit, especially when they wanted privacy. Over the past three days, Anaya was amazed how much easier it had become. At first it was hard to find that little glimmer of light that guided you into a person's head. With practice it had become almost second nature. She didn't need to look into the person's eyes, or close her own, to concentrate. She didn't even need to be in the same room. Yesterday she'd managed to reach Seth in his dorm. Silent talking was also especially useful if, like right now, they needed to save their breath while doing laps.

—*This is definitely not how I imagined turning sixteen,* Anaya said.

—*Maybe Ritter will bake us a cake.*

—*And sing "Happy Birthday" to us.*

Back in her normal life, Anaya had sometimes daydreamed

about having a sweet sixteen party. But she'd never pictured hosting it in an underground bunker with a couple of dozen kids who had tails, wings, and claws. The ones on her own fingers were getting so long, it was hard to hold a fork or scratch her cheek without stabbing herself.

—*My birthday plans also didn't include turning into a Wookiee,* she added.

Petra snorted with laughter. *You are* not *turning into a Wookiee.*

This morning after her shower, she'd taken a good look at herself. She'd been okay when her legs got hairy, less okay when the hairs crept up her torso and down her arms. But today when she'd looked in the mirror, she'd had a brief, terrifying moment when she hadn't recognized herself. Fine dark hairs spread across her forehead, cheeks, and the bridge and slope of her nose. Her ears, mouth, and eyes were still clear. All the other runners were going through the same thing, at least. And it was a small comfort that the facial hairs weren't long and bristly, but soft and sleek.

—*I'd say your look is definitely more kangaroo,* Petra said with a mischievous grin.

—*Thanks a lot!*

Anaya wondered if her friend was secretly happy about her hairy face, but then she felt mean when Petra said:

—*Sorry. It sucks. I could tell you were enjoying being beautiful.*

—*Beautiful?*

She couldn't help glowing with the unexpected compliment.

—*Don't pretend you didn't know,* Petra said.

She was about to deny it, but with silent talking, it was harder to lie. It was too direct, too intimate.

—*How could you tell?* she asked.

—*You just seemed more confident. You weren't hiding your face anymore, stuff like that. And I can tell you like how Charles is always trying to get your attention.*

She couldn't deny any of this—it was all so new to her.

—*Do you like him back?* Petra asked.

She shook her head. It made her feel almost guilty: she liked the admiration, but she didn't feel the slightest bit romantic about him.

—*Anyway, I'm too busy turning into a kangaroo,* she said.

—*And I'm turning into a Komodo dragon.*

Anaya glanced at Petra's tail, jutting through its Velcro flap. It swished side to side as she ran. Anaya knew how hard it had been for her friend to finally let it show. It had simply gotten too uncomfortable to cram down a pant leg. It was almost a foot long. Below her smooth skin, a pattern was starting to show: delicate black-and-gold vines twined hypnotically around each other.

She caught Petra looking ruefully across the gym to where Seth and Esta were having their feathers measured.

—*He's basically dumped us,* Petra remarked.

—*He hasn't dumped us,* Anaya said, though it was true that Seth was spending more and more time with the other flyers. She knew it drove Petra crazy, especially when Seth chose to eat with

Esta rather than them. But Petra would never go over to the fly-ers; she was too proud.

—*Dumped* me, *then,* Petra said. *I can't believe he got sucked in by Esta's wounded-bird routine. I don't buy it. She's all quiet and doesn't talk to anyone but him, and then she goes all psycho and slashes apart punching bags.* She sighed. *Anyway, what guy wouldn't prefer a hot babe with wings over someone who molts?*

—*No one could be hotter than you,* Anaya told her friend, want-ing to cheer her up. *And your new skin is more beautiful than ever.*

It was so unlike her friend to feel sorry for herself, but Anaya remembered, back on Deadman's Island, how Petra had confided her worst fear to her: she was terrified that if her body changed, she'd become monstrous and no one could ever love her. Did she actually think this was what had happened with Seth?

She was about to say something comforting, but Petra looked over, her blue eyes startlingly vulnerable, and asked:

—*I'm still me, right?*

It was something Anaya had promised her friend when they'd started changing: *We're still us.* No matter what happened on the outside, they were still the same inside. But lately she'd caught herself wondering if it was true. Everything that had happened to her body—her speed, her strength, her brain that could talk to an alien species—it *had* started to change how she thought. And wasn't that an *inside* change? But she could see Petra watching her urgently, waiting for her reply.

—*Absolutely,* she said, hoping her friend hadn't noticed her hesitation. *The way we look doesn't change who we are. We're still us.*

"W10!" a White Coat shouted. "Pick up the pace! L9, standing jump station!"

Anaya gave her friend a reassuring smile and pulled off the track.

Every day in the bunker followed the same routine. In the morning, they were woken by guards, who escorted them to the cafeteria for breakfast. Afterward, they went to the gym for exercise and tests. Then lunch.

In the afternoon, they were taken out for interviews with Paul or Ritter, sometimes both. The interview room was windowless, of course, but one wall was papered with a faded panorama of a beach at sunrise. Presumably to make them feel calmer.

The questions rarely changed.

Had she dreamed about the cryptogens?

Had she had any communication with them?

Could she draw them?

Had she ever seen signs of their technology or weaponry?

Was she experiencing any new changes to her body or ways of thinking?

She told them nothing about her telepathy—and nothing about the single word from the cryptogen that night in the antenna farm. Though she thought about it often. *Help* and all the urgency, hope, and kindness carried with it.

During the interviews, Anaya's own questions always went unanswered:

When can I talk to my parents?

Where are they?

Are they safe?

What's going on outside?

What happened with all those eggs that rained down?

Luckily, there were other ways of getting news. Yesterday three new kids had arrived, and at dinner, Anaya had clustered around with the others, asking them what was going on topside.

There was a swimmer from Winnipeg called Nia, whose arms had icy silver patterning. Paolo, a bespectacled runner from Saratoga Springs, didn't say much. The most talkative was Adam, a broad-shouldered runner from Minneapolis. And some of his news was hopeful.

Turned out the herbicide spray was definitely killing the plants. The problem was, the authorities couldn't make it fast enough. So they'd designated Spray Zones around major power stations, factories, highways, rail lines, and farms. Most of the herbicide was used up just keeping these areas plant-free.

Outside the Spray Zones, things were getting worse. Nia said that the vines and pit plants were everywhere, people were losing power and running water, and food was getting scarce. Everyone was trying to get to the Spray Zones, which were turning into giant refugee camps.

And then there were the bugs.

None of the new kids had actually seen any themselves, but they'd all heard stories, mostly about big, winged insects. Quietly, Paolo said that he'd seen a video of a guy getting attacked by a swarm of them, but it was really blurry. There were rumors they drank blood.

Anaya remembered the three tiny hatchlings in Dr. Weber's lab back on Deadman's Island. One of them had looked like it might grow wings. Could that tiny thing have grown into a blood-sucking monster so quickly? What about the other two creatures that had hatched? And who knew how many other kinds of eggs had fallen around the world? Or what they'd become?

Now, watched over by White Coats, Anaya started obediently doing her standing jumps. Atop the stack of tires, she glanced across to where Petra sat, having acid dripped onto her skin. Their eyes met.

—*So, what do you want for your birthday?* Petra asked jokingly.

Anaya chuckled. *A case of hair removal cream. I'd settle for a razor, though. You?*

—*To be normal again.*

PETRA LOOKED OVER AS the gym doors opened and Paul entered, pushing a cart with a big monitor on top. It felt like a long time since she'd seen a screen or clutched one in her hands. It had actually been sort of a relief, not having to look at other people's better bodies and better lives.

"We have a special viewing treat for you!" Dr. Ritter announced, walking into the gym after Paul.

She'd never seen Ritter smile before, and it changed his face, but not in a good way. The contrast between the smile and his lightless eyes made him look like a ghoulish doll. He was really chewing his words today, really enjoying the taste of them.

"I know you've all been anxious about what's going on top-side, so I thought I'd bring you the latest news."

Everyone had stopped running and jumping and gliding and was making their way toward the television like cold, weary travelers drawn to a campfire. Even the White Coats and guards gathered around, looking as surprised as the kids. Petra went to stand with Anaya.

"We thought," said Ritter as Paul fiddled with switches, "you might like to see the first images of a cryptogen spacecraft."

"How?" Petra exclaimed.

"Thanks to L9," Ritter said, nodding directly at Anaya, "we found it. We triangulated the cryptogen signal she received and had a satellite repositioned closer to those coordinates."

The monitor lit up, and Petra's gaze was instantly welded. It took her a while to understand what she was seeing. How could that be a spaceship? It had no metallic surfaces or sharp corners. What was it even made of? It looked like a gray rose. There was a long central stem and, blooming from the top, about ten over-lapping petals. There were no lights she could see. Without any-thing nearby for scale, it was impossible to gauge how big it was.

She'd always known that the cryptogens must have traveled a great distance in *some* kind of ship. And that the ship would need to be close enough to Earth to make it rain down seeds and eggs. But actually *seeing* the ship—something so utterly strange—sandblasted her mind.

"This," said Paul, "is a live feed from the satellite."

"How big is it?" she asked.

"Huge," Paul answered. "Each one of those petal-shaped structures is the length of two cruise ships."

—*Why are they showing us this? Telling us stuff?*

She recognized Seth's voice in her head and looked over to where he stood with Esta and the other flyers.

—*Wondering the same thing,* Anaya said.

When practicing their silent talking, they'd discovered it was possible to have a conversation with more than one person. It took a little more effort to hold two voices in your head simul-taneously. Seth's voice always came in clearest. Anaya's was good, too, but they'd told her that hers was sometimes blurry. It bugged her that she wasn't better at it, but it never felt natural to her, and she didn't like it. Her eyes flicked to Esta, and she wondered if Seth had told her about the telepathy. Probably.

"So all the seeds and eggs that rained down on us," Darren was asking, "they came from this ship?"

"That's our assumption," said Ritter. "We also believe this ship is where your signals have been going all these years. All the intel you've been shooting out to the cryptogens. Whatever or whoever you've been communicating with, they're right inside. And by the looks of it, there's lots of them. Hundreds of thousands."

"If they're the same size as us," Seth said.

This seemed to irritate Ritter. But it startled Petra. She'd always assumed the cryptogens were roughly human-sized—but maybe she was wrong.

"Whatever their size," Paul said, "that ship holds one hell of an army."

"So they're definitely invading?" she asked.

"Can't see any other explanation," Paul replied.

"Have you tried to talk to them?" Anaya asked.

—*Careful,* Petra said to her.

"We have, in fact, tried to contact them," Paul said. "On every frequency imaginable. Without any response."

—*See?* Petra told her silently. *They're not here for some friendly shore excursion.*

"How come it took so long to find it?" Charles asked. "With all your satellites and stuff? I mean, the thing's huge."

Petra saw Paul look at Ritter, as if asking for permission to explain. Ritter nodded smugly. He really did seem in an unusually good mood.

"It has extraordinary cloaking technology," Paul explained. "And no heat signature we can detect. It doesn't show up on any radar system. The only way we found it was through the coordinates"—he nodded at Anaya—"and then visual tracking with various satellites."

"What's that?" Petra asked as a narrow object darted into view from offscreen.

Unlike the cryptogen ship, this thing was decidedly human-made, all glinting metal, emblazoned with the American flag.

"That," Ritter said with his terrible smile, "is the end of the war."

"What do you mean?" she said.

"It's a missile launched from our satellite. It's carrying a nuclear payload."

"We have nukes in space?" Seth asked.

"We have nukes in space," Paul replied, watching the monitor.

"Luckily," said Ritter, "we've been developing a covert space force, and we deployed it fairly quickly."

—*Oh my God,* Petra heard Anaya murmur inside her head.

Her friend sounded genuinely upset, but it was ridiculous. This could solve everything! They'd blast this thing into oblivion!

Petra watched the missile quickly disappear into the inky darkness.

"Where'd it go?" Darren asked.

"It's moving incredibly fast," Paul said. "And the target's a long way away."

Which made Petra realize how truly huge the ship must be, looming there in the darkness.

"Come on!" she said, her eyes fixed on the screen. "Blow it up!"

"Nuke it, baby!" shouted Darren.

She couldn't tear her eyes away. Suddenly the entire monitor flared so brightly that she gave a little gasp. She blinked, still seeing the scalding white corona.

"Touchdown!" Ritter shouted.

All the guards and White Coats in the room, and the kids, too, were whooping and clapping, and shouting things at the monitor: "Hell yeah!" and "See you never, baby!" and "*That's how you do it!*"

"Yes!" shouted Petra, throwing her arms around Anaya in sheer joy and relief. She noticed her friend wasn't hugging her back. She looked at Anaya and saw her troubled eyes.

—You've got to be happy! It's over!

—I am. It's just—

Over Anaya's shoulder, she saw the monitor become a crawling, pixelated mess. Then the image froze altogether.

"What happened?" she asked.

"Electromagnetic pulse," Ritter said. "It's typical to temporarily lose image right after a blast."

With the ship destroyed, what would happen now? The plants were still here, and the bugs, but there'd be no more invasions. Surely they could deal with what was left behind. Her hopes cascaded through her head. Tails could be cut off. Patterned skin could be lasered. None of that would change her DNA, but at least she wouldn't *look* different from anyone else. And with a supply of special water, she could beat her water allergy. Anaya could pass as normal with some hair removal and a good mani-pedi. And if Seth were a little more flexible and had his feathers clipped, he could fit in, too. She remembered how violently he'd reacted when her father suggested it. Well, maybe Seth would have to change.

"When can we go home?"

Petra wasn't sure who'd asked the question, but the sudden silence made it obvious that every single kid was thinking the same thing—and waiting for the answer.

"Soon," said Paul.

"When soon?" asked Nia.

Paul replied, "We should be able to start—"

"We have some work to finish up here first," Ritter interrupted, and Petra caught the surprise on Paul's face.

"What kind of work?" Seth asked.

The question seemed to darken the room. Ritter's smile spread wider, but his eyes grew dimmer.

Petra's eyes were suddenly dragged back to the monitor as the image stuttered to life.

"Ah, we're back online," Ritter said.

Debris sparkled across the screen, like a careening constellation.

"That's the wreckage," said Ritter happily.

After a moment, the barrage thinned, and the hair on the back of Petra's neck lifted. In the distance was the vast, flower-shaped ship.

"It's still there!" she cried.

"Doesn't even look damaged," Paul said, leaning closer to the monitor.

Petra stared, devastated, as the ship serenely tilted and drifted slowly out of sight.

There was another hailstorm of debris, and she realized this was the wreckage of the missile, nothing more. She glimpsed a jagged piece of metal bearing the Stars and Stripes rushing right toward the satellite, and then the image exploded into static.

CHAPTER EIGHT

THAT NIGHT AFTER DINNER, they came to the cafeteria to get her.

"Are you trying to find the ship again?" Anaya asked Ritter as she was handcuffed and escorted down the corridor. The guards were a bit rougher this time. And Ritter seemed angry. Gone was his smile, which was actually a relief. But his eyes, if anything, were more baleful.

Despite her nerves, part of her was eager. She wanted to *talk* to the cryptogen this time; she wanted to know more.

Watching that missile streak toward the ship, she'd been bewildered by how violently her emotions had forked. She'd wanted the ship destroyed, and she'd also wanted it saved. She knew Petra thought she was crazy, but she couldn't forget the aura of kindness around that voice in her head.

As she was marched down corridors and up stairs, she tried to remember the landmarks and turnings. At the elevator to the antenna farm, she watched closely as a guard with a froggy face took out his ring of keys. The one that unlocked the elevator was silver with a round top, shorter than the others.

"Did you warn them?"

She startled at Ritter's voice and looked over, confused.

"When we took you outside last time, did you tell the cryptogens our plans?"

"How could I? I didn't even know what you were planning!"

The elevator clanked as it rose.

"Did you knowingly communicate with them?" Ritter persisted.

"No. I was half asleep!"

He seemed far from convinced. The elevator shuddered to a halt and the doors snapped open. Up the ramp to the outside. The cool gust of fresh air. Electric lamps. Antennae towering into the night sky. The waiting crew of telecommunications people, sneezing behind their masks.

And then she was on the dentist chair, hands locked behind her back. Her eyes measured the height of the fence. Ten feet. With a running start could she clear it? The forest seemed quieter than before. When she pulled her gaze back inside the fence, her eyes snagged on the concrete deck. Was that a seam in the concrete, or a sneaky tendril of black vine pressed into a crack?

There was a sharp prick in her arm, and Ritter was saying: "Knock her out this time. I don't want her chatting with anyone."

She was aware of her heart beating fast, and then—

She was warm and quiet inside. Was she awake or dreaming?

—*Look.*

With a flare of amber light and the smell of damp soil, the

word blossomed in her head. As before, it was only a single word, but Anaya felt like she'd been joyfully greeted by a worried mother.

She had so many questions but was suddenly aware, in her mind, of a light glowing like a small box. It had the feeling of a gift.

—*Look.*

—*Who are you?* Anaya asked silently.

But she was alone now and waking up. Foggy shapes moved around her.

Someone said: "It was too fast! We couldn't get a fix."

Two pats on her cheek, not gentle.

Blearily, she tried to focus on Ritter, looming over her.

"Are you doing this on purpose?" he asked angrily.

Her mouth felt like it was filled with cotton. "Wha—?"

His hands were heavy on her shoulders. "Did you tell them to stop transmitting?"

"No!"

"Dr. Ritter," said another man, and Anaya realized it was Paul, "I think she's telling you everything she knows."

Ritter lifted his meaty hands away, and two guards came and hefted her off the chair. Her legs felt wobbly as they marched her back inside to the waiting elevator. Ritter's face was grim.

"You had no communication with them whatsoever?" he demanded.

"No," she lied.

In her head, the little box glowed expectantly.

When the guards returned her to the dorm, Petra was awake and waiting. Silently, so she wouldn't wake any of the other girls, Anaya told her friend what had happened.

—*You think she left something in your head?* Petra asked.

—*I can see it glowing.* It was clearest when she closed her eyes, like the ghost of a bright light. *It wants to be opened.*

—*Anaya, you have no idea what it is!*

She had no intention of ignoring it. How could she? She leaned back on her bunk and concentrated on it.

—*Anaya, what are you doing?*

—*Shhh. Just let me . . .*

The light had a hum to it, an amber glow, a faint loamy smell that reminded her of the cryptogen. As she stared, the light unfolded itself like some fantastical stage set and filled up her mind.

A planet blazed before her, a blue-and-green ball not unlike Earth.

She fell toward the planet, through the brightening sky. From on high she saw forests of black grass—and realized they must be farmers' fields, because they had such clear edges. Machines hovered nearby, harvesting. And somehow she understood that this black grass was a valuable crop. A food crop. A city was built in a valley and up the hillsides. Low, undulating buildings, like nothing she'd ever seen. Among them were creatures. They were far away and had a dream haziness to them, but she knew instinctively they were like her. Furred, taking great, leaping strides. Like the creature who'd left these very images in her head.

She wanted to go closer, look longer, but suddenly her view changed, and she was above a lake. Built on the water's surface, and beneath it, was a city. Coursing through the waterways were creatures with long tails and angular bodies. When they came out of the water, they walked on four legs, and sometimes two.

Another shift. Now she beheld a mountain, and a city built around its summit like a cone-shaped vulture's nest, but woven out of metal instead of twig. Buildings bristled from the city's jutting spars. And filling the sky were magnificent winged creatures. In her head, Anaya smelled something like gasoline, giddy and dangerous.

"Anaya!" she heard Petra whisper, as from a great distance.

"Go away," she muttered, because she wanted to see more and was afraid it might all disappear like a mirage. She felt Petra shaking her roughly now. Reluctantly she opened her eyes and focused on the anxious face of her friend.

—*Sorry,* she said to Petra. *It was like I was right there.*

—*Right where?*

—*Their home planet,* she said, and went on to describe what she'd seen.

—*So there's three different species,* Petra said. *We kind of knew that already, right?*

—And we're definitely shaped after them.

—Were the swimmers totally gross? Petra asked.

Anaya knew she had to proceed with caution.

—It's not like I was very close up.

Her friend looked at her skeptically.

—Honestly, I was watching everything from a distance! They looked very graceful, she added truthfully.

—But they were like reptiles? Alligators?

—More like dolphins.

—Yay, I've been upgraded to dolphin.

—Dolphins that could walk on two legs. And had cities.

—Did they have machines and stuff?

Anaya tried to remember. *They must've, to build their cities. I think the runners were farming the black grass.*

—Anything else? Petra asked.

—I don't know, 'cause you shook me out of it!

—Sorry. Go back and see if there's more.

Eagerly Anaya closed her eyes. To her relief the light was still there, patiently waiting. She tuned in to its hum, let the amber glow engulf her.

Once more she saw the water city, but the sky overhead was now darkly streaked with winged cryptogens. Light flashed off them, as though they were coated in metal. Their heads were hidden inside helmets with ferocious crests. They strafed the water city, battering it not with explosives but with something invisible that made the buildings crumple like plastic cups. From the city, and beneath the water, the swimmers retaliated with a barrage of what looked like arrows. Some of the winged creatures fell from the sky, but the majority fought on, relentless.

Her view changed suddenly. Now she was hovering above the runners' city, and it, too, was under attack by the winged cryptogens. This time Anaya was aware of a terrible sound that came from their helmets as they swooped low.

Buildings imploded under the sheer power of this noise. Furred creatures, trying to leap to safety, were struck down, their bodies flattened like tin cans. Anaya felt the pure terror of the battle, like a terrible symphony building to a crescendo inside her head. She wrenched open her eyes. Her body was slick with sweat.

"You okay?" Petra whispered. "You were whimpering."

—*There was a war,* Anaya said. *The flyers attacked the other cryptogens. They have some kind of sound weapon that crushes things. The runners and swimmers didn't have a chance. It was really, really awful.*

In the corner of her vision she was still aware of the amber flicker.

—*I think there's more.*

"Maybe take a little break," Petra suggested.

Anaya swallowed, not sure how much more she could take. The inside of her mouth felt grimy, and she wanted to brush her teeth. But she had to see the rest.

Closing her eyes, she saw the ruins of the runners' city. Some of the fields of black grass remained and were being harvested. But everywhere there were winged cryptogens circling overhead, overseeing the runners. The black grass was loaded onto levitating transport vehicles and taken away by the flyers. Anaya followed one of the transports as it skimmed over the landscape toward a vast building at the base of a mountain. Inside, she saw that the black grass was fed into a huge furnace. Not food anymore, but fuel.

Then she was hovering above the water city and plunged deep below it. Swimmers mined the lake's bottom, extracting metal ore. On the surface, more laborers transferred the ore to hovering transports under the watchful eyes of winged cryptogens. Again Anaya trailed behind one of these transports as it approached the same factory. Inside, workers, mostly runners, melted the ore in colossal vats and then began to shape it.

Now she was somewhere else. On a flat, barren landing field, long lines of runners and swimmers were marched through gateways by flyer overseers. All the cryptogens were bulky with armor and gear. The gateways, she soon realized, were actually hatches in an enormous vessel. The hatches closed. The ship lifted off the ground toward other petal-shaped ships. They docked together around a central shaft—and now the single enormous ship resembled the one Anaya had seen orbiting Earth.

She opened her eyes. At the end of her bunk, Petra waited impatiently.

—*The flyers control everything,* Anaya said. *Three species, but one rules. They use the runners' black grass as fuel in their factories. And there's some kind of stuff they get the swimmers to mine underwater. I'm pretty sure it's the same thing their spaceship's made of. I saw them all board it to come here. I don't think the runners and swimmers had a choice.*

—So why show you all this?

—I think she's telling us not all the cryptogens are bad. The swimmers and runners are being forced. Not all of them want to fight.

IN THE GYMNASIUM, BETWEEN slashing punching bags and doing sprints, Seth silently told Esta everything that he'd learned about the cryptogens from Anaya at breakfast.

—So we're the bad guys, Esta said.

He'd struggled with the same dismal thought. At least before, all the hybrid kids were lumped *together* as the bad guys. Now things had changed. According to Anaya's story, the flyers were tyrants, using the other two species as forced labor. For so much of his life, he'd dreamed about these winged creatures. They'd been glorious things. He'd drawn them, wished one day he could *become* them. It was too bitter to think they were vicious dictators.

—She didn't just dream all this? asked Esta.

—She seemed very sure.

—That's an awful lot to pack into someone's head in a split second.

He'd told Esta about the telepathy the same day he'd learned himself. He hadn't felt good about breaking his promise to Petra and Anaya, but Esta half knew already, like he'd thought. He couldn't believe how easy the silent talking was with her. Much clearer and faster than with the other girls. Maybe it was because he and Esta were both flyers, their brains molded to effortlessly respond to each other.

—*Anyway, it doesn't make* us *the bad guys,* Seth told Esta, as much to convince himself as her. *Just because we have some of their DNA doesn't make us* them.

—*Doesn't matter. They'll hate us for it anyway.*

—*Ritter already hates us.*

—*I meant the other kids.*

Startled, he glanced over at her.

—*They're jealous of us already,* she told him. *Because we stick together. And because we're more powerful. Now they'll be scared of us.*

—*Not Petra. Not Anaya.*

—*You sure? They won't start wondering if we might turn against them?*

—*But we won't,* he said.

—*They won't trust you, Seth. Not like I do.*

She brushed her fingers across his hand, and the sensation lingered on his skin. He felt like she'd spun something between them that couldn't be broken.

—*We can't help what we are,* she said. *We can't help that we're the most powerful. We need to stick together. Come on—they want us to do our glides now.*

In the gym, the White Coats had built a launch platform for the flyers, to see how long they could stay airborne. A White Coat ordered Seth to climb up after Siena and Vincent.

When it was his turn, he threw himself off the platform, arms spread, holding his body taut. He felt the drag of his legs. They were heavy and wanted to fall. It took all his strength to hold them straight. He glided toward the far wall and tried a turn, but he botched it and crashed down in a heap on the mat.

He rolled off to make room for Esta. She managed a half turn before touching down on the floor. It was encouraging to see how graceful she was.

—*That was good,* he said.

—*Petra and Anaya aren't going to tell Ritter about this, are they?* she asked him as they headed back to the platform.

—*Petra thinks we should. She's got a point. If there's an invasion, it might mean we have some cryptogen allies who would help us.*

—*I'm afraid what Ritter might do to us.*

Seth had said the same to Petra and Anaya. If Ritter believed the winged cryptogens were the true enemies, he might start punishing the hybrid flyers. And Seth didn't want to imagine what form that punishment might take.

—*I made them promise not to tell,* he said.

—*I don't trust Petra. All she wants is to be normal.*

He didn't like hearing her talk about Petra unkindly.

—Every kid here wants to be normal, he reminded her.

—Not me, she said. *And not you.*

She was right. He loved his feathered arms. He loved the feeling of gliding, the hope it might turn into proper flight. He wasn't horrified by his new body the way Petra was by hers. She talked so much about wanting her tail off, wanting to go back to normal. Seth wanted to stay the way he was.

He wanted to go further.

—She's not like us, Esta said.

Seth watched Vincent's glide, admiring the sweep of his feathers.

"Go again," a White Coat told Seth, and he climbed the steps to the platform and took a running jump. His glide began well, but when he tried to take an upward stroke, he felt his legs pulling him down again. He landed clumsily.

—Maybe we're fooling ourselves, he said to Esta after her jump. *Maybe we're not really made to fly.*

Despite having feathers, he was still the wrong shape, the wrong weight.

—No, she said. *Look.*

She rolled up her pants to show him. From ankle to knee were small bumps beneath her skin. They were quills, ready to break through.

—More feathers! he said.

He ran his hands over his own lower legs, and his heart leapt when he felt the tender spots along the length of his bone. It was happening to him, too.

—*With feathers on our legs . . . ,* he began.

She nodded. *We'll have lift back there.*

—*No more drag!*

—*See?* she whispered inside his head. *We're built to fly. We're special, you and me.*

"THANK YOU, PETRA," PAUL said. "This is very useful information."

Behind him, on the wallpaper of the interview room, the sun set over the sandy beach. Before today, the scene had always made Petra feel calmer and even sort of hopeful. Right now, though, she couldn't help noticing the places where the wallpaper curled at the seams, speckled with mildew. She felt like she had a stone in her stomach.

She'd thought about it over and over. She *had* to tell them.

She was just a *kid,* same as Seth and Anaya, and they shouldn't be keeping secrets from the military. Yes, they'd locked her in an underground bunker, but *they* were human beings, and *she* was a human being, and she should be helping them all she could.

The cryptogens had a ship that was untouchable. The nuke hadn't even dinged it! When the invasion came, the military was going to need all the help it could get. And maybe there were runners and swimmers who might be allies instead of enemies. It could make all the difference.

She was glad it was just Paul sitting across from her. If it had been Ritter, she might've lost her nerve. She trusted Paul more. Which was why she'd sought him out in the gym this morning and asked to speak to him in private. She'd always found her interviews with him strangely reassuring. They were orderly. He used her first name, but he didn't try to make friends with her. Also, his hair smelled of the same shampoo as her dad's.

She'd told him everything Anaya had "seen" last night, and she felt lighter. But already guilt was flooding in to take the place of relief. She'd promised Seth she wouldn't tell. He'd been worried about their safety—and his own, especially, as a flyer. She didn't want anything bad to happen to him.

Even if he *had* been a lousy friend. Mostly he hung out with Esta and Siena and Vincent. Just because they had feathers with super-cool patterns and could sort of fly, they acted like they were special. They'd even started working out together with the ancient weight machines in the cafeteria, doing curls and bench presses. They never invited her over, so she kept her distance. No way was she going to beg to join their little crew.

So yes, she'd broken a promise to Seth. But he'd broken one to her, too. He'd told Esta about the telepathy, and maybe Siena and Vincent as well. Too many times she'd caught them sitting together silently. No one's mouth moving. It could only mean they were using telepathy.

Across the desk, Paul watched her patiently.

"I know you probably still think we're national security threats," she said, "and spies, or whatever, but we're not. We're all on the same side. The *human* side."

She was good at speeches and wanted to convince Paul that the hybrids were loyal. She'd prepared what to say ahead of time, because she needed to nail it. She took another breath, opened her eyes wide.

"We all want to beat these things as much as you do. It was me and Anaya and Seth who helped get that soil the herbicide's made from. We risked our lives to do that. Because we want to win. All of us do. Every single darn hybrid down here. The runners, the swimmers, the flyers. None of us asked for this. None of us want anything but for this to be over, and us to win. That's why I'm telling you this. I want you guys to have all the ammo possible."

"Okay," Paul said.

That was it? She'd delivered a killer speech, and all she got was an *okay*? Frankly, she'd expected a smidge more gratitude and enthusiasm. She'd given him amazing information about three distinct cryptogen species and their relative statuses and technologies. She hadn't expected a medal or anything, but still. Paul seemed done with her, so she started to stand.

Ritter walked in, and the room's center of gravity shifted.

"Sit," he said. "I have some questions of my own."

With a sick turn of her stomach, Petra realized that he must've been listening from another room. She was suddenly aware of her tail swishing nervously against the leg of her chair. She stopped it.

"I wonder," Ritter began, "why L9 didn't come and tell us this herself. Since she was the one to actually receive this information."

Petra had been worried about this question but had an answer prepped. She didn't want Anaya getting into trouble.

"She thought it was probably only a dream, so she wasn't sure it was worth telling you. But I thought you should know. I mean, if it's real, it means—"

"I'm also interested in this cryptogen she's been communicating with."

"It was just the once," Petra lied. "Last night."

"And whether L9 might have transmitted any information."

"No, she didn't!"

"We have no way of knowing, of course, how trustworthy this cryptogen informant is. Or if it's a living cryptogen at all. It might be some kind of AI designed to send us misinformation and propaganda. To make us think there are sympathetic factions within the enemy ranks. To make us hold our fire and confuse us on the battlefield when the time comes."

"Well," said Petra, deluged by all these possibilities, "okay, and that's why I told you, so you guys could decide what was best."

"You did absolutely the right thing," Paul said.

Ritter splayed his hands on the table, as if admiring the sheer size of them, then lifted his gaze to her. "And what about your own communications?"

She looked back at him, confused. "Um, I haven't had any. I haven't even been outside, so how—"

"I mean your own telepathic communications with the other hybrids."

She couldn't stop the blaze of heat in her cheeks, blaring her guilt.

"What do you mean?" she said, knowing how unconvincing she must sound.

"Oh, it was quite obvious. We have very sensitive equipment, and we've been picking up lots of radio activity from the cafeteria and gymnasium and dorm areas. I can't say it comes as much of a surprise. Those radio organs in your brains seem designed for all sorts of communication. How many of you have been using telepathy?"

There was no point lying now. "Three of us, maybe more, I'm not sure."

"You and who else?"

"Anaya and Seth."

"L9 and A4."

Hearing him turn her friends into numbers gave her a chill.

"No one came forward sooner to tell me. Why is that?"

Paul interjected before she could splutter out an excuse.

"I think Petra's shown considerable bravery coming forward. She's given us lots of valuable information."

"No question, no question," said Ritter. "I'm very pleased. Still, it does make me wonder what else you might be with-holding."

"Nothing!" Petra said indignantly. She'd come here with the best intentions, knowing her friends would probably be pissed at her, and now Ritter was treating her like an enemy spy. She took a breath, reminded herself that getting angry would not help her cause.

"I'm really sorry I didn't tell you sooner," she said.

Tears blurred her eyes without her even trying. She'd come wanting to make things better for all of them. And now she feared she'd just made things much, much worse.

CHAPTER NINE

WHEN ANAYA RETURNED TO the cafeteria after morning workouts, the place had been decorated with balloons and streamers. Across the back wall was a big banner that proclaimed: HAPPY 16TH BIRTHDAY!

"This is weird, right?" Petra said beside her.

"I would say yes."

Anaya would've been less surprised if all the chairs were upside down on the ceiling.

Bowls of chips and cheese puffs were set out with paper napkins and noisemakers. There were bottles of soft drinks as well as an enormous punch bowl glowing with some radioactive-looking orange fluid.

"This can't have been Ritter's idea," she said.

"Paul's?" suggested Petra.

Or maybe a committee of White Coats who thought it would be good for prisoner morale. Something sparkly to cheer them up, make them feel like real kids turning sixteen at a fun underground party. Anaya wasn't sure if the whole idea was kind or cruel.

"It's like a party for five-year-olds," Petra said.

"But without chaperones," Darren remarked. And he was right. No guards. No White Coats. They'd been left to have the party on their own.

All the kids gravitated toward a table in the middle of the room where there was an enormous slab cake. Whoever had done the icing was not skilled. HAPPY BIRTHDAY was written in thick, wobbly pink letters. The cake had been precut into squares, and beside it was a stack of paper plates and plastic forks.

"Look, it's even gluten-free," Charles said, pointing to the little handwritten sign.

"Whoever has the first bite of this thing is one brave dude," said Siena.

"You think it's poisoned?" asked Vincent.

"No. Just gross," Siena said. "Way too much icing."

"Are you kidding? I love icing," said Vincent. "Gimme a piece of that!"

The weird thing was, the party *did* seem to make people relax. As kids munched on nibbles and shoved cake into their mouths and hesitantly sipped the punch, Anaya heard more laughter than she had in days. Adam and Nia and a group of other kids launched into a version of "Happy Birthday" that culminated with:

Happy birthday, dear freaksters!
Happy birthday to youuuuuuuuuuuu!

Whoever had organized the party must have left behind some music that wasn't a million years old, because a kid put on an album that Anaya actually recognized. When it got turned up loud, a few kids started dancing, and Anaya felt pulled by the thumping bass.

She'd always loved dancing, though mostly she danced alone in her room, with her headphones on, sometimes on the bed for extra bounce. Now she was in a brightly lit cafeteria with lots of virtual strangers, all of them as weird as her. She had nothing to lose. She stomped, her arms pumped, her shoulders rolled, she whipped her hair around. It felt fantastic.

"You are a crazy messy dancer," Petra said with a grin, joining in.

"I'm a messy person!"

Which was true, and she didn't care. She liked the song and wanted to be filled up with something that wasn't dread.

"Just don't gore me with your claws," Petra said, laughing.

Anaya smiled as her friend started matching her crazed moves with genuine enthusiasm. Charles and Darren joined the dance mess, too. A little ways off Seth and Esta bounced to the music. Swinging tails, furry arms and furry faces, wings, claws, patterned skin. There had never been a weirder sweet sixteen party.

When the music was suddenly turned down, Anaya looked over to see Ritter standing by the turntable. She came to a standstill, instantly chilled by his presence.

"I hope you're enjoying your birthday festivities," he said

chewily, and attempted a smile that didn't go well. "And I'm sorry to interrupt. This won't take long, though I think I have some news you'll like. Consider it a birthday present."

Anaya glanced warily at Petra.

"We know how upsetting these changes to your bodies are," Dr. Ritter went on. "Which is why I've decided to start a protocol to return you to normal."

Normal.

Anaya saw how everyone in the room turned their faces to that word as if it were a glorious sunrise after an endless night.

"The procedures will be simple and safe," he said now. "With the L group we'll be filing back fingernails and toenails. We'll also be using lasers to remove excess body hair and prevent future growth."

A cheer went up from the runners, and Anaya felt her own spirits lift. Finally! She wanted the hair off her face so badly, but every time she'd asked a White Coat for a razor, she'd been turned down. They kept saying they wanted to view and assess all her natural traits. Hair, claws, the works. They wanted to see what she was going to become.

And now, suddenly, this new direction.

"What's changed?" she whispered to Petra.

"For the W's," Ritter was saying, "we'll also be using lasers to see if the patterning on your skin can be safely removed. More important, we will remove tails."

More cheers rose around the cafeteria, none louder than the

"Yes!" Petra shouted as she pumped her fist triumphantly into the air.

Anaya couldn't help smiling at her friend's delight, but she caught the disdainful look Esta slid Petra's way. There was probably no hope these two would ever be friends.

"Since this procedure requires surgery," Ritter continued, "we'll be looking for volunteers."

Again, Petra shot her hand up, like a schoolkid dying to be chosen. Judging by the number of raised hands, Anaya figured every single swimmer was volunteering. Except Darren, whose forehead was furrowed with confusion.

"I don't get it," he muttered. "Why would they do this?"

"I don't know," Anaya replied, "but I don't think they want us as soldiers, Darren."

She saw Ritter take in all the swimmers' raised hands with a little nod. "It's helpful to know the level of interest," he said matter-of-factly. "However, the selection will be made randomly. And some of you will remain controls, which means you will continue to develop without interference."

Anaya heard Petra release a disappointed sigh as she dropped her hand. "No fair."

"Okay, I get it now," Darren said with a relieved grin. "He's weeding out the weak ones. He's keeping the best to be soldiers." He winked at Petra. "We'll make the cut, no problem."

Anaya rolled her eyes and was about to say something, but Ritter was talking again.

"And with the A's, we'll be removing feathers."

Her eyes flew to Seth. His reaction couldn't have been more different from Petra's. His whole body stiffened, like he'd stopped breathing. Revolt blazed from his eyes, which, right now, were locked with Esta's.

"This procedure is somewhat more complicated," Ritter carried on, "so how many of you are interested?"

Anaya's uneasiness contracted into a terrible fear.

—*Put up your hand,* she told Seth silently.

—*No,* came his terse reply.

—*It's a test!*

Across the room, she saw Siena raise her hand and then, more reluctantly, Vincent. Seth and Esta were the only other two flyers in the bunker. Anaya watched Ritter's gaze slide across the room toward them.

—*Seth!* she said urgently. *Do it.*

He didn't. Neither did Esta. Anaya could tell Ritter was looking straight at their blue jumpsuits. And what was he thinking? That the two of them preferred being hybrids? That they'd abandoned their human loyalties?

Anaya had an uncomfortable flash memory of the winged cryptogens decimating cities, killing the runners and swimmers. She looked at Esta and Seth, wondering if they could be capable of such a thing—and hated herself for it.

"It won't change us inside, though," she said, wanting to distract Ritter. Heads turned her way across the cafeteria. "I mean, my claws might grow back, and I'll still be able to jump high and run really fast, won't I?"

Ritter's gaze strayed lazily over to her. "This remains to be seen."

—What're you doing? Petra hissed silently in her head. *Shut up!*

"Regardless," Ritter continued, "my medical teams are investigating a possible treatment that will prevent any further changes to your bodies. If they're successful, you would return to normal in every sense of the word."

"How?" Charles asked. He was, for sure, one of those kids who were never afraid to ask questions in class. "How will that work?" With his facial hair filled in, he looked even more like a nervous meerkat now.

"As our research progresses, I will keep you up-to-date," Ritter said. "Our hope has always been that, when this is all over, you'll return to your lives, and your homes and your families."

Even as Anaya doubted his words, the promise of it was so wonderful that she felt a hot tingle behind her eyes. She swallowed. Mom and Dad. Salt Spring Island.

"Enjoy your party," Ritter said, and left the cafeteria.

Anaya didn't feel like dancing anymore, even when the music started up again. She found a quiet table and sat down. Petra, Darren, and Charles joined her, and even Seth and Esta came over.

"See?" Petra said to Seth. "You said they'd never let us out of here."

Seth made no reply, and Anaya could see the confusion and wariness etched into his face.

"Why's he talking about this being all over?" Charles asked. "Does he know something?"

"They're not taking my wings," said Seth.

"What's wrong with you?" Petra said to him. "He's giving us a chance to be normal again."

"I don't buy it," said Anaya. "We're half cryptogen. How can they change all the DNA in our body?"

She wasn't even sure she wanted to be normal. Lose the facial hair, definitely. But the strength and speed? No way. She could tell Seth felt the same. Wings, he'd called them. Not feathers, but wings. She'd always known how fiercely protective, and proud, he was of his feathers, but calling them wings was something new.

"I agree with you," Charles said to her. "Clipping our toenails isn't going to change us."

"He said they're *working* on it," Petra retorted. "I'm sorry, I didn't know you guys were all brilliant scientists. I say leave it to the experts. They're trying to *help* us."

Esta shot Petra a withering look. "You are so naive."

Anaya could hear Petra's tail thwack out an angry beat against the chair leg.

"They're not trying to help us, Petra," said Seth. "They're scared of how strong we're getting." He nodded at Charles. "I saw you guys in the gym today. You can punch through sheet metal with your claws. And we're getting more feathers, on our legs."

"What?" Anaya said. "Since when?"

"I just noticed mine today. Esta's are further along."

Anaya had grown up with a pilot mother and knew what this meant. "You'll have more lift and be able to steer better."

Maybe they really would fly. The idea was mind-blowing. She thought of all Seth's sketches over the years, the creatures he hoped he might one day become.

"But this is my point," Darren said. "We're getting more powerful. Which makes us even more valuable as soldiers. They don't want to lose that."

"Are you delusional?" Seth said.

Anaya felt exactly the same way, but she wouldn't have said it aloud. The surprise on Darren's face was quickly replaced with a menacing grin.

His tail lifted a few inches above the table. It swayed from side to side, cobra-like.

"You want to put that away," Seth said.

"What?" Darren looked around in genuine surprise to behold his tail.

Anaya leaned closer, squinting. "Did it always have that sharp bit at the end?"

Darren brought the tip closer to his face. "Well, look at that," he said, sounding pleased.

"Oh my God," mumbled Petra, looking queasy. "Is that a stinger?"

"That's what I'm thinking," Darren said. "About time we got a weapon of our own. If it's a stinger, that means venom."

"This is why I want my tail off," said Petra.

"Nah. This is why we're so valuable," Darren said, looking at Seth. "Maybe you don't want to fight for your country. But I do. That's why I didn't put my hand up. It was a test."

"Yeah, it was a test," Anaya said, "but not for that. Ritter wanted to see who *didn't* want to be normal."

"Oh, right, because that automatically makes us dangerous?" Esta said.

"Should've put your hand up," Petra said angrily to Seth. "Ritter's going to be suspicious now."

"Yeah," said Esta, "we might want to help the flyer cryptogens take over the planet, and put all you little runners and swimmers into work camps."

Anaya swallowed, realizing that Seth must have told Esta everything.

"What're you talking about?" Charles asked, his eyes ricocheting between her and Esta.

—*Tell them.*

Anaya's breath caught as Esta's words materialized in her head. They flickered yellow and tasted electric, like aluminum foil in her mouth.

"Tell them," Esta said, aloud this time. "About that little

home movie the cryptogens sent you." Sarcastically, she added, "Shouldn't they all know the danger they're in?"

Charles and Darren both stared at her. Anaya truly regretted keeping secrets from them. She'd tried to do the right thing, but it wasn't right, withholding information that affected every one of them.

As simply as possible, she described what the cryptogen had planted in her head.

Darren looked at Petra. "You knew about this? And you never told me?"

"I can keep a secret," said Charles, sounding hurt, "but this shouldn't be a secret."

"We've got to tell Ritter," Darren said.

"No, we do not," Seth said.

Charles said, "This is pretty vital intel. I mean, who knows if it's true, but if it is, it could change the whole outcome of the war. Anaya, you see that, right?"

"He'll put us in a cage," said Seth.

Anaya felt torn. She wanted to protect Seth, but she didn't want to cripple humanity's chances of winning the war. She glanced over at Petra, who had gone very quiet and was staring hard at the table.

"We can't hide this from them," Darren said. "It's obvious."

"They already know," Petra said. "I told them."

Anaya looked at her friend in disbelief. "Petra! We said we wouldn't."

"Hey, Seth's already told his pal Esta, and who knows who else." Anaya knew Petra well enough to see the guilt behind her friend's defiance. "Ritter needed to know, so I did it."

"When?" Seth demanded, his voice hoarse.

"This morning."

"What else did you tell him?"

"Nothing. I didn't need to. He knew everything else. *Everything*."

"Our telepathy?" Anaya said with a jolt.

"Yep."

"We have *telepathy*?" Charles said, his eyeballs pinballing from person to person.

"I'll tell you later," Anaya said.

Darren paddled his hands against the table. "Woo-hoo, we are really rolling now!"

"This new plan of Ritter's," Seth said, "it's because he's worried we're plotting something. He's going to clamp down hard."

"Why would he punish the runners and swimmers?" Darren demanded. "Seems like it's only the flyers who want to rule the world. I mean, maybe it makes sense to lock you guys up, but—"

"Darren, cut it out," said Anaya.

She could practically feel the heat of everyone's anger and anxiety. She wanted to cool things down.

"I can't believe you ratted us out," Esta was saying to Petra. "It shows where your priorities are."

"Trying to help beat the cryptogens?" Petra retorted. "Um, yeah, *that's* where my priorities are!"

"More like saving your own neck and getting first in line for cosmetic surgery."

"This is not cosmetic surgery, Esta! Maybe you're happy being a freak, but I'm not! I've seen you in the gym. You *like* ripping apart those dummies with your wings."

"Petra, stop!" Anaya said, loud enough so that a few kids sitting nearby turned.

An uneasy silence fell over the table. After a few moments, Seth leaned in and very quietly said:

"We need to escape."

The mere sound of the word *escape* made Anaya's pulse quicken.

"You're crazy," said Petra. "Say we do break out somehow—then what? We don't know where we are. We could be thousands of miles from anywhere."

Anaya shook her head. "No. We're close to an airport. When I was outside, I heard a plane."

"Okay, fine," Petra said. "We're close to a city, whoopie. No one's going to be happy to see a bunch of kids with fur and feathers and tails. We're crypto scum. They'll just bring us right back here. If we don't get strangled by plants first. Or eaten by giant bugs."

"It sounds like a monster movie up there," Charles agreed. "Down here still seems like the best bet."

"Anyway," said Petra, "if we get caught trying to escape, things *would* get worse for us."

"Things are going to get worse for us anyway," Seth said. "Can't you see that? They're going to start chopping off parts of us."

"Parts I don't want," said Petra.

"Seth's right," Anaya said. "We need to get out of here."

Ritter had said the surgery was voluntary, but why would she believe him? He could do anything he wanted to them down here. No one would know. No one would care, especially not with the entire world being torn apart.

And she desperately wanted to be outside again, not only to find Mom and Dad and Dr. Weber, but to talk to her cryptogen again. There was more to learn, so many questions that needed answering.

"I'm staying put," Darren said.

"Seth," said Petra. Her tone was calmer now, and Anaya saw the pleading in her eyes. "Stay here, okay? Nothing good is going to happen outside."

"Nothing good's going to happen down here," said Esta. "Especially with you informing on us."

Anaya saw Petra start to speak, then falter. Her heart went out to her. Probably she'd thought she was doing the right thing. She was about to say so when she tasted Esta's electric words in her head:

—I think we know where everyone stands.

—It's just the three of us, Seth said, his words smelling like rain on hot asphalt.

Anaya could tell that Petra was not being included in this conversation.

—You're not being fair, she said. *We need to convince Petra. The others, too.*

She was aware of Petra watching with a disgusted shake of her head.

"I know you guys are talking about me. Very mature. Just ghost me."

—She's made her choice, said Esta, and her words carried more voltage than usual.

—We need to make plans, Seth said.

—And we need to keep them secret, added Esta.

PETRA PEDALED ON THE stationary bike, going nowhere, fuming.

How could Seth and Anaya do that to her?

They'd cut her out of the conversation. Really, she should be blaming Esta. It was probably her telling them what to do. But why were they letting her? Neither of them made a peep when Esta basically called her a traitor to her face.

She pedaled harder, feeling her tail curl and uncurl restlessly.

She wasn't sorry she'd told Ritter. It was the right thing to do. And now her friends were giving her the silent treatment, just because she thought staying in the bunker was the best option.

She worried she might start to cry. When she'd stormed away from the table, Anaya hadn't even come after her. Some friend. Well, Anaya had been disloyal before; this was nothing new. She glanced across the cafeteria at their little clique. Probably trash-talking her—or worse, not talking about her at all.

—*Hey.*

Startled, she looked over to see Darren wearing a very self-satisfied grin. He'd figured out telepathy.

—*You're blushing,* he said.

It was involuntary and she hated it. It was the sheer surprise of having a new person suddenly inside her head. She didn't want him to think she had a crush on him—though he was conceited enough to assume it. She wrinkled her nostrils. The briny smell of his silent words was pungent, almost too intense. And it made her wonder about her own telepathic scent. *A beach at low tide,* Seth had said. She hoped it was a nicer beach than Darren's.

—*Charles and I figured it out together,* he said. *Wild, huh?*

—*We're just crazy-fun aliens, Darren.*

She didn't like having him inside her head—he was like an uninvited guest in her bedroom. Probably there was some way of blocking him, but right now she was grateful *someone* was talking to her. She watched him doing biceps curls with the free weights. As if his arms weren't big enough already.

—They're nuts if they think they can escape this place, Darren said. *They'll never make it out.*

She resented that Darren's silent voice came through so clearly, much clearer than Anaya's or Seth's did. But she supposed it was because she and Darren were the same kind of hybrid. Lucky her.

—It's weird, he said, *that the flyers are the rulers on their own planet.*

—Why?

—They're kind of spindly. Without wings, they wouldn't be so special.

Typical Darren: reduce everything to a shoving match.

—Anaya said they had some kind of weapon that crushes everything.

—They are so up on themselves, he said. *I figure I could take them.*

—No doubt.

Seth walked over and reclined on the bench press machine. He grabbed the handles and started pushing.

—You all right? he asked her.

His words seemed sincere, but she ignored him. She was still too angry.

—Petra, I want you to come with us, he said.

Her heart softened. The idea of Anaya and Seth leaving without her was like staring into a bottomless pit. The three of them belonged together. *Come with us,* he'd said. But *us* meant something different now. It meant Esta, too.

Petra didn't feel like being added on, maybe out of pity. Did Esta even know Seth was talking to her right now? Or maybe she'd sent him over to find out if she really was a spy.

Darren barged into her head again.

—*Know what else I noticed? I counted all the kids and there's an equal number of guys and girls. You think it's a coincidence?*

She shrugged. What did it matter?

—*Everyone's paired up,* he went on. *It's like some kind of alien mating program.*

—*That's creepy, Darren.*

When she scowled at him, he winked back, then silently said something that made her blush again, this time with shock.

—*Knock it off, Darren. Not interested.*

—*Come on, a little birthday kiss—*

He added something so graphic that her hands flew to her ears, trying to block him out.

"Shut up, Darren!" she said aloud. Her tail, unbidden, had lifted aggressively to her left side. She saw it had the same barbed end as Darren's.

On the bench press, Seth sat up. He looked from her to Darren and seemed to understand instantly what was going on.

"Hey, Darren, whatever you're saying, she doesn't like it."

Darren swaggered over to the bench press and stood looming over Seth.

"Still on the little weights, huh?" He reached past Seth's head, pulled out the pin, and slotted it under a much heavier weight. "Why don't you try lifting something real?"

Seth craned his neck around to see where the pin was set.

Darren smirked. "Can't handle it, huh?"

Seth removed the pin and moved it to an even greater weight. He lay back and, as Petra watched in amazement, did eight smooth presses, his breathing nice and calm.

Then he stood and said to Darren, "You want to try?"

Darren shrugged and sat down. He gripped the bars, took a couple of big puffs, and pushed. He couldn't do even one full press. He let the weights slam down, his face red.

"No way you did that," he muttered, jiggling the pin to see if there was something tricky with it.

"You know how I did it, Darren?" asked Seth. He thumped the center of his chest with his fist. "Flight muscles. Right here. Birds have them to power their wings." He inhaled deeply, and Petra watched his chest swell against his jumpsuit. He'd always had a weirdly large chest for such a skinny guy, but now it looked big *and* muscular. When had this happened?

"Which means, Darren," Seth said, "I can bench-press way more than you. Which means, Darren, you should shut up when I tell you."

Worriedly Petra watched Darren for his reaction. This was not a good idea, what Seth was doing. Surprisingly, Darren grinned. He actually looked happy, like someone had just said yes to him.

He stood, took a step toward Seth, and with one hand shoved him backward.

Seth stumbled over a barbell and went down, smacking his head hard against the weight rack.

"Darren!" she cried. "You jerk!"

Seth stood. The only time he'd looked anywhere close to this angry was when her own dad had suggested clipping his feathers. He swung and whacked Darren across the head with his plastered right arm. Darren staggered, then threw himself at Seth's skinny legs. Toppled off balance, Seth hit the floor again. At once Darren was astride his chest, knees pinning Seth's arms.

"Maybe I break those freaky feathered arms of yours, huh?"

"Darren, stop it!" cried Esta, rushing over with Anaya.

Darren snatched up a nearby barbell and smacked it down on Seth's forearm. Petra gave a shriek when she heard the crack. But it wasn't bone, only the cast. Five sharp feathers sprang through the gap in the plaster.

Seth struck out. Darren swore and scuttled off him. Seth got to his feet and took another swipe at Darren, slicing through his jumpsuit.

Darren grabbed a barbell and threw it at Seth. It hit him in the chest, and he doubled over, gasping. Darren marched closer, another barbell gripped threateningly near his shoulder.

And then suddenly he faltered, wincing. The barbell dropped from his hand, and he pushed his fingertips against his temple. Unsteadily he sank to the floor, eyes crinkled shut.

"Stop!" he grunted. "Please, stop it!"

Petra saw Seth frown in confusion, and when she looked at Esta, the girl was glaring at Darren with such fury that Petra felt scared of her.

Then Esta gave a little gasp and stepped back, looking surprised. Her face went pale.

Petra heard shouts and turned as four guards rushed into the cafeteria. Two of them hoisted Darren to his feet, manacled his hands, and marched him toward the doors.

"What'd you do to me?" Darren called back at Seth. "You freak!"

Petra knew by the look on Seth's face that he hadn't done anything. The two remaining guards had their Tasers drawn on Seth, looking at the sharp feathers of his right arm.

"Hands behind your back," one of them barked.

Seth did as he was told.

"He didn't do anything!" Petra shouted, then watched helplessly as he was marched out of the cafeteria.

WHY DID YOU TWO fight?" Dr. Ritter asked.

Sitting on the bench, his back against the wall, Seth looked up at Paul and Ritter. They'd kept him waiting a good long time in the holding cell, his arms manacled behind his back. He could tell he had a huge bruise on his chest from where Darren's barbell had hit him. It hurt to move, or to breathe too deeply. But he'd had plenty of time to talk silently to Esta and figure out what was going on.

—*It was me,* she'd told him shortly after he was thrown in the cell. *I did that to Darren.*

—*How?*

—*It just happened. I was really angry, and silently shouting at him to stop, and it was like my words got hotter and pointier, and I felt something shoot out of me, and that's when he grabbed his head.*

"Why did you fight?" Ritter asked him again.

"It was stupid," Seth replied. "We were lifting weights and we started trash-talking each other. It got out of hand. It's no big deal."

Early on in life, he'd learned that snitching on people rarely made things better. Mostly it made people hate you more.

Ritter regarded him with his pouchy eyes. "Darren says you did something to his head. Got inside and made it hurt."

"Yeah, right." Seth sniffed, and hoped his response seemed genuine.

He'd figured Darren would tell. Ritter already knew about the telepathy, thanks to Petra, but this sound thing, this *weapon,* was something new. All Ritter had right now, though, was Darren's word.

"Described it like being stabbed in the brain," Ritter said. "It doesn't seem impossible, considering you have a powerful transmitter in your head."

Seth willed himself not to look away, not to sweat.

He shrugged. "I didn't do anything," he said truthfully.

—*It was like making sound in his head,* Esta had explained to him earlier. *A really destructive noise. If I can do it, you can do it.*

The thought startled, then frightened him.

—*Who else knows?* he asked.

—*Petra. I could tell. So I told her, and Anaya, too.*

—*Can they do it?* he asked hopefully. He didn't want to be the only one; it made the flyers seem more like monsters.

—*No. They both tried.*

—*Maybe you need to be really angry,* he suggested. *For it to work.*

—*Oh, I think Petra was plenty angry. She'd love to hurt me.*

—*Don't say that about her.*

—*Only we can do it. The flyers. It's just for us.*

—*Have you told Vincent and Siena?* he asked.

—*Not yet. But I will. When we escape.*

"If I had that kind of power," Ritter was saying now, scratching at his fleshy cheek, "and I were at risk, I'd be very tempted to use it."

"Well," Seth said reasonably, "did Darren do it to you guys?"

"We asked him to," said Paul, "but he claimed he couldn't."

Seth lifted his eyebrows like this proved his point.

"But maybe *you* can," Ritter said.

"I can't! Because it's not a thing. Darren's messing with you."

He told himself: *Don't blink, don't look away, don't sweat.*

Paul said, "I think we're done here, Dr. Ritter. Shall I have the guard escort him back—"

"Not yet," said Ritter.

Seth caught the surprise on Paul's face as Ritter went to the door and opened it. A White Coat carried in a metal chair with a low back.

"Sit here," Ritter told Seth.

Warily he went to the chair and stood in front of it.

"Why?" he asked.

Seth winced as Ritter pushed him backward into the chair. The pressure of the man's fingers against his bruised chest was like a brand. Seth felt his temper heating.

"Arms over the backrest," the White Coat told him, and then produced a roll of duct tape and wrapped several loops around his wrists and the chair back. His feathers jutted through the cracked cast.

"Maybe you just need to be properly motivated," Ritter said.

Seth couldn't tear his eyes away from the shiny silver instrument that Ritter now held so casually in his meaty hand.

"These are actually bone cutters," Ritter said. "They'll have no trouble cutting through the shaft of your feathers. It will be painless."

Seth bucked against the chair, but the White Coat pressed

down hard on his shoulders, and the guards stepped closer, their Tasers drawn.

"Dr. Ritter—" Paul began, but Ritter spoke over him.

"Your feathers mean a lot to you, don't they, Seth?"

"Stop!" Seth shouted.

In horror he watched as Ritter opened the curved blades of the cutter and moved toward his exposed feathers.

"Tell me what you did to Darren."

—*Don't tell them anything,* Esta had said urgently when they last spoke.

—*Of course I won't.*

—*We need to keep this secret. Anaya and I are making escape plans.*

—*I won't tell them,* Seth had promised.

"I didn't do anything!" he shouted at Ritter now, craning his neck to watch what was happening. His heart battered his ribs.

"The feathers are likely still growing," said Ritter, "so there may be some bleeding, but that's easily controlled."

He was bluffing, Seth told himself desperately. A trick to make him tell the truth. Ritter slipped the cutter's blades around the base of a long feather.

"Stop!" Seth shouted.

"Make me stop," said Ritter. "Do to me what you did to Darren."

"This is torture!" Seth shouted hoarsely.

Inside his head he discovered a vibration. It appeared as a thin string of light. He could pluck it like a musical instrument. He could play a tune on it. A terrible jagged tune right inside Ritter's head.

"Sir!" he heard Paul say. By that one word, Seth knew Paul was horrified by what Ritter was doing.

"Just going to clip this one feather," Ritter said.

Seth couldn't help it. He plucked that string of light, and its vibration swelled to fill his mind, and he aimed it right at Ritter.

The bone cutters fell from his fingers, and he staggered back, one hand clamped against his temple, the other held up in front of him, like he was fending off a wild animal.

Instantly Seth stopped himself, cleared that terrifying vibration from his head. Such power.

There was shouting and a guard crowding in on him with a Taser. He heard a crisp pop and his body was suddenly not his own, just a big spasm of pain and darkness.

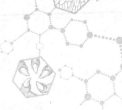

CHAPTER TEN

WHEN DARREN FELL INTO step beside her in the gym, Petra ignored him.

—*I'm sor*— he began to say silently, but she put on a burst of speed and left him behind.

She looked around the gym. If Darren was back, Seth should be back, too. Neither of them had been at breakfast, so maybe they'd only just been released by Ritter. Seth would be along in a few minutes.

Last night, in the dorm, Esta had been talking to him silently. It irked Petra that she was the one talking to him—but she didn't have the range to reach him, and anyway, she was just so grateful to find out he was okay. Last she'd heard, he was still locked up in a solitary cell on Level 300, waiting for someone to come question him. And then she'd fallen asleep.

This morning, when Esta had tried to reach him, she couldn't. Which freaked Petra out. Terrible explanations had filled her head. But maybe he was just asleep or, as Anaya had said, he'd been moved to a different level. No way even Esta's telepathy could penetrate two thick concrete floors. This place was built to withstand a nuclear hit. Still, Petra wondered, *why* had Seth been moved?

—*Seth,* she called silently. *Seth!*

No reply, like all the other times she'd tried this morning. She wished she was better at silent talking.

Darren caught up with her.

"I'm sorry," he said, aloud this time. "The things I said. I was a creep."

An apology was something she hadn't expected, but her anger was a long way from being spent. She didn't know Darren well enough to tell if he was genuinely sorry or merely good at faking it.

"You know where Seth is?" she demanded.

"He's not here?" Darren seemed truly surprised. "I mean, he *shouldn't* be here because the guy's dangerous. It was like someone gouging a hook into my—"

"What exactly did you tell them?"

He looked at her like the answer was obvious. "I told them what happened."

"Which was what?"

"You saw, you know what happened! Seth did something in my head."

She was starting to get seriously worried now. "You told Ritter that?"

"Why d'you look so angry? I thought you wanted to tell them everything!"

"Yeah, but it wasn't Seth who did that to you. It was Esta!"

She saw his eyes skitter around the gym, trying to find the other girl. "She can do it, too? Holy crap, can all the flyers do it?"

She broke away from Darren and headed across the gym toward Paul, who was observing some swimmers getting their acid test.

She glimpsed Anaya, pounding away on the elliptical machine, probably breaking a new world record. Last night in the dorm, Anaya had tried to convince her to escape with them. She'd been tempted—of course she'd been tempted—but she didn't buy that Ritter and Paul were monsters.

What she *did* know was that there were real monsters waiting for them outside, and it made way more sense to stick it out down here. And yes, she wanted her tail removed, and what was wrong with that? Was it so unreasonable? Selfish? No. She could tell Anaya wanted her hair and claws removed, too. She'd caught her enough times sighing at her reflection in the bathroom mirror.

When she passed the glide platform, she saw Esta at the top. The girl's eyes tracked her suspiciously. Petra didn't care.

When she reached Paul, she wasted no time.

"It wasn't Seth," she said.

Paul glanced at her, surprised, and for a second she wondered if she'd made a big mistake. She caught a whiff of Paul's shampoo, her dad's shampoo, and tried to calm herself. She wasn't giving anything away. Darren had already told them about the pain inside his head—he'd just gotten the details wrong.

Why should Seth take the blame for what Esta had done? Seth would never hurt someone. He was too gentle. But she was genuinely afraid of Esta. That girl was boiling with anger. Who else would she hurt?

Paul told the White Coats he'd be back in a second and walked off a few steps with her. Now they could talk in private. Shouts echoed around the gym. Shoes pounded and squeaked.

"It was Esta," Petra said quietly. "She hurt Darren with sound. It's this weird thing she can do."

Paul nodded calmly. "Can the rest of you do it?"

"No," she said. "You're going to let Seth go, right?"

"Listen to me carefully," Paul said. His gaze roamed across the gym, and Petra wondered if he was making sure Ritter wasn't in the room. "None of you are safe here."

Heart galloping, she tried to speak, but her tongue was glued to the roof of her parched mouth.

"He's planning new procedures," Paul said. "I've been in touch with Dr. Weber. I'm trying to help get you kids out."

"When?" she managed to say.

"I need a little more time."

"What about Seth?" she whispered, trying to stop her voice from shaking.

"He's been moved upstairs for a procedure."

"What procedure?"

At that moment, the gym doors opened and Ritter entered with half a dozen guards.

Paul was already walking away from her.

"I NEED SEVERAL OF you for a new test," Ritter said from the gymnasium door.

Anaya watched the guards fan out on either side of him. This was not a good sign. What kind of new test was this?

"Come forward as you're called." In his meaty hand was a slip of paper. He read out a list of ID numbers.

Darren, Charles, Siena, Vincent, Esta.

And her.

"Follow me," Ritter said.

Anaya cut a look at Charles, and they both headed toward the door. What choice did they have? Ritter waited for them, regarding them with his impassive doll's eyes.

"Where's Seth?" she asked him.

She'd been worried sick about him, watching the cafeteria doorway all through breakfast, then the gym doorway. Only Darren had come through it.

"A4 is cooling down," Ritter said, chewing through his words. "I won't tolerate violence."

She looked coldly at Darren. He was the one who'd started the fight, so why was *he* back?

Late into the night she and Esta had discussed escape plans. Before they fell asleep, they had one that felt pretty solid. But without Seth, their plan was pointless. They couldn't leave without him.

And how could they leave without Petra? Their entire friendship, Petra was always the one to talk her way out of things, to bend and kick against rules and grown-ups, especially her RCMP mom. It was so weird that now she wanted to do what she was told—by Ritter of all people! She'd tried to change Petra's mind but failed. Their little group, she and Petra and Seth, was falling apart, and it made her heavy with sadness—and fear. Where was Seth now, and what were they doing to him?

She was about to start silently grilling Darren when suddenly Petra's voice blared in her head:

—*They're going to do something to Seth!*

Involuntarily she looked back into the gym, just as the cafeteria doors slammed shut behind her.

—*Petra, how do you know?*

—*Paul told me. He said—*

—*Why were you talking to Paul?*

What had Petra done now? Distractedly she fell into step with Charles, Darren, and the other hybrids as they were escorted down the corridor, flanked by guards.

—*He's going to help us get out, but—*

—Petra, from the beginning, please!

She turned a corner and Petra's words began to crackle. She heard her say Seth had been moved upstairs for a procedure, but she didn't know what kind of procedure—and then her voice decomposed altogether.

—Petra, I can't hear you! Petra?

A few more shards of words sparked in her head, but she couldn't make sense of them. All she picked up was their fear and urgency.

—They're going to do something to Seth, Anaya told Esta.

—Cut off his feathers? the other girl asked silently.

—Don't know.

—I'll kill anyone who hurts him.

Startled, she looked over. The viciousness in Esta's expression made her believe the girl was deadly serious.

The guards pushed open a set of fire doors, and Anaya was back in the familiar stairwell she'd taken on her way to the antenna farm. The same evil, stale smell wafted up from Level 100.

To her surprise, this time Ritter began descending.

Anaya fought back a shiver in the dank air.

Vault. Machine room. Morgue.

"Where are we going?" she dared to ask.

Ritter gave no answer. She glanced over at Esta, could see the fear and anger in the girl's face.

—Don't do anything, Anaya told her. *Wait.*

At the bottom of the stairwell, the guards pushed through

the doors and continued down a long corridor lit by fluorescent tubes. At the very end a bunch of waiting White Coats stood before a huge metal door. It had multiple spoked wheels and a complicated system of levers.

Charles leaned closer. "I read about this. All these bunkers had vaults for the Federal Reserve Bank. It's where they'd store the gold reserves. In case the world got nuked."

"Because gold's so useful in the apocalypse," Anaya muttered.

"Open it up," Ritter told the White Coats.

With a gust of stale air, the vault door swung open.

"Inside," Ritter said, and led the way, pushing past a heavy plastic curtain.

Reluctantly she followed. The vault was vast, with four mighty pillars supporting a concrete ceiling snaked with wires and pipes. Shadows pooled around the tops of the pillars. She didn't see any other apparatus in the room. What kind of tests were they supposed to be doing in here?

"What's remarkable about all of you," Ritter began, pacing near the doorway, "well, I should say, one of the *many* remarkable things—is your immunity to the enzymes and toxins produced by the cryptogenic plants."

—*Why do we need to be all the way down here to hear this?* Anaya asked Esta.

—*Thinking the same thing,* the other girl replied.

"Many of you have been asking what's going on topside," Ritter continued, his fleshy hands playing chords on his trousers.

"And I must tell you, the news is dire. We have a new guest on the planet."

"Only one?" Anaya asked, thinking of the terrarium on Dead-man's Island.

"Is it one of those winged things?" Charles asked. "The blood-suckers?"

Ritter stretched his mouth into a smile. "You've been getting updates from the new arrivals, I know. And yes, they are winged. And they seem to drink blood, certainly, but that's not what makes them so dangerous. They produce a very harmful virus. My assumption, though, is that all of you will be immune."

With that, he turned and pushed his way out through the plastic curtain.

"Hey!" Anaya started running for the vault door. Guards were already pushing the huge thing shut. It had an unstoppable momentum, and before she was even halfway there, it pounded closed with an ear-popping thud.

"Freaking maniac!" she cried.

"What's that noise?" Charles said.

It sounded like crickets. Anaya listened and tracked it to a long metal box hanging from the ceiling. With a whirring noise, a panel slid open. Something darted out, too fast for her to focus on. More things flitted into the shadows.

"There's lots of them!" she said.

Vincent ran past her and pounded on the vault door.

"Let us out of here!"

"Give it up!" Esta shouted. "He's not letting us out."

Anaya looked around the vault for a weapon, but the floor was bare. Her heartbeat pounded in every part of her body.

"Why's he doing this?" Darren said. "Why'd he risk making us sick?"

"We're not soldiers, Darren," Esta said. "We're lab rats."

"He wants to see what these things do to us," Charles said, pushing hair out of his nervous eyes.

"Stay together," Anaya said, and they turned their backs to each other. "Vincent, get over here!"

He wouldn't come. He'd squeezed himself between the plastic curtain and the door, hoping for protection.

"Wish I had my arms free," muttered Esta.

Anaya wished all three of the flyers did. Their feathers would come in handy right now. She looked at her hands. She at least had claws.

Esta said to Darren sarcastically, "You're going to get to do some fighting."

"I'm ready." Eyes fixed on the ceiling, he stood, legs and arms wide, his tail lifted. In the dim light Anaya saw liquid glint on the tail's pointed tip.

From the ceiling came a creaky little song, like a dozen rusty hinges being nudged. Something darted down, sparrow-sized. Mauve light refracted through its translucent wings. Then it was gone, back into the shadow.

In a blur it came again and was suddenly on her arm, all

vibrating shell and membrane—and a long, needle-like proboscis. She felt the weight of it on her skin, the prick of its skinny legs. The proboscis twitched, ready to pierce her flesh. She yelled and punched it off. Had she even hit it? It zipped back up into the air.

More of the things came flashing down. Their speed alone was frightening, the way they twitched and turned in the air. And the *thought* of them on your skin. *Feeding* on you.

Everyone ran, breaking apart their little group.

Anaya lashed out with her clawed hands, raking her jumpsuit and own skin to clear the things off her. She caught a glimpse of Siena and Esta swinging their plastered arms like baseball bats. Esta connected with a wet smack, splattering one of the creatures against a pillar. Darren was trying to punch them out of the air. His tail swayed and struck out like a snake, but never fast enough.

She saw Charles back up against a pillar, and that turned out to be the worst place, because three or four of the things dropped straight down on him from the shadowed ceiling. Their wings glittered against his brown jumpsuit.

Anaya ran to help him, but Darren got there first and hit them until they all flew away.

"They got me!" Charles said in a strangled voice. "Look, I got bitten!"

He pointed to a small red puncture mark in the soft flesh of his neck.

"It's okay," Anaya said automatically, having no idea if it was true.

No time to think, because there were more now, darting around her face and body. She impaled one on her claw and lifted it, twitching, toward her face. She could barely feel its weight. It looked like a strange skeletal bird, a mosquito bird, except there were no feathers, no beak, no eyes, and no blood. It was definitely an insect, leaking a mucus-like fluid down over her hand.

Before she could flick it off her claw, it jerked its head and, in the blink of an eye, sank its needle-thin proboscis into the skin between her fingers. The needle filled with red before she flung the thing to the ground and stamped on it.

Bitten. She'd been bitten now, too.

Her eyes locked with Charles's, and a current of shared horror arced between them. What was going to happen? Beside her, Darren was still lashing out at a swarm of mosquito birds, oblivious to the three that had landed on his back.

"Darren!" she cried, and rushed to knock them off.

Not fast enough. Two mosquito birds plunged their needles through the fabric of his jumpsuit, then flickered up and away.

"Did they get me?" Darren said, whirling, his face wild. "Did they?"

Across the room came a cry of despair, and Anaya saw Vincent cowering behind the plastic curtain, trying to smack off the mosquito birds that had slipped in with him. He burst out through the curtain.

"They got me!"

"They got all of us," Esta said, scratching her neck.

"They got me on the hands," Siena said.

They'd all instinctively drawn together. Anaya kept her gaze on the ceiling, where the mosquito birds darted excitedly, making creaky noises.

"It's like they're communicating," she murmured.

"Why aren't they coming back for more?" Darren asked.

"Maybe because they've had enough blood," said Esta.

"Maybe it's not our blood they really want," said Charles.

"What, then?" asked Siena.

"Maybe they want to put something *into* us."

"Are we infected, for sure?" Vincent said. "I think they only got me once."

"What'll happen if we are?" Siena asked.

For the first time, Anaya noticed the four security cameras mounted high in the corners of the room.

"They've been watching us," she said.

As if on cue, the vault door swung open.

"Come out now," Ritter called. "Quickly."

She started running with the others but stopped when she heard a pattering sound behind her. On the floor was one of the mosquito birds, wings askew. From the ceiling, another one spiraled down listlessly, wings trembling but not beating properly. It hit the floor, making hardly more sound than a falling leaf.

"Are they dead?" she asked.

A third and a fourth mosquito bird fluttered down lifelessly.

"Come on," Charles said, grabbing her and tugging her toward the door. "Let's get out of here!"

WHEN SETH WOKE UP, blind, it took him a few panicked seconds to realize there was a hood over his head. He tried to move his hands, but they were tied to the bedsides. Ankles, too.

"Hey!" he shouted.

He remembered what had happened in the cell with Ritter and cursed himself. Why couldn't he have held out a little longer? At worst he would've lost a couple of feathers. And Ritter wouldn't have known their secret. But in his panic, he'd struck with sound. And if Ritter knew he could do it, he'd instantly suspect Esta and the other flyers.

—*Esta!*

He had to warn her, to warn all of them.

—*Esta!*

Nothing. He couldn't find a flicker of her light in his mind. Not Petra's either, or Anaya's.

He heard the door open and footsteps. It sounded like two people.

"You're awake."

Ritter. Just hearing his voice filled Seth with rage. He tried to breathe, to calm himself. He didn't want to lash out with that sound again. The power of it terrified him. He was relieved he couldn't see that tempting string of vibrating light. Where was it?

"It's quite an exquisite weapon you have," Ritter said from the foot of his bed. "You must be wondering why you can't use it now."

"Why am I blindfolded?"

"The hood has a microfiber that blocks radio waves. Which means you can't use your telepathy. Or that sonic weapon. I'm assuming you've probably already tried to strike me by now."

"No," Seth said, but he could tell by Ritter's chuckle that he didn't believe him.

There was a strange emptiness in his head. Whatever that microfiber was, it blocked him totally.

"Who else can do this?" Ritter asked.

"No one."

"Ah, well. We'll find out soon enough."

—*Esta,* he called out in vain. *Petra! Anaya!*

He heard someone else sit down beside him. Metal things clinked on a tray.

"What's going on?" he demanded as a blood pressure cuff tightened around his arm. The cold circle of a stethoscope touched the inside of his elbow.

"No need to be alarmed—this is only a pre-op physical," Ritter said.

Seth felt a prick, then something being quickly taped against the top of his hand.

"Hey!"

"We're just setting you up for an IV," Ritter informed him. "For the procedure."

"Don't take off my feathers!" The words surged out of him.

"Don't worry," said Ritter. "It's not your feathers I'm going to remove."

CHAPTER ELEVEN

PETRA'S STOMACH ACHED AS she stared at the cafeteria doors, waiting.

The entire day she'd been worrying about Seth, and now it was almost dinner and Anaya and the others weren't back either. What was Ritter doing with them?

—Anaya! Charles!

She even tried Darren. Wherever they were, they were still out of range. She was the only person in their little group who was here right now. It made her very uneasy. Had Ritter singled her out because she'd been useful to him and passed on information? Was she being rewarded? And if she was, did that mean Anaya and the others were being *punished*?

She tried to banish that possibility from her mind. Whatever the reason, she hated being separated from her friends. She felt desperately lonely. Especially since she knew Anaya was pissed at her for talking to Ritter and Paul. If she lost Anaya as a friend, she didn't know how she'd survive down here.

And what about Seth?

Upstairs, awaiting a procedure, Paul had said. She hoped it was just removing feathers—even though she knew how hard Seth would fight to stop them. But the way Paul said *procedure* made it sound like something so much worse.

Her stomach cramped again. She wanted to move, to *do* something. The thought of them hurting Seth made her furious. Wasn't Paul going to help him? He'd said he'd help them all escape, but how—and when? Another twist of her knotted stomach. She hoped she hadn't been an idiot, talking to him.

Finally the cafeteria doors swung open. She practically launched herself off her chair as Anaya and Charles walked in. Esta came next, then Darren, Vincent, and Siena. Her joy and relief cooled when she realized Seth wasn't with them. Looking at Anaya's eyes, she knew something terrible had happened to all of them.

"You okay?" she asked.

—*Silent talking,* Anaya told her.

Petra didn't need to ask why. Six guards remained inside the cafeteria after the doors were locked. This was new. They'd never had guards inside before. They took up positions along the walls, never staying too long in one spot.

—*What's going on?* she asked Anaya.

Dinner was called out by the kitchen staff, and she collected her meal tray with the others. When they all sat down at their usual table, she listened as Anaya described what had happened to them. Petra's eyes kept getting pulled back to the red puncture marks on their skin.

—I can't believe he locked you in there with those things!

The thought of an alien bug on her, biting her, made her lose her appetite. But when a guard strolled slowly past their table, she forced herself to take a bite of her fish taco.

—But you guys are okay, right?

After they'd gotten out of the vault, Ritter had quarantined them on Level 100 to see if they'd been infected by the mosquito birds. Apparently, the virus was fast-acting, and symptoms appeared within two hours of being bitten. Fever, respiratory distress, possible coma.

—We were just lucky, Charles said, entering the silent conversation. *We're all immune.*

It was the first time she'd had his voice inside her head. It flickered a dark green and smelled like coffee and the slightly dank place at the back of her yard, beneath the cedars.

—Ritter's crazy. We could've died!

This new voice was like burned sugar, so sweet it almost smelled like garbage, and Petra realized it belonged to Vincent. Esta must have taught him about telepathy.

—He doesn't care if he kills us.

That was Siena. And suddenly everyone was talking. Amazingly, having six silent voices in her head wasn't confusing. Each carried its own light, its own smell or taste, which was soon as recognizable as someone's face.

—We need to get out of here, said Esta. *We went over the plan while we were quarantined.*

—*Paul said he was going to help us escape,* Petra said. She figured Anaya would've already told them this.

Esta's gaze landed on her like a hammer blow.

—*Why?* she asked.

—*He said Ritter had plans for more procedures. He said we weren't safe.*

—*So he's going to help us, out of the goodness of his heart?* Esta asked sarcastically.

—*What's his plan?* Darren wanted to know.

—*He didn't say. Just that he needed more time.*

—*We don't have time,* Charles said.

—*It's a trick,* Esta said. *He wants us to keep waiting, doing nothing.*

—*Why would we trust Paul?* Anaya asked.

—*Look. You trust the cryptogen you've been talking to. I trust Paul. At least he's* human!

—*Why were you even talking to him?* Esta again.

Petra pushed her tray away. The smell of the fish was making her feel sick. In her head she sensed everyone waiting.

—*I was worried about Seth. I wanted to know where he was.*

That was the truth, but not the whole truth.

—*What did you tell him?* Esta insisted.

—*Nothing that Darren hadn't already told them!*

—*Hey,* Darren said, *someone was tearing my brain apart. So I told Ritter that—*

But Petra barely heard him, because Esta was talking over him.

—*What exactly did you tell them, Petra?*

There was a sudden vibration in her head that became a small molten ball of pain.

—*I said Seth didn't do anything, all right? He didn't hurt Darren!*

She didn't want to admit what else she'd said, but the noise in her head sharpened to a point. It was like a curved hook, sinking deeper and deeper. All she wanted was for it to stop.

—*And . . . ,* Esta prompted.

—*I told him it was* you! she confessed, wincing.

—*You traitor!*

—*I didn't want them to hurt Seth!*

—*Esta, stop it!* Anaya told her.

The sound made one last jab and then evaporated.

—*They know what we can do with sound now,* Esta said. *They know because of her!*

—*They* know *because you went nuclear on Darren in the first place!* Petra shot back, massaging her temples.

—*I couldn't help it!* Esta said.

—*Yeah, well, I couldn't help protecting Seth. And now he's going to get punished. Thanks to* you!

—*Stop, both of you,* said Anaya. *We don't have time. We need to get Seth and get out of here.*

—*Paul said they'd taken him upstairs for a procedure.* She felt queasy just thinking that word.

—*Makes sense they'd take Seth upstairs,* Anaya said. *It's out of range so we can't talk to him. And Level 400, that's where the surgical suite is. I passed it when they took me outside. We'll get him on the way to the elevator.*

—*You really have a plan?* Petra asked.

—*We'll need to make some changes,* Anaya replied, *now that we have guards inside.*

Petra looked at them. Six very solid men and women, each with a Taser.

—*Do we need to fight them?*

She'd never laid a hand on anyone. What if she couldn't do it?

—*We have some very good weapons,* Esta said.

—*We don't all have the sound weapon,* Petra reminded her.

—*No,* Anaya said. *But we're strong. We can do it. Look what the three of us did on the eco-reserve.*

Anaya was looking right at her, and Petra nodded gratefully. She felt a swell of pride and also confidence. They'd fought venom-spitting water lilies and strangling vines, and they'd killed a massive pit plant. That was just her, Anaya, and Seth. They were amazing. And there were way more of them now. If only Seth were here.

—*First we need to tell the other kids what's happening,* Anaya said. *Silently.*

—*You mean teach them telepathy?* Charles asked in surprise.

—*We don't have that much time,* Esta said.

—Better teach them fast, then, said Anaya. *We're not leaving anyone behind.*

IN THE MIDDLE OF the cafeteria, Anaya jumped, knocking a lightweight ceiling tile out of its frame. She caught it as it dropped and handed it to Vincent, who passed it on to someone else.

"Hey!" one of the guards shouted. "Stop that!"

With a crazy monkey whoop she jumped again. It felt good to use her legs, to give her body something to do with that pounding heart of hers. She couldn't help giggling at the mayhem of it, even as her stomach knotted tighter with anxiety. Beside her, Charles was jumping, too. Together they smacked down more ceiling tiles. Nia and Adam and a bunch of other kids snatched them up.

All the guards were glaring at her, which was exactly what she wanted.

She was the distraction.

Across the cafeteria, Darren did bench presses on the machine. He lifted up a big stack of weights, and Esta quickly slid her plastered arm into the gap underneath. Darren let go, and the stack fell down with a crack. Anaya made a whoop to cover up the noise.

She knocked out two more tiles and saw something slither into the shadows of the ducting.

—*Vines up there!* she said to Charles.

Vines meant a pit plant, but she had no time to worry about that because two guards were strutting over.

"That's enough!" one of them shouted. Both had their Tasers drawn.

—*Here we go,* she said to Charles.

She'd never done anything like this in her life. She'd never been in a fight. She'd certainly never hit a grown-up. All her muscles throbbed.

"I want you sitting on the floor!" a guard shouted.

Her eyes drifted past the guards. Darren lifted and dropped the stack of weights again, this time onto Esta's other arm. Anaya whooped again as shards of cracked plaster danced through the air.

"Sit!" the guard bellowed at her.

A shout dragged her eyes across the cafeteria, where three guards were now charging toward the exercise area. Darren was frantically helping Esta rip off the remains of her cracked casts. She stretched out her arms. Her feathers flared like they'd been waiting forever for this moment. They were quite long now, and their strange metallic colors painted a pattern that made Anaya think: *Dragon.* Suddenly Esta seemed an altogether different creature.

The guard nearest Esta fired his Taser, and the barbs snagged in the feathers of her right arm. With a gasp, Anaya waited for Esta to drop, stunned with high voltage. But she stood tall.

Sparks crackled along her feathers, making it look like her arm was on fire.

Esta struck the guard. The sparks leapt onto him, stunning him. He dropped to the floor. With her left arm, Esta slashed through the two Taser wires, then whirled to face the other guards.

Anaya snapped her attention back to her own guards. One was shouting at Charles, the other into his shoulder mic for more backup. When a guard aimed his Taser at her, Anaya raised her ceiling tile like a shield. She felt the barbs smack against it uselessly, then tossed the tile aside and launched a flying kangaroo kick at the guard, hitting him with both feet. The impact blasted him backward, and a bunch of kids immediately piled on top of him.

The second guard rounded on her now.

—*Vincent!* she shouted silently. *Zap him.*

The flyer squinted at the guard, who instantly let out a moan and fell to his knees. His Taser clattered to the floor, and Vincent kicked it across the linoleum to Petra, who snatched it up and rushed off with Siena to help Esta and Darren.

While the guard was still moaning in pain, Anaya snapped the handcuffs off his belt and manacled his hands. She looked for a ring of keys but didn't see one.

—*You can stop now,* she told Vincent.

Pale, Vincent let out a big breath.

Anaya glanced over at the guard she'd kangaroo-kicked and saw that Charles and the other hybrids had already cuffed him.

Every time he tried to stand up, someone knocked him over again.

Across the cafeteria, Esta was rushing at the last guard standing, slashing her glinting arms. The guard fell back. But it wasn't the razor-sharp feathers that brought him to his knees; it was her terrible sound weapon. He cried out, begging her to stop. Darren dragged the guard's arms behind his back and handcuffed him.

—*Don't kill him!* Anaya called to Esta.

Esta looked over. "This was a piece of cake," she shouted across the room, her face flushed, eyes dangerously bright. "We should've done this sooner!"

"Darren!" Anaya said. "Help Vincent and Siena get their casts off, too."

The cafeteria doors flew open and guards in body armor poured inside.

"Take down the flyers first!" shouted the one in the lead, and they fanned out.

All around Anaya things happened in explosive bursts. A kid hurled a barbell at a guard. Runners punched and kicked with their clawed feet. Siena, only one arm free of its cast, used sound to make a guard clutch his head in pain while a few other kids manacled him. Petra tased a guard, but the barbs bounced off his armored chest. Her tail had better luck. Like a cobra it struck the guard behind the knee and he swore. Then his leg buckled and he fell to the floor and lay completely still.

—*Anaya, look out!*

The moment she heard Charles's warning, she whirled. A guard came at her, Taser pointed. She jumped high, pulling her legs up tight as the two barbed wires whizzed past beneath her. She grabbed hold of the ceiling frame and swung, kicking the guard in the chin, sending him sprawling.

I like my legs, she thought.

She felt the flimsy ceiling give way—*So stupid!*—and plunged down on top of the unconscious guard in a cascade of ceiling tiles and twisted aluminum. On his belt was a ring of keys, and she yanked it off and pocketed it.

Behind her she heard more ceiling tiles clatter down—and then something else landed with a heavy smack.

When she turned, she saw the pit plant, a livid bruised purple, ensnarled in its Medusa nest of black vines. Some of the vines still clung to the ceiling; others were already twitching hungrily across the floor.

Anaya jumped up and skipped away from the questing vines. Nearby a guard had tased a kid and was crouched over, starting to handcuff him. A black vine looped around the guard's ankle and jerked his leg out from underneath him. With a curse he toppled.

Before the guard could scramble up, the pit plant was actually moving, pulled by all the vines flexing on the floor. Maw open wide, the pit plant streaked toward the guard with such speed that Anaya shrieked.

And then suddenly the guard wasn't there anymore. The pit plant had swallowed him whole. Inside its elastic flesh, Anaya saw the guard's thrashing shape, even his mouth trying to scream. But the plant had sealed tight, like someone smirking with a terrible secret. A skinny stream of acid leaked from its smug lips and began hissing and smoking on the linoleum tiles.

"Out!" Anaya shouted to everyone.

Two more guards came rushing through the doors, but Esta and Vincent didn't even break stride. They just looked at the guards and, with sound, crumpled them into moaning heaps.

"Come on!" she yelled.

It was crucial they get out fast enough to lock the door behind them—and trap the guards inside. Kids poured out into the corridor. The one who'd been tased was supported by two of his friends. When the very last was out, Anaya slammed the door.

She fumbled with the keys to find the right one. It took her three tries. Finally the dead bolt shot into place. There were steel rods that locked into the floor and ceiling. Esta did those.

All according to plan. They were out. They had keys. So far so good.

Anaya led the way down corridors, reciting landmarks to herself. Red door labeled FIRE EQUIPMENT, dented gray lockers, TOOL CRIB, and there! The set of double doors labeled A-200.

Hands shaking, she unlocked the doors to the stairwell. From above came the thunder of footsteps. Fast, Anaya ushered everyone down the stairs toward Level 100 and waited out of sight till the guards pounded past. No doubt they were headed for the cafeteria. Once they freed the guards in there, things were going to get a lot worse.

The path was clear: she sprinted up the stairs. She didn't know how many of these security cameras worked, but she hoped no one was paying attention. They reached the landing of Level 400.

—*Guard behind the doors,* she told Esta.

—*On it,* Esta replied.

The guard saw them through the window in the doors and reached for his walkie-talkie. Before he could utter a word, he grabbed his head and slumped heavily on his desk. Esta had him. Anaya found the right key and pushed through the doors.

"Cuff him," she told Charles, nodding at the incapacitated guard. "Take his Taser and walkie-talkie."

"These guys are pushovers," Darren said. "They can't touch us!"

Anaya wished she felt Darren's confidence. Every inch of her vibrated with fear.

"Now," she said, "let's get Seth."

THERE WERE LOTS OF people in the room.

Seth heard them moving around, rolling equipment across the floor, arranging metallic things. Machines beeped. There were murmuring voices he didn't recognize, and one he did: Ritter's, calmly giving instructions.

He lay on a narrow bed, flat on his back, hands and ankles tied. Through the hood, he was aware of a circle of dim light that must have been an overhead lamp.

His heart raced, as much from rage as from fear. He hated being so powerless. He could actually *hear* his pulse, amplified on a monitor. He needed to breathe. He needed to think. If he could only get this hood off. He wasn't sure he'd be able to control his rage then. His heart accelerated even more. Whatever they were planning to do to him, he didn't want it.

There was an IV in his left hand, and he knew enough about operations to know that the anesthetic would flow through it and into his veins and knock him out. That would be the end of it.

Very quietly he tested the plastic fastener around his left wrist. He knew he'd never be able to pull his entire hand free. But there was a bit of wriggle room, and if he could get the plastic fastener over the IV needle, maybe he could drag it out of his vein.

"When do we shave his head?" someone said.

"Not till he's out. The hood stays on till then."

An electric rash of fear swept across Seth's chest.

"Why're you shaving my head?"

"I want to give you your life back, Seth," Ritter said, chewing his words like he was enjoying a particularly fine meal. "I could simply remove all your feathers. And I see you've got more coming in on your lower legs. But they'd probably grow back. I want to see if I can do better. I'm wondering if that transmitter

186

in your brain controls more than radio signals. It's possible it also controls the changes to your body. We can't alter your DNA, but if we remove the transmitter, we might prevent further changes. In effect, you'd go back to being normal. Don't you want to be normal again, Seth?"

"No!" he shouted. "And you don't even know if this'll work!"

"True," Ritter agreed. "That's why we need to try it first."

He heard things clinking close to him. He imagined bright silver instruments. Scissors. Knives with strange curves. A saw.

They were going to cut his head open. The horror burst over him with nightmare intensity.

"You can't do this to me!"

—*Esta!* he cried silently.

He felt so terribly abandoned. Once again he tried to find that scintillating string of light inside his head. The one he could pluck to hurt Ritter. Nowhere to be found. The hood made him powerless.

"It should be fairly straightforward," Ritter told him conversationally.

The last time he'd had surgery, when he was little, they'd taken his feathers. Now they wanted part of his brain—the thing that had given him the only pure joy he'd known his entire life: his dreams, the idea of home and flight. Without it, how was he supposed to find his way? When he was little, he'd had no fight, but he'd fight this time, as hard and as long as he could.

Seth bucked and kicked, wanting to draw attention away from his hand. He managed to slip the plastic fastener over the needle and was now trying to push it out of his vein.

"These aren't easy decisions to make," Ritter was saying—to him, or maybe to all the other people in the room. "In times of war, the rights of the individual have to take a back seat to the good of the many. Especially in cases where the individual in question does not even belong to the human race."

"You think we're monsters," Seth shouted, "but *you're* the monster!"

Working his hand, he felt the taped needle shift. He pushed harder. There. Was it out? He wasn't absolutely sure. He was afraid to push more. He angled his hand to try to hide what he'd done.

"Let's get started," Ritter said. "Put him under."

Seth tensed.

"Here we go," someone said off to his left, and he felt a dribble of fluid down his hand and fingers.

Out. He'd done it!

Seth's heart bleeped fast over the monitor, and he tried to slow his breathing. If he was supposed to be asleep, he couldn't have his heart blasting away. Inhale. Exhale. Pause. Inhale. Exhale. Pause. He heard his pulse begin to slow.

"He's out," the voice on his left said. "You can shave now."

He felt fingers curl under the hood and pull. Air and warm light against his face. He kept his eyes shut, then opened them to the tiniest slits. Enough to count the shapes moving around him. One, two, three, four, five. Behind him, someone started cutting his hair. That made six people.

"Hang on," someone said. "His IV's out."

"What?" said Ritter.

"His IV! It's not in!"

Seth snapped open his eyes. All around him stood people in green gowns and surgical caps and masks. Ritter's sheer size made him easy to recognize. And you couldn't mistake those dead eyes.

"Cut me loose," Seth told him.

"Be very careful what you do," Ritter said. "You can only hurt one of us at a time with sound, am I correct? And there are lots of people in this room. With lots of very sharp things."

Seth couldn't stop his eyes from darting to the tray near his head. It glittered with tools even more terrifying than he'd imagined. At that moment Ritter's hand snatched up a scalpel and held it against his neck.

Seth stared into his eyes, not knowing what to do.

Ritter stared back. "Get that IV back in," he told someone very calmly. "And put him out. Now."

CHAPTER TWELVE

PETRA SURGED DOWN THE corridor with the others. She felt so much safer and stronger in a pack. Look what they'd been able to do together, back in the cafeteria! They'd just taken out a dozen armed guards. All Esta and Vincent and Siena had to do was *look* at them, and they dropped.

And then there was what she herself had done. She couldn't stop her mind from jumping back to it. She'd been so scared, and suddenly her tail had struck the guard and he'd collapsed. She was pretty sure his chest was still rising and falling. She'd almost thrown up afterward, she was so horrified. Over and over she'd told herself, *I'm still me. I'm still me.* But she couldn't deny the sense of power she'd felt. Esta and the other flyers might be able to crumple people with sound, but she could paralyze them.

So far they hadn't run into anyone else on Level 400. No alarms blared, and maybe this was going to be easier than she thought. Maybe all the guards were still down on Level 200. But that wouldn't last for long. They'd come looking. And there'd be more of them.

Seth, Seth, Seth, she thought in time to her heartbeats. They must be almost there by now. Her eyes roved over the passing doors: DEPARTMENT OF FISHERIES, DEPARTMENT OF PARKS, DEPARTMENT OF MORTGAGES. *Mortgages?* During a nuclear Armageddon?

Where was the surgical suite?

She blamed herself for all this. Maybe if she'd kept her mouth shut about Anaya and the cryptogen, maybe if she hadn't told Paul about the telepathy, none of this would be happening to Seth. She needed to fix this; she needed to save him.

A squawk came from the walkie-talkie Charles had snatched.

"Level 400, check in, please. Any sign of the hybrids? Check in, Level 400."

—*Answer it,* Petra said, shooting him a glance.

"All clear up here," Charles said gruffly into the walkie-talkie.

Did guards even say stuff like that? After a few tense seconds there was no reply, and Petra could only hope they'd bought it.

They rounded a corner and there were people. Not guards. Maybe they were off-duty White Coats, or kitchen staff or electricians or accountants—who knew? But it was weird to see them. Like real people in a real world. And on their faces was pure terror. Petra almost looked behind her to see what was so scary—but then understood: it was them.

When Esta flared her wings, all the people ran, some rushing inside rooms and locking doors.

"We're almost there," Anaya said.

Rounding yet another corner, they nearly barreled into a guard. Petra heard the now-familiar pop of compressed air. Twin Taser barbs snagged in Charles's jumpsuit. He pulled back, trying to break the connection, but too late. Voltage coursed through him, and with a loud cry he fell to the floor.

Petra rushed the guard. Her tail swung around and struck him in the arm. He shoved her away so hard she smacked the wall. But the guard didn't collapse. Had she missed? Was she already out of venom? After only one strike?

Right away Esta stepped in and slashed the Taser wires with her feathers. Then she made the guard clutch his head in pain. Petra manacled his hands behind his back and shoved him inside a room.

"We're running out of time," said Esta.

Petra watched anxiously as Anaya looked all around, like everything was suddenly unfamiliar. Were they lost? No, no, no.

Finally, Anaya said, "This way."

She and Darren helped Charles up and steadied him as he walked.

"That was terrible," he muttered. "Feel like I've been struck by lightning."

They passed a dental office, and then Anaya said, "We're here," and stopped outside a door that said SURGICAL SUITE. Through the window Petra saw a small room with shelves of medical supplies, then another set of doors with clouded glass. A blurry figure moved on the other side.

"Petra, wait!" she heard Anaya hiss, but she was already plunging into the first room. She reached the other doors and smashed them open. Six people in green scrubs whipped their heads around to look at her.

In the middle of the room, beneath a cluster of lights, was an operating table. She saw Seth's gawky body on it. He was dressed in a hospital gown and arranged so she couldn't see his face, only the back of his head. Some of his hair had been clumsily cut away.

Over him stood Ritter, with a scalpel to his throat.

"Get away from him!" she yelled.

Seth craned his neck to look around at them all.

He was awake! They hadn't done anything to him yet!

—*You okay?* she asked, but got no reply—probably because he was already talking to Esta, who was beside her now, along with Anaya and Vincent and Siena.

Ritter beheld them all balefully, his scalpel pressing even closer against Seth's neck. Petra could see the artery jumping beneath his pale skin.

"Leave this room immediately," Ritter said. "Or he dies."

—*We've got this,* Esta said.

By *we,* Petra assumed Esta meant the flyers. But that scalpel was so close to Seth's neck.

—*Wait,* she said fearfully.

Ritter's body jerked back in a terrible contraction. His hand clenched into a fist, the scalpel jutting out. He teetered back, then forward. For a horrible moment Petra thought he was going to fall onto Seth with the scalpel. Then, as though yanked by a string, Ritter rose onto his toes, slewed over to the side, and hit the floor. Curled into a ball, he made a whine of anguish.

Petra wasn't sure who was attacking Ritter: Seth or Esta, maybe both. Near the wall, someone in scrubs pushed a red button, and Petra heard an alarm start bleating outside in the hallway. Another person in scrubs made a lunge for the sharp things on the tray, but before she could grab anything, she doubled over, begging for the pain to stop. Two members of the surgical team bolted out a back door. The remaining two crumpled to the floor, hands clamped over their ears.

Petra rushed to Seth. From the tray she grabbed a pair of clippers and snipped through all his restraints. He sat up, panting. She ripped the electrodes off his chest. He tore the IV out of his hand, then grabbed scissors and starting cutting off his casts.

On the floor, Ritter twitched. Petra looked worriedly over at Esta. The girl's face was etched with fierce concentration and hatred.

"Don't kill him," Petra said.

Esta made no reply. Petra shot a glance at Anaya, who was using plastic fasteners to manacle the hands of the stunned surgical staff.

"Esta!" Anaya shouted. "Stop!"

The doctor gave one final kick and then was still. There was foam around his lips and blood dribbling from his nose.

"Is he dead?" Petra gasped.

"Let's go," said Seth, jumping off the bed.

BAREFOOT IN HIS HOSPITAL gown, Seth charged along with the others. The alarm's throbbing followed them down the corridor. The air felt good against his feathers. He was light-headed. They hadn't let him eat or drink anything in a while. When he thought of Ritter on the floor, his stomach felt sick, like he had an oil spill inside him.

Using the sound weapon was terrifying. The power and fury of it. Once you started, and had that vibration in your head, it was very hard to stop. It was difficult to tell if he *had* stopped, especially with Esta blasting Ritter at the same time. Was it he or Esta who'd delivered that final twisting blow? Maybe they'd done it together.

Murderers.

"We're here," Anaya said.

At the end of the corridor was the elevator. Seth's heart jumped. He knew the plan. That elevator would take them to the antenna farm, and then there was only a chain-link fence to get through and they'd be free.

He watched Anaya yank a ring of keys from her pocket and hurriedly thumb through them. She frowned.

"What's wrong?" he asked.

"Not sure which one it is . . ."

She tried to fit a small key into the elevator lock. It wouldn't go. Anxiously, he looked back down the corridor, over the heads of all the waiting hybrids. No guards yet. But it couldn't be much longer, not with that alarm going.

"It's not here," Anaya said.

"What're we waiting for?" called out a swimmer named Letitia.

Anaya looked stricken. "It was silver with a round head. I thought all the guards would have one, but maybe only some of them do." She swallowed. "Or just *one* of them."

"Let me try," said Darren, snatching the keys and jamming them one after another against the lock.

"Which guard had it last time?" Seth asked.

"Both times it was a guy with buggy eyes."

"Was he in the cafeteria just now?" Petra asked.

She shook her head. "I don't think so. There were so many of them!"

"There can't be just one freaking key!" Darren said furiously. "Someone else must have one!"

"We could go back and check the other guards," Anaya said.

"No way," said Petra.

"No time," Seth agreed. The idea of going backward was terrible, especially when the guards would soon be surging forward. "You said you passed a room with vents. Where they were cutting back the vines."

Anaya pointed two doors down the corridor. "There."

"Come on, might be a way out," he said, weaving through the kids clustered around the elevator.

"Hang on, what kind of vents?" Charles asked, catching up.

"I don't know," said Anaya. "Big enough for someone to stand up in."

"That might be an escape shaft!" said Charles excitedly. "A lot of bunkers had one."

Seth looked at him sharply. "How d'you know?"

"School project," Anaya said.

Seth reached the door and tried the handle. Locked.

"What's going on?" asked Adam, the talkative new kid. "I thought we were taking the elevator!"

Seth turned to look at all the frightened faces. "There's another way out." To Anaya he said, "You have the key?"

"Don't need one," she said, and with a single kick blasted the door open, splinters flying.

He rushed inside. Set into the back wall was a red steel door. He hauled it open and ducked inside, flicking on a light switch.

It was like a giant fireplace. The floor was a metal grate over a dark pit. A current of gritty air lifted from the darkness below, and his nostrils flinched with a familiar smell—a terrible, cloying perfume. Vines.

Directly overhead was a large circular hatch.

"That's definitely the escape shaft," Charles said, leaning in. "Fifteen tons of gravel up there. To block the radiation. You need to pull that lever. See?" He pointed to the discolored metal sign that said PULL LEVER TO CLEAR HATCH. "It all pours down through the grate and then we can climb up."

"It'll make a ton of noise," Anaya said, peering in.

"There's vines, too," Seth said.

"Just pull the freaking lever!" he heard Petra shout. "Let's get out of here!"

"Move back." Seth seized the lever. It wouldn't budge. It hadn't been moved in fifty years, if ever. "I need a hand."

It was Darren who ducked in. Seth choked back his dislike. Together they pulled down on the lever with their combined weight. It shifted, then jerked down all the way.

Jumping aside, Seth felt his ears pop as a deafening torrent of gravel poured past, through the metal grate into the pit. Dust billowed up like a desert storm, blinding and choking him. He staggered back into the room with Darren, covering his face.

When the roar of the gravel stopped, everyone was still coughing. The room was thick with dust but slowly clearing. Seth saw three guards in the doorway. They held not Tasers but real guns.

"I want everyone to lie down on the floor!" shouted a guard with buggy eyes. "Right now!"

—*That's him,* Anaya said in his head. *He's got the key!*

Seth saw the ring of keys dangling from his belt.

"Do not try to attack us," the guard said. "We will shoot instantly."

—*What do we do?*

That was Siena asking. Some of the kids were already obediently lying down on the floor. Seth didn't blame them.

Another guard pulled four black hoods from a pocket and flung them into the room. "Flyers, you will pull these over your heads. Now."

—*Those block us,* Seth said. *No telepathy. No sound weapon.*

—*We can take them,* Esta said.

—*What if they shoot first?* asked Vincent.

Seth worried about the same thing. They were all crammed into a small room. All the guards had to do was squeeze a trigger and they'd hit someone.

"All right!" he told the guard. "We're putting them on."

Slowly he bent down to pick up the hood at his feet. This could all go terribly wrong.

—*Seth, what're you doing?* Anaya said.

—*Pick up your hoods,* he told the others. *Esta, you and I are going to take the guard with the buggy eyes. Siena, you take the one on the left. Vincent, guy on the right.*

There was no way he was having a hood over his face again. He picked it up.

Behind him came a wet rasping sound. When he turned, something was oozing out of the escape shaft. Glistening yellow and black, it kept coming, foot after foot, like some disgusting toothpaste squeezed from a tube. Finally it flumped onto the grate with an echoing clang.

"What the hell's that?" cried the buggy-eyed guard.

The thing lifted itself so it filled most of the hatchway and looked out into the room. If it was even looking. It didn't seem to have eyes, or anything resembling a head—until its mouth opened wide.

When Seth saw the spiraling sets of teeth, he knew instantly this had to be the same wormy thing he'd seen in Dr. Weber's lab. This one was a grown-up. It began to hump into the room. One of the kids threw a chair and hit it in the mouth. The worm didn't even flinch, just ate the chair, plastic, metal, and all, inhaling it with its spiral of teeth.

Seth jerked at the sound of gunshots and saw the guards' bullets slug into the worm's corrugated flesh. No effect. Kids were screaming and scrambling out of the way as the worm moved through the room. All the guards' guns were aimed at it.

—*Now,* Seth said.

Guards clutched their heads; guns clattered to the floor. The buggy-eyed guard jerked backward so violently he fell, gun firing into the ceiling a few times before his shaking hands lost their grip.

With surprising speed, the worm surged toward him and swallowed him up to the thighs.

"The keys!" Anaya shouted aloud.

Before Seth could stop her, she raced to the guard, grabbed him under the armpits, and tried to haul him free.

There was a thump, and from the escape shaft a second worm bulged out and into the room.

"We need to go!" Darren was shouting.

Seth ran over to help Anaya. But they might as well have tried to save the guard from a black hole. The keys on his belt jingled violently as he thrashed. Soon the worm's teeth would gobble them up. Anaya darted out her hand and snapped the ring off the belt. The worm's serrated teeth cut a deep gash in her skin.

"Anaya!" Seth cried out as she yanked her hand clear.

He saw the worm falter and give a small shiver, as if it had tasted something disgusting. But only for a second. Seth didn't think it was possible for the thing's jaws to get any wider, but they did. Its body surged forward, devouring the guard up to his neck.

"Elevator!" Anaya shouted to everyone. "I've got the key!"

Everyone poured out of the room and back to the elevator doors. Anaya plunged the small key into the lock, turned it. A clank, and a metallic whirring.

Waiting for the elevator doors, Seth thought he'd lose his mind. His gaze bounced between the doors and the corridor, which was still clear—

Until there was a man. Gun in hand, he'd stepped into the T-junction at the far end of the corridor. He stared straight at them. Seth felt all the kids press closer against the elevator doors.

—*It's Paul!* Anaya cried out.

Seth could hear other voices, still out of sight around the corner, calling questions to Paul: "Are they there? Do you see them?"

—*I'll drop him!* Esta said.

—*Wait!* Petra said. *He said he'd help us!*

Paul didn't lift his gun and take aim. He only turned his head to the unseen guards and said, "Nothing down here! They must've gone to Wing L!"

And then he disappeared in the direction of the voices.

The elevator doors opened and kids started pouring inside. Seth exhaled in relief and followed them.

ANAYA JABBED THE G button, and a dim light flickered behind it. The elevator was crammed. She didn't know how many people it was supposed to hold, but she hoped they weren't too heavy.

"Why aren't the doors closing?" Petra demanded, stabbing at the button.

Down the corridor, a worm lurched out from the escape-hatch room. It was grotesquely swollen. Its blunt head turned away from the elevator, then toward it. With a slippery surge, it came at them.

"Close the doors!" screamed Paolo, the bespectacled runner.

In slow motion the doors began to shut. Crushed against the back of the elevator by a mass of bodies, Anaya watched as the worm humped closer. Anaya saw teeth, so many teeth. Finally the doors clanged shut. The elevator shuddered as the worm slammed against it.

"Why aren't we moving?" Petra wailed.

The sound of a hundred knives being sharpened filled the elevator.

"It's eating its way through!" Charles yelled.

"Go already!" Anaya roared at the elevator.

With a lethargic rumble, it began to rise.

"Thank God," breathed Petra.

"We're going up," Anaya said, like she needed to say it to make it real.

She looked around at all the tense faces. Adam and Jen were talking with some of the other runners. Letitia was crying, in relief or terror, Anaya wasn't sure. There was Charles, scratching nervously at his hairy face. Darren, checking his tail. Esta, using her sharp feathers to help cut off Siena's and Vincent's casts. Petra, staring at the control panel, like she could make the elevator go faster. Her eyes settled on Seth, tearing a strip of fabric off his hospital gown.

"Here," he said, passing it to Anaya. "For your hand."

"Thanks." She wrapped it tight around the bleeding wound and knotted it. "What were they going to do to you?" she asked quietly.

In the dim light, Seth's face looked hollowed out, his eyes haunted.

"Operate on my brain. Take out the transmitter."

Anaya was mute with horror. She heard Darren mutter, "Holy crap."

Seth said, "Ritter thought it might stop us changing. Make us normal again."

"Really?" Petra asked intently.

Esta cut her a scathing look. "Oh, you want to go back, Petra? See what your buddies can do for you?"

"Esta," Anaya said, trying to head off another fight. She was a little bit afraid of the other girl now—a bit afraid of all the flyers, to be honest, after what she'd seen in the cafeteria. She hadn't been able to stop the guilty questions from surging into her head: *What if they* are *dangerous, just like their cryptogen parallels? What if they* like *destroying?*

Petra glared back at Esta. "They're not my buddies. Anyway, I was right to trust Paul. He *saw* us and didn't come after us!"

"It's true," Anaya said. "He got rid of the guards."

"He's probably the reason the alarm didn't go sooner," Petra said. "He's helping us escape."

"We haven't escaped yet," Esta said.

"We can handle whatever they throw at us," Darren added, then looked at Petra. "I saw you sting someone."

So had Anaya. She looked down through the forest of legs and saw Petra's tail give a nervous twitch. That tail was the bane of her friend's existence, and now it turned out to carry a toxic sting.

"I got someone, too," Darren said proudly. "Bet you're pretty glad you have that tail now, right?"

"It doesn't kill them, does it?" Petra asked worriedly.

"My guy was still breathing. Only paralyzed, I think. I don't know how long it lasts."

"It didn't work the second time I tried," said Petra.

"Maybe it takes time for your body to make more venom," said Anaya.

Looking queasy, Petra nodded. "Awesome."

The elevator jerked to a standstill, but the doors didn't open.

"We there already?" Petra asked.

Anaya shook her head. "No. Something's wrong."

Anaya gulped as the elevator dropped a little. From deep below came the anguished sounds of metal twisting.

"Is the worm eating stuff?" she asked. She'd been trying not to think about what it might be doing.

The elevator shuddered.

"If it eats through the cable, we fall," Charles said.

That was all Anaya needed to hear. "Let's get out." She pointed at the maintenance hatch in the ceiling.

"And then what?" Petra demanded.

"There'll be a ladder or something in the shaft."

Someone shrieked as the light suddenly went out. Anaya got jostled by frightened, shouting kids. Breathless, she had a terrible memory of being trapped inside a pit plant. She could almost feel the walls closing in on her.

She staggered off balance as the elevator rattled side to side, like it was being shaken by its cable.

"It's gonna eat us!" someone wailed.

Anaya jumped straight up and punched open the ceiling panel. Mercifully, a pale light filled the elevator from an emergency lamp in the shaft. She jumped again and this time grabbed hold of the sides and hauled herself out. The top bristled with wheels and pulleys guiding cables. With huge relief, she spotted skinny rungs on one side of the shaft, leading up. Far overhead was a line of faint light. The doors. It wasn't so far, not really.

She ducked back inside the elevator and reached down a hand. "There's a ladder. Come on."

The elevator shook and dipped again, and a few kids hollered.

One by one she helped pull them through the hatch. The runners didn't need her help and made the jump on their own. She sent Seth and Charles up the ladder first. Between the two of them—claws and feathers—she figured they could get the shaft doors open from the inside.

"Fast," she told them as the elevator shuddered. Metallic croaks and shrieks rose up from the shaft. Everyone needed to be off before the cable snapped.

"Hurry up!" she heard kids yelling at the climbers above them.

She helped out a swimmer called Ravi and sent him on up the ladder. It was just her now. From below came a crack and the elevator dropped—and kept dropping. Cable shrieked through the pulleys. Anaya's instinct was to lie flat and hold on for dear life, but she forced herself to jump at the rungs flashing past. Her timing was lousy.

A rung struck her under the chin; another knocked her in the stomach, winding her. Gasping, she flailed about, missing another rung as she plummeted. Her hands clawed hold of a rung, and she held tight, shaking all over, as the elevator crashed at the bottom of the shaft with an echoing boom.

CHAPTER THIRTEEN

BURSTING THROUGH THE DOORS, Seth was dazed by the vast twilight sky, the warm, pine-scented breeze. It was suddenly summer. Metal masts and satellite dishes towered around him. Behind him, the other kids poured out into the antenna farm.

Hungrily, he filled his lungs. His legs trembled from the long climb up the shaft. He felt hollow and tired to his core. But he remembered their plan and hurried to the fence. With his feathers he began cutting a vertical gash. After making slashes across the top and bottom, he peeled the chain link back like a door.

"Go!" he shouted, holding it open.

Charles was the first to duck through, followed by a stream of others.

"Where now?" Charles asked from the other side of the fence.

Seth had no answer for him. Had they ever really imagined they'd make it so far?

Anaya, he knew, wanted to find her parents and Dr. Weber; Esta had said they should hide out and avoid all cities and grown-ups, because there was nobody they could trust. He felt torn between their two positions.

Beyond the fence the ground was strewn with dead stalks of black grass. And in the surrounding forest he saw cracked yellow vines among the branches. The whole area must have been sprayed with herbicide. He remembered what the new kids had said about Spray Zones. The bunker was definitely in one of them, though it hadn't stopped black vines and pit plants from invading. Or the worms.

The antenna farm was at the top of a hill, and the land sloped down to a parking lot and a helipad and what must be the main entrance to the bunker itself: a corrugated metal shed built into the side of the hill.

—*We need to get away from here,* Esta said at his side.

—*I know.*

There were still lots of kids waiting to go through the fence. And he didn't want to do anything before he talked to Petra and Anaya. Darren went through the gap, and Seth looked around anxiously. There was Petra, but where was Anaya? With relief, he saw her emerge, panting, from the elevator room. Last one out.

When finally everyone was outside the fence, Seth said, "We need a plan."

"No kidding," snapped Paolo.

"There's cars in the parking lot," Adam said.

"You know how to steal a car?" asked a swimmer called Seema.

"The roads aren't safe anyway!" Letitia said.

Everyone was talking at once now.

"Where even are we?"

"We need a map."

"We need a *phone*."

"We should call the cops on these guys."

"Are you crazy? The cops are all in on it!"

"I want to call my parents," said Siena.

There was a small pause, as if everyone had the exact same yearning thought.

Seth locked eyes with Esta.

—*We have no parents to call,* she said. *It's just us.*

He knew there was no plan that would make everyone happy. The kids' nervous energy crackled from them like electricity. They wanted to *go*. Any second, they were going to split apart like unstable atoms.

A helicopter tore out of the darkening sky and skidded through the air overhead. Blinding beams of light stabbed down at them. Squinting, Seth glimpsed two soldiers crouched in the hatchway, rifles raised. They'd open fire any second. The helicopter turned and hovered low overhead, deafening him.

Through the swirling grit and plant debris, Seth could barely see. A few kids jostled him as they bolted for cover. Where was Esta? Where were Anaya and Petra? Someone grabbed him by the hand, pulling hard.

—Come on!

Together, he and Esta pelted for the woods.

PETRA COWERED AS THE helicopter made a slow, thunderous turn overhead. Caught in a tornado of dust and panic, she shielded her eyes and glimpsed masked soldiers perched in the helicopter's hatchway.

And suddenly, leaning out past them: a woman.

Like the soldiers, she wore a pollen mask across her mouth and nose, and she was so unexpected, so out of place, that it took Petra's brain a few seconds to accept that it truly was Dr. Stephanie Weber.

Dr. Weber pulled off her mask and was shouting something that Petra couldn't hear and pointing at the helipad, where a second helicopter was already landing.

—Anaya! Petra shouted silently. *Anaya! Did you see her?*

—Yes!

Anaya stumbled out of the swirling dust, and Petra gripped her tight in jubilation. It seemed impossible as a dream. How had Dr. Weber found them? And now she was here with two helicopters to rescue them.

—We need to tell everyone! Anaya was saying. *Tell them it's safe!*

It was darker now, and the blinding lights lancing from the

helicopter only made it harder to see. Confusing shadows bounded across the hillside. Petra looked all around at the mayhem of panicking kids.

She shouted at them out loud and then silently:

—*Go to the helicopters! They're here to rescue us! Pass it on!*

Darren nodded at her, but she wasn't sure how many other kids got her message. Maybe their heads were too filled with their own noise and fear. Even if they did hear her, would they believe her? Why on earth would they think military helicopters would help them?

Where was Seth?

With growing panic, she scanned the hillside. He should be easy to spot, the only kid in a hospital gown. When she tried to find him telepathically in her head, she saw no flicker of his light. Was he already too far away? Or was he busy talking to someone else, probably Esta?

The helicopter carrying Dr. Weber drifted off toward the helipad now, and the soldiers were waving at them to follow.

—*I can't see Seth!* she said to Anaya.

—*Me either. Maybe he's already down there.*

A small group had reached the parking lot, and the kids were watching the helicopters from behind parked cars. It was dark and they were far away, so Petra couldn't tell if any of them was wearing a hospital gown.

From the main entrance of the bunker, a lone man came running. He wasn't in uniform, but he gripped a rifle. His mouth and nose were covered by a pollen mask. He turned up the hill-side and headed straight for her and Anaya.

Petra froze. How she wished she had the power to stun people with sound. Her tail gave a restless swish and she hoped she had more venom now.

"It's Paul!" Anaya cried.

In the beam from the passing helicopter, Petra recognized him.

"Get on those helicopters!" Paul shouted.

"We can't find Seth!" she yelled back.

"I'll find him. Go! Ritter's guards are coming!"

Paul continued up the hill, shouting to the other hybrid kids and pointing at the helicopters.

"You can trust him!" Petra shouted at them.

She glanced at Anaya, feeling sick, not wanting to leave until they knew where Seth was. The second helicopter had landed now, its rotor blades still turning. Some kids were nervously drawing closer.

"Petra, we need to go!" Anaya said, tugging her by the hand.

"But Seth—"

She ran anyway. With rescue so close at hand, she couldn't stop herself. She felt like she was running toward a dream mirage that might evaporate any second. Anaya could have streaked on ahead, and Petra felt a swell of gratitude that her friend stayed by her side. She dragged air into her lungs. Her feet hit the asphalt of the parking lot. She looked over at the bunker entrance, terri-fied she'd see guards pouring out.

From the second helicopter a couple of soldiers hopped down with Dr. Weber. Petra was too breathless to call out her name, but Dr. Weber hurried toward her and opened her arms. Petra and Anaya were instantly wrapped up in them. Petra buried her face in Dr. Weber's neck. She wasn't sure she'd ever held anyone tighter.

"You're all right, both of you?" Dr. Weber asked urgently. "You're all right?"

Petra nodded and gulped out a yes.

"Where's Seth?" Dr. Weber asked, drawing back so she could see their faces.

Petra saw the fear growing in the doctor's eyes as she waited for their reply.

"He's not down here?" Petra said, her stomach suddenly heavy as a stone.

"No. Did he get out of the building?"

"Yes. We were all together on the hill—"

"Was he hurt?" Dr. Weber demanded.

Petra wasn't sure if her tone was accusing, or if it was simply her own guilt.

"No, it's—it got crazy once the helicopters came," Petra said. "Everyone panicked and ran."

"I told them not to come in so low," Dr. Weber said angrily. "This is our fault."

Petra looked back up the hill. More kids in jumpsuits were running toward the helipad now, but none of them were Seth.

"We need to find all of them," Dr. Weber told the two soldiers. "Go."

"We'll look, too!" Petra said.

"No. You two stay here," said a voice behind her, familiar even though it was muffled behind a pollen mask.

Petra turned to see the gaunt face of the man who'd torn her away from her parents, interrogated her, and handed her over to Ritter. Colonel Pearson strode over from the other helicopter with four soldiers. In alarm, Petra whirled to Dr. Weber.

"It's all right," Dr. Weber assured her.

"How can it be all right?" she demanded. "He's the one who sent us here!"

"I'll explain later. Trust me, please."

Petra saw the colonel take in her tail, the black-and-gold patterning darkening her arms. Then his eyes went to Anaya. Petra wondered if he even recognized her, now that her face was matted with fine hairs. As usual, Pearson's expression revealed little.

"Get on board," he said. "We don't have much time."

Two of his soldiers took up positions around the helicopters, and the other two hurried up the hill, trying to corral more kids.

Reluctantly Petra climbed into the helicopter with Anaya. Up front the two pilots hunched tensely over their glimmering instruments, ready for a quick takeoff. Petra stayed next to the hatch so she could see what was happening outside.

Dr. Weber was talking quietly to Pearson, but the whole time she watched the hill anxiously. With a tightening of her heart, Petra remembered how Dr. Weber had asked Seth if she could be his foster mother. The very day everything fell apart.

Silently she called for Seth, but nothing came back.

"Have you tried to reach him?" she asked Anaya.

She nodded. "Nothing."

Some more kids, breathless and sweaty, piled aboard.

"Have you seen Seth?" Petra asked them.

"I think I saw him go into the woods," said a tall swimmer named Kawhi.

"You sure?"

"Pretty sure, yeah."

"How about Esta or Charles?" Anaya asked.

"Esta was with him, yeah."

Petra's chest tightened. For the first time she wondered if Seth was doing this on purpose. Hiding away, not answering. Him and Esta against the world.

She leaned out the hatchway and called to Dr. Weber. "Seth might be in the woods. A bunch of kids went to hide there."

She saw a soldier speak into a shoulder mic, relaying the information.

Petra sat back and asked Anaya, "You think all the flyers are sticking together or something?"

More kids climbed inside the helicopter, looking unsure about the whole thing.

"Is this safe?" Paolo whispered, light flickering off his glasses.

"Yes," Petra said.

"But these guys are soldiers, too!"

"They're not working for Ritter," Anaya said, and Petra hoped she was right. She felt her tail tapping restlessly against the back of the seat and stopped it.

Outside, a group of kids were being corralled down the hill by Pearson's soldiers. They were still too far away for her to tell if Seth was among them.

"These are the last," she heard Pearson tell Weber. "Once they're aboard, we go."

—*Seth, are you there?* she called out desperately.

From the bunker's main entrance, guards poured out, then stopped dead in their tracks. They seemed genuinely startled to see the two military helicopters.

Nervously, Petra looked toward the hill. The kids and soldiers were almost at the bottom but still had to cross the parking lot to reach the helipad. There was a shout from the bunker guards, and an abrupt stutter of light and gunfire. Petra heard something ping off the helicopter's fuselage.

A soldier leaned in and told them to buckle up, then slammed the hatch shut.

Petra pressed her face to the small window. The last of the kids were running, crouched over, around cars, as their soldier escort returned fire. None of the kids were Seth.

Her eyes flashed back up the hillside, still hoping to see his shape hurtling toward them.

The hatch was yanked open and she almost toppled out onto Pearson.

"Buckle up!" he roared at her.

Dr. Weber climbed into the cabin, and two soldiers jumped in after her.

"Take it up!" Pearson hollered at the pilots.

"We don't have Seth!" Petra wailed.

The rotor blades whined as they accelerated.

"We're out of time!" Pearson shouted, then slammed the hatch and ran for the other helicopter.

"No!" Petra cried. The rotor's beat became a single urgent note.

Dr. Weber looked at her, mute with misery. Her own cheeks were wet.

"Bugs!" one of the soldiers shouted. "Ten o'clock."

Petra caught a glimpse of yellow-and-black worms breaking through the asphalt like it was tissue paper. The gunfire faltered, then redoubled. These worms looked much bigger than the ones she'd seen inside the bunker. As if drawn by the vibrations— or the smell of metal—two humped across the parking lot toward the helicopters, eating through any car in their path.

"Take it up!" the soldier hollered at the pilots.

"We're heavy," one of the pilots barked. "Didn't know there'd be this many!"

Petra saw a worm open its turbine mouth. She knew it could chomp through them like a pretzel.

"Up-up-up!" yelled the soldiers.

Sluggishly the helicopter lifted. The worm actually reared up on its tail and lunged. Its jaws narrowly missed the landing gear. Petra breathed again. Below her, the worm fell away, the parking lot, the bunker, the woods.

And somewhere down there, Seth.

SETH STEPPED OUT FROM the trees, waving his arms wildly.

"Wait! Wait! I'm here!"

Both helicopters thundered past and kept going. Esta grabbed his arm and dragged him back into the cover of the forest.

—*Quiet!* she told him.

He couldn't find words, his mind was so fogged with grief.

He should've made a run for the helipad sooner. Why hadn't he? When the helicopters first appeared, he'd thought they were reinforcements for Ritter. He'd seen soldiers with guns hopping out! They'd corralled kids and marched them down the hill toward the copters—and *Pearson*.

But then he'd seen Dr. Weber.

Since coming to the bunker, he'd built so many hard thoughts about her, welded together from steel. How she'd given in to Pearson, helped him even. How she'd let Ritter take them away. How she was just using them all along. How she'd told him she wanted to be his foster mother so she could keep studying him like a lab rat. How she was no different from Ritter.

But seeing her now was like an earthquake, shaking the foundations of all these thoughts. He didn't know why she was with Pearson. He didn't know what it meant. But she was here. She'd come.

—*She came to rescue us!* he blurted out to Esta.

—*How d'you know? All we saw was a bunch of soldiers rounding up kids! She's working for the military, Seth!*

—*Paul must've called her! She came for us! She came for* me!

Esta squeezed his hand and said:

—*Then why'd she leave you behind?*

It felt like a punch to the stomach.

—*There was gunfire! And the worms! They had to take off!*

He was trying to convince himself, too.

—*They left all the flyers behind, Seth.*

He looked at the small group of kids around them, crouched tensely among the trees. Charles. Darren, unfortunately. And Vincent and Siena.

Was Esta right? Did the flyers get left behind on purpose? Maybe not even Dr. Weber wanted them anymore. Too dangerous.

A small keening voice welled up inside him. *How could you do that to me? After what you said to me? About being my foster mom.*

What an idiot he was. Whenever he hoped for something, it only made it worse. With his own mother. With Mr. and Mrs. Antos back on Salt Spring. With Dr. Weber.

She'd rescued some of the kids but not him. Maybe she'd even seen him and still gone ahead and left. His sadness burned off under the hot glare of his swelling anger.

—*We have to go,* Esta told him gently.

She was right. Of course she was right. Of all the people in the world, she was really the only one he could trust.

He glanced back at the bunker entrance. Floodlights now illuminated the parking lot and helipad, where two worms humped toward a power pylon and started tearing into the lower struts. Gunfire pocked the night as the guards blasted away at a couple of worms burrowing back into the earth. Flashlight beams started skittering around the hillside. They'd come looking.

"This way," Seth said, and led them deeper into the trees. His bare feet crackled against dead vines, but he kept his eyes wide in the dying light. He didn't know how much of the forest had been sprayed. He remembered the vines from the eco-reserve, snaring your feet, pulling you toward pit plants or hauling you into the air by your neck to let you hang.

"Where we going?" hissed Darren behind him.

Seth wasn't thrilled to have Darren in tow. He'd finked on them, told Ritter about the sound weapon.

"Far away as possible," Seth said.

"We'll make better time on the road." Darren pointed through the trees.

"Not safe," said Seth. "There's pit plants."

"Not if it's in a Spray Zone."

"Then there'll be traffic," said Charles. "And we look like we just escaped from prison."

Esta took a few steps closer to the road. "Train tracks."

Seth saw the crossing up ahead, the rails dull silver in the twilight. He followed Esta out from the trees and walked carefully alongside the road to the crossing. In both directions, the rail corridor passed through forest. Seth noticed that on either side of the tracks, the black grass was dead and cracked. Same with the yellow vines in the trees.

"They're spraying it," said Charles. "Must be important tracks."

It made an irresistible road. "Come on," said Seth.

He ran to the rails. No snarling vines. No pit plants. Who knew which way they were headed? But that didn't matter now. They needed to put as much distance between themselves and the bunker as possible.

They ran along the tracks. When he first heard the blare of a whistle, he thought it was some kind of alarm from the bunker. But it seemed too close, and then he felt the vibration through his feet.

"Off the tracks!" he shouted.

The train still hadn't come into view, but he didn't want the engineer seeing a bunch of panicked kids in jumpsuits. They'd be reported, fast. He took cover with everyone in the trees and waited as the locomotive trundled past.

It was a long freight, a motley collection of tankers and box-cars.

—*Let's get on,* Esta said.

He'd only ever seen this done in movies.

—*We're getting on,* he heard her tell everyone. *This is our express ticket out of here!*

They broke from the trees at a sprint. Charles was the fast-est, with his powerful legs, but Seth and the others managed to match the speed of the train. It felt so good to move, and he couldn't help laughing at the sheer relief of it—the same kind of ecstatic movement from his dreams. Looking back over his shoulder, he saw an open boxcar coming up.

—*That one!*

Seth pulled as close to the tracks as possible, feeling the train's noisy machine heat. Charles beat him aboard, vaulting in like he'd used a springboard. When Seth made his own jump, Charles's hands were ready to pull him inside. Together they helped bring the others aboard.

Catching his breath, he looked at everyone, counting them. Six. That wasn't bad. He wished Anaya and Petra were with him. His wish turned hard. They'd left him behind, too.

But he had Esta. And Siena, and Vincent. *All the strongest ones.* The unbidden thought startled him. Did he truly think of himself as stronger than Petra or Anaya? It was pointless to lie to himself. The sharpness of their wings, the weapons in their heads. Esta was right—they were by far the most powerful cryptogens.

He slumped against the juddering boxcar wall. He felt like he'd been running forever.

"So," said Vincent, "what's the plan?"

Seth shrugged, too exhausted to think.

"Which way are we even going?" Darren asked.

Seth leaned his head out the open door. The tracks ran straight. Dead ahead, the orange rim of the sun was about to disappear over the horizon.

He ducked back in, slamming the door closed.

"West," he said. "We're going west."

CHAPTER FOURTEEN

"WHERE ARE WE GOING?" Anaya asked above the thump of the rotor blades.

In the cramped cabin, Dr. Weber passed around blankets and bottles of water. Every hard, uncomfortable seat was taken, and a few kids sat on the metal floor, scrunched up small, arms wrapped around their knees. Even so, plenty of them had already fallen asleep. Anaya was startled by how young they suddenly looked—these same kids who'd fought guards, climbed an elevator shaft, seen monsters.

Slumped beside her, Petra had cried herself to sleep after unsuccessfully begging the soldiers and pilots to turn around and find Seth.

"We're going back to Deadman's Island," Dr. Weber said.

Anaya nodded. She'd thought as much, though she still didn't understand what had happened to change Pearson's mind. And she was too weary to ask right now.

"Thank you," she said instead. "For coming to get us."

Dr. Weber came closer and put her warm hands over Anaya's cold ones.

"I tried to come sooner. I've been worried sick about you poor kids."

It had been a while since Anaya had heard such kind words, and she was afraid they'd start her crying. She was ashamed at how relieved she felt, because there was so much that wasn't right. Seth and the others, missing. The entire world, falling apart.

"My parents?"

"Fine. They're waiting for you at the base."

This time she did start crying—it seemed too impossibly good to be true.

"After Ritter took you three away, Pearson put me in lockup, same as your parents. He only let me out when the eggs started hatching worldwide and he wanted me to get working on vaccines. Every single day I tried to convince Pearson to get you kids released. But he wouldn't shift. Not until he got the call from Paul Samson at the bunker."

Anaya snuck a guilty glance at Petra. She'd been right all along about trusting Paul, but Anaya hadn't believed her. No one had. Mostly they'd just been furious with her for sharing information with him and Ritter.

Dr. Weber gave her hand a squeeze. "Paul told Colonel Pearson about the experiments Ritter was planning. I'm so, so sorry for everything that's happened."

Anaya nodded. "There's a lot to tell."

"It can wait," Dr. Weber said. "Sleep."

Which was what she wanted, more than anything. To forget for a little while and feel safe. Somehow, folded against Petra's body, she found a comfortable position. Before long came that delicious drifty feeling that heralded sleep. The rhythmic noise of the helicopter became a cocoon that she was warm inside.

And in that half sleep there was suddenly someone with her: an amber light, the familiar deep, earthy smell of soil. This time, it was Anaya who spoke first.

—*What's your name?*

Of all the questions she might have asked, this was not the most crucial. But it was the first to occur to her, and she truly wanted to know who she was talking to.

—*Name?*

The word echoed back, carrying an aura of confusion. And was it even a *word* she heard? No, it was just how Anaya translated the *idea* that was being sent to her. It hit home now: she and the cryptogen had no shared language. Their brains were simply translating their ideas as best they could. She tried again.

—*My name is Anaya.*

But this time she tried to send not just words—which seemed so clunky—but a mental picture of herself, the *essence* of herself, how she *felt* inside her body right now. The ache in her legs, the quick beat of her heart, the excitement and fear coursing through every vein. *This is me,* she tried to say.

She got not words in return, but a renewed sense of that earthy smell, so pungent it almost had a taste, enveloped in amber light. Was this the cryptogen's version of a name?

In the same instant, Anaya saw, in her mind, a pair of large, dark eyes. They had no whites to them, only a beautiful, rich amber with irises of streaked gold. The pupils weren't circles, but horizontal rectangles. Long black lashes fringed the eyelids. The surrounding skin was furred.

—*Where are you?* Anaya asked.

—*Vessel.*

Anaya understood she meant the vast gray-petaled spacecraft. So the cryptogen was still aboard. And suddenly Anaya was being shown *inside* the ship, inside a seemingly endless chamber. Row after row of dark sacs floated weightless. Not all were the same shape. Some were long and thin, others round. They looked eerily similar to pit plants, but their exterior wasn't quite as fleshy. Instinctively she knew that inside each one slumbered a living creature. Like a baby in a womb.

—*Soldiers,* the cryptogen told her.

Anaya remembered all those runners and swimmers being marched onto the ship by the flyers. They'd spent their entire voyage asleep inside these sacs, somehow being kept alive and nourished.

—*When will they wake?* Anaya asked.

—*Soon.*

—*But* you *are awake now?*

Surely not everyone could be asleep on that enormous ship. Even if it was automated, there had to be cryptogens managing those rains of seeds and eggs, and protecting the ship from the nuclear missile. Deciding when to invade Earth.

—*I am awake,* came the reply. *Preparing.*

Words seemed to be passing between them a bit more easily now, like they were slowly learning each other's language.

—*What are you preparing?* she asked.

—*The Resistance.*

In her half sleep, Anaya felt her heart begin to pump harder. It was what she'd suspected back in the bunker. The runners and swimmers had been conquered and were being forced to fight.

—*The flyers. You want to fight the flyers.*

—*Yes. There is not much time. Help.*

She realized she was being asked a question.

—*Yes. Yes! I'll help! Tell me how!*

She was trembling all over and realized there was a hand shaking her shoulder.

"Seat belt on," a soldier said as she opened her eyes. Beyond the windows was the pale light of dawn. "We're coming in to land on Deadman's Island."

AS THE TRAIN ROCKED and tilted through the night, Seth flew for the first time in almost two weeks.

In his dream, he looked for Petra and Anaya. When he couldn't see them, he felt a deep stab of longing. But then he was soaring higher, and beside him were Vincent and Siena. And Esta. Her eyes met his, and he felt an instant connection. Somewhere in his conscious mind, he realized she was seeing him, too.

"We're special," she told him.

He grinned, giddy with the sheer delight of flying and being close to her. Over the years he'd had so many dreams where he was flying toward something and someone, never knowing what or who it was. Maybe all along he'd been waiting for Esta.

When he woke, he was looking right into her eyes, like a continuation of his dream. He hadn't realized they'd fallen asleep with their shoulders practically touching. The train must have jostled them closer together. He wondered how long she'd been awake, watching him. He liked the idea of her watching him.

"We got out," she whispered, smiling. "We did it!"

He smiled back. Maybe it was the morning light filtering through the seams of the boxcar, but things felt different. He felt exultant.

"It was crazy," he said. "I can't believe we made it!"

They talked silently about the escape, because the others were still asleep and he didn't want to wake them. Also, he felt even closer to her when they used telepathy. He wanted it to stay like this, him and Esta, alone and safe in the sunlight, for a little longer. Maybe forever. Forever seemed like a pretty good idea.

—*You rescued me,* he told her.

—*Well, you* were *on the way.* Her grin faded, and she touched his hand. *I would never have left without you.*

Unlike Dr. Weber, he thought. Or Anaya and Petra. He chewed at his lower lip. Was he being fair? The other two had helped save him, too.

—*Do you think we killed him?* he asked her. *Ritter?*

—*I don't know. Do you care?*

He thought about it a moment and nodded.

—*He wouldn't have thought twice about killing us,* she said.

—*I know.*

It was too uncomfortable to dwell on, and he was almost grateful when he heard Charles stir. Vincent groaned as he uncurled and pushed himself upright.

Darren sat and beat a drumroll on the floor. "It is *good* to wake up a free man!"

"Good to wake up alive," muttered Siena. "That place was insane."

"I am starving!" said Darren, who seemed intent on speaking in exclamation points. "You think there's any food in these?"

He walked over to the cardboard cartons stacked behind netting.

"The one thing I didn't mind about that place was the food," said Charles.

"Are you serious?" asked Siena, wiping sleep from her eyes.

"Breakfasts, anyway," Charles said, a bit defensively. "Breakfasts were good."

"The eggs were powdered," said Siena.

"I liked those potato things," Vincent said, yawning.

"The Tater Tots?" Siena said witheringly.

"Is that what they're called?" Vincent asked. "I never had them before."

"They're just hash browns, only ball-shaped!"

"But fluffier," said Charles. "A lot fluffier."

Seth was watching Darren rip into a couple of boxes. "Anything good in there?"

"Like something to eat or drink?" added Esta.

"Nope," said Darren. "But it's something we do need. Clothes." He glanced at Seth. "Especially you, dude. You look like you've escaped from a horror movie."

Seth examined his blood-spattered hospital gown and had to admit Darren was right. He needed to ditch it, and everyone else needed to lose their jumpsuits.

He went over with Esta and dragged aside the safety netting so they could pull down more cartons. The others joined in.

"Not super fashionable," said Siena, pulling out a pair of heavy khaki work pants.

"But oh so practical," Vincent said, holding up a jacket bulky with protective padding.

"Is that Kevlar?" Seth said, tapping it. "It's the same stuff they had us slashing apart in the bunker."

"This must be armor for cops and soldiers," Esta said.

"It's perfect," said Charles. "It'll hide us. Feathers, tail—"

"What about those claws and hairy face?" Darren said to him.

"This'll work," said Esta, tossing Charles a pair of gloves and a helmet from another open carton. It had a protective visor that flipped down. "Until you find a razor."

"We wear this stuff, we're invisible," Seth said, realizing how lucky they were. "People think we're emergency workers, no one hassles us."

Esta and Siena took their new clothes to one end of the car to change. Seth turned his back to them and, with the other guys, stripped down to his bunker-issued tank top and boxers.

"Yours are coming in, too," he said to Vincent, nodding at the quills ready to poke through the skin of his bare legs.

"Yeah, they hurt."

A few of Seth's feathers must've broken through while he slept; there were spots of dried blood around the new quills. They couldn't come fast enough for his liking.

"You still think you're gonna fly?" Darren asked.

"These'll help," Seth said.

He caught Darren sneaking a backward peek at the girls changing, then wince suddenly and grab his head.

"Okay, okay, sorry!" Darren said.

"Next time I'll make it hurt, Darren!" Esta called out.

"Geez," Darren muttered, rolling his eyes. "Lighten up."

As Darren stepped into his baggy work pants, Seth studied his tail. Esta had already told him how the swimmers had stung and paralyzed guards during the cafeteria escape.

"Don't look so freaked out," Darren said with a smirk. His tail lifted itself straight up, its barbed tip swaying snakelike. "This is a good thing. It's another weapon for us."

The tip feinted at Seth and he stumbled back.

"Sorry, dumb joke," Darren said.

Seth said nothing. He didn't like Darren being this powerful. He was relieved when the tail disappeared down a pant leg.

—*We should stun him,* Esta said inside his head, *and dump him off the train.*

Seth fastened his own pants and pulled on an armored jacket.

—*Not yet,* he replied. There were only six of them, and Darren was right. They could use another weapon. He just hoped Darren wasn't stupid enough to use it on any of them.

—*We can't trust him,* Esta said.

"Some boots here." Vincent pushed over a couple of cartons, then went to check out more near the wall.

Seth was rooting around for his size when he heard Vincent say, "Whoa."

He looked up. Vincent was backing away from a low stack of cartons, his face pale.

"What's wrong?" Seth asked.

From behind the cartons came a sloshy sound that did not belong to the train. Seth met eyes with Esta.

—*Hear that?*

—*Yes.*

Together they removed their jackets so their arms were bare. Seth flared his feathers a bit and heard their reassuring metallic rustle. Warily he moved closer to the drippy sound, kicking some cartons out of the way.

Against the boxcar wall were three translucent eggs. One was as big as an ostrich egg, the others slightly smaller. All of them were surrounded by clothes and torn plastic wrap and cardboard, like some kind of makeshift nest. Seth realized that the eggs all leaned against each other and had somehow fused. Cloudy liquid oozed from the spots where they touched and dripped into the cardboard.

"Holy crap!" said Charles, leaning in for a look along with Esta and the others.

"Are these worm eggs or the bird things?" Charles asked.

"I don't get it," Seth said. "The eggs that fell in the rain were tiny. These are something different."

"If the eggs are this big," said Esta, "how big's Mama?"

"And where is she?" Siena asked, looking around.

Cold spiraled down Seth's back as he scanned the boxcar ceiling. There was nothing to see, and nowhere to hide up there, especially for something big.

He looked back at the eggs. They seemed to be melding

into one. Through their semitranslucent shells, he saw their quick, shadowy contents pour together and swirl violently. The sides of the single new egg trembled and bulged, then were still.

"Did something just eat something else?" Charles asked weakly.

"On Deadman's Island," Seth said, "in the lab, there was one thing that hatched and ate everything else, then swelled up."

"What did it turn into?"

"I don't know. It turned itself back into an egg."

"Just get it off the friggin' train!" Siena said.

Esta slid the boxcar door open. Light crashed in, along with the wild clatter of the tracks.

"Don't kick it!" Seth yelled as Charles pulled back his leg. "It might hatch! We've got to lift it out."

"I'm not touching that thing," Vincent said.

It was the last thing Seth wanted to do either. He looked at Esta.

"Together?" she said.

"Yeah. Take a side."

He crouched and put his hands against the egg. It was soft, rubbery, like a cheap beach ball. Inside, something punched against his hand, and he gave a shout.

"Lift," Esta said.

He was afraid to squeeze too hard, in case it burst.

"It won't budge," he said.

"It's stuck," Esta said.

When Seth took a closer look, he realized the bottom of the egg was puddled in a gluey substance on the boxcar floor. Wincing in disgust, he plunged his hands into the goo and started to scoop and peel it away. There was a sticky, tearing sound as Esta pushed the egg.

"It's free!" Seth shouted as it made a schloppy roll toward the open door. Something long and pointy poked out from inside the egg, narrowly missing his face.

"Watch out!" he cried to Esta, jumping to his feet and dragging her back.

A second needle, sharp as a sea urchin's, jutted out. The egg churned like it contained three brawling chimps. It was only a few feet from the door.

"Kick it!" he yelled to Charles.

Charles booted it. The egg made a few sluggish rolls and teetered on the brink of the door.

"Again!" Seth shouted, and as one, they belted the egg and sent it sailing off the train.

He stuck his head out to see the egg bouncing alongside the tracks. There was a sudden spray of liquid, like a water balloon bursting, and for a second he couldn't see anything.

Then he beheld something pale and gawky and with many legs running after the train. It seemed to be growing—and not just because it was getting closer, but because it was actually *growing*. Or at least *unfolding* itself in some terrifying way.

"It's coming back!" Seth whipped himself inside the boxcar and grabbed the door.

"What d'you mean?" Siena croaked.

"It hatched!"

Esta threw herself against the door to help him push. It slammed shut. Seth fell back, staring at it, waiting.

"What is it?" Vincent asked.

"I don't know. It's big. Lots of legs."

"Why would it come back for us?" asked Charles.

There was a thump outside the door.

"Get ready," Seth said, his words clicking in his dry mouth. "You two might want your wings."

Vincent and Siena both shrugged off their armored jackets and flared their feathers.

The boxcar door flew open and crashed deafeningly at the end of its track. A rectangle of trees and sky blurred past. Seth stared. One second, two, three, and nothing but air entered the boxcar. Then Charles gave a shout as something popped up into the doorway.

Head on a stick, Seth thought. Atop a very long neck was a triangular head, about the size of a football, with bulbous eyes and two mandibles. The head swiveled left and right, then yanked itself back down out of sight.

"It's underneath us," Seth said. "It's holding on underneath!"

"Close the door!" Vincent yelled, rushing toward it.

A skinny leg darted over the edge, tapping along the floor. Even though it was thin, it looked dense and strangely muscular. Vincent slashed at it. Instantly the leg pulled out of sight.

Seth ran to help Vincent with the door, but before they could get it rolling, two jointed legs slammed into the boxcar. They were so long they reached the far wall. They flexed and the rest of the creature surged inside.

Stiltlike legs lifted the narrow body to the ceiling. Its long spindly neck snapped down at Seth, and when he took a swing at it, the head pulled back out of range.

"Go for the legs!" Esta cried.

There were six legs, and when Seth struck, he felt his feathers bite, but not deeply. Charles delivered a kick to another leg, and Seth heard a satisfying crack. From the corner of his eye, he saw the creature flick a long limb and send Siena spinning against the wall, hard. She didn't get up.

Seth struck again and opened an oozing split in the leg. Two more quick slashes and the severed limb fell away. The creature staggered, then quickly rebalanced itself, and the head came plunging down on him.

The mandibles closed around his upper arm and squeezed hard. With a cry of pain, he was lifted off his feet. His free arm struck the head, and his feathers slit one of the bulbous eyes.

Rearing back, the creature released its mandibles, and he hit the floor, dazed.

All the frenzied activity was suddenly slow and soundless. He saw Darren's tail make a jab at the bug's underbelly, but it was out of range. Vincent slashed at a leg and got kicked. He sailed out of the boxcar door and disappeared. Charles drove his clawed hand into the joint of a skinny leg. The bug staggered and knocked Esta onto her stomach. As she struggled to rise, the bug's mandibles came down for the back of her neck.

—*No!* Seth cried, but he was silent, because all his energy was in his head now, where that glowing string beckoned. He plucked it hard.

The giant insect veered away from Esta, its long neck twisting in agony. The legs stamped. Seth tasted blood in his mouth as he blasted out more sound. Its long neck sagged like a piece of broken hose, and its head hit the floor beside Esta.

"You okay?" he asked, going to her.

"You killed it with sound, didn't you?"

If only he'd done it sooner, he might've saved Vincent. He staggered to the boxcar door, shaking. His arm throbbed and his entire body felt spent. He looked down the tracks but couldn't see Vincent. With his mind he tried to reach him, but he got no reply. Out of range, maybe?

"He's probably okay," Seth said, wanting it to be true. Would a fall from a moving train kill you? Break your legs?

"Not like we can do anything about it now," said Darren.

It sounded harsh, but Seth knew he was right. No one was going to jump off the train to search for him.

Charles knelt beside Siena, who was sitting up against the wall, holding her right arm.

"I can't lift it," she said, her eyes scared. "It just hangs there."

"I think your collarbone's busted," Charles told her. "Mine broke when I was little. We'll put it in a sling. It heals on its own."

"How long's that take?" Siena wanted to know.

Charles took a breath. "A month?"

Seth caught Esta's worried glance.

—*She's helpless now,* she said.

—*She has sound,* Seth reminded her.

"Let's get this thing off," said Darren, kicking at the dead bug.

Motionless, it didn't seem quite so big. Seth felt a strange surge of pride. They'd all worked together to fight this thing, and he'd delivered the killing blow. They were strong.

"We should eat it," Esta said.

Her words surprised him as much as his sudden, intense hunger.

"Whoa, whoa, whoa, you want to eat this?" Darren asked.

Charles shared his look of disgust, but Seth thought he saw confused interest from Siena.

"We might not find food for a long time," she said.

The body looked surprisingly meaty. With her feathers, Esta sliced away the top layer of spiny skin. The flesh underneath was moist and translucent. She ripped off a strip and offered it to

Charles, who shook his head, same as Darren. Siena took the piece, gave it a hesitant nibble, swallowed, and started crying. But she didn't stop eating.

Seth ate the piece Esta handed him. It was sweet. As he chewed, he felt like the meat was satisfying a hunger he'd never known he had. It tasted *right*.

He couldn't believe he'd gone so long without it.

CHAPTER FIFTEEN

"LET'S GET STARTED," COLONEL Pearson said from the front of the briefing room. Sitting beside him at the table were a couple of other officers and Dr. Weber. "A great deal's happened while you were detained. I assume you were told very little inside the bunker."

"Nothing," Petra said, sandwiched between her mother and father.

"Then we have a lot to talk about," Pearson said.

—*His usual warm and cuddly self,* Petra said silently to Anaya.

—*Notice how he said* detained, *like it was really our fault.*

—*I don't think we're getting an apology.*

All the other hybrid kids were here as well: showered, fed, their jumpsuits traded in for fresh clothes. Petra felt guilty that she and Anaya were the only ones who had their parents.

When she'd arrived at the base and caught sight of Mom and Dad, her first instinct wasn't joy. It was dread. She was afraid of being seen. Afraid of how they'd react. When they hugged her, she knew they were looking at her tail. Her mother ran her fingers over the black-and-gold patterning on her bare arms and said, "Well, you always did want tattoos." And that made Petra laugh and cry at the same time.

Her dad was smiling, but it was just a mouth smile. His eyes tried and failed. What was he thinking? That there was nothing of him in her at all? That she'd become truly alien?

And that had made her think back to all of Seth's hard words about how the hybrids would never be accepted, never go back to school, never be trusted. What if she weren't even trusted by her own parents?

From the front of the room, Colonel Pearson now said, "This base will be your home for the foreseeable future. And your presence here is, and will remain, top-secret. What happened at the bunker was, I believe, improper—"

"*Improper?*" Petra heard her mother snap. "That doesn't even come close!"

"—but your release from that facility was not authorized."

"Neither was what they were doing in that bunker," Dr. Weber interjected. "I don't believe the American military command had any idea what Ritter was planning on doing with these children."

Children. The word gave Petra a start. When was the last time someone had referred to her as a *child*? Or she'd thought of herself as one?

"How many of these detention centers are there?" demanded

Anaya's mother, Lilah Riggs. "How many other children are imprisoned?"

"I don't have numbers," replied the colonel. "All I know is that most countries are rounding up hybrids, and it is completely legal. What *we* did is not. Our own government knew nothing about our stealth mission, nor did the Americans. We used unmarked helicopters so no one at their facility would have any idea who rescued all of you."

"Not *all* of us," Petra said. "Seth and a bunch of others got left behind."

"Yes. That was regrettable but unavoidable," said the colonel sternly.

"You need to go back," Petra persisted.

She felt her mother squeeze her hand, a cue to pipe down. But she wasn't in the mood to pipe down. After what she'd been through, she wouldn't be shrugged off by Pearson, or any other grown-ups with stern faces, or badges on their suits, or important *hats*. She didn't care anymore. She'd trusted them, and they'd betrayed her.

"We can't go back," said Pearson.

Petra ignored him. "Dr. Weber, you want to get Seth, don't you? You were going to be his foster mother!"

She knew she was playing dirty, but she'd use whatever ammo she had. This was *Seth*. For a moment Dr. Weber said nothing.

"More than anything, Petra, yes. But the colonel's right. It's not possible. Seth could be anywhere by now."

"He's all alone!"

"He's probably not alone," Anaya said.

She wasn't sure what was worse: alone, or with Esta. That girl was toxic. And Seth didn't seem to know it. What would she be telling him? What kind of trouble would they get into?

"Complicating matters further," Pearson went on, "is that five personnel were also killed at the bunker. Including Dr. Ritter."

Petra's breakfast shifted greasily in her stomach. She remembered Ritter twitching on the floor, the blood from his ears and nose. So he really was dead. It was Esta, it had to be. She refused to believe Seth could kill someone.

"You kids left quite a trail of destruction," Colonel Pearson said.

—*Who else died?* she asked Anaya. *I can only remember the guy gobbled up by the pit plant. In the cafeteria.*

—*A worm swallowed the guard in the escape-hatch room.*

—*Oh. Right.*

How could she forget *that*? That still left two. Maybe the flyers had killed them with their sound weapon. Or—another queasy lurch of her stomach—the guard she'd stung with her tail? Could he have died? Could she be a murderer, just like Esta?

"I'm sure these kids had nothing to do with those deaths!" insisted Mrs. Riggs.

Petra kept quiet.

"They only did what they needed to," said Mr. Riggs, his voice hoarse with emotion, "to escape with their lives."

"My point is this," Pearson said. "Each and every child here was already considered an enemy of the state. Now they're considered murderers."

"Ridiculous," said Petra's dad.

"That's how it will be seen. If anyone outside my base discovers you're here, we all risk imprisonment, myself included."

"I think everyone here understands the need for secrecy," Dr. Weber said. "Now, we have a lot we need to share with you, and I'm sure you have a lot to share with us."

You have no idea, Petra thought with a sigh. She'd already shared some things with her parents, but there were others she'd held back, like her poisonous tail, and what she'd done with it. She slumped in her chair and stilled her tail, which was restlessly swishing.

"I'll start with some good news," Dr. Weber began. "The herbicide we developed has been very effective at killing the black grass and the other cryptogenic plants. The whole world is trying to ramp up production."

"It's a constant battle," Pearson said, less optimistically. "The spray clears away the plants for a while, but then new pollen blows in, roots spread, and we need to spray again. And again. It's like a sandbag wall against a tsunami. For now, we've designated certain areas as Spray Zones. Key roads and rail corridors. Industrial farms. Hospitals. Fuel refineries. Power-generating stations and transmission lines. Vital factories. Water-pumping stations."

For the first time, Petra began to realize how many things

needed to work to keep the world running. Food to feed cities, and transportation to get it there. Clean water. Electricity.

"What about Saratoga Springs?" one of the hybrid kids asked. It was Paolo, Petra saw when she turned to check. "Is it in a Spray Zone?"

Pearson's brow furrowed. "I'm afraid my knowledge of zones south of the border is—"

"How about Edmonton?"

Pearson's voice was drowned out as, suddenly, all the hybrids in the room were calling out the names of their hometowns.

—*You think Salt Spring is in a Spray Zone?* Anaya asked.

For both of them, the island had been home their entire lives. Petra knew practically everyone by sight, and she wanted them all to be safe.

—*Doubt it. There's nothing important there.*

—*I hope Tereza and Fleetwood are okay,* Anaya said.

Petra shuddered when she remembered how Anaya's two friends had been trapped inside pit plants beneath the school field.

—*They got taken to a hospital in Vancouver, right?* Petra said. *So they might still be over here. Probably safer. I bet Salt Spring's overrun with plants. And bugs.*

"I will try to get answers for you," Pearson said, his voice raised with impatience. "But all of you here are very lucky to be in a Spray Zone."

"And I'm hopeful," Dr. Weber came in quickly, "that if we can produce a critical mass of herbicide, we'll be able to reach more of your communities. The goal is a comprehensive, simultaneous spray that will stop the plants permanently. And I know Mike Riggs, Anaya's father, will be bringing his botanical expertise to help us with that."

"But first we've got a whole new set of problems," Pearson said grimly. "The last rain delivered eggs worldwide."

"We now have some new cryptogenic species on the planet," Dr. Weber continued.

"How many?" Anaya asked.

"We don't know yet. You saw the worms last night during the evacuation."

"They got inside the bunker," Petra said.

Pearson said, "They tend to stay underground. And that's a problem for us. They're hard to kill. And they eat through everything. Gas lines, water pipes, concrete, steel. They're literally eating electrical grids and telecommunications systems. If there's enough of them, they can eat through the foundation of an office tower and topple it. If we don't get a handle on these things, they're going to take us back to the Stone Age."

Petra felt a gulping hopelessness. Dr. Weber's promised good news hadn't lasted very long and didn't seem good enough anymore.

"The other species that's thriving is a winged insect," Dr.

Weber continued. "The bite itself is trivial. It takes very little blood, but it injects a virus into its prey. Luckily the disease doesn't spread person to person. You have to be bitten."

Glancing out the window of the briefing room, Petra saw the mesh fabric that draped the entire army base like an enormous circus big top. They'd told her it was secure from the mosquito birds. As secure as anything could be these days.

"If you're bitten," Dr. Weber continued, "the mortality rate is quite high."

Did she think *mortality* was a less scary way of saying *death*?

"Tens of thousands of people have died worldwide so far," said Colonel Pearson.

"We're immune."

Petra looked over at Anaya, who'd blurted out the words. Colonel Pearson leaned forward slightly on his elbows. "How do you know?"

"Ritter threw a bunch of us into a room with them."

Petra shuddered, even though she hadn't been there.

"He *what*?" Mrs. Riggs said, outraged. "Did you get bitten?"

"We all got bitten," Anaya said. "And we're all fine."

Petra watched as Mr. and Mrs. Riggs asked if she was sure, touching her arm, her head, her cheek, as if their touches could protect her.

"Dr. Ritter's methods were monstrous," Dr. Weber said, her voice hoarse with anger.

"He doesn't even deserve to be *called* a doctor," said Petra's dad.

250

"Or a human being," Mrs. Riggs added savagely.

"Agreed," said Dr. Weber. "But the fact that these children are immune is very valuable to us."

Anaya said, "You think you can make a vaccine from us, right?"

Dr. Weber nodded. "Absolutely. If we can isolate the antigen in your blood. It's going to be a lengthy process. Even if we succeed, we have the problem of producing enough to vaccinate everyone. That's why we need to start right away."

"More tests—yay," Petra said weakly.

"But it still doesn't help us kill these things," Colonel Pearson said gruffly.

"I think I might have an idea how to do that," Anaya said.

IN THE VAULT, AFTER we all got bitten," Anaya said, feeling a pulse of excitement beat through her, "the mosquito bird things started dropping dead on the floor. I'm pretty sure our blood killed them."

"You never told me that," Petra said.

When had there been time? With everything happening so fast and furious during their escape, she'd barely had time to think about it. It was only in the past few hours that an idea had started to take shape in her mind.

"I wasn't sure at first," she said. "I mean, I wondered if maybe the mosquito birds always died after they stung someone—like bees."

"No," said Dr. Weber. "That hasn't been reported."

"So it must be us," said Anaya. "Our blood hurts them. And it might be the same with the worms."

She told them how, when the worm's teeth had gashed her hand in the bunker, the worm had flinched.

"This is incredible stuff," said Dr. Weber, shaking her head, not in disbelief but in sheer amazement and excitement.

"So I'm thinking," said Anaya, "that, sure, you could make a vaccine to stop the mosquito bird virus—but maybe you could also make a pesticide that will kill *all* the insects. Everything that hatched on our planet."

She saw Dr. Weber turn to Colonel Pearson, but he lifted a hand to stop her. His look was almost sheepish.

"You were right, Dr. Weber, these children are an invaluable resource. I'm glad to have them back here."

Anaya was grateful that Pearson had changed his mind, but there was something about his choice of words that gave her a shiver. *Invaluable resource.* She hoped the colonel—or Dr. Weber, for that matter—didn't see them merely as useful sacs of chemicals.

"These kids have been to hell and back," said Mom. "And you'd better treat them right this time."

Mom's arm had been curved around her since they'd sat down and now gave a protective squeeze. Gratefully Anaya leaned into her. She and Petra were so lucky to have their parents here. When the helicopters had touched down, none of the other kids had had anyone waiting for them—except a bunch of soldiers who, honestly, looked pretty much like the soldiers they'd just escaped from.

Jumping down onto the helipad, she'd watched the faces of those soldiers. Even though they must've been briefed, they couldn't hide their amazement—and sometimes their disgust—at all the tails and hairy faces and claws. For a second she'd worried that her own parents wouldn't even recognize her. But they had, right away.

"I want you all to know that you're safe here," Dr. Weber said now. She looked pointedly at Colonel Pearson as she said this, as if binding him to the promise. "The things that Dr. Ritter did, and was planning to do—I would never do those things to you."

"I believe your good intentions," Petra's mother, Sergeant Sumner, said, "but how can we trust Colonel Pearson's? Let's not forget he was the one to hand the children over to Ritter in the first place."

There was a burst of talking among all the kids, and it took a while for everyone to quiet down.

"I'd just like to say," Dr. Weber began, "that the colonel has risked a lot to bring these children to safety. He's risked the lives of himself and his men, and he's broken the orders of his own military command to give you all a safe haven."

Anaya saw Colonel Pearson bow his head for a moment

before looking out into the room. His expression was genuinely contrite. "You have my assurance that no harm will come to any of you while on my base. I made a mistake, and it's one I won't be repeating. It's clear we need each other. But for us to be most effective, we need complete honesty from each and every child here. We need to know about all the changes you're experiencing."

Anaya cleared her throat. There was no point waiting to tell the big stuff.

"We're telepathic," she said.

Pearson's head kicked back a bit. "Is this a joke?"

"We can talk silently with each other. And some of us can make a sound in other people's heads to hurt them. Maybe even kill them. That's how Dr. Ritter died."

"Dear God," she heard one of the military officers murmur.

"Who exactly can do this?" Pearson asked.

"No one here," said Petra. "It's only the flyers. Vincent. Siena. Esta. And Seth."

"This is surprising but not incredible," Dr. Weber said, "considering you all have transmitters in your brains."

Anaya took a breath. "And I've talked to one of them. A cryptogen."

Heavy quiet blanketed the room. Except for Petra, no one here knew about this. She hadn't even told her own parents yet, and she felt them looking at her, stunned.

"Anaya, really?" Mom asked.

Her hair and claws were one thing—and her parents had taken that very well—but the telepathy was different. This was something *inside* her.

"How many times has this happened?" Dad asked.

"Three so far," Anaya told him.

She saw Pearson lean over to Dr. Weber at the front of the briefing room and whisper something in her ear. She shook her head.

"The colonel has suggested we interview all of you in isolation, but, Anaya, if you're comfortable telling the room, I think everyone has a right to hear this."

Anaya was relieved. She didn't want to be taken to another room and interrogated. So she started telling them about what she'd heard and *experienced* when talking to the cryptogen.

"I think they're asking for help," she finished, her mouth parched. Mom passed her a bottle of water.

Pearson's face was like an unreadable desert map. "You *think*?"

She'd doubted he'd be sympathetic toward the cryptogens. She didn't think anyone in this room would, including Petra.

"We're still learning how to talk to each other. Sometimes it's not words. It's pictures, or sensations."

"That you had when you were *asleep*," Pearson stressed.

"*Half* asleep, yes, but—"

"We did suspect there were three distinct species," said Dr. Weber, "given the nature of the children. But, Anaya, you're saying two of these species, the runners and the swimmers, have been conquered and forced into labor by the flyers."

Anaya nodded. "Absolutely."

"How can you possibly know," asked Mr. Sumner, "if they, it, *whoever* you talked to, is telling the truth?"

"Exactly what I said," Petra chimed in.

Anaya knew how weak her answer would sound before she even uttered it. "It *feels* like the truth. I *know* it's the truth."

She saw the doubt in her parents' eyes. Mom turned to Dr. Weber.

"I don't like this at all. We have no clue what the cryptogens might be *doing* to her. We don't want these things in her head!"

Dad asked, "Is there any way we can block these transmissions?"

"That's what the bunker was for," Colonel Pearson said dryly. "I'm not sure our basement here would be adequate to block transmissions. These are very powerful signals."

"At the bunker, Ritter had these hoods—" Petra began.

Anaya shot a furious look at her friend, but Petra carried on anyway.

"They were for the flyers so they couldn't use telepathy or their sound weapon. Something like that might work."

"I don't want to be blocked!" Anaya said, and realized she must've shouted, because everyone was suddenly looking at her in surprise. She forced herself to take a breath. She hadn't known how attached she'd grown to having the cryptogen's voice in her head.

"This is important," she said, appealing to Dr. Weber. "This is a direct link to the cryptogens. Some of them might be allies. And we could learn a lot from them. You can't cut me off."

"I need a full, written account of this," Pearson told her. "And I thank you for your honesty." The colonel took in the room as a whole. "Has anyone else had communications with the cryptogens?"

Anaya looked around the room and saw not a single hand raised.

"Strange that you're the only one who's had contact," Pearson said, and Anaya felt her armpits prickle with sweat. Probably this made her suspicious in his eyes. A sympathizer, possibly even an enemy?

"I think it's because they reached me first," she said. "When Ritter used me for signal-tracking tests at the antenna farm."

"If any of you are contacted," Pearson said, "do not speak to them. Tell them nothing. Share nothing with them. They are a hostile force."

"Why would they bother lying to me, though?" Anaya asked. "What's in it for them?"

"I don't know," said Pearson, looking at her carefully. "Maybe they want something from you."

"Yes, our help!"

"Hard to believe we could be any help," said Pearson, "to a species so much more advanced than us. More likely they're trying to trick us into thinking they're friendly."

"It's not a trick," she said. She turned to her parents, but they didn't look very supportive.

"Anaya," Dad said gently, "these things might be brainwashing you. Look what they're doing to the planet. They want to destroy us."

She felt suddenly childish, like she'd been caught believing in garden faeries. But her instincts told her that her cryptogen wasn't a liar, and that they could help each other.

"If they contact you again, Anaya," Pearson said, "do not speak to them. Do you understand?"

"Yes," she lied.

"WE NEED TO DECIDE where we're going," Seth said.

He'd put off thinking about it, lulled by the clattering momentum of the train, hoping it would never stop. But it would.

"My mom and dad—" Siena began.

At her words, Seth felt a surge of shared longing pass through the other kids.

"Your mom and dad are probably locked up somewhere," Esta told the other girl. "As parents of an evil cryptogen hybrid. Even if they weren't locked up, you think they'd be happy to see you?

With your wings? And the power to explode people's brains? I saw you back at the bunker, Siena—you were ferocious. You *liked* it. Your parents would be *terrified* of you."

Seth watched the girl's face crumple. Her collarbone was clearly giving her a lot of pain, but she wasn't complaining about it, and his heart went out to her.

"Hey, Esta," he said quietly. "Easy."

"My mom and dad would still want me back," Siena said, on the verge of tears.

"Okay, sorry," said Esta. "Forget what I said. Your parents are fabulous people. But there's no way we can go back and live a happy life in Smallville. We'd get turned in and end up in a different bunker."

Seth could sense Esta's anger. It was like a hot steel girder inside her, and maybe sometimes it was the only thing holding her up. He understood it because he shared it. They were the only two without a family that might want them back.

"What about Deadman's Island?" said Darren.

"Are you serious?" Esta said. "Another military base?"

"They came to rescue us," Charles pointed out.

"They handed Seth over to Ritter in the first place," Esta countered.

"That was Colonel Pearson," Seth said.

"And he was on those helicopters, too," she reminded him.

As if he'd forgotten. He'd been thinking about it, trying to puzzle it out, this whole time.

"Look, maybe Pearson's working with her now," he said. "Maybe he's changed his mind about us."

"Or maybe Dr. Weber has," Esta replied. "I know you don't want to hear this, but they all might be against us. Ritter. Pearson. Weber. Maybe it only *looked* like a rescue."

The idea was so terrible that Seth had no words. He was grateful when Darren spoke up.

"No way," the other boy said. "The guys from the bunker were firing at the helicopter! And those dudes were firing back."

Esta shrugged. "It was pretty confusing down there. Maybe they were all just firing at the giant worms."

Seth felt the fault lines in his heart crack a little wider. Despite himself, he still wanted to trust Dr. Weber, but it was getting harder.

"Look," said Charles, "I agree that trying to get back to our homes is not a good idea. That's the first place they'd look for us, right? But we need somewhere safe. And I still think Deadman's Island makes the most sense."

"Who says those helicopters even went back there?" Esta asked. "Either way, I'm not going to another military base. You guys can do whatever you want."

Seth looked at her in alarm. Was she serious? He didn't know if he was strong enough to lose someone else. Especially Esta.

"We've got each other," he said, "and that's the most important thing right now. We do need to find a safe place. Where we can get food and water, and take care of each other, and . . . weather this."

"*Weather* this?" Charles said. "Like a bad storm that's going to blow over?"

"And then what?" Darren asked. "We pop back up when the cryptogens have taken over the world?"

"So what if they do?" Esta mumbled.

Seth sensed the shock rising off everyone, like heat off pavement. He felt startled himself. Darren was the first one to give voice to it.

"What's wrong with you, Esta? You actually want cryptogens taking over the world?"

"Don't you guys get it?" she said. "There's nothing *left* for us in this world. The humans will never stop hunting us."

"*We're* still humans!" Darren said.

"They don't think so!" Esta said. "Maybe the cryptogens will treat us better."

"Our enemy?" Darren said, incredulous.

"Those people we just escaped from?" Esta said. "*They're* the enemy! Ritter and all those guys. They didn't care what happened to us. If we lived or died. They were going to cut Seth's head open! And then all of ours, probably. The cryptogens are *coming,* and nothing's going to stop that. They're going to win. You want to survive this? You might want to reconsider which side you're on."

Seth could still taste the sweet insect meat in his mouth. He wanted more. He had a dangerous feeling of free fall—something from a flying dream, half terrifying, half exhilarating.

"You're crazy," said Darren, glancing around to Charles and the others for support. "You actually—"

"Who says the cryptogens didn't help us escape?" Esta said.

"How?" Charles demanded.

"The vines in the cafeteria. The pit plant that swallowed a guard. The worm that inhaled the other one."

"They also ate through our elevator!" Charles told her.

Esta shrugged. "Maybe they were sent to bust apart that bunker and let us escape! Maybe the cryptogens are looking out for us!"

Seth felt dizzy and took a breath, trying to stop the free-fall feeling.

"First things first. Let's focus on finding somewhere safe," he said, hoping his slow, careful words would steady him.

With a faint shriek of metal on metal, the train began to slow.

—*You know I'm right,* Esta said.

He didn't trust himself to reply.

CHAPTER SIXTEEN

ENVIOUSLY, PETRA WATCHED AS Anaya wiped hair removal cream from her cheek. Even with only a small part of her face clear, she already looked more normal.

"Such a relief," said Anaya.

"Geez, I wish it were that easy for me. A little shave, a little manicure."

"They needed an electric saw to cut off my claws, Petra!"

"Still, basically a spa treatment."

She and Anaya were in the same bathroom, in the same little apartment they'd shared when they'd first arrived at Deadman's Island, a million years ago. Anaya had already made it messy again with all her creams and damp washcloths. Still, the bathroom was theirs alone, same as the bedroom—and it felt like a luxury after the crowded bunker dorm.

She liked being alone with Anaya, watching from the edge of the bathtub. She was glad to be back with her parents, but they stressed her out. They kept checking on her, being concerned about her, *looking* at her. She felt way more like a freak with them than with Anaya—even if her friend was looking more normal by the second.

So unfair! A little cream, and back came Anaya's lovely face, swipe after swipe. And she was still dolphin girl. Maybe scorpion girl now. And also snake girl, since her skin was still molting.

She touched a hand to her neck and felt how scaly the skin was getting. She'd checked in with Nia and Letitia and a couple of the other swimmer hybrids, and a few had the same thing happening. It meant the skin on her neck was going to shed soon, and after that, her face? She wasn't ready to see her entire face peel off.

"Is it weird that I kind of miss the claws?" Anaya asked, inspecting her clipped fingernails.

"Yes."

"I just feel less . . . powerful."

"I get it," Petra said, thinking back to their escape. They'd needed all the fight they had in them. "Still, I'd lose my tail in a second."

"What did Dr. Weber say?" Anaya asked.

"It's going to be weeks before they can take it off."

"I'm really sorry," Anaya said. "That sucks."

"Colonel Pearson said his surgeons are too busy with real emergencies to deal with cosmetic surgery. *Cosmetic surgery!* Even after I told him it's got a stinger with venom! I should give him a little poke, see how he likes that."

Morosely, she picked at the Band-Aid on the inside of her

elbow. After lunch, they'd all given blood—because what could be more fun than being stuck with needles?

Dr. Weber wasn't wasting any time. She wanted to see if she could isolate a substance in their blood to create a pesticide. Petra was starting to feel like they really were lab rats—to everyone. Dr. Weber hadn't even taken the time to set up a special shower for her yet, though she promised they'd have one for her tomorrow.

With a bitter laugh she said, "Bet Ritter would've gotten my tail off sooner."

"Not even funny," said Anaya as she swiped cream off her other cheek. She looked at Petra in the mirror. "Is that why you told them stuff? You hoped they'd somehow make you normal again?"

Petra had been dreading this conversation, but mostly she was glad. Back in the bunker, she'd sensed Anaya drawing away from her. She wanted a chance to clear the air.

"When I told them about your conversations with the cryptogen—all that stuff about the flyers and the war—honestly, I thought they should know. I thought it was stupid to keep it secret. I mean, they were supposed to be the good guys! I was trying to do the right thing."

Anaya nodded. "I know. I believe you."

Petra let out a breath. She'd promised herself she'd be totally honest. "And yes, maybe I also thought if I cooperated, Ritter might take my tail off sooner. Or let us out faster! I swear, I had no idea he was a lunatic."

"I don't think anyone did," Anaya said. "Not at first."

"And when I told Paul what happened to Darren, I was only trying to protect Seth."

"Well, by blaming it on Esta."

"I wasn't *blaming* it on her. She really *did* it!"

She couldn't bring herself to admit how much she hated Esta. That was too shameful.

"Anyway, that was how I found out Paul was on our side."

"You were right about that," Anaya said.

"So you don't hate me?"

Anaya gave her a hug and got hair removal cream on her cheek. "Of course I don't hate you! I never did. Half the time I didn't know what to think *myself*. It was terrible in there."

"The worst," Petra agreed, dabbing the cream off with some toilet paper.

"Probably the worst bunker we've ever been in," Anaya added with a grin.

"I am totally giving that bunker a one-star review," Petra said in a petulant voice that made them both laugh.

Then she felt a sudden stab of guilt. Here she was, joking around with her best friend, *safe,* and Seth was still out there. If only she hadn't lost sight of him in all that chaos. If only they could've waited longer.

"I keep wondering," she said, "do you think he saw us take off in the helicopters? And thinks we abandoned him?"

Anaya winced. "That's too horrible."

"I mean, we kind of did."

"There was nothing we could do, Petra."

Sometimes when she had a quiet moment, she tried to call Seth silently. Concentrating and waiting for his light in her head, and even if she couldn't find it, calling out anyway. Never had an answer come back.

"He won't be alone," Anaya said. "He's probably with Esta and the others."

"Yeah, you've said as much," she replied, feeling the usual stab of jealousy. "But where'll they go? Where's safe for them now? Pearson's such a jerk, not going to look for them."

"Seth's really strong now," Anaya said. "All those guys are. If anyone can make it out there, it's them."

She pictured the fierce faces of Siena and Vincent and Esta. The guards crumpling before them. Ritter twitching on the floor until blood pooled in his ears.

As if reading her mind, Anaya asked, "Do you think differently about Seth now?"

"Because of the sound weapon? It's pretty scary. I mean, Esta jabbed me once, and it really hurt." Petra remembered the sharp poke of pain, and how quickly it might have become unbearable, enough to curl her up into a whimpering ball. "But Seth wouldn't kill anyone with it."

"That's what I thought, too."

"Anyway, what about my tail? I might've killed one of those guards." She felt an overwhelming urge to explain herself, to be forgiven. "I didn't mean to. I hardly knew it was happening!"

"It's okay, Petra. It was self-defense."

Petra wished she felt more reassured. "What if we're more like *them* than we think? Especially the flyers. I mean, maybe not Seth, but Esta seems so angry, it makes me worry. She seems to get off on all the slashing and blasting."

Anaya was silent, and Petra wondered if her friend was remembering those images of the winged cryptogens crumpling cities, killing the runners and swimmers.

"What's she like, the one you talk to?" Petra asked.

"Terra?"

Petra blinked. "That's her name?"

Anaya looked embarrassed. "No, that's just how I think of her. You know how when we talk silently, there's light and a smell or maybe a taste? I think those are their names. Anyway, she smells like soil, so I think of her as Terra."

Petra smiled. "Latin for 'earth.' Very scientific. And she's a runner, right?"

Anaya nodded. "And she seems kind. That's my sense of her. And scared."

"So there's millions of cryptogens on that ship, and she's the only one awake?"

"She can't be," Anaya said. "I was thinking about it. If the flyers are the leaders, why would they leave a runner in charge?

There's got to be a big team of them awake, with the flyers running the show. So she's got to be contacting me in secret, trying to get help."

"With their Resistance, right? So we'll just get rid of the flyers and live in peace together?"

Anaya wiped the rest of the cream off her face.

"I know you think this is crazy, but Terra doesn't want to destroy Earth."

"She actually said that?"

"No, but it's obvious. She's not in charge. She has no say in what's happening. She wants freedom, and she has a plan that needs us."

Petra looked at her friend. It was unnerving to hear her talk so confidently about what the cryptogen thought. How could she really know all this? She worried that Anaya was being way too trusting—or getting brainwashed somehow.

Gently she said, "Hey, Pearson did say you weren't supposed to talk to them, her, *Terra*, anymore."

"She hasn't contacted me again," Anaya said. "Not yet."

"So you *would* talk to her again?"

"I'm the only one they're talking to, Petra. This is important, even if Pearson's too dim to know it. And I want to *do* something to help."

"Geez, we haven't even been here twenty-four hours," Petra said. "Do we have to save the world right away? I just gave blood. Doesn't that count?"

Anaya laughed. "And we did do a lot of exercise in the bunker."

"Didn't you set a world record or something?"

"Two, actually."

"Oh-ho, listen to her!" Petra said, giving her a friendly shove.

"Don't mean to brag," said her friend. "But I can jump on more tires than anyone else alive."

"That is *so* useful," said Petra.

"Especially in today's tough job market."

"And don't forget your other world record, for being the hairiest girl on the planet."

Anaya put on a shocked face and tickled her so hard she fell bum-first into the bathtub. It took them both a good long time to stop laughing.

"Oh, that felt good," Petra said, wiping tears from her eyes.

"Uh-huh," Anaya said, then gave a sigh. "Doesn't it feel weird being here, though, just hanging out?"

Doing nothing. Petra knew how her friend felt. Everyone else on Deadman's Island was already incredibly busy. Mr. Riggs was helping Dr. Weber in the lab, and her own dad was working in the base hospital, which was overflowing with injured soldiers and people from all over Vancouver. Her mom had volunteered to go out on search-and-rescue missions with Pearson's soldiers, and Mrs. Riggs had offered her services as a pilot to reach coastal communities.

As far as world cities went, Vancouver was lucky. It was in a Spray Zone. But the plants had had plenty of time to creep and grow in small, dark places. There were still a million buildings with vines and pit plants that needed clearing.

Petra knew she should be raring to go, chipping in on the war effort, but right now she wanted to do nothing. She felt guilty having a private bathroom, and a bedroom with a window, and a really nice soft bed—but not guilty enough to give it up and bunk with all the other hybrid kids in the general barracks, four to six in a room.

"We should hang out with the others," she said to Anaya. "Have dinner in the mess hall tonight, maybe."

"Good idea," said Anaya. "It must be so hard, being on their own."

"Yeah, and it's not like everyone here's thrilled to see us."

She'd caught some hostile looks from the soldiers and over-heard a few calling them cryptos and even crypto scum. Despite Pearson's change of heart, plenty of people still thought of them as freaks or, worse, enemies.

"You smell that?" Anaya asked, sniffing.

"What?"

"Pine needles. Is it the cream?"

Petra shook her head. Then her friend's eyes got a faraway look. Her hand touched the edge of the sink for support.

"Anaya, you okay?" Anaya's knees were trembling. She looked

like she was having some kind of seizure. Petra helped lower her friend to the floor. "I'm going to get help!"

"No, wait," Anaya gasped. "She's talking to me."

BEFORE, IT HAD ALWAYS been when she was asleep.

Awake, it was much more wrenching—and frightening.

The smell of soil filled her nostrils, and she tasted pine needles. At the edge of her vision pulsed an amber light, and she knew she was being greeted. Instinctively she closed her eyes to focus.

Dimly she heard Petra saying, "Pearson said not to talk to her! Anaya!"

How could she not talk to Terra? The colonel didn't understand how urgent these mind conversations were, and how personal. Maybe she could block them, like you could block the silent talking. But it would be difficult with Terra, like barring a door against an elephant. And anyway, she didn't want to. She *wanted* to talk.

—*Hello.*

This was new: an actual word greeting.

—*Hello,* Anaya replied.

—*You are in a new location.*

—*Yes.*

She almost told Terra where she was, but Pearson would be

furious if she said she was on a military base. Maybe Terra already knew anyway.

—*Are you safe?* Terra asked.

—*Yes. Are you?*

—*We will come soon.*

—*The invasion?* Anaya asked, thinking of all those strange black wombs filled with cryptogen soldiers.

—*No. Three of us only. To collect the substance.*

—*What substance?*

—*You.*

The word sent an icy surge through her veins. She was a substance? About to be collected like a lab sample?

Terra seemed to sense her alarm and confusion, because right away Anaya started seeing images.

Veined fleshy walls pumped vigorously. A heart! She was inside a heart, and now she was traveling through a tunnel. An artery filled with blood! And it seemed like her attention was being directed at the blood itself, and all the cells and chemicals and proteins contained within it.

—*Blood,* Anaya said, naming it.

—*Blood.*

—*Blood is the substance?*

—*Your blood.*

So was this the help Terra wanted all along? Her blood?

—*Why?* she asked.

—*To create the weapon.*

SETH LED THE WAY across the rail yard, all five of them wearing their protective gear. Work crews unloaded the boxcars with forklifts. The workers were dressed pretty much the same as them, and Seth hoped they wouldn't attract attention. Siena had a sling, but Seth figured broken bones were nothing unusual these days. And they all had their visors down, so no one would notice the fact that Charles's face was practically all hair.

In the distance, a worker lifted a hand in greeting. Seth waved back and kept walking. He wanted to get out of here.

Underfoot crackled the yellowed stalks of dead cryptogenic grass and vines.

—*We must be in one of those Spray Zones,* he silently told the others. *Look.*

Up ahead was a parking lot where a couple of semitrailers were being loaded. Trucks meant roads. Roads safe enough to drive on. As they passed closer, he looked at the license plates on the trucks.

—*Washington State,* Charles said. *We know where we are now.*

—*But where?* Darren asked. *It's a pretty big state.*

—*Near a city,* Seth said. He'd lived in enough crappy neighborhoods to know that rail yards were usually on the outskirts.

The road led to a high fenced gate. Beside it was a security booth. With dismay Seth saw there was someone manning it.

—*What do we do?* Siena asked.

—Keep walking, or it looks suspicious.

Would the guard buzz the gate open, or would they need to talk to him? Seth didn't want to talk to anyone.

—I could stun him, Esta said.

—Wait.

Behind them a truck honked, and they moved to the side as it rumbled past.

—Maybe we can get out with him, Seth said.

The truck stopped at the guard booth. Seth saw the driver lean out and speak to the guard, and then the gate slid open.

—Keep walking, Seth said, following the truck as it began to pull slowly through the gate.

The guard stepped out of the security booth. There was a gun holstered in his belt and a walkie-talkie with a shoulder mic. Seth's pulse beat hard in his throat.

—I'll stun him, Esta said.

"You guys need transport?" the guard asked.

Seth was still trying to think of the best reply when Darren said, "Nah. They're picking us up on the other side."

"Okay. Watch out for the birds."

Darren tapped his helmet. "We're good."

The guard retreated inside his booth, and Seth kept walking, forcing himself not to look back. He heard the gate clang shut behind him.

—Good one, he told Darren.

They came out on the highway. Off to the right, Seth saw the truck driving away. It was the only vehicle in sight. To the left, the highway was completely blocked with fencing and concrete barriers and a huge sign that said:

DANGER
YOU ARE LEAVING THE SPRAY ZONE

Beyond the fencing, it was like another world. Black grass soared high. Golden pollen glittered in the air. Vines snaked through defeated trees and climbed power poles, the lines snapped under their weight. The road itself was a cratered mess. Snarled vines grew through the windows of abandoned cars and over a jackknifed semi.

Seth sensed a restless, relentless hunger to all of it. Already, a few vines had twined through the fence and started to obscure the warning sign itself.

"Holy crap," said Darren, staring out at the cryptogenic jungle. "So we've got *out there* or *in here*. This is not a hard choice to make, is it?"

No one said anything, not even Esta.

"There might be something good in those cars, though," Seth said.

"I'm not going in there," Darren said.

"Stay here, then," Seth said. They could use a phone, money, food. He grabbed a long piece of rebar and squeezed through a gap in the fencing. Esta and Siena followed. Esta rolled back her sleeves to expose the feathers on her forearms. Seth did the same.

He banged the ground ahead of him with the rebar, checking for pit plants. The vines across the asphalt were mostly still, and he tried to avoid stepping on them, but it was hard because there were so many.

The first car they came to didn't have anything interesting inside, so they moved on to a minivan with its sliding door wide open. Through the driver's window, Seth spotted a portable GPS unit, still suctioned to the windshield. Gingerly he opened the door, leaned in, and snapped it off.

"There's a knapsack," he heard Siena say as she climbed into the back.

The knapsack was on the back seat, and Siena grabbed the strap. Only it wasn't a strap but a black vine, and immediately it coiled around her wrist and tugged. She was pulled deeper into the minivan, crying out as she fell on her broken collarbone.

With a bang it was suddenly darker, and Seth realized the vines had somehow pulled the rear door shut. The entire back seat flipped down, revealing a pit plant in the cargo area. Its lips trembled open as more of its vines twined around Siena to pull her in.

Seth dropped the GPS and plunged between the front seats, slashing with his feathers at the tangle of vines. He severed one after the other, but still Siena was getting dragged closer to the pit plant. Light poured in as Esta wrenched open the rear door and grabbed Siena, pulling hard. Seth slashed a few more vines, and Esta hauled Siena out of the van. Amazingly, Siena managed to snatch the knapsack on her way out. Seth scrambled to the driver's seat, got the GPS, and then threw himself out the door.

"What happened?" Charles asked when the three of them pushed back through the fencing and joined the others on the safe side of the road.

"Pit plant," Seth said.

"Hope it was worth it," Darren said.

Siena was paler than ever and winced with every step. As Charles adjusted her sling, she clutched the knapsack with her good arm like she never planned to let go.

"Can we check what's inside?" Seth asked her gently.

Reluctantly she handed it over. "Maybe there's some pain-killers."

From the main pouch Seth pulled out a couple of bottles of water and a ham sandwich in a ziplock bag. It made him sad suddenly, imagining someone going to the trouble of making a sandwich and cutting off the crusts. Darren opened the bag hungrily, took a sniff, and winced.

"Rotten," he said, and tossed it on the ground.

"There's some granola bars," Seth said, rummaging some more.

He opened one and passed it to Siena, then offered the others around. Charles and Darren took them. He was still full after the insect meat. He opened a bottle of water and had a long drink. He felt good. Strong. Maybe he was just happy to be outside again.

He unzipped the knapsack's small outer pouch and found a couple of fives and three twenty-dollar bills.

"That'll buy us some real food," said Darren. "Not all of us can eat bug."

"I'm going to need some razors or hair removal cream," Charles said, touching his face.

"You're assuming there are stores open," Siena said.

Darren shrugged. "If they aren't, we can break in."

"Siena needs a doctor," Charles said.

"What can they do?" Esta said. "You said yourself, it heals on its own."

"She needs medicine at least. For the pain."

"Would help if we knew where we were exactly," Darren said.

"I found this." Seth pulled the GPS from his pocket. When he switched it on, by some miracle it still had power—and a signal. A blue dot pulsed their location on the map. With two fingers Seth zoomed out.

"Tacoma," he said as the others gathered around.

"Where's that?" Esta asked.

"Just below Seattle," Charles told her. "So we're not too far from the Canadian border."

Seth zoomed out some more and saw the familiar outlines of southern British Columbia. He found Salt Spring Island, then crossed the strait to the mainland. His gaze settled on Vancouver.

"And Deadman's Island is right there, huh?" Darren said, leaning in. "What is it? Like two hundred miles?"

"Turn it off," said Esta. "Save the battery. We should move. We'll look weird if we keep standing around."

The road went only one way, and they started walking. The black grass on either side of the highway was dead and yellow, and there were lots of gravel patches in the asphalt where repair crews must've dug out pit plants. A truck passed by on its way to the rail yards and honked its horn at them. Seth heard the drone of a propeller plane and looked up to see one flying low in the distance, mist billowing behind it.

"Herbicide," he said. Maybe over a neighborhood, or fields of crops.

"Are those birds?" Charles asked, pointing to a different spot in the sky.

It was hard to know. It looked like a flock of small birds, but there was something about the way they moved that didn't look right to him.

"It's those mosquito things," Charles said tightly.

"They can't hurt us," Esta said.

They soon disappeared from sight. The road climbed, and at the top of the rise, Seth stopped. He could see for miles. Off to the left were fields, all of them clear of black grass. Some of them had crops, mostly low green things. He thought he recognized corn. Another airplane buzzed low and delivered its payload of herbicide.

Off to the right were the curling roads of a subdivision. The houses were cobwebbed with dead vines, and their lawns and backyards were a patchwork of yellow stubble where the black grass had once thrived. Craters of dead pit plants were everywhere, but there were work crews here and there, filling them with gravel. Seth saw hardly any cars on the road, or any people. But he did spot several police motorcycles.

"What're those things poking out from the handlebars?" Darren asked.

"Oh, wow, I bet they're some kind of sonar thing," said Charles. "So they know if there's pit plants under the road. That's so smart."

"They're really fighting back here," Siena said.

There was a genuine hopefulness in her voice, and Seth felt it, too. Fields growing food. Safe roads. People living their lives.

"And check that out," said Darren, tilting his chin.

Past the subdivision was a shopping plaza. The entire thing was tented with see-through mesh. Probably to keep the mosquito birds out. The parking lot was mostly empty, but lots of people pushed grocery carts and pulled wagons, going in and out of the superstore. Seth picked out a couple of police cars near the main entrance.

A shopping center open at the end of the world.

Esta said, "We stay clear."

Seth could see the yearning in the others' faces and the fierce disapproval in Esta's. They all looked at him, as if he were the leader.

"We're disguised," he decided. "We'll be okay. We go in, get some painkillers, some food, whatever else we need, and get out."

CHAPTER SEVENTEEN

"I WAS VERY CLEAR: no more communications with them," Colonel Pearson said.

Anaya took another sip of water, her hand trembling slightly. She was still shaken after her conversation with Terra, and by the urgency and strangeness of what she'd been told. She was glad to have Dad's warm arm around her shoulders.

Mom was there, too, in the living room of the apartment, along with Petra, Sergeant Sumner, and Dr. Weber. They hadn't needed to call Colonel Pearson; his telecommunications team had already picked up the powerful barrage of radio signals during her conversation with Terra, and he'd appeared at the door, wanting answers.

"She contacted me," Anaya said. "I couldn't block her!"

"Couldn't, or wouldn't? And why are you referring to it as a she?" Pearson demanded irritably.

"Because I can tell. She's like me."

"She's given it a name," Petra added.

Anaya turned to her friend. "Why would you tell him that?"

"I thought we weren't doing secrets anymore!"

"This isn't a secret," Anaya shot back. "Just personal."

"She calls it Terra," Petra informed the colonel.

For the first time Anaya wondered if Petra might be jealous of her contact with Terra. It didn't really make sense: Why would Petra want to talk to a cryptogen when she hated being a hybrid? But even when they were little, they'd been competitive.

"*She.*" Pearson's mouth compressed in distaste. "And did *she* say when they were coming?"

"No. Just that three of them would come."

"To get your blood?" Pearson asked.

"Well, not *all* of it," she replied, trying to make a joke, but her laugh came out a dry crackle. "I hope."

She turned to Mom and Dad, suddenly scared. She sensed that Terra was kind and meant her no harm. But hearing herself described as a *substance* made her much less certain.

"And this weapon they mentioned," asked Dr. Weber gently, "did Terra say what it was intended for?"

"I got the feeling it would be used against the winged cryptogens."

"The *feeling*?" Pearson said.

Anaya sighed. "It's like we're translating for each other. We're getting better at it, but it isn't so easy to get exact meanings."

"It makes sense," Dr. Weber said. "If your blood is toxic to the insects, it might also be a weapon against the cryptogens themselves."

"Or a weapon against us," Pearson countered. "For all we know, they might be making a biological weapon to wipe out humans."

Anaya faltered. It was possible. Of course it was possible. She was talking to a species from a different planet and *wanting* to believe that they shared something. Some common humanity. But *humanity* was a human word, and who knew if it existed on a different world? All she had was her instincts, and they were impossible to shrug off.

"Terra says she's part of a Resistance. If they want a weapon, it's so they can fight the flyers."

"Good aliens versus bad aliens," said Sergeant Sumner skeptically. "A good story."

"A true story," Anaya insisted, "and it might help us stop the invasion. Imagine if we had a weapon that could defeat the flyers."

"Sure, but why can't we cook it up ourselves, then?" asked Mom.

"Possible," said Dr. Weber. "But I'm assuming their technology would be much faster."

"Enough theories," said Colonel Pearson. "The hard proof is that the cryptogens have only one thing in mind: our destruction."

"Terra knows exactly where we are," Anaya said. "If you're right, why haven't the cryptogens blasted Deadman's Island to pieces already? I saw what they're capable of. They don't need my blood to destroy us. But the Resistance might need it to destroy the flyers. Terra's offering us a chance. And allies."

"So all she wants," Pearson said with icy sarcasm, "is to come down for a meeting. Just herself and two other like-minded rebels, to take some blood samples."

"Hang on," said Petra, looking like something horrible had only occurred to her that very second. "Do they want *your* blood, or blood from *all* of us hybrids?"

"Deal with it," Anaya told her.

Petra was shaking her head. "I've given blood to *a lot* of people the last few weeks, but I am not okay with giving it to cryptogens."

"It's not happening," said Pearson. "None of it. It's a trap."

"What would change your mind?" Anaya persisted.

Outside the window, the protective netting over the base billowed in the wind. Beyond, clouds scudded across a sunny sky.

"Information," said Pearson. "The time and locations of all their planned landings for the invasion. Numbers of troops. Technical specs on their weaponry. And that's just a start."

"I don't know if Terra knows all that," Anaya said. "She's only one person. But I can ask next time."

Pearson said, "I'm not convinced there should be a next time."

For a terrible moment, Anaya wondered if he was going to send her to another bunker. Or put one of those hoods over her head.

There was a sharp knock on the door, and a soldier entered.

"Colonel, the sentry tower's spotted something in the harbor."

"Bugs?" Pearson asked, standing.

"No, sir. Eggs. Floating on the water."

PETRA FROWNED. "HOW COULD you see them from so far away?"

"They're big," the soldier replied tersely.

Dr. Weber said, "We're starting to see much bigger ones now. But not on water before. I'll need to take a look."

"We don't have any boats available," the soldier said.

"I'm not waiting until they hatch," said Dr. Weber. "I need them in the lab, fast."

"If you've still got that floatplane at the dock," said Mrs. Riggs, "I can take you out. Probably safer anyway, inside a plane."

"You'd still need divers," Pearson said, "and all my Navy SEAL teams are elsewhere. It'll have to wait."

"Is the harbor water acidic?" Petra asked. "Like the lake at the eco-reserve?"

"Very much so," replied Dr. Weber.

"I can go," she said, surprising herself. "I'll grab the eggs."

"No," her mother said firmly.

"Seriously, it's fine. The water won't hurt me."

"And what about the lilies and the mosquito birds?"

"Immune to both," said Petra. "You guys just stay inside the plane."

Dr. Weber said, "Petra, I can't ask you—"

"You're not. I'm offering. It'll take like five seconds. Mom, I can do this."

"I'm coming, too, then," her mother insisted.

"It's your call," Pearson replied. "But protective gear for everyone who goes outside the base." He looked at Petra. "You included."

Twenty minutes later, Petra was on the dock wearing boots, heavy pants, a vest, and a helmet with a visor.

"They're by that old buoy," said the soldier who'd first spotted the eggs, pointing out into the harbor. "I heard some splashing, but by the time I got eyes on it, all I saw was bubbles on the surface and the eggs. Whatever laid them was gone."

Petra's eyes roved uneasily across the harbor. Rafts of lilies drifted slowly like small islands of sleeping black swans. Overhead a flock of small birds contracted and dispersed above the city. She noticed a few gaps in the skyline where buildings had collapsed, leaving piles of rubble and twisted metal. She shuddered to think of how the worms could undermine entire skyscrapers.

Her gaze was pulled back to the water. Just smelling it, even with its rotten-egg stink, she felt some of her unease disappear. And she realized why she'd volunteered to come.

Despite everything, the water still lured her. She wanted to be in it and *under* it again.

She climbed aboard the floatplane. Mrs. Riggs was already in the pilot seat, Dr. Weber beside her. In the back Petra sat down between her mother and the soldier from the dock.

"Seat belt," Mom told her.

"We're not even taking off!"

"Doesn't matter."

She was about to do an eye roll but instead said, "Okay, Mom," and buckled up. Her parents, especially Mom, had been super protective since she'd returned to Deadman's Island. Mom barely let her out of her sight and wanted to know where she was at all times. A month ago, it would have driven Petra crazy. Now she sort of liked it. After everything that had happened, she was greedy to be cared for. She could wear a seat belt for her mom.

When the engine kicked, she felt a squeeze of nausea. She reminded herself that they were just taxiing. They rumbled over the water. After a few minutes, the plane slowed and came to a stop.

"We're alongside," Mrs. Riggs told them.

Petra stood, and the soldier approached with a safety line that was tethered to the plane's ceiling.

"I don't need it," she said.

"You're wearing it," her mom told her, in a voice that would not take no for an answer.

"Fine," she muttered, and let the soldier clip it to a metal loop on her waistband.

Dr. Weber ducked back into the cabin and opened a cooler

filled with ice. From inside she took a set of tongs and handed them to Petra.

"You should be able to reach them from the pontoon," Mrs. Riggs said from the cockpit. "Hold on to a strut, okay, Petra?"

"Ready?" the soldier asked her, then opened the door.

With her mother feeding out her safety line, Petra stepped carefully onto the pontoon. She wished she weren't wearing all this bulky gear. The stupid helmet squished her vision. She crouched, holding on to a strut for balance.

Bobbing on the water were four gray eggs, each about the size of a stubby cucumber.

"Are they some kind of fish?" Petra asked over her shoulder.

When she was younger, back before she was allergic to water, she'd spent a lot of time looking at marine life. Weren't shark eggs long and leathery like this? Her stomach gave a quick growl of hunger.

"Could be," said Dr. Weber from the doorway.

With the tongs, Petra reached for the first egg. When she tried to grip, the egg squirted away out of reach. She tried another one, but it, too, spurted away. Like they didn't want to be caught. As she reached for the third egg, all four began to sink, sending up trails of bubbles.

"What happened?" Petra asked in amazement. "Did I break them?"

"I don't think so," said Dr. Weber. "May be a survival mechanism, if they're disturbed . . ."

Petra unclipped her safety line and pulled off her helmet. She heard her mother shout out, but she'd already tipped herself forward. She went right under, heavy with all her clothing. She shrugged off the vest, kicked her feet free of her boots. They wanted the eggs, she'd get them the eggs.

She shivered, but not from cold. From sheer excitement. It wasn't the eggs that had made her do this rash thing. She *wanted* the water. Her legs and arms propelled her deeper. She wished she'd freed her tail before she went in so she could feel the sway and push of it. Her pupils dilated, drinking in the underwater world.

Below her the eggs were sinking. She kicked, wondering how long she could stay under, which made her also wonder how long the real swimmer cryptogens could. Could they stay down forever? If she herself went deep enough, would anyone be able to find her?

Such a strange thought, and she flushed it away.

The eggs sank into a grove of seaweed. It was like a little forest.

Bobbing like pale Christmas ornaments from each strand of seaweed were more eggs. They were tethered by cobwebby goo. She hovered in the water, staring. There were dozens of them. No, hundreds!

For the first time she felt unease. What had laid these? She looked all around but saw nothing except the shadow of the floatplane above her.

Her stomach rumbled again, and her fear was overwhelmed

by a sudden, crazed hunger. It was like nothing she'd ever known. As though she hadn't eaten for days and this was the only food in the world she wanted.

Her hand shot out and grabbed an egg. The cobwebby strands holding it to the seaweed were surprisingly strong. After three tugs the egg tore free, and she crammed it into her mouth.

Teeth clamping down, she crushed the gelatinous shell and felt something thrash frantically around in her mouth. She chomped again and again until it stopped moving. It was crackly and tasted deliciously salty. After three gulps she swallowed. A single word blazed in her head. *More.*

In a frenzy, she ripped off a second egg. And this time she realized that the eggs were attached not only to the seaweed but to *each other* in a complicated fibrous web. The grove of seaweed swayed suddenly as though blown by a strong wind.

The egg in her hand vibrated so violently, she let go. The skinny end opened and something streaked out too fast for her to see. Her eyes darted back to the grove of seaweed. All the eggs were trembling.

It was like awakening from some terrible dream, only to find it was real. Why had she done this? Tugged them off? A deep shame swept over her. She'd *eaten* one of those alien *things*! There was no denying the strange taste echoing in her mouth. She worried she might vomit.

I'm a monster!

And now look what she'd done! One after the other, all the

eggs were opening. Skinny creatures blasted out in a cloud of air bubbles. Impossible to get a good look at them.

Frantic, she kicked for the surface. When she came up, her mom and Anaya's were crouched anxiously on the pontoon, shouting to her. It looked like her mom had been on the verge of jumping in. She swam closer, and the two mothers hauled her onto the pontoon.

She felt incredibly weak all of a sudden, and her mom had to help her stand. She'd never seen Mom so furious, but there were tears running down both her cheeks. Roughly, she was pushed inside the plane. She collapsed into a seat, dripping.

"We need to get out of here!" the soldier shouted, peering up at the sky.

Still outside on the pontoon, Mrs. Riggs ducked to enter, and a mosquito bird landed on her shoulder.

"Look out!" Petra cried.

There was a small unprotected patch of skin where Mrs. Riggs hadn't fastened her collar fully. She swatted at the bird, but it was already gone in a whirl of shell and wing.

Left behind was a tiny blood-red dot on her neck.

INSIDE THE SUPERSTORE, SETH let out a sigh of relief.

The two police officers at the entrance had barely given them a glance. After all, most of the people here were bulked out in weird protective clothing with hats and helmets and masks. Seth and the others looked like everyone else.

The place was packed. Maybe it was the only store open for miles around. People pushed grocery carts and wagons filled with everything from breakfast cereal to chain saws to frozen popcorn shrimp. No one was really talking to anyone else. They were all focused on one thing: getting what they needed, fast.

Playing over the PA system were xylophone versions of songs that were popular a long time ago. It was like some bizarre Black Friday sale for the apocalypse. Lines at the cash registers were very long.

Seth spotted a police officer walking slowly past the aisle ends, probably making sure people didn't start looting.

—*This was a mistake,* said Esta.

—*We're fine,* said Seth. *As long as no one does anything weird.*

"There's a McDonald's," said Darren in a tone of awe. He tilted his chin at the golden arches at the very back of the superstore.

"It won't be open," Seth told him.

"You don't know that. Can I have a few bucks?"

When he hesitated, Darren said, "Come on. I just want a freaking hamburger, all right? I haven't eaten anything real for two days."

Seth handed over one of the fives.

"Thanks, Dad," Darren muttered. "Promise I'll bring back all the change."

"We meet at the checkout, ten minutes," Esta called after him.

Seth divided up the rest of the money. Charles went off to get shaving cream and razors. Esta said she'd get more bottled water and protein bars.

"Let's find you some painkillers," Seth said to Siena.

"Feel so useless," she murmured, wincing as her arm jostled with every step.

"You're going to be fine," he told her.

The shelves were quite empty, but Siena picked out a couple of bottles of ibuprofen.

Seth gave her the last of the money. "I'll go check on Darren. Meet you at the front."

At the back of the superstore was a small food court, and the McDonald's was the only restaurant open, aside from a place that made giant pretzels. For the end of the world, the McDonald's was doing great business. There were lines for both cashiers, a teenage boy and girl, each wearing a freaky forced smile. Darren was still waiting to place his order.

At the scattered tables in the food court, people hunched over their burgers and fries and giant drinks, intently sucking and cramming, like this might be their last meal. They might be right. Their eyes were all lifted to a big TV screen, watching the news. Seth saw pictures of the cryptogen spacecraft—the same one he'd seen inside the bunker—and then some footage of soldiers opening fire on a worm at the bottom of a construction site.

A police officer, sitting alone, tidily worked his way through an oozing burger. He turned and looked straight at Seth, and his gaze lingered. Seth's eyes dropped to the cop's gun, and his pulse kicked up.

He turned back to Darren, who was only now stepping up to the counter. Seth sidled closer. He didn't trust Darren and wanted to make sure he kept his mouth shut.

"We only have the Big Mac and the McChicken today," the cashier told Darren. "Everything else is sold out."

"Fries?" Darren asked.

"Oh, we always have fries," the girl replied.

"Big Mac and fries," said Darren.

"Would you like to add a drink and make it a combo?"

"Nah, I don't have enough."

"It's actually cheaper if you have the combo."

"I don't get it, but okay. I'll have a Coke." He handed over his money and moved off to the side to wait.

—*You my bodyguard?* Darren asked silently without looking at him.

—*Once you get your burger, we're out of here. There's a cop.*

—*What're you worried about? There's trouble, you zap them with sound.*

Seth didn't want to tell Darren that he was terrified of using his sound weapon. Despite everything that had been done to him, the idea of hurting someone made him feel sick. His eyes strayed back to the big TV and got stuck there.

". . . accident at a detention center resulted in the escape of over twenty hybrid cryptogens. The army reports multiple casualties. The hybrids present as teenagers and are considered extremely dangerous. . . ."

A hot prickle worked its way from Seth's armpits down his flanks.

"Freaking weirdos," a customer grunted at the screen.

"Typical hybrid markings," the newscaster continued, "include feathered arms, excessive body hair, clawed toes and fingers, and distinctive skin patterning."

"They're helping the aliens," Seth heard one man tell another. "They put them down here as an advance army."

On the screen flashed pictures of hybrids from the bunker—including one of Darren, showing the black-and-gold markings on his arms.

Seth dared not look at the cop, in case he was staring right at him. He turned to find Darren. He was sitting at a nearby table with his back to the TV, eating his burger out of the paper bag.

—*Let's go,* he told Darren.

"It doesn't taste that good," Darren said aloud, looking wistfully at his burger.

"It never did," Seth said.

"This used to be my favorite burger."

—*Come on,* Seth told him. *You're on TV.*

Darren turned his face to the screen, then slowly stood and

followed Seth. At the front of the superstore, Esta, Siena, and Charles were waiting in a cashier's line. Another cop was doing his slow back-and-forth along the aisle ends.

—*There's a picture of Darren on TV,* he told Esta.

—*We need to go,* she replied. *Right now.*

—*Pay first. We run now, they'll chase us.*

He didn't want to wait for the others outside; those cops guarding the door might take a closer look at him. So he stood nearby with Darren, who nibbled at his burger and fries with less and less enjoyment until he scrunched up the bag and dropped it into the garbage.

Esta was paying the cashier when a scream wrenched Seth's gaze to the deli counter.

There was something on the ceiling. It looked like a pale armadillo with six insect legs. It had no fearsome jaws; in fact, it hardly had a head at all, only two globular eyes sunk in the fleshy folds of its body. It stood very still, its eyes flicking to and fro, tracking the people who were running away, shouting and screaming—including a little boy and his mother rushing in Seth's direction.

Something big and yellow hit the boy in the back of the head and oozed around his face and neck. With a gasp, Seth realized the yellow goo was actually the end of a very, very long tongue. It originated from the gaping mouth of the armadillo insect on the ceiling, some thirty feet away. The tongue stretched diagonally across the store like a meaty clothesline—and then snapped back.

The boy was yanked off his feet and flew through the air. Halfway to the creature's mouth, he hit the top of an aisle-end display, sending glass jars of pasta sauce splattering red all over the floor. The insect's tongue slackened for a moment, and the boy bounced on the ground, giving his mother a chance to throw herself on top of him.

"Help me!" she screamed, trying in vain to pull her son free.

Seth ran. Maybe it was because the boy was so small and gangly; maybe it was because the mother's anguish struck a deep, echoing chord in him. Shrugging off his protective jacket, he flared his feathers.

"Move back!" he shouted at the mother.

With a quick slash, he cut through the thick yellow tongue, sending the severed end snapping back into the creature's mouth.

Gunshots rang out, and Seth jerked, half thinking he was the target. But when he looked, he saw two police officers firing on the creature. The bullets sank into its flesh, and it sagged, but fast as a cockroach, it scuttled back through the swinging doors behind the deli counter.

Suddenly Seth was aware that all eyes were on him, even as he tried to tuck himself back inside his protective jacket.

"Look!" he heard someone shout.

"His wings!"

The small boy looked up at Seth fearfully, still dragging the gooey bits of tongue off his face.

"He cut me!" his mother cried out.

Startled, Seth saw the blood on her hands. He must've nicked her accidentally with his feathers.

"I didn't mean—"

"He's a hybrid!" she shouted.

—*We're leaving!* Esta cried out to him. *Run!*

The cops were looking only at him now. One lifted his gun. Seth heard the shot and the bullet's dull smack in the cans behind him.

Suddenly everyone was running and shoving. Shopping carts toppled; people tripped and went sprawling. A huge panicked knot of people jammed the main exit.

—*This way!* Seth called out, and pelted down one of the aisles, deeper into the store.

He saw Siena and grabbed her hand, pulling her along, even as she cried out with the pain of running. He heard cops shouting, saw people staring at them in horror. One big shopper tackled him, but Esta must have stunned him with sound, because the guy grabbed his head, and Seth was up and running again.

He vaulted over the bakery counter and burst through the kitchen—flour and the smell of fresh bread. He checked behind himself to make sure the others were all still with him, then smashed through a loading door to the outside.

They were in luck: no one was around. Seth made for the mesh that tented the entire plaza and cut a slit. One by one they pushed through.

They skirted the edges of a neighborhood. A few lights shone behind windows. A face peered out of one. Seth heard the drone of a distant helicopter, but it quickly faded out. Before long they reached a street that dead-ended with a sign:

DANGER
YOU ARE LEAVING THE SPRAY ZONE

Seth looked at Esta, then at the doubtful faces of Siena, Darren, and Charles.

"Are you kidding?" Siena asked.

"It'll be harder for them to find us outside the Spray Zone," he said.

Then he climbed the barrier and kept going.

CHAPTER EIGHTEEN

WHEN ANAYA BURST INTO the infirmary, Mom was sitting on an examination table, a blood-pressure cuff around her arm and a sensor clipped to her index finger. Dr. Weber pulled the thermometer from her ear.

"I'm fine, really," Mom said as Anaya threw her arms around her. "It was just one bite, and it barely got me."

Anaya whipped a look at Dr. Weber, wanting reassurance, but didn't get it.

"You've got a fever, Lilah," Dr. Weber said. "I think we should start a course of antivirals. We've had some success reducing—"

"Is she infected?" Anaya asked, her voice breaking. *High mortality rate:* those terrible words careened through her head.

Dad put his hand on her shoulder. "I don't think we know for sure yet, sweetie."

Nearby stood Sergeant Sumner and Petra, who looked utterly miserable in her wet clothes.

"It's because I dived for the eggs," her friend said, "and I stayed down too long."

Petra started to cry, and her mother put her arm around her. Anaya could only stare; she couldn't bring herself to go comfort her friend. She didn't even trust herself to speak.

She turned on Dr. Weber instead. "Why was my mom even outside! She was just supposed to fly the plane!"

"Anaya—" Mom said. "I was helping. We were all worried."

"About Petra, yeah," she muttered.

"Anaya," Dad said gently but firmly.

She didn't care if Petra was still crying. She looked at the red mark on her mom's neck—and remembered how horrifying those mosquito birds felt on her skin. Her poor mom.

"It was an accident," Mom said with force. "If anyone's to blame, it's me. I didn't have my collar done up properly."

Mr. Sumner arrived with a stand carrying a bag of intravenous drugs and started setting it up. "Would you like me to get the IV going?" he asked Dr. Weber, and she nodded.

Anaya watched her mother give a little shiver. Her skin had a waxy sheen to it.

"Mom," she said helplessly.

She'd seen terrible things the past few weeks, but this was the worst. She needed her parents safe; they were the pillars holding up her entire life.

Her mother gave her hand a quick squeeze. "Come on, let's be a little optimistic here. This isn't a death sentence."

Anaya wished she hadn't used that word. She felt herself start to tear up—and then caught a whiff of dirt and pine needles. She looked around the antiseptic sick bay in confusion and realized the smell was in her mind, as was the amber light trembling at the edge of her vision.

Terra.

She was less startled this time, but it still pulled the breath from her lungs and she gasped in surprise.

"Anaya, you okay?" asked Dad.

"It's Terra," she said, sinking down into a chair.

She wanted to see if she could keep her eyes open this time. She felt her focus splitting. Before her was the infirmary, her family and friends, but *inside* her mind was Terra's silent and shimmering presence. Could she hold them both?

—*Hello.*

Anaya was too upset to stop the anger and fear that poured out of her.

—*My mother's hurt. She got bitten by those stupid mosquito bird things and now she might die!*

The silence seemed to stretch out a long time. Had Terra even understood her frantic gabble? It was still a mystery how her words got translated inside the cryptogen's head.

—*Trust,* Terra said.

—*Trust?* Anaya retorted. *Right now? How am I supposed to trust you? How do I know anything you've said is the truth?*

—*I will help you trust,* Terra replied.

Even though Anaya still had her eyes open, her focus was suddenly consumed by the growing amber pulse in her head. It was a bit like the box that Terra sent her at the bunker's antenna farm. And now she did squeeze her eyes tight so she could concentrate.

"Anaya?" she heard Mom say. "Are you in pain?"

"I'm okay."

She tried to block out the sound around her. Before her mind's eye she watched a shape draw itself with light, and instinctively she knew this was important.

"I need something to write with!" she called out, and a moment later felt a pencil and pad of paper pushed into her hands.

She traced the image taking shape in her head. It began with a hexagon. Some of the sides were a single line, some double. More lines radiated from the hexagon at different points, branching and spawning new geometric shapes. She hurried to keep up. The growing image flared very brightly, then faded to nothing. She felt suddenly alone. Terra was gone without even a good-bye.

Blinking, she stared at what she'd drawn. "Looks like something from chemistry class."

"You saw this in your head?" Petra asked.

"They're molecules," Dr. Weber said. "May I?" She took the pad and showed it to the others. "Carbon, hydrogen, potassium . . ."

"Why'd she want you to see this?" asked Sergeant Sumner.

"To help me trust her," Anaya replied. "It felt like she was giving me a gift."

"How?" Petra asked.

Dr. Weber started scribbling notations around the diagram. "It may well be a gift. It's a chemical compound."

"A medicine?" Anaya asked hopefully, looking at Mom.

Dr. Weber glanced up with a quick nod. "I think it's the formula for an antiviral drug."

PETRA WOKE UP IN total darkness.

Her eyes were open, she could feel her eyelids fluttering, but she saw nothing. Even if it was the middle of the night, where was the pale glow behind the curtains from the base's floodlights? Or the simple line of light underneath the bedroom door? Was there a power outage?

No, there was definitely something *over* her eyes. Her eyelashes were brushing against it. She reached up and touched thick scales. Her heart battered her ribs. She sat up and cried out for Anaya—

Except she couldn't open her mouth. Her fingers flew down to her lips.

Where was her mouth?

Her entire face was encrusted. She dug her fingernails between her lips, cracking through the scaly stuff, tearing it away in strips, spitting it out of her mouth in disgust.

"Anaya!" she gasped. Her voice made a weird whistly sound through the hole she'd made. "Anaya!"

"Hmm?" her friend murmured, half asleep.

"There's something on my *face*! I can't see!"

She heard her friend moving, then the click of the lamp—and then Anaya's shriek.

Which made *her* shriek. "What? What is it?"

"Your face, it's—"

"What! Oh my God, what's wrong with it?"

"Okay, calm down," Anaya said, sounding very much like she was trying to calm *herself* down. "I think it's what happened to your skin, you know, on your legs and arms. I think your face is . . . molting."

Petra's hands touched her chin, cheeks, forehead. She gouged out her ear holes. All this had happened overnight while she slept! The only bit that was clear was her nostrils, which explained why she hadn't suffocated.

"Okay," she panted, "so I'm not blind."

"No, just . . . crusted over."

"Is it really hideous?"

The shortest of pauses. "No."

"You're lying!"

"It's hideous."

"Anaya! You're not supposed to say that!"

"I thought you wanted the truth!"

"I want to see!"

"Don't scratch at your eyes!" Anaya told her. "Maybe you should wait for Dr. Weber."

All she could see was a vague glow and a blurred shadow that was Anaya.

"I'm being punished," she gasped.

"What? You are not being punished, Petra."

She could barely think. Huge, jagged thoughts ricocheted off the walls of her head.

"It's because I ate the egg! I *ate* one of them! I couldn't stop myself."

She could still taste it in her mouth, the spurt of flavor each time she'd bitten down. Crunchy and sweet, and utterly delicious. She'd wanted to stuff more into her mouth!

"And I stayed down there way too long. I *wanted* to be in the water, Anaya! So it's my fault your mom got bitten!"

"No, Petra! I'm sorry I was mean about it. I was really upset. It's not your fault."

Anaya was just being nice. Petra did calm breathing, a trick she'd learned from a therapist in a different lifetime. It wasn't working.

"I'm a monster," she said.

"You are *not* a monster," Anaya said, then added quietly, "I've done it, too."

"What have you done?" she asked, astonished.

"Last night. Coming back from the sick bay, I saw a vine growing up from a crack in the pavement. I ripped it out so I could show Dr. Weber. But when I saw the berries on it, I had to eat them. And then I ate the vine itself, all of it." Her friend paused. "I couldn't help it. It tasted so good."

"Why didn't you tell anyone?"

"I did. I mean, I told them where the vine was growing so they could spray. But I didn't tell them I *ate* it."

"Why not?"

"I felt ashamed. It wasn't the first time."

Petra exhaled slowly. She wasn't alone in craving cryptogenic food.

"Wish you'd told me," she said. "Still, doesn't make it better. We're changing. We have no control over ourselves. What're we going to do next?"

"It makes sense, though," said Anaya. "We're half them. They probably eat this stuff, so we want it, too."

"Remember when you said, *I'm still me?* What if it's not like that? What if we're *not* going to stay the same inside? What if we're going to change on the outside *and* the inside? What if we start *thinking* like them?"

Anaya said nothing, and Petra felt uneasy, wondering what was going on in her friend's head. She worried that all these transmissions with Terra had unbalanced her. Anaya believed everything she was told! She was way too trusting. It was like she saw everything from Terra's point of view instead of theirs. Did that mean Anaya was becoming more like the cryptogens?

And was she, too?

She felt Anaya take her hand and hold it for a few quiet seconds.

"I don't know what's going to happen to us," her friend said. "But I feel a lot better knowing I'm not alone."

"Yeah." It was a comforting little thought, but she couldn't help wishing Seth were with them, too.

"You want me to go wake up your parents?" Anaya asked.

She sighed heavily. "Thanks."

A few minutes later, she felt Mom's arms around her and heard her dad saying he'd call Dr. Weber right away. She relaxed into her mother's embrace, glad she couldn't see how people were looking at her. If only she could disappear entirely.

When Dr. Weber arrived, she said, "You're fine, Petra. It's definitely the same process we saw with the rest of your skin."

"Shedding like a snake, you mean."

"More or less."

"Can you get it off, please?"

"I think so. Let's go to the bathroom. There's more light. Could the rest of you wait here?"

"I want Anaya."

The three of them went inside the bathroom, and Dr. Weber sat her down on the covered toilet.

"I'm going to remove a piece on your cheek first."

"You're not using a scalpel or anything, are you?" she asked.

"Only a pair of tweezers."

She felt Anaya squeeze her hand as the tweezer tips crackled through the crust.

"It comes off easily," said Dr. Weber. "Close your eyes now."

She felt the tweezers peel the scale away from her right eye, then her left.

"How's that?" Dr. Weber asked after clearing a little more of the surrounding skin.

She opened her eyes and saw Anaya smiling at her reassuringly.

"Wow, your skin is so smooth," her friend said.

"I want to see."

"Maybe wait until—" Anaya began to say.

She went to the mirror and choked back a yelp. The sight was truly frightful: a scaly red shell covered her entire head. She squinted.

"Where—is—my—hair?"

"Maybe it's just underneath?" Anaya said uncertainly.

She gripped the edge of the sink. She wasn't sure which was worse, being blind or being bald.

"It's underneath the scale," Dr. Weber said, looking more closely. "I can see it."

That was good. She had hair. Petra looked at her reflection, Her new skin *was* beautiful. She could already see the hint of patterning. She'd have a tattooed face as well. She could live with that, as long as she had hair.

She stared herself in the eyes and thought: *Am I* really *still me?*

SETH LOOKED AT THE donuts behind the glass and didn't want any of them. He'd had his fill last night and still had their oily aftertaste in his mouth.

After leaving the Spray Zone, they'd sprinted, then jogged, then walked, and finally reached a desolate industrial strip. The long road, cratered with living pit plants, was flanked by warehouses and self-storage lockers and car lots. Asphalt and gravel and chain-link fences crawled with black vines and razor wire. Charles had kicked open the door of a miserable-looking coffee place, and they'd sprawled in the back room, eating stale donuts, until they fell asleep.

Morning now, light slanting through grimy windows.

Seth had slept poorly, woken in the middle of the night by the pain of his new leg feathers poking through. He couldn't help wondering if eating all that bug meat had somehow hastened the feathers. Maybe the more cryptogenic protein he took into himself, the faster his body changed into what he was meant to be.

He'd wiped away the blood, and when he'd finally fallen back to sleep, he'd been woken again by Darren's hollering. His entire head had crusted over, and they'd all helped him clear away the scaly skin. His new skin was incredibly smooth and already had a faint pattern on it. After that, Seth had managed maybe an hour's more sleep, but without the flying dreams he'd hoped for. His own nightmares had crowded them out.

He was haunted by what had happened in the superstore. The bug on the ceiling was scary, but not as scary as the way people had looked at him. That little kid he'd saved. The mother he'd accidentally cut. The cops. Their horror. Their hatred.

"We need to get going," Esta said when the others were stirring.

"Where?" Charles asked.

"As far away as possible," she answered. "They're going to keep looking for us."

"I want to try for home," Siena said.

Seth looked at her, startled, even though she'd talked about it before. "Quebec City's a long way."

"I don't expect you guys to come," she replied.

—*Let her go,* Esta said to him. *She's only going to slow us down.*

"It's too dangerous, especially alone," Seth said to Siena. "We've got to stick together. We have a much better chance that way. There's only five of us as it is."

The idea of their already small group getting smaller filled him with true sadness. The entire world hated and wanted to kill him. These people, in this room, were some of the only ones who didn't.

"I still think we should go to Deadman's Island," said Charles.

"Agreed," Darren said.

"No," said Esta.

"Who made you leader?" Darren asked.

"She's right," Seth said. "Your face is on TV. They're looking for you, for all of us. You saw what happened at the superstore. I saved that freakin' kid from getting eaten, and he and his mom started screaming at me! That cop *shot* at me! You think it's going to be different anywhere else?"

"So what about Anaya and Petra and the rest of them?" Charles said. "What's happened to them?"

"I don't know! And I don't care!"

They'd left him; they were as much to blame as Dr. Weber. He was finished with people leaving him behind. For all he knew, Dr. Weber could be continuing Ritter's work, just on Pearson's army base. Or maybe Esta was right, and the helicopters hadn't even taken the kids to Deadman's Island.

"We're not going back there," he said.

"We don't need your permission," Darren said.

Seth saw the other boy's tail twitch impatiently against the fabric of his pants. Esta's chin tilted up ever so slightly, eyes hooded like a falcon's. He worried she might strike with sound. And as much as he disliked Darren, he didn't want that. They needed everyone they could get right now.

"Okay," he said, trying to step things back, "right now, we need to move or we're going to get caught."

"We passed a car lot," Charles said.

"You know how to steal a car?" Darren asked him, turning his aggressive gaze to Charles.

"No, but there's probably keys there."

"You saw the roads outside the Spray Zones," Siena said. "We wouldn't get far. Walking's the only way."

"Water," Seth said. "We're on the coast. We get a boat, we could really move."

Darren was nodding. "We had a boat back home. I can drive one."

Seth turned on the GPS—saw the battery light flashing red—and found their blue dot. He zoomed out. There were lots of islands.

"Maybe one of these," he said, pointing. "A good place to hide."

"Doesn't look like there's even towns on some of those places," Charles said. "How're we supposed to get food if there's no stores?"

"There's other kinds of food," Seth told him.

Darren looked at him, confused, then said, "Oh, right. Bugs, you mean. That's not going to work for me."

"There's berries from the vines," Seth added. "They're good."

"You guys can go full-out alien all you like," said Darren. "Go crazy. But I need human food."

"I know how to fish," Charles said.

"Okay, so we have a plan, then," said Seth, looking at Siena. "Get to the water, find a boat. Stay together, stay safe."

The sudden trilling sound was so strange and unexpected, it took him a second to figure out it came from a cell phone. He homed in on Siena. Her face blazed with guilt, but also hope, as she dragged a mobile from her pocket.

"Where'd you get that?" Esta demanded.

Siena glanced at the screen and moved her thumb to accept the call.

"Don't!" Esta shouted, too late.

"Dad?" Siena said, her voice breaking as she lifted the phone to her ear. And then her face became very still and pale. "Who is this?"

Esta snatched the phone from her and whipped it against the wall.

"That wasn't my dad," Siena hiccuped through sudden tears.

"Who was it?" Seth asked.

"Some woman asking where I am and who I'm with."

"They've got your parents under arrest—don't you get it?" Esta said. "That was probably the army calling!"

"I just want to go home," Siena said, barely audible.

Gently, Seth asked, "How long have you had that phone?"

"It was in that minivan, jammed between the seats. Last night I called home when you guys were asleep. There was no answer, so I left a message."

"Can they trace it?" Darren asked worriedly. "In the movies they can do all sorts of crazy crap."

"Definitely," said Charles. "They'll know exactly where we are. Right now."

"We're leaving," said Esta.

She looked at Siena so fiercely that Seth was afraid she might hurt her.

—*Don't*, he told her.

"I'm sorry," Siena murmured. "I don't think I can run anymore. It really hurts."

"You can run," said Seth. "Come on." He held out his hand to her. "We need you. Stronger together, remember?"

CHAPTER NINETEEN

DR. WEBER PLACED A fluid-filled syringe on the tray.

"It's untested," she told Anaya and her dad.

Inside that syringe, Anaya knew, was the chemical that Terra had drawn in her mind. She turned to her sleeping mother in the hospital bed. A tube across her face hissed oxygen into her nostrils, but her breathing was still a labored rattle. Other tubes were connected to her arms and hands, keeping her hydrated, feeding her drugs that, so far, weren't helping.

"You're sure it's actually an antiviral?" Dad asked Dr. Weber.

"It shares definite similarities, but it's not one that's ever been created."

"If we do nothing, what's the prognosis?" Dad asked.

"Her oxygen saturation is getting very low. We'd need to intubate her soon."

"What's that mean?" Anaya asked.

"Hook her up to a machine that does her breathing for her."

Anaya still couldn't believe how much Mom had deteriorated

overnight. From a slight fever to a cough to shortness of breath to unconsciousness.

"And then what?" she asked bluntly, feeling her throat tighten. "Will she die?"

"It's likely."

"Dad, we should give her the drug!"

He looked at her searchingly. "You trust this . . . Terra? She actually told you it was medicine?"

"She didn't say that word, but yes, it was definitely something to help Mom." She knew how unsatisfying this sounded. "And yes, I do trust her, absolutely. Dad, Mom needs this!"

Dad rubbed hard at the center of his forehead. "Okay. Let's try it."

"All right," Dr. Weber said. "I don't know the ideal concentration, but I've made my best guess." She slotted the syringe into a valve on the IV line and started it dripping.

Anaya looked at Mom's lovely face. She wanted her rapid breathing to smooth out. She wanted her fast, skippy heartbeat to slow. She wanted Mom to open her eyes.

"YOU MADE A *ZOO* for them?" Petra said, staring through the wide observation window in bewilderment.

Inside the biodome was a little world that she hoped she'd

never have to enter. Black grass grew tall alongside a big pond, slick with cryptogenic water lilies. Her skin crawled as she watched mosquito birds flit through the pollen-speckled air. A water lily arched its swanlike neck and blasted acid-coated seeds at the mosquito birds. One plunged into the pond. Water lilies serenely swirled over the top of it, to eat it.

The biodome wasn't on the army base itself but a short trip by van to the Vancouver Aquarium in Stanley Park. The whole park was now a military Spray Zone. Right before the world went to pieces, the aquarium had finished a new biodome: a giant golf ball that was supposed to showcase all kinds of exciting new animals. And now it did, thanks to Dr. Weber and her team—only the animals weren't from Earth.

"This is incredible," said Mr. Riggs. "You've re-created an entire ecosystem for them."

Dr. Weber nodded. She looked exhausted. It was no wonder, Petra thought, working on so many things at once, including the new treatment she'd just given Mrs. Riggs. That's where Anaya was right now, at her bedside, waiting. Mr. Riggs would've been there, too, but Dr. Weber had asked him specially to come.

"We thought it would be the best way to study the new insect species," Dr. Weber said. "And they all seem to be thriving."

Petra believed it. Everything in the biodome looked terrifyingly alive. Black vines snaked everywhere, even onto the observation window. Dr. Weber pressed a button on a console, and the reinforced glass was misted with herbicide. Immediately the vines recoiled and began to yellow.

"Are you sure this is a good idea?" asked Petra's mother, who'd insisted on coming along. After what had happened in the harbor, Petra doubted Mom would ever let her out of her sight again. "What if what's in there gets out?"

"The biodome's completely sealed," said Dr. Weber. "And someone's here monitoring it around the clock."

"Are there worms in there?" Petra asked nervously.

"No," Dr. Weber said. "They're too destructive. They'd bore right through the walls. But we've managed to collect quite a few other species."

"You mean there's *new* bugs in there?"

"We're starting to see variations of the original three specimens that rained down. I brought you here because you're the only one who's seen an aquatic species. Take a good look in there and tell me if you see anything similar."

Peering inside, Petra frowned. "Those aren't eggs, are they?"

Clustered on the ground were several baseball-sized objects.

Dr. Weber nodded. "A lot bigger than the ones that first fell, aren't they?"

"How'd they get so big?"

"They're evolving, every time they lay eggs. It makes it very hard to predict what's coming next. I'm trying to see if there's any logical progression."

Petra gasped as a yellow tongue splashed around one of the eggs and snatched it through the air. The tongue and egg disappeared inside the mouth of a creature she hadn't even noticed, it was so well camouflaged. It clung to a thick stalk of black grass and looked a bit like an ugly, headless armadillo.

"What the heck's that?" she cried.

"Did the underwater bugs look anything like it?" Dr. Weber asked her.

"No, not at all."

As she watched it chew dopily on the egg, the black grass rustled. At first she thought the tall stalks were actually *moving*, actually *walking*, but then she realized she was seeing very long, skinny legs. And on top of those legs was a narrow body with a bulgy-eyed head and a set of pincers. They plunged down, impaled the armadillo thing, and cut it clean in half.

"I wish I hadn't seen that," murmured Petra.

The stilt creature stepped out from the excellent cover of the black grass and started ripping into its kill.

"Familiar?" Dr. Weber asked her.

"The ones I saw underwater were definitely long and skinny, but no pincers."

"Legs or fins?" Dr. Weber prompted.

"Legs. I think."

"How many?"

"Couldn't tell."

The stilt-legged thing lifted its head and seemed to stare in their direction.

"Can it hear us?" asked Petra's mom.

"I don't know," said Dr. Weber.

Petra instinctively took a step back. The creature took a step forward—and staggered into a hole that hadn't been there a second ago. A pit plant's fleshy lips closed around two of the bug's legs. After a lengthy struggle, the bug yanked out the stumps of its acid-melted legs and scuttled back into the grass.

"It's great that they all get along so well," Petra said.

But truly, it was very satisfying that these cryptogenic bugs and plants also ate each other.

"As I said, it's a complete ecosystem," Dr. Weber remarked.

"Which seemed to be their plan from the start," Mr. Riggs commented.

"First the plants, then the animals," Petra said.

"You think the actual cryptogens eat all this stuff themselves?" her mom asked, glancing over at her.

Petra felt a throb of guilt. Yes, she'd eaten the egg. It revolted her that she'd been designed to eat the same food as the swimmer cryptogens—*designed*—but it was totally out of her control.

"What we're seeing," Dr. Weber said, nodding at the biodome, "is the way the cryptogens want our entire world."

"Including the atmosphere," Mr. Riggs said. "You must be noticing some pretty major atmospheric changes in there."

"That's what I wanted to ask you about," Dr. Weber said, handing him a printout. "These plants exhale different gases from Earth plants."

Petra remembered the rotten-egg smell rising from the water lilies on the eco-reserve.

"Definitely," Mr. Riggs said, his eyes skimming the chemicals listed on the piece of paper. "We're not quite at toxic levels for humans, but getting there. Unless we get these plants under control, we're going to see serious global changes."

"How serious?" Petra wanted to know, alarmed by the look that passed between Mr. Riggs and Dr. Weber.

"I can run some models and timelines for the kinds of changes we might expect," he said.

"Seems like we've got more pressing problems right now," Petra's mother said, staring into the biodome.

"True," admitted Dr. Weber wearily. "We have no idea how many other new species are out there, or what's coming next."

Petra looked at the shadows under Dr. Weber's eyes and felt a flood of sympathy.

"But you're going to figure out a way to kill them," Petra said, hoping to hear something reassuring back.

"It's slow-going," Dr. Weber said. "I think I've isolated the agent in your blood that's toxic to the bugs. But I'm not having much success keeping it alive."

"You will," Petra said.

"And after that we need to culture it. And create a delivery medium so we can spray it onto the bugs."

"Sounds pretty straightforward to me," Petra said, trying to lighten the mood. It did sound like an overwhelming task.

"Piece of cake," said Dr. Weber, chuckling as she rubbed her eyes. "And then all we need to do is produce tons of this stuff worldwide. If these bugs are as fast at reproducing as I think, we'll need a lot of pesticide."

"UP AHEAD WE HANG a left, cross over the highway, and then we should hit water."

Seth turned off the GPS to save the battery. They were moving along an industrial road at a slow jog—the fastest pace Siena could handle with her broken collarbone. The buildings had thinned out, and between them Seth could see the highway, running through a valley.

A little farther on, they reached an intersection. To the left was the bridge that would take them over the highway—and west to the coast.

"I can smell the water," Darren said, and he seemed almost excited. "We're pretty close."

Starting across the bridge, Seth looked down at the eerily silent highway. He made out some exposed pit plants, waiting for more food. Their vines grew across the road, over abandoned cars and trucks, hungrily seeking.

"Hear that?" Esta asked him.

Seth made out the faraway sound of engines. Motorbike engines.

"Getting closer," Siena said.

They were halfway across the bridge, and terribly exposed, but Seth wasn't sure which way the bikes were coming from. Down along the highway, or higher up on some nearby road? The answer came with the flash of motorcycles between warehouses on the industrial strip they'd left behind.

Seth started running. When he whipped a look over his shoulder, he saw four police motorcycles with the same long sonar arms that he'd seen on the bikes near the superstore. They turned onto the bridge and came straight at them.

He tried to send a blast of sound at the helmeted drivers, but it wasn't working. Maybe they were going too fast, or he was too scared. He ran all out. Two bikes blasted past and, at the far end of the bridge, skidded around to face them.

Seth brought himself up short, not knowing which way to run.

He glanced back to see the other two motorbikes idling at a distance. There was a muffled pop, and a metal canister clattered against the asphalt and came spinning toward them, spraying out thick smoke. A second spewing canister hit the ground even closer.

"Run!" Darren cried, and bolted for the far end of the bridge.

Charles bounded after Darren, outpacing him almost at once with his huge leaping strides. Seth ran, too, Esta and Siena close behind.

Smoke boiled up around them, and almost immediately his

eyes were streaming. He coughed so hard, he retched. He felt Esta grab hold of him and glimpsed Siena off to his right, her eyes scrunched shut.

—*Jump!* he shouted silently at both of them.

He pulled them close to the guardrail.

"Lie down on the ground, arms out!" a voice boomed nearby. "We have live rounds and will use them."

—*Jackets off!* Seth yelled, shrugging off his own.

When he tried to help Siena off with hers, she shook her head.

—*Can't*, she said. *Broken wing.*

—*Hold on to me*, Seth told her, not even knowing if it would work. If he could bear her load.

But she shook her head and started lying down on the road.

—*Leave her*, Esta said.

As he climbed onto the bridge's railing, he heard people yelling at him to stop. Saw helmeted shadows moving through the smoke toward him. He jumped.

He spread his feathered arms. Falling too fast. He angled his arms, tried to keep his body straight, not let his legs drag. He wished he'd had time to shed his pants so his small leg feathers could catch air.

Clear of the smoke, he saw Esta gliding beside him, her own arms and feathers magnificently spread. He felt the air pushing against his wings—yes, they were finally wings—and he actually lifted.

Off to the west, beyond the trees, he saw water, stippled in the sunlight. And along the shoreline, not so far away, a spidery webwork of docks. The marina disappeared from sight as he glided down. He was tempted to flap, but his guts told him no. He didn't think his arms were strong enough yet, and he didn't want to send himself into a fatal plunge.

The deserted highway was coming up fast. His landing was a clumsy thing. He dropped his legs too soon and tumbled hard on his side. He felt one of his feathers crack, and cursed.

—*Hurry!*

Esta was already crouched over, running for the tall black grass on the west side of the highway. They slashed their way into it until they were among trees. A snaky slither of vines, the sickly whiff of their perfume.

He didn't stop. With Esta, he rushed through the woods, slicing through the vines that tried to snare them.

—*There's a marina this way!* he said.

—*I saw it, too!*

A crashing sound in the undergrowth made Seth duck. Beside him, Esta took quick whistling breaths through her nostrils. Then, in his head, a desperate calling out:

—*Seth? Esta? Siena?*

—*It's Darren,* Esta said inside his head.

He'd made it over the bridge somehow. Not Charles, too?

—*Let him go,* Esta said.

Seth felt the grip of indecision. He could say nothing and let Darren careen past. He didn't trust him. But he felt sick at the thought of Charles and Siena left behind. *He'd* left them behind, just like he'd been left at the bunker.

—*Darren, we're here,* he said, standing up.

"Oh man," said Darren, staggering toward them.

—*Silent talking,* Seth told him. *Charles?*

—*I don't know. He got away, though. He did this amazing jump. Man, is he super fast.*

—*Siena?*

He pictured her lying on the asphalt, defeated, and knew it was too much to hope for. Darren shook his head.

—*We need to move,* Esta said. *They'll come for us.*

They reached a narrow road near the water and listened for the sound of motorbikes before crossing. The marina was fenced and locked. Seth slashed the chain link and they squeezed through.

The dock dipped as he stepped onto it. There were still several boats tied up, most of them very small. From out on the water he heard a familiar creaking sound that sent a shiver down his neck. He saw the slow swirl of water lilies, clustered near the shore.

—*We need to be very quiet,* he said. *The water lilies spit acid.*

—*Aren't we immune?* Esta asked.

—*Yeah, but the seeds can take out your eye. Darren, which boat can you drive?*

—*That one.* He pointed to a larger boat with a windshield and a driver's seat. It had a steering wheel, same as a car. Wouldn't they need keys?

Darren stepped aboard first and gave a strangled shout.

Sprawled on the bottom of the boat was a man's body that had become a garden. Bat-shaped leaves grew from his chest and face. Seth's nostrils wrinkled at the sickly smell of rot. A thick stem lifted with amazing speed, and its flowered head angled itself at Darren.

With a quick slash of his arm, Seth decapitated the plant. Wilting, the severed stem pulsed clear fluid.

"Bad plant," Darren muttered.

Seth heard the velvet plash of rippling water as more lilies drifted closer.

Near the body was a key on a foam bob. Seth snatched it up and tossed it to Darren. The other boy sat in the driver's seat. When he turned the key in the ignition, nothing happened. Not even a weak whine.

—*Battery,* he said.

—*Dead?* Seth asked in alarm.

From the distance came the sound of motorcycles. Seth listened long enough to know they were coming closer.

Darren hurried to the rear of the boat and yanked up a long, narrow cover. He reached inside, turned something, then sprinted back to the driver's seat. He didn't bother sitting down.

Seth heard the promising sound of a fan somewhere inside the boat, but no roar of an engine.

—*Why isn't it starting?* Esta demanded.

The motorcycles were getting closer.

—*Gotta ventilate the gas fumes first!* Darren said. *Four minutes.*

Seeds clattered against the boat's hull. Seth felt one bite into his shoulder and tore it out. He pushed Esta into the shelter of the windshield. Through the trees flickered motorcycle headlamps. Almost here.

—*We don't have four minutes!*

—*Just go!* Esta yelled.

The engine burst into a triumphant roar.

—*Cut the lines!* Darren said.

There was one at either end of the boat. Seth did the one at the bow; Esta took the stern, shielding her eyes from the seeds.

Outside the marina fence, two motorbikes pulled up. Cops in helmets and protective gear jumped off and took aim. The sound of gunfire drowned out the hail of seeds against the boat.

Darren turned the wheel over hard and opened up the throttle. The boat lurched away from the dock, and Seth crouched to avoid falling overboard. The boat straightened out, narrowly missing another dock, then shot into open water.

CHAPTER TWENTY

WHEN ANAYA CAME BACK to the sick bay after a few hours' sleep, Mom's bed was empty. In a nearby chair Dr. Weber sat with her hands clasped in her lap, lost in thought.

Panic squeezed so hard at Anaya's throat she could barely speak. "What's happened? Where's Mom?"

Dr. Weber smiled and nodded across the room, where Mom was returning from the washroom, Dad at her side, pushing along the IV stand. There were bruised shadows under her eyes, and she shuffled, but her face had lost its awful waxy sheen, and she was *walking* all by herself!

"Mom!" Anaya rushed to her and threw her arms around her. Ear pressed against her mother's chest, she heard her steady heartbeat—and no wheezy rattle when she breathed.

"You're better!"

"I sure feel a lot better."

Anaya turned to Dr. Weber. "So it worked?"

"No one's ever documented such a dramatic improvement. Oxygen saturation is normal, blood pressure great, no fever. We'll do a chest X-ray to make sure her lungs are clear, but they sound very good to me."

"So it's a cure, then!"

Dr. Weber nodded. She looked pretty wiped herself. "I think it's safe to call this a cure."

Such a swelling relief Anaya felt. And triumph, too. Terra hadn't lied to her. Far from it. She'd sent her a medicine that was going to help the entire planet—and Anaya had had a small part in relaying it. She wished she could thank Terra right now, but she had no idea how to initiate contact.

Colonel Pearson walked into the infirmary and actually smiled when he saw Mom sitting up, sipping water.

"This *is* good news," the colonel said.

"I've sent the formula to every public health agency worldwide," Dr. Weber told him. "The biggest challenge, as always, will be producing it fast enough."

"Well done," the colonel said, and he turned to include Anaya in this.

"Terra was telling the truth," she said. "We *can* trust her."

"I still need more," he said.

"She gave us the cure to a plague!"

"A plague they sent. And why didn't Terra send this cure earlier, if she wanted to be so helpful?"

That was a fair question, and she didn't know how to answer it.

"Have you been contacted again?" Pearson asked.

"No."

"This meeting she wants with you. If we were to agree to this—"

Anaya's eyebrows lifted hopefully.

"—and it's a very big if," Pearson cautioned, "I would need to know when and where, in advance. And not only that. I need details of the ultimate invasion force. The ships. How many soldiers. Landing sites. Weaponry."

"This is a lot to put on a kid, Colonel," Dad said.

"It's a lot to put on anyone," he agreed, "but your daughter's the only person they're talking to, so it has to be her. Then we'll see if this Terra is someone we can truly trust. I hope she is."

"I'll do my best," Anaya said. She wasn't sure she'd be able to get answers to all of Pearson's questions—or even if Terra *knew* the answers.

"You don't have to do this, you know, sweetie," Mom said with a pained expression. "You don't have to talk with them, or meet with them."

"I know."

"We have no idea what it might be like."

She'd avoided thinking about it. About actually having Terra and the other cryptogens in front of her. She still wasn't sure how they looked up close, or how big they were, or how they smelled—or how exactly they intended to take her blood, and how much.

But she didn't believe for a second Terra would harm her. And she couldn't stop her cautious flight of happiness and optimism.

Dr. Weber and Dad had already made a herbicide that killed the cryptogenic plants. And with luck now they'd be able to make a pesticide. Mom was going to be fine. And Anaya was together with her family and Petra.

It felt like they all had a chance.

Like Earth had a chance.

UNTIL TODAY, PETRA HADN'T given much thought to summer. It was like something happening far away, without her.

But this afternoon, outside on the army base's field, the warm air tinged with the scent of freshly mown grass—*real* green grass!—it was finally *summer.* Stretched out on her back beside Anaya, she closed her eyes and enjoyed the heat of the sun on her cheeks. It was very bright behind her eyelids. She tried to figure out what color the light was and decided maybe yellow. It dimmed slightly as a cloud crossed the sun, then came back an intense white. She felt some of her guilt lift: Mrs. Riggs was going to be okay.

There was a shout, and she cracked open her eyes to see Adam and Letitia and a bunch of the other hybrids playing Frisbee. After so long in the bunker, everyone was pretty eager to be outside as much as possible. At first glance they all looked like normal kids. But look a second longer and you'd notice the excessively hairy legs and arms. And you'd definitely notice the tails, and the skin patterning, and a few kids whose necks and faces were starting to scale over.

So, yeah, apart from all that, and the guard towers, and the mesh tenting, and the soldiers who sometimes gave them dirty looks and called them cryptos—apart from that, Petra could imagine it was recess in June, back when there was a thing called school. And you would slump on the grass with a backpack behind your head, and someone would be playing the new songs on their phone, and you'd talk about how insane your latest homework was, and gossip, and make fun of the teachers' clothing choices.

"You want to play Frisbee?" Anaya asked.

"Nah. I just want to bask a little longer."

Like a lizard sunning itself after a long, cold night. *Lizard.* She winced. If only she were one of those lizards that could drop their tails.

Her eyes tracked a dark clot of mosquito birds deflecting off the base's protective tenting. The sight of them still made her skin crawl, but they didn't seem half as terrifying now that there was a cure for the virus.

She tried to clear her mind and find Seth. She spoke his name into the void and listened, but there was nothing. She'd always been lousy at silent talking. But several times each day she searched for him.

"You ever try to talk to Seth?" she asked Anaya.

"Yep."

Sometimes she wondered if he even *wanted* to be found. The thought of him and Esta together made her insides clench.

When the alarm sounded, Petra's gaze flew to the guard tower nearest the harbor. The soldier held binoculars to his eyes, then tilted his head to speak into his shoulder mic.

Petra scrambled up and hurried closer to the shoreline with Anaya and some of the other hybrids. What was out there?

"Inside!" the soldier shouted down at them. The alarm's grating metallic pulse filled the air. "Get inside now!"

Near the shore, she scanned Vancouver's gap-toothed skyline, but her gaze was pulled quickly down to the harbor.

In the distance, a big raft of water lilies crested, and a large creature broke the surface. Its narrow, tapered shape made Petra think of an alligator, until it sprang clear of the water on six long legs. Two of them, the ones in the middle, began to row, skimming the creature over the surface with horrific speed.

"Holy crap!" she said.

All across the harbor, more of these things leapt up and rowed toward the base. If these were the things she'd seen hatch underwater, they'd grown a thousand times bigger.

"They're like giant water strider bugs," Anaya said.

Petra's whole body shook, but it wasn't only fear. It was rage, too. Rage at herself for releasing these things; rage at the cryptogens for ravaging the planet.

From the buildings and barracks poured soldiers, armored and masked. A tank rumbled onto the field. A helicopter lifted off and skidded over the harbor, gunfire flashing from the open doors.

"Get inside!" soldiers were yelling at them, but when Petra looked around, she saw most of the other kids still on the field.

After being locked up and helpless for so long, they wanted to *do* something. They wanted to *fight*.

And so did she.

"You in?" she asked Anaya, swishing her tail back and forth.

"I'm *in*!" answered her friend, checking her still-sharp fingernails.

"Fight!" Petra shouted, and heard her call echoed across the field by the other hybrid kids, all of them now freeing their tails, baring their claws, getting ready.

"Our blood's poison to them, right?" a swimmer called Kai said.

"Yeah," Anaya said. "But they don't know that yet. They'll go for us."

The first water strider reached the rocky shoreline and leapt high onto the base's protective netting. One after another, more of them landed, scuttling over the mesh.

"Can they get in?" Petra wondered.

She couldn't tell if these bugs even had jaws. Their heads narrowed into a very long, sharp nose. Her breath caught as a water strider plunged its nose through the netting and, with a whipping motion, sawed through it. A flap drooped down above the guard tower.

A bug plunged down on top of it. The soldier inside opened

fire through the roof, but the bullets seemed to pass through the bug without harming it. Like wasps descending on a piece of meat, eight more water striders piled atop the tower, and inside it, until Petra couldn't see the soldier anymore.

From new gashes cut in the netting, bugs dropped down everywhere. Each stood ten feet tall, on legs that looked like they were made of wire cable.

"Use your tails!" Petra shouted to the other swimmers. "Sting them!"

"Go for the legs!" Anaya called to the runners.

Petra saw a water strider kick over a soldier, then scoop him up with both front legs. It was a weirdly tender gesture, until the bug drove its needle-like nose into his chest. Petra gasped as the soldier's belly swelled, like it was being pumped full of something. Even as the other soldiers barraged the bug with bullets, its syringe nose vibrated furiously, as if inhaling, then turned red. The impaled soldier collapsed, like his very insides were being vacuumed up.

Petra felt her own insides quake. They were all going to die.

"Look out!" Anaya shouted at her.

She barely had time to move. Inches from her foot, something long and skinny planted itself in the soil. She thought it was one of the water striders' wiry legs until she realized it was actually the thing's needle-like nose. It whistled back up into the air.

Petra threw herself out of the way. She saw Anaya aim a kick at the bug's middle leg and heard a very satisfying snap. The bug listed over. Petra scrambled up, her tail lashing out, but the bug's body was out of range. She struck its rear leg instead. With a jarring pain, her stinger deflected off steely flesh.

When Anaya kicked and broke another of its legs, the water strider's rear end sagged. Petra saw her chance and struck. This time the tip of her tail sank deep, and with a surge of satisfaction she felt the venom pumping in.

Instantly the bug went rigid, its limbs frozen midstride. It keeled over.

"Wicked," Anaya panted, looking at her tail admiringly.

"Good kicks," Petra said.

Everywhere, soldiers and kids were battling the water striders that had infested the base.

"Petra, get inside!"

Startled, she turned to see her mother across the field. She was clothed in protective gear, armed with a rifle, and taking cover behind an empty jeep.

Petra knew that her mother was in way more danger than she was and went running toward her. A bug got there faster. It slipped its skinny front limbs under the jeep and flipped it over.

"Mom!"

Her mother scrambled out of the way, completely exposed now. She fired off two shots before the bug smacked the rifle out of her hands with a steely leg. Then it scooped her up.

Petra ran so fast she had no voice. Her tail was raised like a spike by her shoulder, ready to strike as soon as she got close.

Maybe the bug saw her coming, or smelled her murderous intent, because it turned and sprang away, carrying Petra's mother with it.

Petra gave chase, ignoring the people shouting at her, only wishing she had Anaya's speedier legs. The bug ducked through a gash in the netting and leapt down the shoreline into the harbor. The water dimpled under its steel wire legs, and with its middle ones, it began rowing itself swiftly away from Deadman's Island.

Mom was still alive. Petra could see her trying to break free. There was still time. No way was this thing stealing her mother.

She threw herself into the harbor and felt a surge of energy as she slit the surface and went under. Her entire body undulated in a way she'd never swum before, driving her forward.

Eyes open, she saw the water strider's shadow ahead of her. She kicked harder until she was directly underneath. She grabbed the bug's rear leg. It pulled her along. Then she seized hold with her other hand and exhaled all the air in her lungs. As she sank, she dragged the creature under with her.

This thing might've been born underwater, but it wasn't built to live here. Its spindly limbs flailed uselessly. Blindly, it lashed out with its needle nose, but Petra held tight and struck it viciously with her spiked tail. She pumped venom until she knew she had no more. The bug's legs contracted violently and then were still.

Silhouetted on the surface was her mother's drifting body. A thin bright ribbon of blood unspooled from her chest. Petra kicked to the surface and grabbed her. Mom's lips were blue and she wasn't breathing. Treading water furiously, Petra tried to give her mouth-to-mouth.

"Mom!" gasped Petra, taking a break. "Mom!"

She pressed her ear to her chest, heard a distant murmur, and started swimming her mother back to shore, fast.

"OKAY, LISTEN," SAID DARREN, above the boat's engine. "We need to rethink where we're headed."

A fine drizzle fell. Seth glanced at Darren, then returned his gaze to the water. Esta was taking a turn at the wheel, and he was spotting, pointing out debris and half-submerged boats and rogue log booms.

And rafts of slumbering water lilies. Their sulfurous smell tinged the air as the boat passed. Sometimes their swanlike necks would arch and fire seeds at the boat. Whenever they did, Seth swabbed off the hull with a towel to keep the acid from burning through. Still, he figured it was only a matter of time before they started taking on water. He hoped they'd make it to Whidbridge Island before then.

They'd dragged the dead man's body over the side. Seth hadn't felt good about it, setting him adrift on the water, but the smell was unbearable, and Seth didn't want anything else sprouting from his chest and trying to kill them.

He lifted his eyes skyward, dreading the sight of a helicopter.

So far they'd passed a few other boats, none of them military. Some people had waved from their decks—a kind of sad salute that said, *We're still here—good luck.*

It was cool on the water, and Seth missed his heavy protective jacket. He'd rummaged around in the seat lockers and found a few windbreakers. His was too small, so the feathers near his wrist poked out.

He checked the compass in front of Esta. He figured as long as they were going north, they were headed in the right direction. Up ahead, mist layered the horizon.

Darren said, "I really don't think roughing it on Whidbridge Island is going to work."

"Sure it is," said Esta.

"What about all the bugs?"

"We'll eat them."

"I agree, the people we've seen so far are total dicks," Darren said. "But they can't *all* be bad."

"Darren, we're not going to Deadman's Island," Esta told him.

The name still filled Seth with a complicated mix of yearning and anger.

"Charles agreed with—"

"Speaking of Charles, I can believe he got away. He's really fast. But you aren't."

Darren frowned and shook his head, confused. Seth looked at Esta, not sure what she was getting at either.

"What *really* happened?" Esta demanded.

"I told you, we both got away. We were lucky."

For the first time, Esta looked directly at Darren. "Did you make a deal with the cops? Tell them you'd lead them to us? They found us pretty fast at the marina."

Darren swore under his breath. "You're crazy." He shook his head at Seth. "Why would I do that?"

As much as he disliked Darren, he'd never thought Darren would do such a terrible thing. But now that the idea was in his head, he couldn't dislodge it.

"What's in your pockets?" Esta asked him. "You got a tracking device or something?"

"No!"

"Empty your pockets, then."

"Fine!" He pulled out some granola bar wrappers and the cap of a water bottle. "Happy?"

"You should check all his pockets," Esta said to Seth.

Darren held up his hands. "You know what? I've had it. Just drop me somewhere, okay? The first dock you see."

Seth was about to agree when Esta said, "No way. You know where we're going. You'll tell them."

"I won't tell anyone anything!"

"We don't trust you, Darren. You snitched on us once. You'll do it again. Are you going to check his pockets?" she said to Seth.

Darren looked at him wildly. "Why're you listening to her? She's going to get us all killed!"

Seth felt an unwelcome twinge of sympathy with Darren. He seemed genuinely bewildered—and desperate.

"Come on," Seth said, stepping closer, "let me check you. If you've got nothing to hide—"

"Don't touch me," Darren said.

"You want off," Esta said, "jump off."

"What?"

Seth looked at her, equally startled. "Esta—"

"Jump. Off," she said, her voice pure steel. "Or I'll make you."

Seth saw Darren's tail arch, the tip swaying at shoulder level.

"Don't try it," Seth said. Darren was within striking range of both him and Esta.

"You guys try to hurt me with sound, and I will stab you," said Darren. "Just change course and take me to that quaint little island right over there."

Esta sniffed. "What makes you think your venom even hurts us?"

Seth saw Darren swallow. "Let's find out."

—*I can drop him faster,* Esta said silently.

She must've struck, because Darren winced and gasped, but his tail, as if acting on its own, hit Seth in the chest. He felt the icy puncture through his windbreaker and T-shirt, right into the flesh between his ribs. The tail pulled out and swung fast toward Esta. She threw herself clear, and the spike struck the fabric of the driver's seat.

Esta rounded on him, and Darren staggered toward the back of the boat, hands clamped around his head.

"Stop, please, stop!"

Seth grabbed the wheel and narrowly avoided a collision with a deadhead log. He throttled back. From the rear of the boat he heard a splash. Before he could turn to look, Esta was beside him.

"You okay?" she asked, gripping his shoulder.

"Yeah," he croaked.

"You don't look okay."

The cold at the center of his chest was spidering out along his arms and legs, and with it came a terrible weakness. He was suddenly on the deck, and when he tried to push himself up, his arm buckled. He stared helplessly up at Esta as a silent mist closed around her, and she was gone, and then everything was gone.

CHAPTER TWENTY-ONE

WHEN PETRA REACHED THE rocky shallows of Deadman's Island, she knew her mother was gone.

She pulled her onto shore and sank down, exhausted, beside her. Only dimly was she aware of the gunfire and shouting from the base. She brushed away the wet strands of hair plastered across Mom's face. A mosquito bird dived down and bit Petra on the arm, but she didn't bother to swat it. She let it flutter away to die from her toxic blood.

Numbly, she watched as one giant water strider after another, as if on command, came leaping out through the slashed netting. They weren't at all interested in her as they retreated across the harbor, some cradling lifeless human bodies in their front legs. Farther out, among the thick rafts of water lilies, they flattened their bodies and became practically invisible.

She heard a cry and turned to see Anaya rushing toward her with a medic and another soldier. When her friend put her arms around her, she couldn't even feel their weight, or understand what was being said to her. She watched, as from a great distance, as the medic started giving her mother chest compressions and mouth-to-mouth.

The medic looked at her and shook her head.

Her mother was lifted and carried inside the tenting, across the field.

Anaya helped her up and walked beside her, asking questions. But Petra didn't hear them. Couldn't even feel her feet touching the ground.

An injured soldier limped past.

Ribbons of shredded tenting dangled down from overhead.

An empty boot sat askew on the ground.

There was the overturned jeep behind which her mother had taken cover.

There was Colonel Pearson shouting orders.

And then her father was running toward her. She saw the twisted look on his face, and suddenly all her senses came exploding back to her and she buried her face in his chest, eyes clenched. Over and over she heard herself sobbing, "I'm sorry, I'm sorry."

Maybe if she hadn't eaten that egg, and touched the others, they wouldn't have hatched and none of this would have happened, not so *soon* anyway. Not today. They wouldn't have attacked. They wouldn't have killed Mom.

"Shhh," her father said against her head. "I love you. Thank God you're all right. I want you to go inside—there might still be some out here." His voice was hoarse. "Please, Anaya, will you take her inside?"

She felt Dad shifting her to Anaya, and watched as he helped carry Mom's stretcher toward the sick bay.

That was her mother, going away from her.

Anaya had her arm around her and was guiding her across the field to their apartment. How could the sky still be blue? Nearby lay a dead water strider, and Petra felt something fathomless in her stomach—and couldn't tell if it was hatred or hunger.

Trembling, she went closer, glaring at its narrow body, its needle-sharp head. She kicked at it, and then again and again, cursing. She dug her fingernails into the bug's flesh and ripped off a strip of meat. Taking a bite, she recognized the same salty taste as the egg. Devouring more, she looked over and saw Anaya's surprised expression.

"What!" she shouted angrily, meat still in her mouth. "I'm a monster, didn't you know?"

She was a hybrid freak, half cryptogen. Her mother was the only human part of her, but she was dead now. She felt like she'd been thrown overboard into a frigid, churning sea.

"You're not a monster," Anaya said softly.

"I ate the egg! I made all this happen!"

"They would've hatched anyway."

"We're *all* monsters! We're just pretending not to be."

"Petra."

"But you actually think there's some nice monsters up there who want to help us!"

"I do."

"Because *your* mom lived? Well, they didn't help *my* mom. How come *your* mom got to live?"

Anaya said nothing.

Fury filled Petra. It was insane, the idea that the cryptogens wanted anything but their destruction. But no, Anaya had her special relationship with Terra, and got all this special information, because she was *special.* Anaya with her special relationship and knowledge.

"If they're so nice, how come they're not stopping stuff like this?" She waved her hand at the grisly slaughter on the battlefield.

"Maybe they can't, Petra."

"You're so naive! They've gotten inside your head and messed you up! We need to kill *all* of them!"

She crammed more bug meat into her mouth, not caring who saw or what they thought of her anymore. They could whisper behind her back all they wanted. They could stare at her tail and her tattoos. They could call her a crypto scumbag. She felt half deranged but also strangely powerful, not caring anymore.

"And I'll tell you something else," she said. "Until we wipe them all out, no one's cutting this tail off me!"

ANAYA TILTED HER FACE up to the shower, washing away the dirt and bug guts from the battle. She wished she could also wash away the images jammed in her head: that impaled soldier on the field; Petra sitting beside her dead mother; the torment in her friend's face as she raged.

She'd never seen Petra like that and couldn't blame her one bit. She was right: it wasn't fair that her mom survived and Petra's died. Anaya couldn't even imagine how terrible it must have been for her friend, swimming her mother's body back to shore.

And Petra was right about something else, too. They *had* changed. They weren't the same people, even on the inside. Petra craved cryptogenic insects, she loved being underwater, and she had a venomous tail that seemed to act on its own. And she, Anaya, felt the same kind of hunger for cryptogenic plants. But the biggest change for her was the powerful mental connection to Terra, which seemed to guide her own thoughts.

Was she being brainwashed?

Six soldiers had been killed, four others badly injured, and two of those needed limbs amputated. The hospital was chaos. She'd overheard Dr. Weber say that the giant water striders injected their victims with an enzyme that liquefied tissue, then sucked it out.

Despite the warm water, Anaya shivered. So gruesome. How could she still trust Terra after all this?

She didn't want to leave the shower. Didn't want to see Petra's stricken face, or hear any more news. She just wanted the water to keep hitting her face. It felt cowardly, though, hiding away in here. She had to get out and see what she could do to help.

An amber light pulsed in her head. She grimaced at the taste of dirt in her mouth. It wasn't pleasant this time; it made her think of decay, of coffins in the ground.

Only yesterday she'd longed to talk to Terra, to thank her for the medicine that had saved Mom's life. But she didn't want to talk to the cryptogen right now. She tried to stop Terra's silent words from blooming in her head—without success.

—*What is wrong?*

—*We were attacked!* Anaya said. *By giant water insects. Did you know about this?*

—*No.*

—*So you don't control the bugs?*

—*No.*

—*People died. My friend's mother!*

—*Many have died. Many more will.*

It sounded so callous, and in anger Anaya tried again to slam the door on Terra. Maybe these cryptogens didn't have emotions. Maybe she'd been stupid to think Terra was capable of kindness or fear or empathy. But as Terra's words echoed in her head, their blunt meaning expanded. Sergeant Sumner's death was a personal tragedy, but countless thousands, maybe millions, of people had already died on Earth. And each one of those deaths was a mind-crushing personal tragedy for someone else. And there would be so many more unless they could stop the flyers.

She had many things to ask, and Colonel Pearson had given her his own list of questions, but before she could begin, Terra said:

—*We are coming.*

She was startled by the simple force of the statement. It wasn't a request. It was happening.

—*When? Now? Right now?*

In her mind she saw the sun cross the sky into darkness, then rise once more to its apex.

—*In two days?*

—*Two days. Then we will take the substance.*

Fear prickled her neck like a rash. She needed to remind herself that, even though their communication was getting clearer and faster, sometimes Terra's words came across differently than intended. But *we will take* made it sound like she had no say in the matter.

—*Why do you need my blood?* she demanded. *What's so special about it?*

—*The code.*

—*What kind of code? How did it get into my blood?*

—*We hid it there, long ago. Now we need to extract it. To make the weapon.*

—How does the weapon work? she asked Terra.

—I will explain. When we come.

—Wait, I have questions now. There are things you need to tell us first.

—When we have landed, Terra said. *When we know we are safe.*

ESTA FROWNED DOWN AT him. "Seth? Seth!"

Gasping, he tried to sit up but felt too heavy. There was a cold burn in the center of his chest. Everything rushed back to him. Darren. His stinger. Collapsing.

The last thing he remembered was Esta getting swallowed up in mist—he'd thought it was the mist of death or something, but it was real mist. It swirled around them now, enveloping the whole boat.

"Darren," he tried to say, but all he heard was a strange sound from his mouth. It felt like he'd been shot full of dental freezing.

—I thought you were going to die, Esta said. *You were paralyzed. You were barely breathing.*

He tried again to push himself up, and Esta helped him rise onto his elbows. All his limbs tingled painfully as feeling returned to them.

—How long was I out?

It was much easier to talk silently than to try to use his clumsy mouth.

—Almost two hours.

Whatever venom was in Darren's tail was something else.

—Where is he? he asked.

Esta's expression was unapologetic.

—I made him jump off.

He remembered the splash he'd heard before collapsing.

—I thought he'd killed you! Esta said. *I was scared he'd sting me, too. I hurt him until he jumped. Then I gunned the boat as far away as I could.*

Seth had no kind feelings for Darren, but he felt a pang. He was one of them, a hybrid, and now they were one less.

—Was he conscious? Seth asked. *When he hit the water?*

Esta nodded, and Seth let out a deep breath. If Darren was conscious, he could swim and survive.

Something bumped against their boat, and Esta jumped.

—Just a log, she said, and leaned over to shove it away.

The boat was drifting. He could barely see past the bow, and only a few feet off either side. He liked it. It made him feel hidden and safe. It was very quiet. He bent his knees and wiggled his toes, relieved his body worked again.

Esta sat close beside him.

—I was so worried, she said.

He had never seen her look so vulnerable, or tender. He thought of how terrible those two hours must have been for her, staring down at him, waiting.

—I'm sorry, he said.

She threw her arms around him, and he felt the heat of her cheeks and her tears and her body trembling against him. He hugged her back. Such a good, warm thing to hold.

—*I thought I was going to be all alone,* she said.

She kissed him.

No one had ever kissed him like this. He felt like she'd given him something amazing. He touched her lips with his fingertips, her wet cheeks, her eyebrows. He looked into her eyes.

—*Will you stay with me?* she asked.

The exact same question had welled up in his head.

—*Yes.*

—*Promise,* she said.

Aloud he said, "Yes, I promise." His voice sounded normal now.

"It's just the two of us." Her words carried loneliness but also a sense of purpose, even pride. "For the best."

Seth wanted to believe her. He let his head rest on her shoulder. He felt like he was setting down a huge burden. For a long time they held each other.

—*We're going to be fine,* he told her. *We'll be safe and we'll be together no matter what happens next.*

—*Yes. We won't get pushed around anymore, or put places we don't want to be.* He wondered if she was talking about the bunker or even further back, to her aunt and uncle. More than anything, he wanted a home, a place where he could feel he'd finally arrived and didn't need to do anything else. A place he could share with Esta.

He felt the strength returning to his arms and legs. They could go find a safe place. They would be careful and live in secret and no one would find them and try to hurt them. Esta was strong and he trusted her, and things were possible again.

Something knocked against the boat. This time it wasn't a log.

CHAPTER TWENTY-TWO

"THEY WANT TO SURRENDER to you," Anaya told the colonel in his office.

As soon as she'd finished her conversation with Terra, she'd told her parents and, after that, Dr. Weber. All three of them had accompanied her to tell Pearson.

Doubt was etched across the colonel's face. "Surrender," he said.

Anaya wasn't entirely sure this was the perfect translation, but it was the closest meaning she got.

"They're coming, three of them," she said. "They're coming because they need our help, and we need theirs. *To learn and teach*—that's how Terra put it."

"When?"

"In two days, at noon."

"Did the cryptogen—"

"Terra," Anaya insisted. It was important that he use her name, even if it was one she'd invented. In the bunker Ritter had given all the hybrids numbers, and she knew it was a way of turning people into things. She wanted everyone to think of Terra as a person.

"Did *she* answer any of my questions?" Pearson asked.

"No. But she said she would after they've landed. After they're safe."

She saw the colonel's eyebrows rise, but he gave a little nod, as if he respected the decision. It was Terra's insurance. Information in exchange for a safe landing on Earth.

"They have some requests," Anaya added.

"Ah, I see."

Anaya waited for him to ask what they were, but he didn't, so she continued.

"They need us to build them some kind of enclosure with their own atmosphere. They can breathe ours, but it's still a bit toxic to them. And they want your assurance they won't be attacked when they come to land. The ship they're arriving in has no weapons."

Colonel Pearson actually laughed, but it came out more as a bark.

"Anything else we can do to make them more comfortable? Any dietary restrictions we should know about?"

"I think they already have what they need to eat down here," said Dr. Weber. "They've sent their crops and food ahead of them."

"I'm amazed," Pearson said, "that this cryptogen thinks we'd trust anything she says, after the attack on my base."

Anaya had been expecting this. "She had nothing to do with it!"

"I find that extremely hard to believe," the colonel retorted.

"They were bugs!"

"Explain to me how bugs mass together in an attack on a military installation when there are easier, undefended targets all over this city."

Anaya had no answer to this. Pearson had a very good point. "Even if the cryptogens can somehow control the bugs, Terra's not in charge! She's a rebel. She wants all of this to stop as much as we do."

"So she says."

"She gave us a cure—"

"And right afterward, we're swarmed by giant bugs. Every time you two talk, they pinpoint you here at my base. Has it never occurred to you that *you're* being used as crosshairs?"

Anaya looked desperately at Dr. Weber and her parents. She'd already tried to explain, as best she could, how much she trusted Terra. Clearly she'd failed.

"She's promising us a weapon," Anaya said. "Something that might help us win the war!"

"I'd rather rely on Dr. Weber and our own scientists to develop it. So far we've managed an herbicide. A pesticide may be next."

Anaya sighed, wishing Petra were here. She was always better at convincing people of things.

"If they have some magic bullet, why don't they simply send us the recipe?" Pearson asked.

"Terra said there was a code in me, in all the hybrids, that they hid. And now they need it back."

"Your trust in Terra is starting to concern me."

Anaya felt her pulse quicken. Was Pearson suggesting she might be a spy?

"Don't even *think* of locking my daughter up again," said Dad.

"I'm also worried about her welfare," Pearson said, "and whether she's being manipulated and used as a mouthpiece by our enemy."

"No one's manipulating me!" Anaya insisted. "If Terra only wanted me for my blood, she knows where I am. She could swoop down anytime and take me and blast everything else to pieces. She's coming because the rebels need our help, and they want to help us, too." She took a breath. "Anyway, they're coming, whether you like it or not. What're you going to do? Blow the ship up?"

Pearson nodded. "That is an option, yes."

"We couldn't even touch the ship in orbit!" Dr. Weber pointed out. "What makes you think you could hurt one of their other ships?"

"Strike as they come in to land," Pearson said. "It might be our only chance."

"You do that," Anaya said, "they'll think we're hostile, and we lose an ally—and a weapon."

Pearson studied his hands a moment. "It doesn't seem there's any stopping their arrival. Where do they plan to land? Did she give you coordinates?"

"I'm the coordinates."

Saying it, she felt a shiver ripple beneath her skin. They were coming right to her. Mom's arm slid around her shoulders.

"They must have requirements for a landing site, though," Pearson said.

"A clearing." Anaya remembered the image Terra had shown her. "At least two hundred feet long, fifty feet wide."

"That's all?"

"It's a small ship."

"Hang on," Mom said to Pearson. "Suddenly you're agreeing to this?"

"It doesn't seem my agreement is necessary," Pearson replied. "We'll do it in Stanley Park. It's been sprayed, and it's close to the base, in case we need support."

Anaya knew *support* meant weapons. "You won't need support," she said firmly.

"We also don't know anything about what kind of radiation or energy the ship might produce," Dr. Weber said. "Or biohazards."

"You need to prep a team," Pearson told her.

"You'll need me," Anaya said.

"No," said Pearson. "The moment the cryptogens touch down, you're out. Military personnel only."

She'd feared this would happen. "Terra wants me there. And *you* need me there. I'm the only one who can talk to them."

Triumphantly she looked around at all of them, Mom and Dad, Dr. Weber, the colonel.

"She's right," said Dr. Weber with a sigh. "We have no way of communicating with the cryptogens without her present."

"Anaya, are you sure?" Dad asked, taking her hand.

Despite her fears, she *wanted* to be there. To meet Terra. To finally see her, this creature in whose image she was partly made. The urge was primitive and strong.

"I'm sure," she said. "There's no way around it. I'm your translator."

THE OTHER BOAT WAS much bigger than theirs, and the impact sent Seth sprawling across the deck.

He made out the words POLICE MARINE UNIT on the boat's hull. Poised at the edge of the deck were three officers wearing armor and gas masks.

Twin Taser wires snagged Esta in the chest. She dropped to the deck, flinching as the voltage coursed through her. Instinctively, Seth crouched and shielded himself with his feathered arms. He felt the Taser barbs hit his feathers and saw sparks crackling along their tips. With a swipe he cut himself free of the wires.

Two officers had jumped aboard and pulled a hood over Esta's head. They dragged her limp body onto the police boat.

"Let her go!" Seth roared.

He looked one officer in the eyes and struck hard with sound. When he collapsed, one of his fellows grabbed him under the arms so he didn't fall overboard.

"Go, go!" someone cried, and the police boat veered away into the mist, taking Esta with it.

—*Esta!* Seth shouted, and waited for her returning cry. *Esta!*

Then he remembered the hood—it had to be the same kind Ritter had used on him. Or why wasn't Esta blasting everyone on that boat right now? Why wasn't she calling out to him?

—*Esta!*

Nothing.

He threw himself into the driver's seat and followed the wake of the police boat, but it dissolved before long, and he couldn't hear the sound of its engine above his own. He shut down, listened, aimed, and gunned it, not caring what he might hit.

—*Esta!*

No reply.

The mist pressed in on him, and he could barely see in front of him now. He killed the engine again, listened. Heard nothing. He cried and swore and banged his hand against the steering wheel, until he couldn't feel the pain anymore.

CHAPTER TWENTY-THREE

PETRA'S MOM WAS BURIED in the makeshift graveyard at the far end of the army base, along with all the soldiers who'd died during the battle. A bugle was played at the funeral service. Guns were shot off. Then the bodies were lowered into the earth of Deadman's Island.

Petra didn't like to think of Mom down there. Terrible things lived in the ground. Pit plants. Giant worms. Dad held her close, whispered, "It's all right," but it wasn't all right. Mom had wanted to be cremated and have her ashes sprinkled in the ocean. But there was nowhere to cremate her right now. Her body would have to stay here. Petra couldn't cry. There must be something wrong with her. Maybe she had changed so much, she didn't have normal human feelings anymore.

She stared at the graves and wondered about all the other mothers and fathers and children around the world. Hundreds of thousands of them by now. Where would they find space for them all?

She felt immensely tired. She didn't want it anymore. None

of it. The cryptogens and their plants and bugs and rebels and her own mutant DNA. All she wanted was to crawl into bed and never come out. She wanted oblivion. She didn't care what happened anymore.

The funeral was over. Colonel Pearson was already giving orders. Officers and soldiers dispersed. Her father hugged her and told her he had to get back to the hospital. Numbly she nodded. Mrs. Riggs came over to give her another hug and a kiss on the forehead.

"I'm piloting a medical supply flight to Vancouver Island," she told her daughter.

"Are you well enough?" Anaya asked worriedly.

Mrs. Riggs nodded. "They need a pilot. I'll be back later this afternoon."

Petra gave her friend's shoulder a squeeze as she watched her mother walking away.

"Do you want to go back to the apartment?" Anaya asked.

She was about to nod, but surprised herself by shaking her head. Did she really think she'd be able to sleep? Make everything magically disappear? She wanted to *do* something.

She saw Dr. Weber turn away from Colonel Pearson and Mr. Riggs and approach them.

"We're ready to do a trial of the pesticide," Dr. Weber said.

Petra hadn't known they were so close. "It's ready?"

"It's a prototype," Dr. Weber said cautiously. "Likely it will fail. We're going to do a test in the biodome. Petra, I'll understand if you don't want to—"

"I want to see," Petra said.

It was her blood that had helped make the pesticide. Her blood and Anaya's and all the other hybrid kids'. And if some tiny part of her could kill these cryptogenic bugs, she wanted to watch.

The jeep took them into Stanley Park. Inside the biodome, Petra looked through the observation window and was surprised to see a new resident. Her throat tightened. A water strider, pressed flat against the surface of the pond.

"We managed to capture an injured one," said Dr. Weber, catching her look. "With its proboscis severed, it probably won't live long," she added, like she was trying to make her feel better.

At one end of the observation room, lab technicians were connecting a canister by a hose to the ventilation system.

"Is that the pesticide?" Petra asked, and Dr. Weber nodded.

She looked back into the strange alien zoo, hating everything she saw: the black grass, the stilt bug lurking among the stalks, and the mosquito birds flitting through the air. On the ceiling of the dome, the armadillo bug with the long yellow tongue snapped up a bird.

"We're ready," said the lab technician.

"Let's start with a single unit," said Dr. Weber.

There was a faint hiss, and Petra expected colored mist to fill the biodome, but there was nothing to see until she noticed dew on the other side of the observation window.

The stilt bug took a few steps in the grass. On the ceiling, a vine tried to snare the leg of the armadillo thing, but it scuttled nimbly away.

"Nothing's happening," Petra said.

"It might take some time to work," said Mr. Riggs, glancing at the stopwatch on his phone.

Everyone waited in silence until Dr. Weber said, "Release another unit."

Once more a fine dew settled over the observation window, clouding Petra's view until the windshield wipers cleared it.

Mosquito birds flitted across the biodome, and one fell, as though its wings were glued to its sides. It landed in the water and was quickly swarmed by lilies.

"Look, there's more!" Anaya cried out, pointing.

Petra's gaze whipped up to the mosquito birds as they plummeted to the ground.

One species down, she thought with grim satisfaction.

The stilt bug emerged fully from the grass, tilted because of its two missing legs. Its body glistened with pesticide dew. It opened its mandibles to snatch up a dead bird and then keeled over, its legs pulling up against its thorax.

Two down.

"It's working!" Anaya said, squeezing her arm.

The armadillo thing on the ceiling fell and shot out its tongue, as if to save itself. The tongue stuck to the ceiling of the biodome, and the creature swung back and forth lifelessly.

That's three.

Petra looked over at the water strider, snuggled down against the water. With its middle legs it rowed across the pond.

"Why isn't it dying?" she demanded, looking at Dr. Weber.

"Maybe the water's diluting the pesticide," she said.

"No," said Anaya, "look!"

The water strider's legs churned and the creature hurtled to shore, as if trying to escape something. On land it kept running, straight for the window. Petra took a step back as it crashed against the glass. It rammed the glass again, then staggered back. Its legs curled up, and it flipped over on the ground and stopped moving.

"All of them," Petra said. "It works on all of them!"

"I call that a success," said Colonel Pearson, turning to Dr. Weber and shaking her hand. "We can kill these things."

Mr. Riggs was smiling, too, and hugging Anaya.

Petra hadn't been able to cry at the funeral, but for some reason she was crying now. It was like she'd been holding her breath and could finally gasp air. She cried out of relief and hope—and wishing they'd had this a little bit sooner so maybe Mom would still be alive.

Anaya put her arms around her until she stopped sobbing.

"I'm really sorry," Anaya said into her ear.

Petra nodded, forced a smile. "This is good news."

Anaya smiled back. "*Very* good news."

"We'll need to do some safety tests," said Dr. Weber, "to make sure this stuff isn't too harmful to humans, but this is a huge breakthrough. I'll get the results out through our government channels. With luck, we can ramp up production as soon as possible."

"I'd like to place the first order," Pearson said. "Can you keep making it on-site?"

"Not in very big quantities," Dr. Weber told him. "But enough to arm a few of your men."

Petra stared through the window at all the dead bugs. Vines were already nosing at them, entangling them. The lips of the pit plant opened as the water strider was dragged toward it.

"We need to prep the biodome for the cryptogens now," said Colonel Pearson.

"What?" Petra looked at him, confused, then turned to Anaya, who didn't look confused at all. "What's going on?"

"They're coming tomorrow," her friend said.

"How come no one told me?"

Anaya looked pained, and Petra knew the answer: that she was too grief-stricken, that she'd find the whole idea too upsetting. And they were right.

"You're actually *letting* them come *here*?"

"We don't have much say in the matter," Pearson said.

"And what, they're going to *live* in there?" she said, pointing through the observation window.

"It's the right atmosphere for them," Anaya said.

"That's great you're making them so nice and cozy. Should we put chocolates on their pillows?"

"I know you don't think that—" Anaya began.

"This is insane! We have a pesticide!" she said. "We can kill everything now. What do we need the cryptogens for?"

"Because there's worse coming," Anaya said.

"And Terra might be part of it! I can't believe how trusting you are." She turned to include Pearson. "All of you. This is a big mistake. The best thing you can do is blow them out of the sky before they even touch down."

ANAYA LAY IN BED, unable to sleep.

Tomorrow she was going to meet them.

Tomorrow she was going to come face to face with Terra and the other two cryptogens. Her thoughts ricocheted from excitement to hope to outright terror. Every time she glanced at the pale blue numbers of the clock, she recalculated the countdown to the landing. Nine hours, sixteen minutes.

She closed her eyes, tried yet again to breathe deeply and let her thoughts blur into sleep, but they were too insistent.

All yesterday, crews had prepared the biodome and the landing site. The entire area had been sprayed with pesticide and herbicide to make sure it was safe. The protocol for moving the cryptogens from their ship to the biodome had been finalized.

She thought again about how she'd only ever seen distant glimpses of the cryptogens. She had no idea how she'd react when the time came. She hoped she could hold it all together and not flip out.

Yes, she wanted to meet Terra, this being who'd shared space in her mind. And she was hopeful this meeting would give them what they needed: allies, and a weapon.

But as she lay here, sleepless, she was getting more worried. What if she'd been wrong about everything? What if Petra was right, and she'd been tricked? What if Terra wasn't coming to help them but to destroy them? She wasn't only putting herself at risk: there was Dr. Weber, Mom and Dad, Petra—everyone else on the base. Everyone else on Earth.

"I want to be there."

Petra's words from the next bed surprised her, but she kept her eyes closed. Maybe it was best to say nothing, pretend she was fast asleep. After Petra's outburst at the biodome yesterday, the two of them hadn't talked much.

"Anaya?"

Nice smooth breaths.

"A-nayyyyy-a. I know you're awake."

"How do you know?" she said, opening her eyes.

"Your breathing. It's the way people breathe when they want someone to think they're asleep."

Anaya had to smile. "That's good to know."

"When they arrive, I want to be there with you."

"I don't think it's a good idea, Petra."

"Worried I'll go crazy and try to kill them?"

"Something like that, yeah."

"I know I've been saying some harsh stuff—"

"No," she replied. "You haven't. I've thought about every single thing you've said."

"Really?"

She nodded. It was true. "And if I didn't have Terra talking to me, I'd probably think exactly like you. But I trust her, Petra. I really do."

"She saved your mom."

"It's not just that. What she says makes sense to me. And yes, maybe they're really good at messing around in people's minds, but I can't help believing her. I know none of this is super convincing."

Even though it was dark, she could tell Petra was listening carefully. There were a few moments of silence before her friend replied:

"I want to meet them, too, you know."

"You sure?"

"I'm part *them*. It's like they're our creators. Oh God, I hate how that sounds!"

"I know what you mean." She'd had the same thought, more times than she cared to admit. "Half of whatever we are comes from them."

"Right. So I want to meet the other half of me."

Anaya still wasn't entirely convinced. She knew how good her friend was at speeches.

"How do I know you're not coming to hurt them?" she asked Petra bluntly.

"You'll have to trust me. If you can trust an alien, can't you trust me?"

"Fair enough."

"Anyway, whatever's going to happen, good or bad, I want us to be together. It's bad enough Seth's not here, but the two of us, at least we can stick together."

Anaya reached across the gap between their beds and met Petra's hand halfway. Since that terrible day at the school field, back on Salt Spring, the one thing that always made her feel safer was having Petra and Seth with her.

"I hope he's okay," Anaya said.

"I still try to talk to him every day," her friend replied. "He's never there. But this morning, it was weird—I felt like maybe I reached him."

Anaya leaned closer. "You heard something?"

"Not really. But it was kind of like the way you pretended to be asleep."

Anaya gave a sniff of amusement. "I'm sure if he heard you, he'd talk back."

"Hope so. He should be here for the arrival. Anyway, *I'm* going to be there."

"Pearson might fight you on that."

"I'll convince him he needs a backup translator," Petra said.

"In case I get eaten."

"Exactly."

"That might work," said Anaya. "Good idea."

"Remember the way we were on the eco-reserve, how we beat the vines and killed the pit plants, all of us, together?"

Anaya squeezed her friend's hand. "We were awesome."

"I want us to be like that again," Petra said. "I want us to *win*."

AS DARKNESS SLOWLY BLED from the sky, Seth tore a strip of meat from the water strider. It had made the mistake of jumping onto his boat, and before it could strike, he'd cut off its needle nose, then finished it off with a sonic sledgehammer.

He'd given up trying to find Esta. Careening around in the fog, he'd twice almost collided with wreckage that would've torn out the bottom of the boat. He couldn't risk it.

All night he'd motored north at a snail's pace, staying clear of land, too afraid to try to dock anywhere in the dark. The fog had lifted, but once he'd reached the Strait of Juan de Fuca, he'd been hit by a strong wind from the west. It had chilled him to the bone and made steering difficult. The wind blew him one way, and the tide pushed him the other, so it was like being churned in a washing machine. Water slopped over the sides; spray soaked his pants. It was almost dawn before he'd reached calmer water. He was cold and exhausted.

He swallowed more of the dense meat from the bug's underbelly. It was strange, but he felt like he could feel the energy dispersing through his body, into his blood and his cells, making him stronger. And maybe making him different, too? More like the cryptogens?

It made sense, didn't it? When the black grass arrived, he'd started to change. If sniffing the pollens could make his feathers regrow, imagine what eating all this meat could do.

When he heard the voice in his head, his heart leapt—and just as quickly sank. This voice didn't have the familiar taste and smell of Esta; it didn't have her light. This voice was faint and clumsy.

—*Seth? Seth? It's Petra.*

He knew who it was. Instinctively he looked northeast toward the haze hiding Vancouver, but he made no reply.

It was strange to have Petra in his head again. It felt like it'd been a long time, though he knew it hadn't, really. The salty taste of her silent words gave him a pang of sadness and longing.

—*Seth, if you hear me, we're on Deadman's Island. It's safe. As safe as it gets, anyway.*

If he'd heard this news a few days earlier, it might've moved him more. Too much had happened. After the superstore, after all those hostile, horrified faces, he'd known he had no place in the human world. So why would he return to Deadman's Island?

Even if Petra said it was safe, it was still run by the same kind of people who'd ripped Esta away from him.

—*We got attacked by giant water bugs. My mom died.*

He swallowed and throttled up, hoping the engine noise would drown the voice in his head.

—*Please come, Seth.*

He steered away from Deadman's Island, putting more distance between the two of them, wanting her voice to fade.

—*Seth, are you close? I feel like you're there.*

Her voice was crackling now. Good. She'd never been very good at telepathy.

—*I miss you, Seth.*

Another sharp tug at his heart, and then she was gone. He was glad. He didn't want to be tempted.

He gunned the motor, not knowing where he was going. The boat shook, and he realized it was his hands on the wheel, gripping so tight they were trembling.

He wiped the tears from his face, startled by the sounds he was making, halfway between cursing and sobbing.

Sharply he turned the wheel and aimed the boat north again, toward Vancouver.

CHAPTER TWENTY-FOUR

"YOU'RE SURE YOU GOT the time right?" Colonel Pearson asked irritably.

"It wasn't exact," Anaya told him. Did he actually think Terra had given her Pacific Daylight Time? "The sun was in the middle of the sky. That's what it looked like to me."

It was half past noon. For almost two hours, Anaya had been anxiously waiting inside the trailer that had been set up as a field office at the landing site. Outside, flags marked the perimeter, along with sensors that measured radiation and toxicity in the air. A van waited nearby to transport the cryptogens to the bio-dome, whose roof Anaya could see curving above the trees in the distance.

Inside the trailer, it was a small group. Anaya was glad that Petra had managed to convince Pearson she should be there. Her friend sat on one of the plastic chairs in front of the windows, her tail restlessly tapping against the floor. Anaya wondered if she was regretting her decision; she looked nervous, her eyes darting across the sky. Dr. Weber paged through a binder of notes. There was a radio operator present and two other soldiers. Anaya wasn't happy about having soldiers at all, but Pearson was adamant. At least they were only armed with spray canisters of pesticide, in case they ran into any cryptogenic bugs. Along the wall hung a row of orange hazmat suits, one for each of them when they went outside. Not for the first time, she wished Mom and Dad were here.

"You all right?" Dr. Weber asked her quietly.

"A little nervous."

An understatement. At breakfast she hadn't been able to eat a bite, and she still felt like she might throw up. She took a sip of cold water and let it sit in her dry mouth before swallowing.

"Anything?" she heard Pearson ask his radio officer.

"Nothing's entered our airspace yet, sir."

Anaya wasn't surprised. She doubted they'd see anything on their radar. The cryptogens had managed to park a city-sized spaceship in orbit for years without being detected.

"And you haven't been contacted?" Pearson asked her.

"I'll tell you as soon as I am." She was starting to get worried, too. Had she got the time wrong? Had Terra changed her mind? Had something terrible happened?

In a quiet, singsong voice, Petra said: "The aliens are running just a little bit late."

Anaya had to laugh, and everyone else did, too, except Colonel Pearson, whose scowl lines merely deepened.

Finally, inside her head an amber light pulsed. She breathed damp soil.

—Coming.

Anaya felt her pulse sprint. Terra's silent voice was not as clear as usual—like a radio tuned slightly off station—but the urgency emanating from that single word was unmistakable. Terra sounded frightened, too, and Anaya didn't know whether this should reassure or worry her.

—We're ready, she replied, and then Terra's presence flickered out in her head.

"They're on their way," she croaked.

"Still not getting anything," the radio officer reported.

"Suits on," Pearson said.

Anaya was glad to have something to focus her. Before she zipped up her hood, the radio officer fitted everyone with a headset. They all did a quick sound check, and after that she was sealed up completely.

Even before she stepped outside, she was sweating. The suit stank of plastic. Her rapid breath through the filter rasped loud and unpleasant. Despite the tinted visor, the sun was hot on her face. Everything looked slightly unfamiliar to her. Grass. Trees. Clouds. She suddenly felt as if *she* were the alien, peering out at Earth's landscape for the first time. Her steps were slow and clumsy in the baggy suit.

—This is weird, she said to Petra, looking at the rectangle of her friend's face.

—Very weird.

—I wish I could ditch the suit.

—Keep that thing on!

Dr. Weber said the cryptogens might be carrying germs. But it seemed unlikely to her that she and Petra could catch something. Wouldn't they have the same immune system as the cryptogens?

The two soldiers flanked their little group, holding their long spray nozzles at the ready. Anaya could only hope Terra wouldn't think they were weapons meant for them.

Turning in a slow circle, she tilted her head to the sky. Wispy clouds. A dissolving vapor trail from a passing jet headed east. She really had no idea what shape the cryptogens' ship would be, how fast it would move, whether she'd even be able to see it.

Rising from the trees bordering the landing site came the quick flicker of mosquito birds.

"Bugs!" she said into her mic.

In a swarm they attacked. The soldiers took aim and released twin plumes of pesticide. The effect was instant: as if the bugs had been coated in cement, they fell dead to the grass.

"Love that stuff" came Pearson's voice over her headset.

A few mosquito birds limped through the air back toward the trees, only to drop before they reached them.

"Let's hope we don't get any more uninvited visitors," Dr. Weber said.

The soldiers split up to patrol the perimeter of the landing site.

—Did Terra tell you who else is coming with her? Petra asked.

—You mean the other two rebels? No.

It seemed strange that she hadn't even thought about it until now.

—I was just wondering, Petra said, *if they're all runners, or if there's a swimmer, too. There's no flyers, right?*

—No. They're the enemy!

—I want to see a swimmer, Petra said, *but I'm also kind of terrified.*

"Something here" came a soldier's voice over Anaya's headset.

She looked over to where the soldier stood near the trees, poking at something with his spray nozzle. As she drew closer with the others, she heard a buzzing sound. On the ground was a gory mess blackened by flies. Anaya swallowed. The metallic smell of blood reached her even through her filter.

Her first thought was, *Dead animal.* But once the flies cleared, she couldn't make out a leg or a head. In fact, it looked more like a big jumble of loose skin, with a skinny cord sprouting from it.

"It's a placenta," she heard Petra say.

"Definitely," said Dr. Weber. "Something gave birth, and not long ago."

With the spray nozzle the soldier unfolded and flattened out the placenta to get an idea of its size.

"Maybe a raccoon," Pearson said.

"Too big," said Dr. Weber, "and most mammals birth earlier in the year. And they usually eat their placenta, to hide the babies from predators."

Anaya swallowed. "Maybe this one isn't worried about predators."

She met Petra's eyes and knew her friend was thinking the same thing: whatever had been born, it didn't come from Earth.

"How can this thing be cryptogenic?" Pearson demanded. "They only dumped eggs, and this definitely didn't hatch."

"All along they've been evolving," Dr. Weber said. "This is the next stage. Live births."

From the forest came a shrill yip that made Anaya's skin crawl. It sounded like an animal—only not quite right. She stepped back with the others as undergrowth crackled, and something emerged from the trees.

AT FIRST, PETRA THOUGHT it was one of the armadillo bugs she'd seen in the biodome. It had the same dog-sized humped shape. But it took her only a second to realize this thing had hair instead of armor. It did not have spindly insect legs but six thick, furry ones with oversized paws tipped with claws the length of paring knives.

When it turned its squat head to them, its face was all wrong. It looked like it had been terribly injured, cratered in the middle, its surrounding flesh shredded into stubby red tentacles. They vibrated hungrily, and Petra wasn't sure if the weird yelping sound came from the tentacles themselves or the dark hole in their center, which had to be the mouth. If there were eyes, she couldn't see them.

"Is this the baby?" Petra said, voice shaking. She didn't know which terrified her more, the claws or the tentacles—or the fact that if this was the baby, there must be a mother.

"Kill it," Pearson told his soldiers over the headset.

They blasted it with pesticide. The spray coated the creature's head and torso. It cowered and made a weird sound that might have been coughing, then collapsed.

But it was only rolling around, scraping its face against the earth, cleaning itself. Its tentacles licked away the last of the pesticide on its head. It stood with an energetic hop that, in any other animal on Earth, might have seemed playful.

"The stuff doesn't work!" Petra gasped. "Why doesn't it work?"

"It wasn't designed for mammals," Dr. Weber said.

Petra slowly stepped backward, unable to rip her eyes away from the creature. Why had they come out here without more soldiers, without proper weapons? Were they insane?

It wasn't her knees trembling; it was the ground. From the trees came a diabolical trumpeting. In an explosion of branches and undergrowth, another creature burst into view.

Mama, Petra thought, her heart racing so quickly, she worried she'd pass out.

It was the size of a rhinoceros, its blunt head a writhing nest of tentacles. Each of its claws was like the Grim Reaper's scythe.

"Go!" Pearson shouted. "Get inside!"

Petra ran. Over her headset the colonel barked orders for an airborne weapons unit. She heard the gasping breaths of Anaya and the others as they pelted for safety. Anaya was fastest, way in the lead. She reached the trailer first, swung the door open, and turned to urge everyone on.

From the corner of her eye Petra saw the two soldiers running, shrugging off their heavy pesticide canisters, and then suddenly there was only one soldier. She didn't stop, didn't look back. She reached the trailer and piled inside with Dr. Weber. Pearson brought up the rear, dragging the remaining soldier after him.

"Where's Fischer?" the soldier was shouting. "What happened to Fischer?"

Colonel Pearson slammed the door and shot the bolt, which Petra didn't think would be very useful at all. She rushed to the windows.

The hulking creature stood, its flanks heaving, about twenty meters from the trailer. Its tentacles writhed, shoving something into the dark crater of its mouth. Petra caught a glimpse of a boot disappearing.

"It just swallowed Fischer whole!" the surviving solider said.

Petra started unzipping herself from her hazmat suit.

"What're you doing?" snapped Pearson.

"I want to be able to use my tail."

"And I want my claws," Anaya said, taking off her own suit. "If we need to run again, I don't want this thing slowing me down."

"Can't see properly in it anyway," said the soldier, removing his helmet.

"Where's my helicopter?" Pearson barked at the radio operator.

"ETA two minutes."

"Should've brought weapons," Pearson muttered.

Outside, the baby creature butted against its mother impatiently. The mother regurgitated a molten hunk of food, and the baby eagerly bent its head to it.

"Oh my God," murmured Petra.

The mother creature stood tall on its rear legs, head turning. Was it tasting the air with its tentacles? Petra had the eerie feeling it was looking right at them, even though it had no eyes.

"Stay away from the windows," Dr. Weber said.

From the dark crater of the creature's mouth, Petra caught a bright flash. The trailer's plexiglass window exploded into crystals, and something struck her face, blinding her. It seeped over her eyes, her nose, her mouth, stifling her scream of horror. Her entire head and shoulders were now encased in this warm, wet, living thing. A pulse beat through it. A tongue! This whole thing was an enormous tongue! Her hands flew up and tried to peel it off. The flesh hardened suddenly, then tensed.

"Petra!" she heard Anaya shout, and felt her friend's arms wrap tightly around her waist.

But she was wrenched away, dragged headfirst out the window. She sailed through the air and hit the earth. Her head still encased in slimy goo, she was dragged fast. Even though she couldn't see, she knew exactly where she was headed. The hole in the center of that cratered face.

She clawed at the tongue, like digging her hands into an endless block of modeling clay.

"Petra!" Anaya must be running alongside her. "Sting it with your tail!"

In her terror she'd forgotten her own weapon. Instantly her tail was alive. She whipped it toward the creature's tongue, struck, and felt the venom pumping in.

Almost right away she stopped being dragged. Anaya jostled against her, helping peel the tongue off her body. Petra tore it away from her face and could suddenly see again. Blinking, she scrambled to her feet.

She was stunned by how close they were to the rhino creature. Another ten feet and she would've been inside its mouth. The long, pale tongue lay paralyzed on the ground. It was thick as her leg. The tip, the part that had engulfed her head, was the fattest bit of all, marbled with veins.

The creature made a number of jerking coughs, as if trying to pull its tongue back into its mouth. It wouldn't budge.

As Petra watched in horror, the creature clamped down with its black-hole mouth, severing its own tongue, leaving it lying in the dirt. Then it charged on its six legs, its long claws splayed. Without a doubt, Petra knew it would run her down before she reached the trailer.

Anaya was already streaking on ahead, but she glanced back to check on her and faltered.

"Go!" Petra shouted. "Keep going!"

But Anaya turned and ran toward her, then right past her, and straight at the creature. With an awesome leap, she soared over the creature's head and onto its armored back. The creature bucked, trying to throw her off, but Anaya crouched and grabbed a handful of its bristly hair and kicked her clawed feet into its hide for better purchase.

—*You have any venom left?* Anaya asked her.

—*Not sure!*

—*Sting it!*

Even if she had any venom left, would it be enough to drop this thing?

The creature reared and turned, but somehow Anaya held fast. From the side, Petra saw her chance and rushed in to strike, but the baby lunged from between its mother's legs. Its narrow tongue slapped against Petra and yanked her off balance.

She didn't want to waste venom on the baby. She managed to yank its tongue off with her hands. The baby came at her, its butcher-knife claws clumsily slashing. Petra scrambled away, but a claw cut across her leg. Her tail struck. She felt the venom pumping out of her. The baby gave a shiver of surprise, then froze.

The mother roared so loudly that Petra clamped her hands over her ears. The creature rounded on her. She raised her tail, hoping there was something left.

Suddenly, like a mirage, Seth stood beside her.

She couldn't even say his name, only stare in incomprehension. His gaze was locked on the creature's head. He spread his arms. His feathers blazed with color. The creature faltered, as if mesmerized. Its tentacles curled up, and its head dropped. It writhed, clearly in agony. Anaya vaulted off its back and landed in a crouch as the creature toppled over, shaking the earth.

Petra turned to Seth. "Did you kill it with sound?"

He gave a nod and lowered himself to the ground, trembling violently.

"Seth! You okay?"

His face was pale and dewed with sweat. He dry-heaved twice, then wrapped his arms around his legs, like he was trying to stop himself from shaking apart. His teeth chattered.

"I'm okay," he panted. "That thing was just . . . so freakin' big."

She threw her arms around him, squeezing tight, wanting to warm him up, wanting to convince herself he was really, finally here.

HIS HEAD THROBBED WITH the fast beat of his heart. The bug on the train had been hard to kill, but this thing had taken all his strength. He felt Petra's arms around him, and then another set of arms that he knew must be Anaya's. He relaxed into them for a moment, then warily drew back to look them in the eyes. The last time he'd seen them had been on the hill outside the bunker's antenna farm, just before the helicopters created a tornado of noise and dust and confusion.

He was still out of breath, and he knew that if he spoke aloud, his voice would shake.

—*You left without me.*

—*No! Pearson made us!* Petra said. *And he wouldn't go back! I asked so many times!*

—*It's true,* Anaya said.

In his mind, their silent replies blazed with raw grief. He believed them. He'd tried to tell himself the same kind of stories over the past days, to explain how and why he got left behind. It wasn't Petra's fault, or Anaya's. He still wasn't convinced it wasn't Dr. Weber's.

—*I tried to reach you every day,* Petra said. *Did you hear me?*

He nodded. *I'm sorry about your mother.*

She pushed his shoulder hard. *You heard me? Why didn't you say anything?*

The sound of rotor blades made him flinch, and he looked up to see a helicopter flying low. Its underbelly bristled with a rocket launcher, and soldiers leaned from the open doorways. All his muscles tensed for flight.

—*It's okay!* Anaya said. *They're not going to hurt you. You're safe.*

"Seth!"

Dr. Weber was rushing toward him in an orange hazmat suit

without its hood. He felt a pressure behind his breastbone. He wasn't sure if it was joy or grief.

"Let me have a look at you," she said, and peppered him with medical questions while she checked his eyes, made him follow her finger, took his pulse. Then she hugged him. He hung his head and let himself be embraced. He didn't know what he felt.

He watched as the helicopter landed on the field and soldiers sprang out, warily circling the rhino creature, making sure it was dead. Seth saw some of them glance at him, his feathered arms, and their expressions ranged from amazement to hostility.

"You know that we didn't leave you behind on purpose," Dr. Weber told him.

Her eyes were wet, but Seth wasn't sure he trusted her. With telepathy it was easier to tell if people were lying. Aloud, it was harder. He *wanted* to believe her, but that was as far as he could go right now.

"What about Pearson?" he asked, looking over her shoulder as the colonel walked toward them from a trailer. He, too, was in a hazmat suit, his gaunt head uncovered.

"He okayed the rescue mission, Seth," Dr. Weber told him. "Once he found out what Ritter was doing, he sent those two helicopters. We got as many kids as we could. I'm so, so sorry you weren't one of them."

There were tears on her cheeks now, and he was afraid he might cry, too. He had so much inside him, feelings and thoughts flapping through his head like crazed bats. He was dimly aware of Pearson chewing out the helicopter team for their slow response. Telling them a bunch of kids had done their work for them.

"Seth," the colonel was saying to him, "you killed this thing with sound?"

Seth nodded.

"Impressive. Glad to have you back, son."

If Pearson felt guilty for sending him to an underground bunker run by a maniac, he didn't show it.

"What is that thing?" Seth asked, nodding at the creature he'd killed.

"Another charming addition to our planet," Anaya said. "How did you even get here, Seth? Who else is with you?"

"No one."

He told them the bare bones of his journey: the train, the superstore, the bridge, the kids lost on the way. He felt so heavy, telling it. The boat, the fight with Darren, and then Esta being kidnapped.

He looked at Colonel Pearson. "We need to find her."

"We need to find *all* of them!" Petra said.

"This is a discussion for later," the colonel said. "We have more pressing matters at hand."

Seth's mind boiled with sudden anger. "Like what?"

He felt Anaya touch his shoulder. "They're going to land. Three of the cryptogens."

"What?"

It was his turn to listen now. Anaya told him about Terra and the cryptogen rebels who wanted to overthrow the flyers. He remembered how, in the bunker, Anaya had figured the flyers were brutally forcing the other cryptogens to work for them. Now it seemed they were being used to fight in the upcoming invasion. She told him how Terra had sent the formula for a medicine to save her mom and cure the mosquito bird plague. And how Terra and the rebels needed something in her blood—all the hybrids' blood—to create a weapon.

"To kill the flyers?" he said dully.

"We don't know how it works yet," Dr. Weber said.

"And me?" he asked. "Is it supposed to kill me, too?"

Anaya looked horrified. "No! Of course not!"

"Even if it worked on you, we'd never let that happen!" Dr. Weber said.

Seth wasn't in a hurry to trust humans again. He realized he'd put himself in another category. Maybe Ritter had that right all along. Seth *wasn't* human. He was something else. All the hybrids were. Esta was smarter than him and had already accepted it. *He* was only starting to.

"And these three rebels," he asked, "they're coming now?"

He wanted to see them, he knew instantly. Face to face. Wanted them inside his head, like Terra had been inside Anaya's.

"I'm having my doubts they're coming at all," said Pearson. He pointed at the rhino creature being dragged off the field by soldiers. "I'm wondering if it was a trap."

"How could it be?" said Anaya.

"Are you serious, Anaya?" Petra said. "It's like that thing was *waiting* for us! Maybe we got sent here to die!"

"It's an animal!" Anaya protested. "The cryptogens can't control stuff like that."

"Right. Like the bug attack on the base?" Petra said bitterly.

Doggedly Anaya said, "A coincidence!"

"I'm tired of coincidences," Pearson said. To his soldiers he shouted, "Get the chopper up and back off, but keep eyes on us."

"I promised them no weapons!" Anaya protested.

"I don't care anymore."

"They won't come if they don't feel safe!"

Dr. Weber said, "Are you sure it's a good idea to antagonize them, Colonel?"

"We will not fire the first shot," Pearson promised. "But if they do, we won't be empty-handed."

Seth was too bewildered to know what to think. He felt like he'd been given a puzzle with too many pieces missing. He saw Anaya, close to tears, turn to Dr. Weber.

"Do you think this was all a trap?" she asked. "Was I tricked?"

"I don't know, Anaya. I hope not."

"We can't trust any of them!" Petra said savagely. "We need to kill them all!"

"So that's why you really came?" Anaya demanded.

"They killed my mom, and they'll kill all of us unless we stop them!"

Thunder spanned the sky, and Seth glanced up at the dark-bellied clouds. Another great crack came from directly overhead and echoed off the North Shore Mountains.

"No lightning," murmured Dr. Weber.

She was right, but Seth felt an electrical current travel over his skin.

"It's them," he said.

"They're coming now," Anaya said quietly, a faraway look on her face.

He knew instinctively that someone had just spoken silently to her. He wished someone would talk to him, too. Explain things. Tell him what to do.

"Hazmat suits back on!" Pearson shouted.

"No time," Anaya said.

Seth followed her gaze. A shape threaded itself in and out of the clouds. Shielding his eyes, he guessed it was the size of a small jet, though a completely different shape. It looked like some kind of complicated seashell. Suddenly it was lower, and making a wide circle of the park. Maybe making sure it was safe to land. It passed right overhead, plowing so much air before it that Seth was blown off his feet, along with everyone around him.

It banked sharply over the inlet and came back, lower still.

He heard a searing crackle and looked over his shoulder to glimpse a missile shooting from the helicopter. It struck the cryptogen ship. Flame enveloped it.

"No!" Anaya screamed.

Trailing smoke, the cryptogens' ship hit the field and cut a deep furrow, spraying earth ahead of it as it came to a smoldering standstill.

"Why'd you do that!" Anaya shouted at Pearson. "They didn't do anything!"

Pearson ignored her and was shouting into his headset. "I gave no order! Stand down! Whoever fired that missile, arrest them! No order was given!"

The colonel looked genuinely stricken. "Someone acted alone. I did not tell them to open fire."

Anaya started to run for the crashed ship, but Seth caught her arm and held her back.

"They're going to think we attacked them!" he told her.

"We *did* attack them!" she said through her tears.

"They're going to be angry," Petra said, looking terrified.

"Terra's in there!" Anaya cried, wrenching herself free from Seth's grip. "She might be hurt. We need to help her!"

Seth was startled by her anguish and realized how deeply his friend cared for this cryptogen.

"Anaya! Wait!" cried Dr. Weber.

The ship was not on fire. Only one part of it was dented and scorched by the missile. It was hard to know which was the front or back, it was so oddly shaped. There was nothing that looked obviously like an engine or a cockpit. But suddenly he saw an opening that hadn't been there before.

"There's a hatch!" Pearson shouted. "Stay back!"

Something burst from it. Seth felt like all the oxygen had been sucked from his lungs. He saw feathers with the deep, dazzling luster of gold. Breathlessly, he watched as it made an upward spiral into the sky. Fury wafted off it with every stroke of its massive wings.

"It's a flyer," said Anaya in disbelief.

"Oh my God," said Petra, her voice choked. "It was a trap!"

Seth stared. High in the sky, the magnificent creature spread its wings to their full span. Its torso was encased in blinding silver armor, and its head was concealed inside a white helmet that spiked up at the back like the crest of a horned dinosaur. And from this helmet came a vibration that Seth sensed, at any second, could unleash utter devastation.

Gleaming like an angel, the cryptogen folded its wings and plunged toward them.

ACKNOWLEDGMENTS

I would like to thank my early readers, who saw this book when it was a clumsy hatchling and gave me valuable feedback: Philippa Sheppard, Kevin Sylvester, Kevin Sands, Jonathan Auxier. And huge thanks also to my editors, Suzanne Sutherland and Nancy Siscoe, whose thoughtful critiques helped me wrangle this rampaging menagerie of a tale.

I'd also like to give a special thanks to my publishers, who oversaw the release of the first title in the series, *Bloom,* at a very difficult time. To Kristopher Kam and the whole sales and marketing team at Knopf Books for Young Readers, and to Maeve O'Reagan and her associates at HarperCollins Canada—thanks for being so resourceful and going the extra mile for these books!

THEY. ARE. HERE.
ARE YOU READY?

Touching down May 2021

From outside came the faint rumble of thunder.

"Weird," Anaya said. "Thunder in summer?"

"It's not stopping," Petra said.

Pearson said something into his headset and then looked at her and Anaya.

"We need to get back to the base, now."

"What's wrong?" Petra asked.

"It's beginning."

Everyone in the control room inside was talking at once. The lights flickered. Petra felt the thunder's vibration through her feet.

". . . another sighting over the South China Sea . . ."

". . . multiple entries reported now . . ."

"What's happening?" Anaya demanded.

No one heard her over the babble of coordinates, as people talked into headsets and pounded at their laptops.

The air was shuddering. Years ago, there'd been an earthquake, and Petra had heard the old wooden banister rattling in their house, and then in the floor and the walls. She'd stood there, frozen, knowing there was some massive force at work, and she was absolutely powerless against it. This shuddering was no different. It seemed to come at her from all directions, and it was inescapable.

"It should be right over our heads now . . . ," someone was saying.

Petra felt like all the bones had suddenly been removed from her body. She grabbed a desk, afraid she might fall. *Oh my god, it was really happening.*

Anaya headed for the exit after Pearson, and Petra followed them. She wanted to move, afraid if she stayed still, she'd literally collapse. Down a corridor, through the doors, and into the shuddering outside.

Shading her eyes, Petra tilted her gaze skyward.

It was like a lid sliding over the top of the sky.

Beyond the mosquito netting, the ship came in from the west.

It curved like a rose petal, curling slightly at the edges. It wasn't smooth like a flower, though, but rough-textured, like some kind of volcanic stone. It trailed streams of vapor. High against the clouds, the ship's dimensions were a mystery. She remembered the huge ship in orbit and its array of petals. This was just one petal. What was it Ritter had said—"the length of three football fields"? It had no lights, no engines, no doorways, no jet trail.

The entire sky echoed. She felt the low rumble in her molars.

Weeks ago, she'd seen this ship on a television monitor in the bunker. There had been lots of these petal-shaped ships, all connected to a central, flower-like stem.

But that had been on a screen, seen from a great distance.

Seeing it now, spanning the sky, was something else entirely. It was real, and it was right here.

"I want to get back to the base," she said.

The words flew from her mouth. She wanted to be with her father for whatever was coming next.

"We'll get you in a car," Dr. Weber said.

But no one was moving, not even her—it was like they were all mesmerized by the ship passing overhead. She couldn't turn away.

It was like watching something momentous: thundering Niagara Falls, or a rocket blasting off. It demanded your full attention. Swirled up with the sheer terror was a racing excitement in her stomach.

She knew what was inside. Anaya had described all those rows upon rows of pods plugged into the fleshy walls. Thousands of slumbering cryptogen soldiers. Or were they awake now? Wide awake and ready.

The ship moved with eerie slowness. When it blotted out the sun, a huge shadow dashed itself against the earth. She could almost imagine a sound accompanying it, like a clash of cymbals. She shivered.

Everyone from the observation room was now outside the biodome, faces turned upward.

"We have ten reports so far, ten ships," an officer with a headset was saying. "Baltimore, Mexico City, Rio de Janeiro, Brussels, Cairo, Jakarta, Mumbai, Seoul, Shanghai. And here."

"They're picking human population density," said Pearson. "And putting themselves within easy striking distance of multiple targets."

"Sir," said another officer, holding a phone to his ear, "we have incoming fighters from CFB Comox."

"No!" said Anaya. "They'll get annihilated!"

The two warplanes tore strips through the sky, trailing vapor from their wingtips as they closed on the cryptogen ship. Each swooped up sharply after releasing a missile.

Petra wasn't sure they even touched the ship. There were small pulses of purple light, and both missiles exploded, but when the flame and smoke cleared, there didn't seem to be any damage to the vast ship at all. It moved on, as indifferent as an elephant to a mosquito.

"Some kind of shielding," Pearson said.

The planes, spent of ammo, veered off and disappeared. The ship hadn't even bothered to return fire, which was worrying. They weren't even concerned the human warplanes might come back with something worse?

As the ship passed directly overhead, Petra staggered to the side, light-headed. She sat down on the grass, the world spinning.

"It's a low-gravity field," said Dr. Weber, crouching beside her.

"We've lost comms," Pearson said. "Power's down, too."

"Probably an electromagnetic pulse," said Dr. Weber.

Petra wrapped her arms around herself and held on tight. The ship passed directly over the base, and it seemed to take an eternity. It cast huge shadows over the ravaged buildings of Vancouver. People watched from balconies and rooftops as the ship headed off to the south.

She couldn't help feeling relief that it was moving on. She'd feared it would hover over Vancouver and unleash a torrent of destruction.

"Do we have a landing site for this one?" Pearson asked.

"Based on trajectory and velocity, somewhere between Vancouver and Seattle."

Grimly, Pearson said, "Easy striking distance of both."

And Seth, Petra thought.